A JUST DECEPTION

PRIVATE PROTECTORS SERIES

ADRIENNE GIORDANO

ALG PUBLISHING

Edited by Gina Bernal

Copyedited by Elizabeth Neal

Cover Design by Lewellen Designs

Author Photo by Debora Giordano

Print Edition ISBN: 978-1-942504-59-7

Digital Edition ISBN: 978-1-942504-58-0

For my mom, who knows all about challenging, good-hearted partners and how to love them.

A JUST DECEPTION

PRIVATE PROTECTORS SERIES

ADRIENNE GIORDANO

ALG PUBLISHING

1

FROM HER CROUCHED POSITION FILLING THE COPY MACHINE drawer, Isabelle spied her cousin Kendrick in the doorway and knew the next few minutes would be worse than a bad case of chicken pox. Irritating as hell and no scratching allowed. Already he blocked her only exit from the cramped room—that was no accident. She drew a searing breath and straightened to her full height, determined to confront him.

Kendrick wore black slacks and a white Oxford shirt, but the tailored clothes couldn't hide the predator. With a shudder, she remembered everything about him she would rather forget. Despite her resolve, the small room pressed in, and she backed away.

Damn.

His leer forced her to dig her heels into the floor and a relentless gnawing tore at her stomach.

Lawyer mode. Now.

"Kendrick, it's been a while."

Three years, two months and thirteen days.

"I'm here to see my father," he said. "I saw you in here. Thought I'd say hello."

She leaned against the copy machine, folded her arms and squeezed until her fingernails bit into her biceps. After years spent grappling to rise above her brokenness, something in his tone—that confident, you'll-never-get-me attitude—shattered her. "Well, I'm sure your father is waiting for you."

"I'm a few minutes early."

"Your father prides himself on the comfortable waiting area. Maybe you can find something to read while you wait."

Kendrick ignored her suggestion and moved into the compact room. She remained still, but tracked him with her eyes, watching him until he halted a foot from her. *Too close.*

A quick glance across his shoulder revealed the safety of the outer corridor where two associates spoke in hushed voices. Assistance was nearby if needed, but screaming for help against the boss's son? How humiliating. Not to mention having to explain it. "I have a client in my office."

He inched closer, and Isabelle held up a hand to stop him. Silly her for believing he would let her leave. She had to get away.

"I need to talk to you," he said.

Okay. Deep breath. She concentrated on diffusing the internal bedlam this man caused. *Get a grip. Don't give him the control. Don't look at him.*

After a few seconds, her thundering pulse settled to its normal rhythm. She could do this.

"I'm in the middle of a client meeting." She turned, made the copy she'd come in for, grabbed her papers and attempted to push by him.

Kendrick sidestepped to block her exit. Unbelievable. She was trapped. Close enough to feel his breath on her skin.

"I only need a couple of minutes, Isabelle."

Never. He didn't deserve it. Not after what he'd taken from her.

She met his gaze straight on, their eyes locking for an instant. "I don't have time, Kendrick."

"I have an offer for you."

Any offer from him could result in her losing a slice of her soul. Her answer would certainly be no. She found triumph in that. Telling him no. Definitively.

She'd let him say what he needed to, indulge in saying no and then boot him out. "Two minutes."

"Oh, Isabelle. You do amuse me."

She made a show of checking her watch. "Now it's one minute."

"You know I've bought property in Ohio, correct?"

Oh, she knew. She was thankful every day that the state of Pennsylvania *normally* provided a barrier between them. Living on the Jersey Shore rewarded her with a sense of ease, and Kendrick being in the area chipped that comfort. "If you need legal advice, talk to someone else. I won't be objective."

He laughed, his big white teeth flashing. Isabelle ground the heel of her black pump into the floor. Her leg ached from the pressure, but the pain would keep her focused.

"*Anyway*," he said. "I'd like to have you visit. Take a look at the place. Maybe stay in one of the bungalows. It's a wonderful piece of property."

"No."

He held up his hands again. "I know you're still angry over the misunderstanding, but let's put it behind us. We're family. I *know* my father would appreciate you letting go of the hostility. Come see the compound. Stay awhile. You'll be taken care of. Any need or want you have will be fulfilled by one of the staff members."

What was all this babbling about his compound?

She narrowed her eyes and let his comment about his father—her boss—roll off her. Convincing herself to accept a job from Kendrick's father hadn't been easy, but working at one of New Jersey's top criminal defense firms would catapult her career. Her cousin's goading wouldn't jeopardize that. "I need to get back to work."

"Not staff, really," he continued. "Tenants, I guess. Fifty of us live on the property. Some in the main house and some in bungalows scattered throughout the hundred acres. You'd have your own place, of course."

A flicker of perverse excitement twinkled in his blue-green eyes, and sickness swirled in her stomach. She needed to get him out of there before the toxic waste he spewed consumed her. "I'm not interested."

Kendrick reached down and tugged at the sleeves of his shirt, but made no move to leave. Idiot.

And yet, she remained wedged in the room. With a client waiting in her office. The brutal pressure of these few minutes finally overtook her, and a chill penetrated her bones, puckering her skin.

Don't let him win.

He tried the slick smile that always worked on the little girl she'd once been, and she imagined him bursting into flames.

"I need you, Isabelle. There are...things happening and I could use your legal expertise. I promise I'll take good care of you." He dragged his gaze over her body. "I always did."

Sick, sick, sick.

She fisted her free hand until her knuckles popped. Her only other choice would be to pummel him. Probably not a good idea in his father's building.

A knock on the doorframe brought deflating relief to her

tense body. Her assistant stood there, her eyes shifting to Kendrick and back. "Mr. Parker is looking for you. I would have made the copies."

"You were away from your desk. Besides, we're done."

"I'll give you time to think about it," Kendrick said.

"Don't bother. My answer will still be no."

No. No. No.

After her meeting with Mr. Parker concluded, Isabelle dialed a familiar cell phone number. Vic Andrews, a long-time family friend, lived in Chicago, but he'd come through for her. He answered on the second ring.

"Ah, the lovely Isabelle DeRosa."

She sat back in her desk chair. The late afternoon sun blanketed her arm, and she shifted toward the window for the full effect. Between the sun and Vic's Southern charm, a comforting feeling enveloped her.

A long, piercing car horn sounded and Vic let out a stream of creative swearing. All righty, then.

"What's going on?" Vic asked after his verbal tirade ended.

"Where are you?"

"I'm attempting to pick up Lily from day camp. I gotta tell ya, Cambodian jungles are easier to get through than this line. I should put some of these moms on my staff. They'd be world-class operators."

Isabelle snorted. A former special ops guy, he'd seen a lot of action in his lifetime.

"What's up?" he asked.

She swallowed hard and fiddled with her pen. Vic was one of the few people outside the family that knew her secret. "Kendrick is back."

"Son of a bitch. Is it a permanent thing?"

"No. He wants me to visit him in Ohio."

Silence. She knew how he felt. Helpless and stunned.

Vic finally spoke. "What the fuck?"

"Exactly. He's as nuts as ever. He cornered me in the copy room at the office."

"Did you beat the crap out of him?"

"I wanted to," Isabelle said.

"What can I do?"

Kill him. Heaven help her. That would be all she needed. Thinking back on the years she'd lost and what Kendrick did to her, she probably did have that much anger. Scary.

She tossed her pen on the desk and picked a piece of lint from her slacks. "I need a security system on my house."

"Done," Vic said. "I'd rather hit him with a double pop between the eyes, but if you want a security system, it's yours. I've been telling you that."

"Nag, nag, nag."

"You know it, darlin'. I've got a guy out there on vacation in Nosrum. I'll get him over to your place ASAP."

She had no doubt she could defend herself, but the alarm would be added protection. She knew damn well Kendrick wouldn't go away so easily.

2

PETER STORMED THROUGH THE GATES OF HIS PARENTS' ESTATE with the roar of the Challenger's four hundred twenty-five horsepower engine sounding like heaven. He imagined the look on his mother's face and grinned. She despised loud cars. Particularly those driven by one of her sons. Another thing they didn't agree on. The cars he'd collected over the years were part of the draw of coming home to Jersey where he kept them stored in a climate-controlled garage built on his parents' property.

He pulled up the drive, but his mother's Cadillac was nowhere to be seen. He needed to stop and get his surfboard from the upstairs bedroom closet so at least he could say he'd been there. It would save him the lambasting she'd give him for not coming around enough. His father would be at work this time of day, and he made a mental note to call him. Dad at least gave him a break from the constant verbal pounding about living up to the Jessup name.

Peter stepped from the car, shielded his eyes against the blistering August sun, and scanned the three-story brick house—mansion really—he'd grown up in. Red, yellow and pink flowers dotted the front garden. He'd never once spied a weed on this property. His mother ran a tight ship.

He glanced at a four-foot potted tree to the right of the stone stairs, and a clanging erupted in his ears. Had the tree been there when he drove by yesterday? Definitely not. He'd have noticed it.

Possible hiding places no longer got by him. Not anymore. His blood pumped and his brain snapped until his nerves flew into overdrive. He fired a sideways kick at the tree and—*bang*—sent it barreling to its side.

Nothing there.

Shit.

He leaned forward, bracing his hands on his knees. Now he was seeing terrorists behind greenery? Vic was right. He *was* losing his mind.

Springsteen's "Born to Run" erupted from the pocket of his cargo shorts. He dug his phone out and checked the ID. Vic. The guy must be a mind reader.

"What's up?" Peter said, still eyeballing the toppled plant.

"You sound pissy. You got a bug up your ass?"

"Yeah. A six-foot-five one. Calling to check on my mental status?"

"Monk, don't be an asshole. Mike agreed with me. Most people would love their boss to give them an extended vacation."

Well, Peter—Monk, as the guys called him—wasn't most people. As a former Navy SEAL, he needed some kind of action at all times. When he walked into a room, everyone knew he was the alpha dog. The alpha dog didn't like being told he was on the verge of a breakdown. He considered it an insult.

Then again, he'd just kicked over a plant.

"This is a social call then? I'm fine, thanks, gotta go." He hung up, slid the phone back in his pocket and squatted to reset the plant.

The phone rang again, and he straightened to answer it.

Vic laughed in his ear. "Dickhead."

Peter grunted. Vic bullied his way around every damn thing. They'd worked together for three years now, since Peter joined Taylor Security after leaving the navy. The Chicago-based company handled residential and corporate security, and Vic's team did government contract work. When the government needed plausible deniability, they called Taylor Security. Everything from protection details for overseas diplomats to badass counter terrorism assignments—leveling chemical plants, destroying enemy caves, snatching a bad guy—Peter thrived on. His last two assignments were the reason for this extended vacation.

Peter pinched the bridge of his nose. He didn't need this. "Can I call you back when I don't want to tear your head off and shove it up your ass?"

"I need a favor."

A *favor*? The guy had stones the size of Texas.

"You're kidding, right? Three days ago you called me into your office and told me to hand over my weapon and enjoy my family for a few extra weeks after my brother's wedding. It's gonna take me longer than three days to work that off. Call me back in a week. Maybe then I'll do your favor."

"I saved your life last summer," Vic shot back.

Dammit. Peter threw his head back and closed his eyes. "You only get to play that card once. Make it good."

"A friend of mine called. She lives in Monmouth Beach and needs a security system ASAP. I can't do it. Gina has an ultrasound tomorrow, and she wants me there. I *want* to be there. Have I mentioned we're having twins?"

Peter rolled his eyes. "Yeah, yeah, I know, your boys can swim."

"You are crabby, my friend. Not getting any?"

"Getting plenty." Not true, but Vic didn't need to know that.

"Seriously, can you meet with Isabelle tomorrow? She usually gets to work early, so you'll have to meet her at her office. She'll take you to the house from there. All you have to do is tell me what she needs, and I'll fly some guys out there to do the install."

The potted plant drew Peter's attention again, and he nudged it with his boot. "Why can't the North Jersey boys do this? That *is* why we have an East Coast office, correct?"

Vic huffed. "Her father is a good friend. I don't trust anyone from North Jersey for this."

"Oh, but you trust me? The guy you made hand over his weapon?"

"Are you done yet, Mary? My wife never whines like this."

"Speaking of Gina," Peter said, "I'll do this for her. Because she deserves to have you at that appointment. I still can't figure out why I didn't move on her first."

"My man, I owe you one. You just ensured I will continue to get laid. And I'll forget that comment about hitting on my wife."

Peter laughed. He couldn't help it. Vic was one fucked-up son of a bitch, but he was aces in a war zone. They'd become closer since Tiny—Vic's cousin and Peter's closest friend—died during an op last summer. They were both grieving a loss they'd probably never get over, and in that, found common ground. Peter supposed that was the reason he was so royally pissed at Vic for putting him on R&R.

"Is that it?"

"Yeah. I'll email you Isabelle's info. Be at her office at nine. Uh, and wear business clothes."

"What?"

Vic hung up.

Shit.

Peter hated business clothes. His basic wardrobe consisted of cargo shorts, jeans and T-shirts. Usually, his beat-up combat boots and a do-rag finished off the ensemble. Lucky for him, he kept a stash of dress clothes in an upstairs closet of his parents' home.

Peter marched up the stone steps, opened the oversized door and yelled for Marguerite, their long-time housekeeper.

"Have I ever responded to screaming?" she called from the kitchen.

He snorted. Good old Marg. The aroma of fresh-baked cookies attacked him, and he hauled ass to the kitchen to find Marg pulling a batch from the oven.

"Hi. Where's Mom?"

"She went to lunch at the club and had errands."

Peter grinned. "I guess I'll sample some cookies while I wait."

"There's plenty of milk. I figured you'd be by, so I stocked up."

He smacked a kiss on her cheek. "Ah, Marg. You're the best."

Her pixie-cut gray hair spiked up today and looked a little radical, but it suited her in an off kind of way. She'd gained a few pounds since he'd seen her last and, on her small frame, it showed.

After snagging a few cookies and a monster glass of milk, Peter planted himself at the island to commence dunking. Nothing he loved more than dipping chocolate chip cookies in an ice-cold glass of milk.

When a few white drops hit the granite countertop, Marguerite laughed and handed him a paper towel.

"Some things never change."

"Take comfort in it, Marg." He swiped at the drops and crumpled the paper towel.

"I remember the first time you ate my chocolate chip cookies," she said.

"Yep. I was seven, and you'd been here less than a day. I got busted for climbing Mr. G's trellis and my mother locked me in my room for the rest of the night. I still haven't figured out how you snuck those cookies in without her knowing."

She laughed and moved a cookie to the cooling rack. "A lady never shares her secrets. Hard to believe that was twenty-five years ago."

From the moment Marg first smuggled him cookies and milk, Peter loved her. Their partnership had been sealed that day. Marguerite had always been his supporter when the "Oh, Peter" moments became too much.

"Yeah," he said. "And how about that time the principal wanted to expel me for trying to rappel off the school roof?"

Marg shivered. "There weren't enough cookies in the world for that transgression."

The utility room door off the kitchen opened. His mother. She had her country club look going. All spit-and-polish in a blue pants suit and diamond earrings. Her ash blond, shoulder-length hair combed to perfection and tucked behind her ears. At fifty-eight, his mother could easily pass for ten years younger. And no doctor had ever touched her face. An impressive feat in her social circle.

His mother slipped off her jacket, hung it up and glanced at him. "Hello, stranger." She entered the room shaking her head. "Oh, Peter, as usual, you have that silly napkin on your head."

She clamped her hand on his head, slid the do-rag off and dropped it in his lap. He didn't bother with a suffering sigh. Not his style. After all, the do-rags had been driving his mother batshit since his navy days. The always put together Lorraine Jessup couldn't have one of her sons walking around with "that thing" on his head. So instead of arguing with her yet again, he put the do-rag on and ignored *her* suffering sigh. He'd grown used to not being what she needed him to be. And escaping her derision.

"Mom, don't tax yourself. You've oh-Petered me *and* ripped on my attire, and you've only been here a minute and a half."

Marguerite stifled a laugh. "You just missed it. Peter was reminding me of the time he jumped off the school roof."

"I didn't jump!"

"I don't want to think about that," his mother said.

Probably because it had been one of the few times she'd defended his restlessness. "You were aces that day, Mom. You marched in there wanting to know how I got on the roof in the first place and threatened to sue them for endangering my life."

"It was a valid point. I seem to recall punishing you for a month after that fiasco. You never could sit still, Peter."

Marg sighed. "I made a lot of cookies that month."

His mother turned to him; her eyes sharp. "You've been back two days and we've barely seen you. You're staying for dinner, I hope."

No request there. That was a classic guilt-infused order.

He stood. "I was here *last* night. I can't tonight. I just stopped to get my board and some clothes for tomorrow."

The response he received was the stricken look. The one

where she puffed out her lower lip and stared at him. "Your father will be home soon. I'll call Stephen, and we can all eat together like we used to. I *know* Stephen will come."

He always does.

That wasn't fair. If anything, Peter appreciated his younger brother. Stephen, the golden boy, always managed to take the heat off him. Peter was able to live his life the way he chose, while his brother fulfilled the family obligations. Peter owed Stephen for that.

"Not tonight, Mom. I'll come for dinner another night. Leave me a message at the cottage when you guys are eating at home, and I'll make sure to be here."

He made a beeline for the staircase. Time to get his stuff and run.

"And that's another thing," his mother said, scooting up behind him. "Why do you have to stay in the guest cottage? We have ten bedrooms here. Surely, if you don't want to sleep in your old room, you can find another suitable one."

Before reaching the stairs, he stopped and she plowed into the back of him. His mind screamed to keep going and head right out the front door.

He grabbed the oak railing and zipped around. Her big blue eyes gazed up at him. She was tall for a woman—five-nine—but he still had a few inches on her. Why did it always have to be this way between them? The constant pushing. Probably his own fault, but at some point he had learned to duck and cover. He didn't fit in his parents' world, and rather than embarrass them or cause himself grief, it was easier to steer clear.

"I like the cottage, it's quiet. And I've been living alone a long time. I like the privacy."

"We wouldn't bother you here."

He stifled a laugh. *Yeah, and Santa will drop a flock of nymphomaniacs at my door tonight.*

"Fine." She backed up a step. "I'll have Marguerite make a plate for you. We'll leave it at the cottage."

Now she was pissed. Again. *Shit.*

"Mom?"

She waved, but kept walking. "It's all right, Peter. I should know by now not to pressure you."

He should say something. He knew it. But he also knew anything he came up with would be gas on fire, and he'd spent years letting the fire burn out on its own. It was better that way.

At least he thought so.

No. He'd go on his way now, handle this thing with Vic's friend and then deal with his mother. He was stuck here for a few weeks on this forced R&R because, apparently, he couldn't function at work. He might as well make himself useful and try to understand what his mother needed from him. At least he'd get something accomplished, and fixing something—anything—was all he needed now.

3

AT EIGHT FORTY-FIVE THE NEXT MORNING, PETER PUSHED THE
elevator button in the Edmonds, Baker and Associates law
firm building and rubbed a hand over the back of his neck.
These big corporate centers with their marble floors and
cavernous lobbies gave him a rash. And him without his
Benadryl.

Not to mention the dress shirt and slacks. He pulled the
stiff collar off his neck. Marguerite, as usual, had saved his
ass and gotten everything cleaned and pressed. Even with
the lightest possible starch, the shirt irked him.

The stainless steel elevator doors slid open. Peter and an
overweight, middle-aged guy stepped on. And hellooooo to
the smoking hot brunette showing just enough cleavage to
make a man want more. She stood toward the back of the
elevator and must have come up from the lower level
parking entrance.

A stone-cold fox.

Dark, chin-length hair, green, laser-sharp eyes and
cheekbones belonging on a magazine cover. Stunning. Typi-

cally, women like her didn't notice Peter until they saw his bank account.

The schmo that entered the elevator with Peter pushed the button for two and, out of the corner of his eye, Peter saw the brunette roll her eyes. He couldn't take the stairs one flight?

The number eight was already lit up. He and the hot brunette were going to the same floor. Must be fate.

He shifted right to surreptitiously admire her. Why not? He had to wait for the jackass to get off at two anyway and couldn't resist watching how the overhead light made her hair shine. The rest of her was a definite bonus.

She carried her briefcase over one shoulder and her sleeveless blouse showcased one hell of a coiled biceps. She spent serious time in the gym. He could appreciate that because maintaining his ten percent body fat had become a priority. She gave him a sideways look.

Yep, she'd caught him, but he couldn't help admiring a physically fit woman. Hell, he'd been known to get a hard-on at the gym when he saw a toned woman sweating like a linebacker in the fourth quarter.

The elevator door dinged and the jackass got off. When the doors closed, the brunette swung to her left and faced Peter.

He smiled.

She pursed her lips.

Oh baby, what he'd like to do with those lips. Good, pouty lips that he could imagine doing all sorts of things in all sorts of places. This could work out just fine.

She gave him a long, slow once-over and his belly seized at the thorough inspection. He might have even started to sweat. Forget about her zeroing in on his crotch and *smirking*. This woman was clearly uninformed.

A nice tactic to cause a man an instant soft-on though. A more insecure man would have pissed himself, but Peter stood there, absorbing the little lesson she'd given him.

He laughed before reaching into his pocket and pulling out a white handkerchief. He waved it in the air. "I surrender. Point taken. I apologize for staring."

The unsmiling woman nodded and turned front.

Peter took a deep breath and jumped in headfirst. "In my own defense, I'd like to say it wasn't a sexual thing."

She angled her head, obviously not believing it anymore than he did.

"Well, not *totally* a sexual thing," he corrected. "I happen to appreciate people taking care of themselves and you clearly do."

"Apology accepted." She didn't bother to look at him again. Her voice though, with a smoky, purring edge only added to the fantasy he had going. She'd make a great sex line operator.

The elevator doors opened, and Peter waved her forward. She nodded and stepped into the office's swanky reception area with its plush carpeting, shiny oak trim and leather seating. Peter knew big money and plenty of it had been thrown around this office. He headed for the efficient-looking redhead sitting at an oversized reception desk just a few feet in front of them. The brunette turned right toward a long hallway lined with offices.

"Good morning, Ms. DeRosa."

Oh, shit. Did his balls just disintegrate?

"Good morning, Jeanette," Ms. DeRosa said.

Please don't let her first name be Isabelle.

"I have an appointment with someone from Taylor Security. Just send him back when he gets here."

Double shit.

"Will do, Ms. DeRosa."

Peter closed his eyes. Laughing right now probably would not be his best course of action, but this was hilarious. Vic would fry him.

"Good morning, sir," the receptionist said after Isabelle had turned and started down the corridor.

Peter stepped up and gave her his best hundred watter. "Good morning. I'm Peter Jessup from Taylor Security."

And, yep. Ms. *Isabelle* DeRosa skidded to a stop, waited a full ten seconds and spun back around. "Just shoot me," she said.

The receptionist glanced at her, saw her giving Peter the evil eye and turned back to him.

He grinned. "We've already met."

Isabelle remained still; her face devoid of any emotion. *Awkward.*

Then she burst out laughing and rocked his world. His mind went straight to the gutter, dreaming about hearing that throaty laugh while he screwed her brains out.

Oh, hell, could he stop thinking about sex for five seconds? He needed to get laid. In a bad way.

She jerked her head toward the offices behind her. "Come on, Peter Jessup from Taylor Security. Let's try this again."

"You got it, Ms. DeRosa."

ISABELLE KEPT HER HEAD HIGH AS SHE MARCHED DOWN THE hallway, hoping the floor would open up and swallow her. Just suck her whole body up. Tension pooled at her shoulders and she silently willed it away.

Men had been ogling her for years and she'd used that staring trick a hundred times to back them off. They tended to freak out when strange women scrutinized their parts. Maybe it was the *Fatal Attraction* vibe, but it always worked.

Until today.

Now she wanted to die of embarrassment because, not only did it not back Peter Jessup off, it pushed him to explain why he was staring at her. The man had a spine, for sure. Not to mention an all-around killer body—albeit a typical big-chested, slim-hipped build—but he could fill out a shirt. His dark, wavy hair fell in a frenzy around his face, leaving her with the urge to rifle her hands through the curls.

"So—" Peter walked beside her and jolted her out of her mortified state, "—what do you say we forget about that elevator thing? My boss won't be too happy about it."

She halted and waited for him to do the same. What an interesting face. Movie star handsome he would never be, but something drew her in. He reminded her of someone who had lived on both the good and bad side of life. She spotted the L-shaped scar on his right cheek, but the blue eyes were the kicker. A deep, haunting blue that left her yearning to see more of them. Totally unacceptable for a girl who liked to separate the physical and emotional aspects of her feelings toward men.

"I don't know," she said. "I think Vic is twisted enough to see the humor in it. Plus, he's always been a ladies' man. He'd probably be proud of us."

A lightning-quick smile took over Peter's face, and suddenly this man became more than average in the looks department. That smile could brighten an alley on a rainy night.

"Holy cow," she said.

He drew his eyebrows together. "What?"

She shook it off. "Nothing."

What the hell was she doing? Bad enough about the elevator and now this?

"Hello, Isabelle," Kendrick said to her back. His monotone voice never left her memory. Never.

A sizzling rage overtook her. Leave it to Kendrick to spoil her relatively normal reaction to an attractive man. Damn him. She spun around.

"What?" she asked, wanting him only to go away. She sensed Peter shifting behind her.

Kendrick glanced over her shoulder at Peter. "I'm Kendrick Edmonds. Isabelle's cousin."

Peter held his hand out and the men shook hands. "Peter Jessup."

"Jessup Industries?"

"Yep."

Jessup Industries. What the heck was this guy doing working for Vic when his family's company built half the destroyers floating in the ocean?

Isabelle turned to him. "You *are* surprising me today."

His mouth curved into a smile and a thrumming in her ears knocked her a little daffy. "Here to please, ma'am."

She turned her attention back to her cousin. "Mr. Jessup and I have a meeting."

"Have you considered what we talked about?" Kendrick asked.

The only thing she'd considered was how to kick his ass from every possible angle. "I gave you my answer and it's still no. Goodbye, Kendrick."

He narrowed his eyes and Peter moved sideways, probably reminding her he was there. He must not know she could take care of herself, but if he had half the skills Vic did, it would be fun to watch him work. An oily smile spread across Kendrick's face before he held his hand to Peter. "A pleasure."

Peter hesitated, took it but didn't speak.

Interesting. Kendrick would be a complete dope not to see whose side Peter Jessup was on. She hitched her shoulders back a little further.

"Let's go, Peter." Isabelle grabbed his elbow and turned him toward her office. She didn't dare glance back, but felt Kendrick watching them. Despite the freezing cold office, perspiration beaded and rolled down her back. Sick, sick, bastard.

"I'm guessing he's the problem."

Isabelle picked up the pace. "He's the problem all right. You're here to help me fix it."

4

ISABELLE DEROSA DROVE LIKE A KAMIKAZE PILOT ON HIS—*ER* —her last mission. They tore down Ocean Avenue with the top lowered on her Audi and Peter hanging on to what was left of his balls after the elevator incident.

He turned his face to the sun and sucked in the salty ocean air. He couldn't help it. He'd never get enough of fast cars.

She took a hard left and swung into the gravel driveway of a baby blue oceanfront cottage.

"This it?" he asked as she came to a stop in front of the house. He admired the white trim around the oversized windows and the bright white Adirondack chairs on the porch. Beach grass surrounded the house on all sides and, with the ocean as a backdrop, the greens and blues and white mixed together to make it all picture perfect. And for Peter, love at first sight.

"This is it," Isabelle said.

"Will you sell it to me?"

She gave him a half smile. "You haven't even seen it."

"I've seen enough. This baby is a classic."

They got out of the car and paused to admire the house.

"It was my grandmother's," she said, her voice soft. "She died a few years ago and the house sat empty. My uncle wanted to sell it. My mother didn't, so I moved in. I'm working on buying it. In the meantime, I'm doing all the renovations. I just finished the kitchen."

"You sound proud of it."

With the key dangling from her fingers she waved him forward. "I love this house. It'll be spectacular when I'm done. The front door is original and weighs about five thousand pounds."

She opened the five thousand-pound door and ushered him into the large, open living room. Her spike heels clicked against the shiny hardwood floors, but Peter couldn't move.

She must have knocked out a couple of walls because three white support

columns separated the front of the house from the back. French doors lined the rear and, from where he stood, he could see clear to the ocean. He *had* to have it.

"I will buy this house right now. Call whomever you need to and tell them you have a cash buyer."

She stopped, leaned against one of the beams and looked around.

"No," she said. "This house is priceless. Thank you for the compliment though. Come on. I'll give you the tour and you can tell me what kind of security I need."

Peter strolled into the living room and admired the blue-and-white striped chairs and oversized cushions. Isabelle had phenomenal taste. He stepped close to the wall and nearly put his face against it trying to determine the color.

"Is this white paint?"

She laughed. "Possibly."

"What does that mean?"

"It started out as white, but I didn't like it. I had them mix a few darker whites in. Sort of my own creation."

"It's a great color. Not plain, but still white. I hope they wrote down the percentages for when you need to repaint."

She scanned the room. "Hopefully that won't happen for a while. It was a job. Took me three weeks."

She painted the house herself. A capable woman. Why wouldn't she hire someone? More than that, though, he wanted to know why her friends didn't help.

They walked down a short hallway to the two bedrooms. Peter snapped photos and jotted notes about the house's vulnerabilities. Touring the two bedrooms—one of which was hers—sent lascivious thoughts through his head. He got out of there quick as Isabelle walked him to a third room.

"This is the gym." She pushed the door open and sunlight flooded the room.

A heavy bag hung from the ceiling in one corner and hand weights, lined like soldiers, sat next to a workout bench along the far wall. Large mats covered the floor and walls, offering a perfect set up for sparring. Maybe she was into martial arts? It would explain her physical shape.

The kick-ass ocean view got his engine going, but all those windows could be trouble.

Peter noted the number of windows along the back of the room. "You like to work out at home instead of the gym?"

She nodded, her dark hair swinging. "I'm not crazy about the gym."

"Guys hit on you, huh?" He couldn't blame the poor schmucks, considering his own thoughts were leading him down that road.

She shrugged. "It's been known to happen."

Peter gave the heavy bag a shot. "Let's talk about what

you want versus what you need. I'll talk to Vic and we'll come up with something that'll work for you."

"Good. Let's sit in the kitchen. It's my favorite spot these days."

He followed her into the kitchen and let out a soft whistle over the maple cabinets and speckled granite counter tops. If he hadn't seen it himself, he'd have thought the white appliances against the quasi-white walls would be too much, but with the blue of the ocean as a backdrop through the oversized windows, it made a perfect beach home. Peter pulled one of the ladder-back chairs and sat at the oak farm table.

"This really is a great space. I can see why you love it."

"You like the beach?" she asked.

Man-oh-man she had those devastating eyes aimed right at him. Something he'd like to see as he buried himself deep inside her.

Ho-kay. Not going there. He gave himself a mental head slap.

Killer, killer eyes, though.

"I love the beach," Peter said. "Actually, I like to surf. Can't surf in Chicago unless the weather kicks up. I wind-surf there, but it's not the same."

"So move back."

Now there was a thought he hadn't entertained in a while. He'd spent years rejecting his life here, not wanting the pressure of his family's status, but he did miss the ocean.

"It's complicated. Maybe someday." He flipped to a fresh page on his legal pad and checked his watch. "How are we on time? You need to get back?"

She stretched to glance at the clock on the wall. The motion pulled her blouse tight against her body.

"No. I told them I'd be gone a couple of hours."

When she turned back, she busted him staring at her tits and rolled her eyes. "Again, Peter?"

That earned him a self-induced head pounding with his fists. "I'm sorry. I'm a single guy, and you're a beautiful woman. It's hardwired."

She shook her head and laughed. At least she had a sense of humor.

"Back to work," he said. "Do you want motion detectors or glass break? Both probably?" He answered his own question and made a note. Easy. "What about the locks? Who has keys?"

"My uncle and my mother. After I changed the locks, my uncle, Kendrick's father, insisted on having a key. He and my mother are technically the homeowners."

Peter eyed her. Call him crazy, but Kendrick's father having a key wasn't sitting right with him. "Do you have a problem with me changing the locks?"

"Right now, no. I'll give my father the spare key and, if there's a problem, my mother can get it from him."

Interesting that she chose not to give her mother the key.

She plucked at her bottom lip with two fingers. "What did Vic tell you about all this?"

He shoved the pad away and sat back. "Nothing. He told me you needed a security system. I got a bad feeling from your buddy Kendrick though. What's his deal?"

While she drummed her fingers on the table, Peter forced himself to stay silent. If *he* seemed relaxed, *she'd* relax and then the curiosity driving him batshit might get satisfied.

"Hang on." She grabbed the cordless phone from the cradle and walked away.

Peter blew out a breath. *Okee-dokey.*

. . .

"Can I trust this guy?" Isabelle asked when Vic answered his cell.

"Monk? Why? Everything all right?"

"*Monk*?"

Vic cracked up. "That's what the guys call him. He'll have to tell you the story. And yes, you can trust him. I wouldn't have sent him otherwise. He's not hitting on you, is he? I'll kick his ass."

Of course he was hitting on her. She wasn't sure she minded, either.

"He's fine. We're at the house and I wasn't sure if he knew about Kendrick."

"I didn't think it was my place to tell him. If you choose to tell him, he'll keep it quiet. He's a good guy."

"Okay. That's all I needed. I think we're almost done here. I'll call you later."

Isabelle clicked the phone off, tapped it against her lips. She could trust him. A new concept considering she didn't have many friends who knew about Kendrick. She'd lost countless friendships over the years trying to walk the line between total disclosure and self-protection.

Unease snaked around her and she shivered against the building fear. Would he give her the pity face? Or the disgusted face? Could she risk it?

She dipped her head in shame. There was her answer.

Absolutely not.

She couldn't tell him. She liked him, actually liked him, and didn't want to taint his opinion of her. She breathed deep, marched into the kitchen, tucked the phone back into the cradle and sat. Peter entertained himself by doodling on the legal pad, his face completely relaxed.

"Sorry about that," she said. "I remembered an important call I forgot to make. So, where were we?"

Please don't remember where we were.

Peter grinned, a targeted message that told her he was well aware of her attempt to avoid talking about Kendrick.

"What?" she asked. *Right. Play dumb.* That *always* worked.

The grin turned into a soft laugh. "I'm going to make a wild assumption that you're not comfortable talking about Kendrick. Am I right?" A moment passed before he sat back, tore a piece of paper from the pad and wrote down two phone numbers. "No problem. I'll back off, but these are my numbers. Call if you need anything. Doesn't matter what time. Or the problem. Got it?"

The tension inside her broke. He wouldn't push *and* he'd help her. Yes, she liked Peter Jessup. A lot.

She folded the paper, shoved it into her pants pocket. "They call you Monk? I can't wait to hear that story."

He shrugged. "During my military days, when we got weekend leave I was so dog-tired I stayed in the barracks. All the guys went storming out in search of women and booze. All I wanted was a good book and a beer."

"And Monk was born?"

"Yeah. It stuck. Now I'm Peter in Jersey and Monk in Chicago." He cracked a smile. "It's tough keeping my identities straight, but somehow I manage."

Isabelle laughed. "Oh, please."

"Really, it's not a big deal. It's probably the same thing for you when people call you Iz or Izzy."

That would be the day. "Absolutely not. No one calls me Iz. And definitely not Izzy. My name is Isabelle."

"Then we're gonna have a helluva problem because if I have to call you *Is-a-belle* all the time, it's gonna take a while to have a conversation. I like Izzy. It's short and sweet."

"You're kidding, right? Considering I just told you I don't like Izzy."

"Yeah, but *I've* never called you Izzy, *Izzy*. See, it's got a nice ring to it."

Could this guy be for real? Still, she couldn't resist laughing. Peter Jessup's mind must be an exciting place. His laid back, yet somehow assertive nature fascinated her. This man was no dummy.

He waved her off and picked up his notepad again. "Izzy isn't so bad. I've been living with Monk for ten years. At least Izzy is obvious."

"When did you join the military?"

Peter smiled. "Now that's a good story, because I almost didn't survive telling my mother I'd enlisted."

"She wasn't happy about it?"

He raised his eyebrows. "Uh, no. I guess I understand it now. I don't suppose many mothers would like their sons dropping out of Yale their sophomore year to join the navy and blow shit up."

Holy cow. Yale? Definitely not a dummy. "I'm not a mother and it just shocked the hell out of me."

"To compound the problem, I flew off to Vegas and got married before I reported."

"Oh, wow," she said. "The navy and a wife? How old were you when this happened?"

"Nineteen."

Married at nineteen. Yikes. The wife must no longer be in the picture. He did say he was single.

She shook her head. "I'd have murdered you. Don't you think that was a lot to dump on your mother at one time?"

He raised his hands. "First off, I was young and stupid and in love. I wanted to join the navy, but I didn't want anyone stealing my girl. Marriage seemed logical. I'd fly off to who knows where while Tricia stayed home being faithful to her devoted husband. At the time it made perfect sense."

Ah, young love. Too bad at nineteen a man couldn't think with anything but his penis. "So what happened?"

"She left me."

Isabelle winced. So much for the faithful wife. And suddenly, her heart ached for him. He'd been betrayed by someone he loved. She knew all about that. "Ouch."

"It sucked. Big time. Now I'm older and I get it. I'd been stationed overseas, and she wanted to finish school and be near her family. The problem was she didn't know enough about life to stay with a husband she saw twice a year—if she was lucky. Plus, I had to concentrate on my job and didn't want to be worried about my young, unhappy wife shagging someone else." He gave her a no-teeth grin. "I don't share."

"How long were you married?"

"Three years."

"Did you still love her?"

"Absolutely. Some marriages survive military life. Mine couldn't. It hurt like hell, but I accepted it."

This was one interesting man. He knew himself and made no apologies for what he believed. Something told her Peter Jessup always offered the truth. Good or bad, he would give an honest assessment.

"So, are there any gray areas with you?"

"Nope. I'm a pretty simple guy."

She doubted that.

He leaned forward, propped his elbow on the table and stuck his chin in his hand. "I like you, Izzy. There's no bull-shit with you. You laugh when you want, you say what you want and, my guess is, you do what you want."

The focused intensity in his eyes sent a juicy ripple up her arms. She was definitely attracted to this man. Not good. Unless, of course, they could keep it light. No emotional entanglements.

"No fair talking about me when we were talking about you dropping out of one of the best schools in the country and getting married."

He shrugged. "I didn't belong at Yale anyway. I made the grades easy enough, but I've never fit into the blue blood set. All I've ever wanted is to jump out of airplanes. My parents can't figure it out. Sometimes I wonder if they found me on the side of the road. My brother coasted into that life when I've spent most of my time avoiding it."

She must have given him the "poor baby" face because he held out his hands.

"Don't get me wrong," he said. "The money is great. I'm thankful for it every day. I just don't like the crap that goes with it. All the snobbery and judgments. The women hitting on you because they're trying to land a rich husband. I like living in my scarcely furnished two-bedroom condo in Chicago. Nobody there cares about my decorating skills. In my parents' world you need to be on the lookout for the flesh-eating predators."

"Flesh-eating predators? You like these people, huh?"

He laughed. "Love 'em. I'm not whining about it. I just don't fit. I need real friends. The ones who stick when you've screwed the pooch. Like Vic. And Tiny. Tiny was great in screw-the-pooch mode."

Vic's cousin, Justin, aka Tiny, had been killed last summer on an assignment for Taylor Security. "I never met Tiny. Vic talked about him often though. What a tragedy. Were you close?"

Peter hesitated before clearing his throat. "You know—" he poked at his notepad, "—I think I'm all set here."

Did Peter even know he was running from grief? He had to. People always knew. Consciously or not, somewhere inside, they knew. Isabelle was an expert on that. She could compartmentalize with the best of them.

"Right," she said. "I need to get back to the office anyway."

She rose from the table and pushed in the chair, but he didn't move. He just sat, watching her.

"Yes," he finally said. "We were close."

He and Tiny.

A burst of sympathy propelled her forward and she touched his hand. The warmth of his skin wrapped around her, and gave her comfort when all she intended was to offer it. "I could tell. I'm sorry."

He nodded, one solid jerk of his head. "Yeah. Me too."

The silence lingered and with that one moment of hidden weakness, Peter Jessup bulldozed his way under her skin.

Yes. Definitely attracted to him. Maybe it wasn't a bad thing. After all, he lived in Chicago. In a few weeks he'd be gone. Maybe they'd have a fling, he'd go home and Isabelle would go back to her life of solitude. No emotional complications to deal with on his end, and she had learned to separate the physical from the emotional. Isabelle never worried about becoming attached. She didn't have it in her.

Sex was a way to pass time, something to do and, until a few years ago, she did it a lot and with different partners. A desperate attempt to find a man who would make her feel something other than total numbness. She finally gave up on the useless quest. Now she chose her sexual partners with care.

Peter Jessup would do nicely. And he was probably a great fuck. She didn't call it making love. Making love meant something else, something more intimate and cherished. Two people coming together and losing sight of where one began and the other ended. At least that's what Isabelle imagined, but how could she know? She'd never experienced it. Emotional intimacy would cause the bottom to drop out of her carefully crafted life. She just called it what it was.

Fucking.

That's what they'd be together. A good fuck.

5

ISABELLE SLOUCHED OVER HER KITCHEN TABLE READING THE response to the motion to dismiss for the Parker hearing. Her right shoulder nagged at her. She dropped her pen and stood to stretch.

The clock chimed 1:00 a.m. Another late night where her gritty eyes begged for sleep. And she didn't need Kendrick's presence distracting her. The jerk couldn't wait to show up until after her first shot at second chair? Just her luck.

Coffee. The jolt of caffeine would keep her focused during the remaining hour of preparation for the hearing. She stared out the French doors into the blackness of the Atlantic Ocean. If she opened the door, she'd hear the waves of low tide breaking against the shoreline. A sound that always pleased her.

But smart women didn't unlock their doors in the middle of the night.

She set the pot to brew and sat again. Back to work. Maybe she'd start on the list of discovery needs. She probably wouldn't finish, but it would be a start. The repetitive sound of the coffee dripping soothed her overactive brain, and she yawned.

"Oh, Isabelle. You need to get it together, honey," she said, tugging on the bottoms of her favorite boxer shorts.

Maybe she'd just close her eyes for a second. Yes. Stellar idea. Just a minute to refocus. She folded her arms on the table and rested her forehead against them. Her body almost sighed.

Don't fall asleep. Too much to do.

"Wake up sleepy head," a low, breathy voice said against her ear.

"Hmmm?"

"I said *wake up!*"

A sudden and fierce pain blasted the back of Isabelle's head.

"Ow!" Her sleepy body roared to an instant state of alert. *What the hell?*

Someone was in her house. The force of someone pulling her hair snarled her thoughts.

"That got your attention." The man, his fingers brutally clenched around her hair, yanked her from the chair and dragged her toward the living room while ice picks of pain shot down her neck.

Oh, God. Oh, God. Oh, God. That voice. The one that had haunted her for years. She hacked at his arm to free herself. "Kendrick, let go. You're hurting me."

With a grunt, he shoved her to the floor, and she landed on her side, the sting rocketing through her hip. Scrambling her sock-clad feet into action proved futile as they slipped against the hardwood and thwarted her escape.

Kendrick, in a panther-quick move, jumped on her, forcing her to her back and straddling her. She slammed her eyes shut and her body sent conflicting signals to her brain.

Fight.

The clanging in her head began.

No. Not again. *Don't let him do this.*

She threw a punch. He leaned left and the punch skittered off his shoulder.

Dammit!

The relentless adrenaline pounding her system sparked her instincts and she bucked her hips, thrashed her legs. Anything to get him off her.

"No!"

Kendrick laughed that sick little laugh he used when he knew he could control her.

Not tonight. Never again.

"Shhh." He leaned forward, pinning her arms and bending his face close to her ear. "Easy, Isabelle."

His disgusting weight pressed her into the floor as she tried to yank her arms free.

"Just like old times, sweetheart," he said. "You know you want me."

A sob crawled up her throat.

No crying. Focus. You know what to do.

She stopped thrashing. Relaxed her body. She needed him to sit up. Then his little fucked-up world would quickly change.

Still holding her, Kendrick lifted his face from her ear. Now nose to nose, his hateful gaze scorched hers.

Bile replaced the sob in her throat and she closed her eyes to quiet her ravaged mind. She went still.

"That's my girl."

He sat up, released her arms and kneaded her breasts with his filthy hands. "Now, let's have a look at you. It's been so long and you've grown."

Isabelle flipped the switch in her head. The one that

made her go numb. She barely heard the sound of her shirt tearing.

"Oh, yes," Kendrick said, rocking forward so his erection rubbed against her belly.

Her stomach pitched, but she forced herself to study him and analyze her surroundings.

His gaze remained locked on her breasts. "You have definitely grown, my Isabelle."

Rage swarmed her, and she focused on gathering all that virulence into a ball.

Kendrick leaned forward.

The eyes.

Now.

She jabbed her thumbs into his eyes, digging in hard before he got too close to her face.

Kendrick howled. He reeled backward and she shoved him onto his back.

She darted to her feet as he struggled from the floor, swiping at his blistering red eyes. He blinked a couple of times and came at her swinging, but she sidestepped out of his reach.

Focus.

The balls.

With straining lungs, she stepped toward him and drove her knee into his groin. He doubled over and grabbed his crotch. She raised an arm high and thrust her elbow deep into his shoulder blades.

He went down, rolled for a second and slowly got to his feet.

Shit.

She blasted him with a palm strike to the nose. A hideous crunch, blood splattering over his cheeks. Broken.

Good. Somehow he found the energy to remain standing, but staggered back and covered his nose with his hands.

Isabelle was too far gone to stop. She had to put him out of commission. She nailed him with a roundhouse kick to the ribs, sending him to one knee.

"You don't have enough hands to defend yourself."

Hate burned in his eyes. At one time, she would have cared, but now, almost eleven years later, it meant nothing. For insurance, she popped him with a hammer fist on the sweet spot at his temple and watched him hit the floor.

The Vic Special she called it, but had never had the opportunity to use it.

Kendrick didn't move. Not an inch. She squinted at him, blinked a couple of times, as the rush subsided and the reality of her situation settled in.

Oh, God. Oh, God. Oh, God.

Her legs turned liquid and, panting, she dropped to her knees. Kendrick remained motionless.

Could she have killed him?

It would serve him right, but wouldn't that be some irony? She'd go to jail for murder, the life she'd built blown, all because of Kendrick and the evil he brought. A cry escaped and she sucked in a breath as her arms began to shake. Drool slid down her chin and she swiped at it.

She scrambled to him, pressed two fingers to his neck. Please. Please. *Don't be dead you son of a bitch*. The rhythmic bumping of his pulse hit her fingers.

She should call 9-1-1. Boosting herself off the floor, her feet struggling for traction, she ran to the kitchen for the phone.

No.

The police would come. She'd have to tell them and, after

all this time, she didn't want the secret out. She'd left that life behind and wanted it to stay there. The scandal would be disastrous. She had a promising career ahead of her.

If you need anything, just call. Doesn't matter what time.

That's what Peter had said. Somehow he knew.

With trembling fingers, she grabbed her purse and dug the scrap of paper from her wallet.

Her mind raced as she ran for the front door. She began dialing, but stopped before pressing the final button. Should she involve him? Maybe she should call her uncle? He would never take her side though.

The last number being pressed made a sharp, piercing sound in the silent house.

Peter would help her.

Hopefully.

A HARASSING SOUND BROUGHT PETER OUT OF ONE HONEY OF A dream and he fought to pry his eyes open. The image of Izzy riding him like a rodeo queen disappeared and he swore he'd annihilate whoever dared to wake him. *Dammit.* He shot a look at the digital clock. Two-fourteen.

He grabbed his cell phone and checked the ID. Isabelle DeRosa.

"Get outta here," he said with a big-ass smile on his face. Maybe his dream might come true after all. His raging hard-on hoped so.

"Hello?"

"P-P-Peter? I'm—I'm sorry to—"

Crying. Blood rushed from his head—the one on his shoulders—and he vaulted out of bed, grabbing clothes wherever he could find them.

"Izzy, what's wrong?"

"I—I need help. Can you come? Quick? My h-house."

"Are you hurt?"

He shoved his legs into a pair of tighty-whities.

"No. Kendrick is. He's unconscious."

Oh, shit. Basketball shorts were next along with flip-flops. "Is he alive?"

"Mmm-hmm."

"Okay."

"Peter, please hurry."

"Ten minutes. Get out of the house. Get away from him."

She didn't say anything.

"Izzy?"

"I'll wait on the porch. Can't talk now. Hurry."

She hung up.

What the hell was up with her and Kendrick? Did she shoot him? Hell, Peter didn't even know if she owned a gun. And what was he going to do when he got there? He'd figure it out later. He just needed to get there. He grabbed a T-shirt and flew out the door.

Peter pulled his Explorer into Isabelle's driveway, his headlights lighting up the darkened porch and the woman sitting on it. Izzy squinted against the glare. Her face resembled a starched tablecloth, stiff and white. She shoved her hair away from her eyes and stood.

He killed the engine and jumped out. With the cool wind coming off the ocean she must be freezing in a tank top and boxers. The tank top was tied at her waist, clearly torn from the front. He didn't want to think about that right now. A sick feeling made him a little dizzy. He held out his hands and she grabbed them in a shivering grip.

She jerked her head sideways. "He... He's in there. I just checked him and he's still out, but I think he's waking up. I nudged him with my foot and he groaned. I don't know what to do. I can't call 9-1-1. I don't want the police involved if I can avoid it. My family will freak."

Poor thing. If there was one thing he understood it was family pressure.

Peter wrapped his hand around the back of her head and pulled her trembling body into his shoulder. After burying her face in his shirt, her body lurched and she began sobbing. Not just crying, but hardcore sobs that should have cracked a rib. "You're safe now. Let's see what's what." He climbed the two stairs leading to the front door. "What happened?"

"He broke in. Well, he used my uncle's key."

He *knew* it. *Dumbass, should have changed those locks right then.*

Peter stepped into the house and saw Kendrick on the floor, shadowed by a light from the kitchen. A small side chair had been knocked over, and the coffee table was out of place, but otherwise the room was intact. "What did you hit him with?"

Izzy sniffled and scrubbed at her eyes. "What do you mean?"

"Take a breath and think a minute. What did you knock him out with? A lamp? A hammer? What?"

She shook her head as Peter flipped on the lamp and got his first gander at old Kendrick. Well, he assumed the bloody, swollen face on the floor was Kendrick's. He kneeled next to him, checked his pulse and breathing. Someone beat the royal fuck out of this asshole.

He looked back at Izzy. "*You* did *this*?"

Standing a little taller, she narrowed her eyes at him. "Yes, I did it. What was I supposed to do? He was trying to rape me."

Rape. Every cell in his body became a seething inferno.

He snapped his jaw shut, locked his teeth together and scraped his hands through his hair. Losing his temper wouldn't help her.

He forced what he hoped would be a reassuring smile. "You beat the shit out of him. I'm proud of you."

She jerked her head. "What should I do with him? Does... Does he need to go to the hospital?"

"He should probably get checked out, but are you sure you want to be the one to do that? They'll ask questions." That got him a big zippo. "What about your uncle? Can you call him? Or we can drive Kendrick over there and dump his sorry ass."

Her eyes suddenly caught fire. "Yes. Let's do that. Let my uncle clean up the mess."

"I'll carry him out. How did he get here? There's no car in the driveway."

She held out her hands. "I have no idea. He must have parked on the street. I don't even know what he's driving."

Peter boosted Kendrick into a fireman's hold and he groaned. "Shut up, asshole." He angled back to Izzy and tried not to stare at her chest. "Uh, you might want to put something else on."

Considering her nipples were standing at full attention and poking at the torn tank top. She glanced down and slapped her arms across her chest. Her obvious embarrassment kept her eyes to the floor. This poor woman was a freaking wreck. Time for a tension buster.

"Hey, listen," Peter said. "It's working great for me, but I'm not sure how your uncle will feel about it."

She offered a scarce smile before she took off to her bedroom. He hefted Kendrick a little higher and stepped toward the front door.

So much for a quiet vacation.

. . .

ISABELLE POUNDED UNTIL HER UNCLE FINALLY OPENED HIS front door. He stood before them in a silk bathrobe, his full head of gray hair rumpled from sleep.

"What happened?" He watched as Peter dumped Kendrick on the floor. "Who are you? What the hell did you do to my son?"

"Not me, chief." Peter jerked a thumb toward Isabelle.

Uncle Bart spun toward her, his eyes dark and menacing. She'd seen that look in court when he went after a hostile witness. "Isabelle, what is going on?"

The calming meditations she'd done on the drive over failed miserably because the blood stormed back into her cheeks. She gritted her teeth, wanting to scream at him that his sexual deviant son should be in a cell instead of on the floor. "He broke into the cottage using your key." She held the key ring up and handed it over. "He's a menace. Keep him away from me or I'll kill him."

"I don't believe it," her uncle scoffed.

Isabelle took a step forward. She and her uncle, all five foot eight of him, were the same height, and she stared right into his eyes. "You believe it. You know you do. Just be glad I didn't call the police and have him arrested. You thought the scandal eleven years ago would have been a disaster. Imagine the mess it would create now that you're the managing partner of one of the top criminal defense firms in the state. You should be kissing my ass."

His eyes turned a shade darker. "Isabelle—"

"I'm done here. Let's go, Peter."

She turned and, with Peter right behind, marched out.

"Keep him away from me," she shouted over her shoulder.

6

PETER UNLOCKED ISABELLE'S FRONT DOOR AND STEPPED IN, holding it open as she trudged by. She had tucked her swingy dark hair behind her ears and her normally bright eyes appeared gutted. Hollow.

"Are you sure you won't stay at my place for the rest of the night?"

He'd broached the subject in the car—the only conversation in an otherwise silent ride—but she declined the offer.

Her gaze fixed on the coffee table sitting on its side and she shook her head before turning to him. "I have to be in court at ten. More than that, I can't let him put me out of my house. He's taken too much from me already."

A quick check of his cell phone told Peter it was nearly 4:00 a.m. He couldn't leave her alone. Not like this.

He ran a hand over his stubbled chin. "Okay. How about you get some sleep and I hang out here until daylight?"

"I'll be fine, Peter."

"The guys are coming to install your alarm anyway. I can

let them in. I'm changing the lock on the front door. Is that the only door with the old lock?"

She nodded. "You don't have to do this. You're on vacation and I'm not your responsibility."

Amazing. She was ready to fight this herself. She could probably do it too. He needed to get to know Isabelle DeRosa a whole lot more.

"The minute Vic called me, you became my responsibility. You're his friend and he cares about you. If something happens to you, when I should have helped, I'll go insane. Plus, I'll never hear the end of it."

She stepped to the coffee table, set it to rights. "I never imagined he'd break in here like this. He's never been violent with me."

"What *has* he been with you, Izzy?"

TENSION WRAPPED ITSELF INTO A ROCK BETWEEN ISABELLE'S shoulders. She'd dragged him into this mess. He deserved the truth. Even if he treated her differently afterward. Everyone else did. Besides, she owed him. If Kendrick decided to press assault charges, Peter could be implicated. Wouldn't that be a kicker?

She drew in a breath, lowered herself to the ottoman and motioned for him to sit. He dropped onto the couch in front of her.

Draped over the back of the sofa was one of her grandmother's afghans. Yes, this was still her space and she would again be safe here.

Here goes. She prayed he wouldn't give her the pity face.

"Kendrick is ten years older than I am. He sexually abused me from the time I was eight until I was fifteen. He's a sick bastard who now lives in Ohio and wants me to come live with him. He said he needs legal advice. I'm guessing he's in trouble."

The rush of words left her feeling flattened. She'd been carrying the vile weight of Kendrick's offer since her initial conversation with him, and now something inside told her it would be all right. That the man sitting in front of her, the one that ogled her in the elevator less than twenty-four hours ago, would help her.

Peter's face remained a blank canvas. Nothing. Not a wince. Not an iota of a curled lip.

He finally sat forward and narrowed his eyes. "I knew it had to be something twisted. I could tell by your body language."

The breath she'd been holding came hurtling out, and she threw her hands over her face.

When Peter rubbed his rough fingers over her arm, she flinched and he snatched them away. *No.* She reached for his hand. "I'm sorry. I didn't mean to pull away. It startled me. *You* startle me."

She rose, paced the floor and reached for the afghan while Peter watched, his face a cross between curiosity and concern. She enfolded herself in the softness of her granny's hard work and went back to her seat.

"I don't tell people because they either pity me or they're disgusted."

He shrugged, inched a little closer until his leg brushed hers.

"I don't pity you. Look at what you've accomplished. This house, your education. He's the sick fuck. And there's a special place in hell for him. Did he serve time for this?"

She shook her head and Peter's eyes bulged.

"Why the hell not?" He kept his voice quiet, but the slow rumble seemed to strangle him.

"My mother worried I couldn't endure a trial. My uncle, of course, being the top criminal attorney in the state, didn't want the bad publicity. He's the one who found us. Kendrick was having sex with me in my uncle's study during a family party and he walked in on us."

"Oh, Jesus."

"They decided to send Kendrick away. Uncle Bart got him a job with a client's company in Ohio. That's why my parents are divorced. I guess my father felt helpless and resented my mother for agreeing to let Kendrick walk away. And my younger sister left for college out West. She doesn't come back much. I don't know if it's because of the situation or if she's embarrassed or what. Thankfully, Kendrick never put his hands on her. At least she's never admitted it."

"Do you think she would?"

Isabelle nodded. "Yes. She and I are close. She'd at least tell me."

"I can't believe your uncle let a child molester go free. I don't give a shit that it's his kid, he's still dangerous."

Didn't she know it? She'd spent years wondering if there were other victims. Children who would have been safe if Kendrick had paid for his crime.

"I lose sleep wondering if he's abused others. Part of me hopes it was just a sick attraction he had to me. Then I'd be the only one. It makes me nervous that he's back and that attraction still exists."

Bile curled in her throat and she swallowed it back.

Peter leaned forward, put a hand on her shoulder and pulled her toward him. She let it happen. A light embrace. Not too close, not too distant. Just enough so she'd know he wasn't repulsed. A good man. The faded woodsy scent of his soap soothed her rattled nerves and she snuggled into his neck.

Since when did she need comfort from a man?

"We'll take care of the security pronto," he said. "Who else knows he wants you to visit him?"

"Only Vic. I told him when I called about the security system. It's too disgusting to even think about much less tell my family. I just never thought he'd get violent with me."

Forcing sex with a child isn't violent? Peter shook his head in disbelief. "You've never said no to him. He didn't have control this time."

She scrubbed her hands over her face, and the blanket inched down her shoulders. "Maybe you're right. I can't figure out why he came home. It's been three years since his last visit. Even if he's in legal trouble, there are plenty of defense attorneys he could go to. I don't get it. I'm probably just tired."

"Hey." He squatted in front of her and pulled the afghan back into place. "You kicked his ass. Where'd you learn to fight like that?"

"When I started college at NYU, my father wanted me to learn self-defense. Vic was in town on business and Dad asked him to show me a few moves. My dad has never dealt with his own anger about this situation. I think I feel most sorry for him. He has no outlet." She paused a minute and took a breath. "Anyway, that's when Vic found out about the abuse. My dad confided in him. It shocked me because we don't talk about it. Ever. My dad didn't want me to be victimized again, though, and he was worried about me being on my own. Vic showed me some Krav Maga moves. I liked the power it gave me. It became an addiction for me. It helps me get rid of the rage when I think about Kendrick. I told Vic I wanted to get better and he hooked me up with a guy who'd been in the Israeli Army. Ian trained me well."

"I'll say." Peter scratched his head. "Your uncle's quite a guy. I don't get how you can work for him after everything that's happened."

She shrugged. "It's not rocket science. My uncle feels guilty about what his son did. He's also the founding partner of a law firm. I've worked hard at my education and I don't want to depend on anyone. For anything. Defense lawyers make more money than prosecutors. I'm a former victim who has to defend criminals, and I have to live with that. But it gives me freedom."

In a sick sort of way, it made sense. Peter also had ways of channeling his anger. Unfortunately, his ways stopped working recently. "I give you credit. I couldn't be near him every day."

"Yeah, you could. If it meant getting to where you want to be, you could do it. My relationship with my uncle is strained, at best, but I'll use him to build a career. I don't feel bad about it either. I sacrificed for his career, and he can do the same for me. I won't be there forever. Just a couple of years. All I need is the experience at a prestigious firm and I'll be able to go anywhere."

He reached up, tucked the hair that had come loose back behind her ear.

She brought her gaze up and it fused with his. *Oh, crap.* The look he'd been thinking about all day. He started to pull his hand away, but she grabbed his wrist and held it there while his good sense went to war with his horny body.

"You're okay," he said.

If she made a move on him he'd be screwed. He would *not* shag her. Not after what she'd experienced tonight. She focused on his mouth and closed her eyes for a second.

When she opened them, something changed. An odd shift he couldn't decipher. Heat filled her eyes, but she'd become distant when it should have been the other way around. Weird.

She inched toward him. He backed away.

Nope. Not gonna do this.

"Izzy, let's not confuse two issues here."

She laughed. "I'm not confused."

"I'm glad. Overjoyed actually." She'd never know how much. "But, let's wait and see how you feel tomorrow. Adrenaline sometimes makes me want things I shouldn't have. You may think you want sex tonight, and believe me, I'm happy to oblige, but I couldn't take it if you had regrets tomorrow."

Silence. She kept her gaze locked with his though, and he saw the confusion behind it. Did she have a clue how much talking her eyes did?

She screwed up her lips to smother a smile. "Where the hell are you from, Peter? I have never in my life had a man say that to me."

He snorted. "I'm a bit blown away myself. Considering I've been thinking about nothing *but* having sex with you. I don't want it like this. Not after what happened tonight. I'd be damned happy to revisit the conversation at a later date though."

She leaned forward and the blanket slipped off when she pressed her ice-cold hands against his cheeks. And kissed him. Not a crazy, lust-ridden kiss. More of a soft, lingering kiss. Confirmation that they would revisit the conversation. *Haza!* He could only hope. Otherwise, he'd beat himself to death with a ball pein hammer for losing the opportunity.

She backed away, giving his wrist a squeeze. "I'd appreciate it if you stayed awhile. I'll get you some blankets. The couch is comfortable."

He cleared his throat. Nodded.

She headed toward the bedroom, but stopped. "Thank you, Peter. For everything."

"No sweat," he said. "You don't happen to have a hammer, do you?"

7

Isabelle waited as Peter pulled his SUV into the circular drive in front of her office building.

"That's a look if I've ever seen one," she said when he walked over to her. The camouflage cargo shorts, white T-shirt and beat-up combat boots left her wanting to duck and cover. Why, oh why, did he have a do-rag hiding that gorgeous hair?

He handed her a set of keys. "Huh?"

She gestured up and down with her hands "Your outfit."

"Oh, yeah. This is standard wear for me. My day *and* night look, so to speak."

After skimming the getup one more time, she tapped her finger against her lips. "I like the rogue look. It suits you."

A car pulled up and Peter stepped onto the curb, nudging her back a few steps. The intensity of all that male heat so close sent a buzz shooting up her legs.

"Thank you for running the keys over to me," she said. "My court appearance was cancelled, so I could have met you at the house and gotten them."

Ten minutes earlier, he called to say he'd changed the lock on the front door and had new keys for her. Could he come by the office and drop them off? Him going so far out of his way left her wondering why he was being so kind. Vic's words echoed in her mind and she shook off the negative thoughts. She could trust Peter.

He waved his hand. "I knew you had a busy day. I figured I'd run them by. Plus, if I'm not at the house later, you won't be able to get in. Well, you could use the back door I guess. It is your house and you probably have a key."

She burst out laughing. "Peter, you're babbling." She put her hand against his forehead. "Are you feeling all right?"

He snatched her hand away, brought it to his lips and kissed it. *That is quite lovely.* But the kiss ended and he stood there holding her hand as if he'd done it a thousand times before. She didn't fight it. Where had this ease come from in one short day?

Holy.

Cow.

"I feel great," he said. "Gotta go though. I need to stop at my mother's on the way back to your place. The guys are finishing the alarm and I wanna get back before they're done."

She nodded. "I can't tell you how much it means to me that you're taking the time."

"Izzy, we talked about this last night. I know you're grateful. Stop saying it."

She held up her hands. "I just wanted you to know."

"When you get home, I'll show you how to work the alarm." He stepped away from her. "Uh, you care if I do a little surfing by your place?"

Was he kidding? She didn't own the ocean. He could surf wherever he wanted. She knew what he meant though.

He wanted permission to be in her space for reasons outside of installing an alarm. A smart man.

"You can do whatever you'd like at my house."

He raised his eyebrows and grinned.

"Within reason," she added. "If I find you in my bed with a woman, you're a dead man."

He grinned bigger.

Her stomach knotted. "Did I say that?"

He continued to grin.

She *had* said it. Must be the fatigue. Three hours of sleep didn't cut it.

He stepped closer. Oh, boy.

"Izzy, the only woman I want in that bed is you."

Some alternate force propelled her forward and she slid her arms around his neck, pressed herself against the hard planes of his body and kissed him. Tongue and all, right in front of her office building.

Holy.

Holy.

Cow.

What was she doing?

Peter didn't seem to mind the PDA because he steel-armed her around the waist and returned the kiss with just as much enthusiasm. When he pulled away, his gaze stayed glued to hers and the fire shot to her core.

He eased back. "I'll take that as a maybe."

When he got to the car, he smiled that amazing movie star smile and blew her a kiss.

Smart-ass.

Still though, his thinking was spot on about the maybe.

. . .

PETER'S SUV WAS IN HER DRIVEWAY WHEN ISABELLE PULLED in at six o'clock. She breathed in the salty ocean air—nothing compared to be being home. She drummed her fingers against the steering wheel while the suddenly slow process of raising the car's roof took place. Could she be excited about seeing him? Hmm, something new.

As she approached the front porch, she glanced back toward the car in the no-parking zone by the public beach access. She had driven past and spotted a man sitting behind the wheel staring out at the ocean. Maybe he was waiting for someone. She shrugged it off and turned her attention to the new silver lock gleaming in the evening sunlight. Assuming Peter would be on the beach, she unlocked the door and opened it. A beep sounded and she hoped it only meant someone had entered. Otherwise, the alarm would blare and she had no idea how to turn it off. She dropped her keys in the dish by the door and glanced toward the spot in the kitchen where Kendrick had grabbed her.

No.

She wouldn't let him take the safety of this house from her. Her grandmother's afghan on the sofa caught her attention and she breathed in. Her house. Her space.

"Peter?" she called, perusing the mail she'd grabbed on her way in.

Wow. Calling out for a man in her house was a new experience. She needed to decide if she liked it. In this case, maybe so.

No answer.

She brought her briefcase to the kitchen and dumped it on the table, where she spotted a note written in what she now recognized as Peter's scratchy, all caps handwriting. *ALARM IS IN. WAVES ARE GOOD.*

She laughed. A man of many words. She stepped to the French doors and peered out. Three surfers sat atop their boards waiting for the promise of a next wave. She spotted Peter in a sleeveless, red wetsuit. Yowzer. Without a doubt, she needed a closer look.

Maybe she'd change clothes and sit on the beach with a glass of wine. She had work to do, but mental and physical fatigue had set in hours ago, and her body ached from head to toe.

No sense wasting a wind-free, eighty-degree evening.

Ten minutes later, armed with her beach chair, a couple of oversized towels and a glass of wine, Isabelle stepped off the back deck and headed down the beach to her favorite spot.

The afternoon's blazing hot sand had cooled and her feet nearly sighed with joy. Sometimes warm sand was better than a foot massage. The sound of breaking waves crashing into the shore helped release the stress of the last couple of days and her body hummed.

Her space.

She watched Peter grab a wave and ride it in, deftly handling the process. She held her hand up. He waved, but headed back to the water. Apparently, nothing came between Peter and surfing. Just as well. She could enjoy her wine and watch, which couldn't be considered a hardship with him in that wetsuit.

One of the other surfers, Doug, came out of the water and dropped his board to the sand. He surfed here often and they'd chatted a few times. Seemed like a nice enough guy. His surfer-boy blond hair and tanned body didn't diminish the package and, recently, she found herself contemplating his maybe-we-should-get-a-drink-sometime suggestions.

Isabelle's attention turned back to Peter, who caught another wave and promptly got tossed. Ouch. His head popped out of the water and he shoved his hair from his eyes before reeling in his board and heading to shore.

Sorry, Doug, you don't have fantastic hair.

She stuck her wine in the sand and pondered greeting Peter at the shoreline, but with Doug standing not four feet away, she didn't want an awkward situation. Not that they had anything going, but he'd showed an interest, and she'd prefer to avoid being rude by ignoring him while talking to Peter. Men. Such complicated creatures.

Peter solved the problem by coming to her. "Hey," she said.

"Hey yourself."

She tossed him one of the two towels and eyed him as he ran it over his face and rioting hair. She had to get her hands in that hair. Soon.

Doug, his board tucked under his arm, chose that moment to walk by. He slowed his pace but didn't stop. "Hi, Isabelle."

"Hey. Good ride?"

He smiled, his straight white teeth and dimples shining. "Pretty good." He jerked his head at Peter. "Howzit, brah?"

"Good," Peter continued drying himself off and rolled his eyes. He watched the other man walk toward the street and turned back to her. "Surfer speak. Has he ever even been to Hawaii?"

Isabelle laughed. "I couldn't say."

"He a friend of yours?"

That's right. Peter the caveman didn't like to share. He'd said so yesterday when he talked about his ex-wife. "I know him a little bit."

Peter spread the towel on the sand and reached back to

unzip his wet suit. Oh, this would be a pleasure. She already had a nice view of his rock-solid arms and, given what she saw in that clingy wetsuit, the rest had to be good.

Focused on shoving the wetsuit down his arms, he peeled the suit off his body to reveal his chest and abs. Yummy. Springy dark hair, perfect pecs and one hell of a six-pack. The heat of something truly amazing happening stole her breath. Had the sun just risen inside her chest?

Oblivious to her staring, at least until he'd gotten the suit pulled to his waist, he glanced over at her just as she licked her lips.

Their eyes met. There would be no denying she'd been checking him out.

"*Again*, Izzy?" he mimicked from the day before.

Playing along, she thunked herself on the head. "I'm sorry! I'm a single woman, you're a hot guy. It's hardwired."

He cracked up and dropped onto the towel he'd spread on the sand. "Yeah. I've heard *that* before."

Grinning at him came too easy. *Shoot*. She liked him.

"I see the alarm is in," she said.

"All hooked up. I'll show you how to use it before I leave. Damn, this is a perfect evening. If every day could be this good, I won't so much mind this month off."

A month? "Vic must love you if he gave you a month off."

For some reason, Peter grunted and continued to stare at the sky.

Finally, he rolled to his side and propped himself on his elbow. "Vic put me on R&R. I was coming back for my brother's wedding and Vic felt it would be in my best interest if I took a few weeks off. Speaking of Stephen's wedding, I don't have a date. What are you doing Saturday night?"

"It depends."

"On what?"

"On whether you're asking me to your brother's wedding."

He opened his mouth. Shut it again. "Guess I screwed that up." He put his hand on her ankle and squeezed. "Izzy, would you like to be my date for my brother's wedding on Saturday night?"

The answer came to her immediately. When the hell had she turned into a flake?

She should think about it. For no other reason than to get it straight in her head that what was happening between them could only be a physical attraction.

"I'd love to. Thank you for asking."

So much for thinking about it. With him stretched out on that towel, that incredible body, the curly hair and the killer smile, how could she resist?

"You're welcome," he said. "And thank you. It'll be fun. Vic and Gina are coming in."

"Is Gina showing yet?"

"It's not quite a bump." He grinned. "A pebble maybe."

She retrieved her forgotten, now tepid wine from the sand. "Why is Vic coming to your brother's wedding?"

"Steve's been out to Chicago a few times and he and Vic get along."

"Ah." She sipped her wine, put it back down. "You haven't told me why Vic put you on vacation."

"You caught that, ay?"

She caught it all right. "You're good at deflecting the things you don't want to talk about, Peter. It's your rotten luck I've been doing it for years and can spot it a mile away."

He dug his fingers into the sand and let out a breath. "My last assignment turned bad and I went a little crazy."

Her pulse kicked up but, deep down, she couldn't

picture Peter going off his rocker. He'd been the prince of cool during her ordeal the previous night.

"What happened?"

He frowned at a seashell he'd dug out of the sand then tossed it away. "I switched shifts with one of my teammates one morning. We were protecting a diplomat on a Middle East trip. I had the stomach flu and couldn't walk two feet without puking. I asked Roy to cover the shift for me and, while they were transporting the big shot, someone opened fire. The diplomat lived, Roy didn't."

Isabelle's legs melted. And she thought being a lawyer was hard. "I'm so sorry."

He tossed away another shell. "He had a wife and two kids. He was my friend."

First Tiny. Then this. She could see why Vic forced him to take a vacation. She scooted off the chair to sit next to him. "You were sick. There was nothing you could have done."

He looked up at her, those dark blue eyes a little haunted. "Tell that to his family."

Silence hung between them until he finally turned toward the ocean. His damp hair pooled around his face, and she gave in and slid her hand through it. He inclined his head sideways, into her hand.

Isabelle closed her eyes. She could do this. She'd flip the switch in her head and forget how much she liked him. Making it a physical thing shouldn't be hard. Not after all her years of practice. They'd be good together and both needed the release.

Opening her eyes, she realized he was watching her. She pulled her hand from his hair, dragged it down his cheek, over his shoulder to the dark swirling hair on his chest.

Forget how much you like him. She bit her bottom lip before moving in for the kill.

"WHAT ARE YOU DOING?" PETER ASKED, HIS HEAD—BOTH OF them—about to explode. He grabbed her hand before it completed its journey south.

She'd done it again. That closing her eyes thing where her demeanor changed and she became distant. What the hell?

"Did we have a signal malfunction?" Izzy asked. "I mean, I think I have pretty good radar and I thought we had, um... chemistry, I guess...between us."

He squeezed her hand. "There's no malfunction."

She slid her hand away. "Then what's the problem?"

She wasn't the only one perturbed. "Creepy Izzy is the problem."

She opened her mouth and left it hanging for a second. "Did you just call me *creepy*?"

"No. I called the person you turned into creepy. I'd love to give Fun Izzy a good shagging, but Creepy Izzy I'll pass on."

She drew her head back. "Huh?"

"You change. You did it last night right before you kissed me. But when you kissed me at your office, it was Fun Izzy."

She sat and stared at him, either thinking he was completely whacked or that he'd nailed it.

"I...I can't believe you noticed that. No one has ever noticed."

Nailed it.

An insane flickering started under his skin. "Then they weren't paying attention because you definitely check out."

"No, Peter." Her voice hitched and she moved an inch

closer. "It's not you."

Yeah. Nice try. "I'm the only one here."

She scrubbed her hands over her face. Stalling probably.

"It's a coping thing I do."

"A coping thing?" He sat up. "You need a *coping* thing to have sex with me? Jesus, Izzy, you should stop talking right now because this is going off the rails."

"No." She waved her hands at him. "That's not what I mean. It's the sex. I have to separate the physical from the emotional. I flip a switch. It comes from the abuse. Please understand."

"I *don't* understand." But, shit, he'd like to because the disappointment might just kill him.

"No one has ever figured it out. I've told you things I haven't shared with people I've known for years. I'm freaking out. Very much so."

All he could do was lay back and throw his forearm over his eyes. Could he be any more of a selfish prick? She was a victim of abuse and he was letting his dick do all the thinking. He had no idea what went on in her head...or her heart. He got rid of the thought and sat up to face her. "I'm sorry. I shouldn't have jumped to conclusions."

She nodded. "I'll try to explain it, but I don't know if it'll make sense to you."

"Give it a shot."

She sighed, gathered sand in her hand and let it slip between her fingers.

"Sex for me has never been about making love. Being abused by someone I loved caused a...a malfunction... between sex, love and trust. Sex, just for the physical gratification is good for me, but if I start to get emotional, I get scared." She brushed sand off his knee. "I loved Kendrick, and he exploited that love.

"Three years ago I had my first serious relationship and the sex brought back all the pain. For the first time since the abuse happened, I cared about someone. As soon as the sex became more about an emotional connection rather than a physical one, I ended the relationship. I just didn't know how to deal with it. I still don't."

Separating the physical from the emotional. Holy hell. He *could* relate. The knot in his chest eased. He separated his feelings every day when he thought about all the lives lost at his hands. His job meant eliminating people to make the world safer and, somehow, over the years he'd learned to justify it.

Izzy could have casual sex, no problem. But she turned into Creepy Izzy to do it. If he wanted to, he could have her. Creepy Izzy was a major turnoff though. Talk about flipping a switch. Maybe he had his own switch, because Fun Izzy was the girl that got him firing.

He tucked a finger under her chin and tilted her head up. "We're moving at light speed here. We don't have to. I'm crazy attracted to you, but Fun Izzy is the one I want."

Tears welled up in her eyes. Jesus. He was screwing this up.

"But, Peter, you still don't understand."

Yes. He did. At least he thought so. "What?"

She locked those beautiful, watery eyes on him. "Fun Izzy has never experienced making love. Emotionally speaking, she's a virgin. Creepy Izzy always takes over. I don't know how to change that."

Okay. He could tackle this one. "Yeah, you do. You did it today when you kissed me. *That* was Fun Izzy. You didn't think about it. You just plastered one on me and it rocked my world."

No kidding there. He got hard thinking about that kiss.

"Really?" She smiled a little. "You're sure it was Fun Izzy?"

He laughed. What a freaking conversation. "I'm positive. You have this thing you do when Creepy Izzy takes over. You close your eyes and, a few seconds later your attitude changes. That didn't happen today. You didn't close your eyes before you kissed me and you definitely weren't distant."

She jerked her head up and down, her eyes getting brighter. "I didn't think about it. I just did it. And I liked it."

"Yeah, because it was Fun Izzy." He squeezed her hands. "We need more Fun Izzy."

"So, what do we do?"

He shrugged. "Hell if I know, but I'm not having sex with Creepy Izzy. I'm waiting on Fun Izzy. That okay with you?"

She snorted. "I guess. You may wind up taking a lot of cold showers though."

Ain't it the truth? He sighed. "At the rate I'm going, I'll turn into an ice pop."

Wouldn't that be fun?

The ocean breeze blew her hair across her face. She pulled her hands free from his, put them on his cheeks and ran her thumb over the faded scar near his mouth. "You could leave, you know? Just forget the whole thing. You didn't sign on for this. We could just be friends and I won't hold it against you. I don't want to pull you into my mess."

"Babe, I'm already in your mess. And I don't want to just be your friend. I'd screw it up by constantly hitting on you."

She cracked up. Did he say something funny?

"Let's slow down and see where we wind up. We have our first date on Saturday night. It's a start."

A smooth smile slid across her face. "Sounds like a plan."

Unable to resist, he ran his index finger down her cheek and tucked her hair behind her ear. "Hell yeah, it does."

When her stomach growled she rubbed her hand over it. "I'm hungry. I could order pizza."

He rolled to a standing position, reached his hand to her and pulled her up. "I'll buy. Let me get my clothes out of the truck and get cleaned up."

"There's a shower around the side of the house."

"Got it." He picked up the towel, flung it out to get rid of the sand, and suddenly she was in front of him, snagging the towel and wrapping her arms around him. Fun Izzy.

Perfection. The way she fit in his arms. The way her head tucked in just below his chin. The way she made him feel like he never wanted to let go.

But then she backed away. Too bad.

"I'll meet you inside," she said. "By the way, did you happen to notice that car parked by the beach entrance?"

Peter turned toward the street. "No. Why?"

"I don't know. It's probably nothing, but people don't usually park there. There was a man in the car." She shook her head. "He was probably picking up his kid or something."

"I'll check it out."

"Nah. It's not a big deal."

But she'd brought it up. "You wouldn't have said anything if it wasn't bugging you. I'll check it out. I have to get my clothes anyway. I'll meet you inside."

He hefted his board and walked up the beach to the entrance. Whoever was sitting there when Izzy came home was gone.

And Peter had a nagging feeling it hadn't been someone waiting for their kid.

8

A<small>FTER PIZZA WITH</small> I<small>ZZY, FATIGUE DRAGGING AT HIM,</small> P<small>ETER</small> drove back to his parents' estate and spotted a large appliance box—*what the hell is this now?*—on the porch of the cottage. He wasn't expecting any deliveries.

He parked in the driveway and sat eyeballing the box. Had his mother mentioned anything? Nothing came to mind. *Damn.* He blew out a breath, ran his cupped hand over his mouth and scratched his neck. He'd just check it out.

Except his heart was damn near beating itself to death. He'd probably have a coronary before he even reached the porch.

Another deep breath. *It's a box, asshole.*

He got out of the car, stole a glance around the side wall and waited. No movement. Definitely not anyone hiding behind the box. Inside maybe? Peter reached for the weapon that should have been at his waist. *Shit.* No weapon. Vic took it from him. Psychos shouldn't carry guns.

The resourceful prick even boosted the one in the safe at his condo. For backup reasons, he had given Vic the safe's combination after Tiny died. Tiny had always kept the combination so someone could open the safe in case Peter got injured or killed.

Not a problem. Wearing his boots had come in handy because he could take a flying leap and land feet first on top of the box. The boots would do some damage. He could snap a neck with these boots.

Sweat trickled down his face and he swiped at it. Time to go.

He blasted from his spot, got some speed going and leaped. He landed on his feet—a solid ten for sticking it—and pulverized the box.

Empty box.

Fucking idiot.

The front door of the cottage smacked open. "What are you doing?" his brother yelled. "You just wrecked Mom's box."

"What?"

Stephen pointed at the destroyed cardboard. "She wanted that. The new dishwasher got installed and she sent me down here to get it. I figured I'd wait for you."

Peter bent at the waist and sucked in air. Who the hell did he think would be in there? Almost as bad as knocking over the deadly potted plant. He either needed to get back to work or deal with this freaking anxiety.

Laughing at himself, he straightened up and shoved past Stephen, who still wore dress slacks from work, but his jacket was off and nowhere to be seen. The sleeves of his white shirt were folded to his elbows.

"So, you decided to make yourself at home?"

The pretty boy's face lit up. As he aged, Stephen's looks had come to resemble Elvis in his prime—the long straight nose, angular face and dark hair had the women going wild.

"Why not?" Steve said.

Peter stalked to the kitchen for a couple of beers. "Do you people not understand boundaries?"

That's it, redirect the conversation so he won't ask about the assassinated box.

"Sure, we understand boundaries. We choose to ignore them."

Peter made a scoffing noise. "Of course. What a perfect explanation."

"Mom sent dinner for you. It's in the fridge."

Peter glanced toward the fridge. "I already ate. Thanks though. She does this every night. I come home and find a plate in the fridge. She's killing me with guilt."

"That's the plan, big brother."

He walked back to the living room and handed Steve a beer. They clinked and took a slug while Peter moved to the cushioned side chair.

"How do you handle her? She's never pissed at you."

That got Steve puffing up his chest and Peter laughed.

"I love this," his brother said. "Two Silver Stars and you can't figure out how to make our mother happy."

Peter held out his hands. "What can I say? I'm not doing the people around me much good lately."

Stephen narrowed his eyes. "Oh, boo-hoo. I'm guessing we're talking about Roy. And maybe Tiny. After all, you're the Emperor of Fix-It Land. If you can't keep two men from dying, you must be doing something wrong."

The smart-ass comment earned a flip of the bird. "I'm not the Emperor of Fix-It Land."

That seemed to amuse Steve because he let out a sarcastic laugh. "If that's all you've got, you're fucked. You are priceless. They were grown men who liked to live on the edge. Just because you were there doesn't mean you were responsible for their safety."

Tell that to their families.

Peter slouched against the chair. "What if Vic's right? Maybe I'm losing it."

"I know Vic's not laying that on you. It's you doing this. After Tiny died you threw yourself into that overseas assignment. You're kidding yourself, Petey. You can't avoid thinking about your dead friends. *I* think, when Roy died, it knocked you on your ass. And now, with Vic putting you on R&R, you've got no place to run. *And* you're destroying boxes."

Don't forget the potted plant.

But thank you, Dr. Phil. Stephen's idea of a rough day entailed canceling his manicure. He'd like to tell him to fuck off. To get out of his sight, but something needled him, made his shoulders lock up. *You've got no place to run.*

Fucking Stephen was right. Peter was trapped within his own mind. Afraid to admit the weakness.

"I freaked when I saw the box. I thought someone might be hiding in it and grabbed for my non-existent gun. I'm losing it. I kicked over a fucking plant the other day."

Steve waved him off. "You're tired. You just lost a good friend. Give yourself a break and take it easy."

"That's your advice? When I tell you I'm going insane? You want me to take a nap?"

"No. I want you to stop thinking you can fix everything."

"Fuck you."

"No. Fuck *you*."

A minute, maybe two passed until they reached the critical point of impasse. Stephen held up his hands, but Peter's cell rang and he stood to retrieve it from the breakfast bar.

Vic. They'd been voice mailing all day. "Yo."

"What the fuck?" Vic said. "I give you one simple assignment and all hell breaks loose."

"One simple assignment? You are whacked, my friend. She laid that asshole to waste last night."

After a healthy slug of his beer, Stephen looked over, curiosity most likely eating him alive. Good. He deserved it for telling him to take a goddamned nap instead of offering some semblance of actionable advice on retrieving his mental stability. A *nap*.

"She's tough our Isabelle," Vic said.

Our Isabelle. Peter liked the sound of it.

"Is she okay?" Vic asked.

"Yeah. I just left her. The alarm is hooked up. It's like Fort Knox over there now. He won't bypass that system unless he knows the code."

"I feel horrible she had to deal with that."

Peter shrugged. "What are you gonna do from Chicago? I was here and wasn't much help. He's one sick bastard."

"No shit. Thanks for taking care of her. I'm not telling her father about this. She asked me not to. I don't know how I feel about that, but I'll make some time this weekend to see her and I'll get a read."

"Yeah, about that. You'll get plenty of time. She's going to the wedding with me."

"You fucker," Vic yelled, and Peter laughed his ass off. Vic would fume about him hitting on Izzy.

"Gotta go." Still laughing, he hung up.

The phone immediately rang again. He assumed it was Vic, but checked the ID anyway just in case it was Izzy. Nope. Vic. No way he'd answer.

Peter headed back to his chair. "That was your buddy Vic."

"What's this crap about bringing a date to my wedding?"

Stephen circled his hand in the air. "You're screwing up the seating chart."

Peter rolled his eyes. "Like you worked on it."

"Hell no, but I had to listen to all the complaining. This one can't sit with that one because she had an affair with that one's husband, and this one can't sit with that one because he banged that one's daughter. Not for nothing, Pete, but can't these people get laid outside their own social circle? It's a nightmare."

Could his brother actually be bitching about this?

"Anyway," Stephen said. "Who is this person screwing up my seating chart and who'd she lay to waste?"

"Her name is Isabelle DeRosa. She's a friend of Vic's. He asked me to help her out with a security system, but she had a problem before we got it installed."

Stephen held his hands wide. "Petey, you've been here three days. What could you possibly be into already?"

To ward off the burning in his eyes, Peter jammed his knuckles into them. "Tell me about it. I'm freaking exhausted."

"So, what's up with this woman?"

"Her cousin is harassing her. The guy broke into her house, and she beat the crap out of him."

Stephen's grin widened. "No way."

"Yeah, she's a Krav expert. I saw the guy after she got done with him. He got his ass handed to him."

"Good for her. She hot or what?"

The long huff Peter let out only threw gas on the fire because his brother gave him a crooked grin. The one that warned he was going to push buttons.

"Petey, you gonna ball this girl?"

Bingo. "To think I used to wonder why you and Vic got

along. Seeing as you're both assholes, it shouldn't be a shock."

"Yeah, but Vic's gone soft since getting hitched. He's lost his edge."

"You'll lose *your* edge too."

"Nah. I'm training to stay sharp."

"Good luck with that," Peter cracked.

Stephen stood, stretched his arms and brought his beer bottle to the kitchen. "I gotta run. We're closing a deal in the morning. A monster one. You're gonna be a little richer, big brother, and you have me to thank for it."

Actually, he had Stephen to thank for a lot of things. Things they didn't talk about, but both understood. Stephen handled family issues, not to mention fulfilling the obligation of joining the family business, while Peter stormed the world. He stood, shook Stephen's hand and walked him to the door. "Thank you. For everything. And don't tell Mom I killed her box. Tell her I didn't know and broke it down for trash."

"Yeah, whatever. Just don't screw with my seating chart again."

9

AT THREE-FIFTEEN SATURDAY AFTERNOON ISABELLE HEARD A knock on her front door. *Damn.* Peter was early. She'd just finished slipping into her dress and hadn't put her shoes or lipstick on. Of course, she'd been late getting home from her hair appointment and spent way too much time worrying about what to wear or she'd have been ready by now.

She'd opted for the black halter dress with a long braid of silk down the middle of her back connecting the top of the dress to the waist. She spun, faced herself in the mirror and adjusted the neckline, which went clear up to her collarbone. No cleavage tonight. Not for meeting Peter's blue-blooded mother.

He knocked again. Harder this time. Mr. Impatient.

"I'm coming!" She rushed to the door, flung it open and held her arms out to show him the dress.

Kendrick stood in the doorway.

No.

A frigid chill penetrated her limbs and she shoved the door closed, pressing her body against it.

"Leave, Kendrick. I'm expecting someone."

He pushed on the door, and she put her weight into it. She couldn't hold him off long. The cordless sat on the entry table not six feet away, but she wouldn't be able to reach it without letting go of the door.

"Isabelle, please. I'm sorry about the other night."

"Just leave. We can forget about the other night, but leave me alone."

"Can I talk to you a minute?"

He leaned into the door from the other side and her bare feet desperately dug into the floor. No chance. Kendrick outweighed her by at least eighty pounds. She could fight him off though. Even in a cocktail dress.

The distinctive growl of an engine sounded. Peter.

A car door slammed and then, seconds later, an *umph*.

The opposing weight on the door vanished and, with her weight against it, the door slammed shut, throwing Isabelle off balance. Her blood pressure plummeted.

"Peter?" She closed her eyes and wished it to be so.

"Yeah. You're good."

She yanked the door open, sent it flying into the wall. Peter stood on the porch, his hands on his tuxedo-clad hips while Kendrick, face battered from the beating she gave him earlier in the week, lay slumped at his feet. With Peter in a tuxedo, it looked like a scene out of a James Bond film. At some other time, the sight would be amusing.

"What's he doing here?" Peter asked, his voice a little harsh.

But was that anger aimed at Kendrick for showing up or her for being stupid and opening the door without checking it first?

"I don't know. I thought he was you. He said he needed to talk to me. What'd you do to him?"

"I tapped him. He'll wake up in a while."

"Dammit." She punched her fist into her other palm. "I should have been the one to knock him on his ass."

Peter shook his head, but laughed. "Sorry, babe. I got there first."

Which was just too bad.

She stared down at Kendrick in his preppy clothes. *Bastard.* "Why won't he leave me alone?"

Peter shrugged. "He wants something, and he's not giving up. Call the cops. Get a restraining order."

Not something she wanted to deal with, but would if necessary. She reached for the phone. "I'll call my uncle. He can come get him. I'm not letting this ruin my night. I'll call the police later and see what we can do about him."

She started dialing and turned back to Peter. Sweat from the oppressive heat beaded on his forehead, and his hair fell around his face in a riot of waves. "You look very handsome. Of course, Kendrick had to spoil my first sight of you."

"Get your uncle on the phone and let's get out of here. We still have to pick up my grandmother and get over to the church for pictures. My mother is barking orders and driving everyone batshit."

Look who's talking. When Peter was on a mission, nothing got in his way. Even an unconscious man on the porch.

Kendrick groaned.

"My uncle isn't answering." She hung up.

Peter nudged Kendrick with his foot and squatted in front of him. "Hey, asshole, you awake?"

Her cousin's eyes shot open.

"Listen up," Peter said with brutal control. "This is fairly simple. You come here again and you're toast. Got it?"

"Yuh," Kendrick said.

Peter lifted the unwelcome guest over his shoulder. "I'll

get him in his car and he can sleep it off. Get your stuff and let's get out of here."

F<small>UCKING PEOPLE</small>.

That was all Peter could think when he pulled in front of Beach Haven, the assisted living facility where his grandmother resided. All he wanted was a good time at Steve's wedding, and his mother was stroking out while Izzy had her asshole cousin stalking her.

He glanced over at Izzy applying bright red lipstick. Nice. She wore little eye makeup and the red lipstick was hotter than melting asphalt. Her hair was different too. Poker straight. A low moan caught in his throat.

"By the way," he said. "You're stunning. I didn't get a chance to tell you at the house."

"Thanks. I worked on it. How do you like the hair?" She swung her head back and forth and her hair fanned out. "I had my stylist straighten it."

After throwing the Challenger into park, he leaned over and nuzzled her neck. "I love it."

Her hand brushed over his hair and he started counting backward from a hundred to get his mind on anything but a hard-on. He pulled away. Far away.

"I'm sorry about Kendrick," she said. "I won't let him ruin our evening."

"No sweat. He'll be gone by the time you get back."

"I'm worried about the house."

"Nah. The worst he can do is some property damage. In which case, the alarm will go off and the cops will be there in minutes."

He shot a look at the dashboard clock. Three-fifty. He had to get their asses moving.

"Come in with me. I'll introduce you to Gran."

They hustled to the lobby door and he pulled it open for her. Hellooo to the back of that dress. Jeez Louise. All that tanned, bare skin showing off her sculpted back and he had to try and keep his hands off her? The dress fell over her lean hips and clung to every tight little curve. *Yow.* He couldn't think about the four-inch stilettos. The guys called them fuck-me heels and he suddenly understood why.

He made a mental note to add the shoes to his Izzy list. Night after night she'd been invading his dreams and he couldn't risk forgetting any of what she'd done to him in those dreams he started keeping a list. His sexual to-do list. Sick, yes, but at least he'd remember everything.

"Izzy."

She glanced over her shoulder as they went through the lobby door. "Yes?"

"You are smoking in that dress."

After flashing those green eyes at him, she blew him a kiss. "I'm glad you like it."

What's not to like? A grin found its way to his face. He couldn't help it.

At least until he spotted his grandmother in front of the lobby desk in her bathrobe.

Crying.

A blazing throb began inside his skull. "Gran, what's wrong?"

"Oh, Peter! Thank goodness. Tell them they have to fix my air-conditioning. I can't even shower in there it's so hot. The windows don't open and there's no air."

He spun to face the man standing in front of Gran. "Why is my grandmother crying?"

The asshole held up his hands. "Just a problem with her air-conditioning. We're working on it."

"For two days," his grandmother shrieked. "I got no sleep last night."

His eighty-five-year-old grandmother stayed in a sweltering hot room all night? She's lucky she didn't have a heat stroke.

Someone was going to die.

"Hi," Izzy said, stepping up and holding her hand out to the prick in front of him. "You are?"

The prick eyed Izzy. "Daniel Richards, the manager."

She flashed a smile and the man-killer eyes. What the hell was she doing? She slid him her business card. Could she possibly be hitting on this overweight, fifty-year-old schmuck in order to get the damned AC fixed?

"I'm Isabelle DeRosa." She gestured to the card. "Attorney-at-law."

Ah, yes. Attorney-at-law. Peter wanted to kiss her. Well, he usually wanted to kiss her, but this was extra special.

"I'm sure this is just an oversight," Izzy said, "but I'm hoping that by the time we return this evening Mr. Jessup's grandmother will be much more comfortable in her room. Am I correct?"

She laid her hand on the prick's shoulder as an added bonus. Peter hadn't noticed it before, but she could amp up the sex when necessary. He wasn't sure how he felt about it.

"Uh, of course," the manager said, slipping the card in his pocket.

"It better be fixed," Peter added. "For what this place costs, you need to get on it." He turned back to Gran. "Let's get your stuff. We'll run you back to the house so you can get ready. Mom's gonna blow a gasket, but I'll take care of it."

The manager hustled over to the lobby desk. "We'll get this straightened out in no time, Mr. Jessup."

That Izzy. She knew how to work a man.

10

ISABELLE SUCKED IN AIR AND HELD IT AS PETER DROVE through the gates of his parents' home. Estate. Something this big couldn't be called a home. The lush blues, yellows and reds of the landscaping sailed by her, and she marveled at the beauty of the property. She'd never experienced this kind of wealth. Her family had always been middle class. Except for her uncle. His wealth had grown over the years, but didn't come close to this. When Isabelle's lungs started to protest she unleashed the breath she'd been holding.

The house loomed tall and imposing as they pulled in front. A woman that had to be Mrs. Jessup stood on the stone porch in a floor-length sky-blue gown with a diamond-encrusted belt at her waist. They couldn't be real diamonds—could they? Either way, this woman, with her shoulder-length blond hair and perfect posture, appeared every bit the queen guarding her castle.

Peter, still in mission mode, parked behind a limousine, jumped out of the car, pushed the seat up for Isabelle to get out and offered his hand as she crawled from the backseat. He really needed a four-door car for special occasions.

"Sorry you got crammed in," he said before turning to the woman coming down the steps to greet them. "Hi, Mom."

"What happened?" Mrs. Jessup asked.

"She's got no air-conditioning," Peter said, helping his grandmother out of the car. "No air-conditioning. In this heat. We're lucky she didn't get sick."

"There's no reason to yell," his mother said.

Isabelle stepped back. The lady ran a tight ship.

"Ma," Peter waved his arms. "I'm not yelling, but let me tell you, I was about to start if Izzy hadn't jumped in and threatened to sue their ass." He stopped said yelling. "Where's Dad?"

"He went on ahead. We'll meet him at church." Mrs. Jessup motioned to Peter's grandmother. "Mother, are you all right?"

"Oh, I'm fine. I feel awful about this."

"Don't sweat it, Gran."

Mrs. Jessup turned to her left, gave Isabelle a welcoming smile. "Since my son has forgotten his manners, I'm guessing you're Izzy?"

"Yes, ma'am." Isabelle stepped up, held out her hand. "I'm Isabelle. DeRosa."

"Sorry, Iz. This is my mother, Lorraine Jessup. Mom, this is Izzy. I think she might be the love of my life."

Mrs. Jessup laughed. "I did a good job with you, Peter."

Isabelle's mouth slid open before she could stop it, but Peter, already on to the next task, pulled his phone from his pocket. Probably an incoming text because he immediately put his thumbs to work.

"He *can* be charming." Mrs. Jessup said. "He also gets emotional about his grandmother."

"Nobody messes with Gran," Peter cut in.

Mrs. Jessup's blue eyes twinkled. "Did you really threaten to sue them?"

Isabelle snorted a laugh to ward off the heat rising in her cheeks. "Not in so many words. I showed him my business card. I'm an attorney. The manager got the message."

"Don't be shy, Iz." Peter continued working that phone like a madman. "She threatened to sue. His. *Ass*. It was aces, Mom."

A wry grin quirked the corners of Mrs. Jessup's mouth and Isabelle suddenly felt nine feet tall. Amazing how a mother's approval, even when it's someone else's mother, could do that.

"Well, thank you for handling the situation," Mrs. Jessup turned to Peter. "Where are we, Peter?"

He slid the phone into his jacket pocket. "That was Steve. We'll do pictures after the ceremony. He's not gonna let anything start without us."

Mrs. Jessup nodded. The cool-under-fire presence Peter *usually* had must have been inherited from his mother. The woman could lead an army into battle.

"All right," Mrs. Jessup said. "Let's get organized." She turned to Gran, still in her bathrobe. "Mother, I'll help you upstairs so you can get dressed. Peter, you and Isabelle go on. We'll meet you at church. Maybe they can get the pictures of the bridal party out of the way and it'll be less we need to do after." She finally sighed. "It's always something."

Something told Isabelle this woman would never be convinced to do anything she didn't want to do. Wouldn't it have been wonderful to have had Mrs. Jessup as a mother eleven years ago, when her own mother had been convinced to let a child molester go free?

Things would have been so different. Isabelle blew out a

breath and stepped over to Peter, who was staring at a potted bush with narrowed eyes.

"What are you doing?" she asked.

"See this plant?"

"What about it?"

A moment passed, but Peter didn't respond. She turned to him and the menacing hatred carved into his face stung her. "Peter?"

"I hate it." The strength faded from his voice, leaving only slaughtered remnants of the confidence normally found there. Something was very, very wrong.

"Peter, it's a plant. A fiddle-leaf fig bush actually."

Nose-scrunching bafflement took over his face. "I'm scared that you know that." He waved the thought away and gestured toward the bush. "It irritates me."

Okay then. Peter going crazy. What an interesting concept. She rested her hand on the back of his neck and gently squeezed. "It's been a stressful hour. Are you okay?"

Another moment passed and he closed his eyes. She imagined him sorting his thoughts into nice little compact drawers. Suddenly, he opened his eyes, threw his shoulders back, rolled his head around and gave it shake. Peter had just glued the broken pieces of himself back together.

"I'm good," he said.

Such a liar.

11

"DANCE WITH ME," PETER SAID, GRABBING IZZY'S HAND AND nearly hauling her ass out of the chair.

The club's ballroom, with its crystal chandeliers and plush drapes, was loaded down with five hundred guests, and the band had just kicked into the after-dinner music.

"Ow. Peter, I don't want to dance."

He did a sideways glance toward the approaching enemy. *Shit.*

"Please, Izzy."

He tugged her hand again, had her half off the chair before she started laughing. "What is *with* you?"

"Hi, Peter," said an irritating, chirpy voice from behind him. His stomach went south.

Still holding Izzy's hand, he turned to face Lindsey Patterson. The redheaded, knockout daughter of his parents' closest friends and the bane of his existence. She pursued him relentlessly, and it had nothing to do with her unyielding attraction to him. She wanted to merge their bank accounts.

His tight-lipped country club face came out of the dusty box and Peter leveled it on her. "Lindsey, how are you?"

"I'm wonderful, but this is our dance." She aimed her snooty brown eyes at Izzy. "I'm sure your *date* won't mind if a couple of old friends share a dance."

Izzy, seemingly confused, looked up at Peter. *Come on, Iz. Help me out here.*

"He's a big boy," Izzy said. "He can dance if he'd like."

Not the answer he wanted.

"Great," Lindsey said, dragging him to the dance floor.

A sick feeling twirled in his stomach. He knew what dance Lindsey would want. Not too fast. Not too slow. Her way of trying to force him into a situation. She'd been doing this to him since high school when their parents had sent them for ballroom dance lessons.

He turned back and caught Izzy's eye. He hoped she could see the apology there.

"So," Vic said. "You've had a busy week."

Isabelle sat back against her chair. "You're not kidding."

A tuxedo-clad waiter came by and filled coffee cups.

"Are you all right?" Gina, Vic's wife, asked. Isabelle had never met her before today, but knew enough about her to know she was someone special. She had to be if she convinced Vic, stud of the century, to settle down. Gina's full mane had been pulled into a hair clip at the base of her neck and the curls sprung wildly out the back. The tiny baby bulge, barely evident under her simple navy sheath, tempted Isabelle to reach over and rub her hand on it.

Some things in life were a mystery, and Gina and Vic as a couple fit that category. Not that she wasn't attractive or worthy. She wouldn't necessarily be considered gorgeous, but her warm friendliness drew people in. Gina probably made a great best friend. Maybe the odd union wasn't such a mystery after all.

Then again, who was Isabelle to judge? She had yet to experience a relationship she couldn't kill.

"I'm fine," she said, getting back to Gina's question. "Peter's been a big help. It'll all work out."

Vic's gaze was trained on the dance floor. "Monk is doing it again. He's blowing my mind."

Gina patted his shoulder and said to Isabelle, "Vic can't handle seeing Monk ballroom dance."

Understandable. She couldn't fathom it either.

Vic laughed. "It goes against everything we believe."

"He taught us the Viennese Waltz for our wedding," Gina added.

"I sucked at that."

"Yes, honey, you did."

Isabelle cracked up. Vic didn't like to fail. But Peter doing ballroom? This she had to see. She turned and found him and the tiny redhead on the dance floor, their bodies moving in perfect sequence. Something inside Isabelle broke apart as she watched their hips roll in an obviously practiced routine. Clearly it wasn't the first time they'd danced together. The erotic and sensual rhythm brought to mind other things their hips might have done together, and Isabelle's face burned.

Could she be jealous? *Jealous?* Of a dance?

Not. Possible.

The music pounded at her ears and she stuck her fingers in them for a second, but the pounding continued. She pressed harder until the whooshing in her head made her stomach tumble. She hated this feeling. This yearning for a man not to be touched by any woman but her.

She turned back to Vic as her conflicting emotions created unshed tears.

Gina, who stood with her hands resting on his shoulders, wrinkled her nose and stared into the crowd huddled on the dance floor. "That little bitch."

Don't look. It can't be anything you want to see.

Of course, Isabelle turned back to see what had Gina riled. How could she not? Lindsey made use of Peter by grinding her hips into him until he finally spun her under his arm. The flaming bitch swung her head back at Isabelle and jerked her haughty chin in a see-what-I-have gesture.

Unable to resist, Isabelle reached down, squeezed her cushioned chair once and let it go. She would *not* let this witch get to her.

The misery on Peter's face reached Isabelle, and he kept his eyes locked with hers until an ice chip of understanding cooled her fire. She got the message. This was why he'd been in such a rush to get her on the dance floor. He must have seen Lindsey coming.

"Hey," Vic said, leaning forward and getting right next to Isabelle's ear. "You know he hates this woman, right?"

Unsure of how to respond, Isabelle nodded, but she'd only known Peter a few days and although he'd admitted his dislike of the wealthy social circuit, the redhead and her fancy dancing seemed more suited to a man of Peter's means than a sexually abused train wreck.

"I'm fine." Isabelle said. "It's only a dance."

"I don't understand some women," Gina huffed.

"You're telling me," Vic said.

"Oh, shut up," Gina and Isabelle said in unison. Gina added a smack on the arm for effect.

The dance finally ended—*thank you, Lord*—and Peter

made a beeline to the table, his actions bordering on rude by leaving Lindsey standing on the dance floor.

Someone reached for him, obviously to say hello, but he held up a finger and kept moving. A man on a mission.

"Hey," he said, bracing his hand on Isabelle's chair and leaning over. "I'm sorry about that. Will you dance with me now? Please?"

She hated dancing, mainly because she didn't know how. All she could do was shuffle her feet back and forth. Totally inept. "I can't dance."

"It's okay. It's a slow one." He took her hand and pulled her toward the dance floor.

The snappy music, an old Sinatra tune from the orchestra, settled her embattled nerves.

Peter twirled her into his arms and slid his warm, calloused hand under the braid of material stretching the length of her back. A working man's hand. The rough texture of his fingers tickled as he slid his hand down her back, and the skin to skin contact nearly melted her. She didn't mind.

He pulled her tight against his body leaving not an inch of space between them.

"Have I mentioned I love this dress?" He nuzzled her neck.

Second time today. Peter was a neck man. Isabelle, her breasts tingling, was beginning to think she might be a neck woman.

This she would enjoy. She rested her arm on his shoulder and pressed herself against the solid wall of him seeking comfort from the inadequacy she'd experienced minutes before.

"Lindsey is a pain in my ass," he said.

"Peter, it's okay."

He drew back, his eyes searching hers. "No, it's not. It's inappropriate. I tried to talk her out of the rumba, but I knew she'd argue with me and cause a scene. Then I'd get 'Oh-Petered' because I couldn't suck it up and dance with her. I hate these people."

"I should have danced with you. It happened so fast I didn't understand."

He grunted his frustration. "Can we forget it? I don't want you pissed at me all night."

She smiled. "Nope. Not me."

She settled her chin on his shoulder, her feet barely moving, while the other dancers twirled and box stepped around them to "I've Got You Under My Skin."

Yes, she had Peter under her skin. She just didn't know what to do now that he was there.

"Will you teach me the rumba?"

He laughed and dropped a kiss on the side of her head. "The lady likes the rumba."

"I like watching *you* rumba, but not with someone else. I guess I need to learn."

He leaned back and focused on her. "That's about the nicest thing anyone has ever said to me."

The intensity of his stare became too much. Like a piercing spear, leaving her exposed, vulnerable and bleeding. She moved closer, setting her chin back on his shoulder.

"I'd love to teach you the rumba."

The woodsy scent of his soap lingered and she wanted to be closer. An impossible task considering an inch of space didn't exist between them.

Not an inch of space.

An epiphany dawned.

This wasn't just a dance. Not the way he held her. He'd spent the entire dance with Lindsey trying to put space between them, but now, with his feet barely moving, he sent a silent message. This dance didn't have the drama or technical excellence of the rumba, but the way he snuggled close, whispering to her, spoke of what the dance with Lindsey meant. Nothing.

A lump lodged in the center of Isabelle's chest. No air. She couldn't breathe.

"What?" Peter asked, leaning back and drawing his eyebrows together.

Unsure of how to explain it, she reached up and pushed her hand through the hair on the back of his head. Something inside her demanded she get closer, but there was nowhere to go. "Thank you."

"For what?"

Closer.

She kissed him. Not with the fierceness of the other day. Just a light brush of her lips against his, but it made sense now. Her heart and body had always acted as independent agents, guiding her along the trouble spots. The splitting of her physical and emotional being became her survival mechanism, gave her strength.

Tears oozed from her eyes. She couldn't do this. She couldn't give herself over. What would be left if she gave it all?

Peter brushed her tears away with his thumb. "Whatever I did, you're welcome."

Fun Izzy.

Fun Izzy was trouble.

12

PETER DAMN NEAR SKIPPED BACK TO THE TABLE. Miraculously, the world inside the despised four walls of the Nosrum Country Club had become a beautiful place. Go figure.

"Izzy," Gina said. "The prego needs a bathroom break. Come with me."

Peter pulled his chair from under the table and dropped into it. "Why do women go to the bathroom together?"

"Don't ask me," Vic said as they left. "I'm having a hard enough time tonight. All kinds of crazy shit going on here. That whole thing with the redhead? You had to hear the conversation at this table. I mean, kill me now."

"That's the one I told you about. She's a flesh-eater."

Vic leaned into the chair next to Peter. "What's the story with you and Isabelle? Isabelle, who never lets anyone call her Izzy."

Where's this going? Peter and Vic had only discussed a relationship once, during a crisis, and it was Vic's relationship, not his.

"Nothing to tell. I like her."

"Uh-huh."

Peter shrugged. "What?"

Vic scrubbed his fingers across his mouth. "Here's the thing with Isabelle. She's a great girl, right? And that body? Unbelievable."

Oh, shit. No. No. No. Somehow, in the course of the last ten seconds, the world's largest wave pummeled him. Vic was about to tell him that he'd shagged Izzy.

Peter didn't want to know. Absolutely not. He'd just work around it, so to speak. But, son of a bitch, he wanted this woman like he wanted his next breath and the thought of her getting it on with Vic would drive him batshit. Vic had found the promised land before him.

He took a breath before he said something stupid. "Did you..." Peter waved his hand in front of him. "You know... with Izzy?"

Where the hell did that come from?

Vic hesitated. "You want to know if I fucked Isabelle?"

Mr. Crude, at his best.

"Actually, no. Whatever you did before Gina is your business."

Peter picked up a half-filled water glass, probably Izzy's, and slugged it.

"I thought about it. Once," Vic said, as if they were discussing what to have for dessert. "I was here on business five years ago—"

Five years ago? Isabelle was twenty-one-years-old five years ago. A goddamned baby.

"She asked me to spar with her," Vic continued. "We're alone, in the gym, and she's going to town on me. Just kicking my ass. And the more she's kicking my ass, the harder she pushes herself. I think she likes having control of a situation that's not necessarily in her favor."

Peter dug his fingers into his forehead hoping the bashing going on in his head would cease. "Vic, I don't need to hear this."

"Right. And fuck you for telling me to stay out of it. I told her she could trust you, and I don't want to be put in a jackpot with her."

Peter huffed out a breath.

"Anyway," Vic said, "she was all sweaty and panting from the workout and I started to panic because my baser needs took over. For a split second, I thought about banging her right there on the gym floor."

The pounding in Peter's head worsened. His blood pressure must have hit record heights. This conversation had to end before he stroked out in the middle of Stephen's reception.

He stood, curled his hands open and closed while his blood nearly seeped out of his skin. "Are you out of your fucking mind telling me this? Do you have any idea how inappropriate this is?"

Vic stood and, being four inches taller than Peter's six-one, peered down at him.

"Hey, dickhead, you asked. Now shut up and listen. I *thought* about it. For a second. And then it occurred to me. She's the daughter of a good friend. She's got issues regarding sex. She *trusts* me."

The packed ballroom drew Peter's attention. Or maybe he couldn't stand this conversation. Having Vic, a guy who, before he got married, would have taken home the gold in the Player Olympics, lecture him, just fried his ass.

"Isabelle," Vic said, "is not a girl who trusts easily. You cannot fuck her and run. She comes across as strong and self-sufficient, but you could seriously screw her up. She deserves the best life she can carve out for herself, so whatever your intentions are, keep that in mind." Vic poked him, not so lightly, in the chest. "You get my drift?"

Did he get it? How the hell could he miss it? Vic just told Peter he'd kick his ass if he hurt Isabelle.

And he hadn't shagged her. Peter's buzzing pulse quieted and an honest burst of laughter popped out. Relief maybe, because for a few seconds he'd been terrified Vic would tell him Izzy had been the best fuck of his life. Or vice versa.

Don't go there.

Peter didn't want to think about Izzy with anyone else. Primitive, yes, but oh well. He popped Vic on the arm. "I get your drift. No worries. It's under control. You flaming asshole."

"Well, this looks interesting," Izzy said, tossing her purse —if that little beaded thing could be considered a purse— on the table.

Vic's eyebrows headed to the sky and they both cracked up.

13

PETER GOT OUT OF THE CHALLENGER AND FOCUSED ON THE empty space in Izzy's driveway where Kendrick's car had been. Gone. Good. The warm ocean air slipped over him and he drew in the salty smell. Gentle breaking waves sounded from behind the house and he made a mental note to check the charts for high tide.

He opened the car door and watched Izzy's dress ride up her thighs when she slid out.

Yow.

Instant hard-on.

It didn't help when she dragged her hand across his stomach and scooted by him. Throw in the eyes and pouty lips and he was done. Cooked.

He suddenly found himself praying Creepy Izzy had gone on sabbatical for the night.

The gravel driveway crunched under their feet and he marveled at her ability to balance on the fuck-me heels. His hand grew a mind of its own and skimmed her bare back while a jolt of heat blasted him.

They stopped on the dimly lit porch while she shoved the key in the lock with one hand and reached back to touch him with the other. Truth be told, she was probably aiming for his hip, but nailed an eager Monk Junior instead.

Helloooo, baby.

"Oh, my." She turned, hooked her hand around the back of his head and pulled him in for a mind-melting kiss.

And, oh yes, a good shagging was definitely the order of the day. Particularly because he'd been thinking about it nonstop from the moment he saw her. How much waiting could a guy take? He flattened his hands against the door and leaned into her, the heat of her body nearly scorching his.

"Ow," she said.

He jumped back, but she pulled him close again. "The key stuck me."

Peter heard the lock tumble. She must have turned it with her free hand, because the door opened and the inside light she'd left on washed over them.

Izzy threw her arms around his neck, pressed against him and slammed her tongue into his mouth. Demanding and hot. His breath caught and he couldn't release it. *Thank you, Jesus.* He'd never known anything better than this kiss.

He backed her through the doorway, kicked the door closed behind them and shoved her against the wall. Her slinky hair flew around her face and her chest heaved with each breath. When she slid her leg around his and gave him a wicked-ass grin, every bit of self-control crumbled.

That's it. She was going to get it. *Right here. Right now.* Fuck off, Creepy Izzy.

A beep echoed in his head.

What was that?

"The alarm," he said.

"Who cares?" Izzy was clearly riding the same euphoric wave because she started clawing at his shirt buttons.

He reached behind him to the keypad by the door. Couldn't reach. *Dammit.*

"Iz, the alarm will go off in about five seconds. Just let me..."

WHAAAAAAAAA!

Too late. The shrieking wail of the alarm permeated the house, but Izzy didn't seem to hear it. She now had his shirt unbuttoned and his T-shirt pushed up.

Those lush lips trailed kisses across his chest and his body went ballistic. Seriously fucking insane.

He had to get that alarm off, but moving would be a freaking tragedy.

With one arm around her, he dragged her with him to the keypad and punched in the code. Silence shrouded the house.

"Good. Back to business," Izzy said, pushing his shirt off his shoulders and down his arms until it hit the floor. The undershirt came off next and she raked her hands and mouth over his chest again.

"They'll...call," he said, trying to concentrate on anything but what she was doing to him.

"Who?"

"Dispatch."

The phone rang and he glanced in the direction of the cordless on the entry table.

Figures.

He'd been dreaming of this every night for five days and had his fantasy list completely up to date, tucked safely in his wallet where no one would find it. The phone rang a third time.

"Izzy," he said, shoving the phone at her while she

headed south. "You have to answer and give them the code or they'll send the cops. And right now, the cops are the dead last thing I want."

No, what he wanted was to rip that dress off, shove her against the wall and pound his aching body into her.

Just as she reached to unfasten his pants, she stopped. *No. No. No.* If his body could talk, it would be screaming for her to keep going. *Screaming.*

Too bad his brain was in charge at the moment. He punched the speaker button on the handset and she straightened up before shoving her rumpled hair out of her face. Major league hot and totally shaggable.

"Hello?" she said and kissed him again.

Tongue and all.

No longer able to keep his hands still, Peter slid her dress up and his fingers skimmed her bare ass.

A thong.

Good thing he hadn't known about that all night or he'd really have to be committed.

"Ms. DeRosa?" a voice asked, filling the room from the speaker.

"Mmm-hmm."

Peter mentally checked his willpower and pulled back. "Just talk to her."

"Ms. DeRosa, this is Connie from Taylor Security. Are you all right?"

Great. Connie from central station in Chicago. Ballbuster of the year.

"We are *fine*," Izzy said giving him the nymphet smile again.

"Can you give me the code?" Connie asked.

But Izzy had no interest in Connie or the code. She had

her arms wrapped around him and was busy kissing his neck.

"Iz, give her the code." *Please, give her the code. Now!*

"The code?"

Oh, come on.

"Connie?" He rolled his eyes because Izzy had her hands all over him and was moving down his body. *Good God.* He had to get rid of Connie. "This is Peter...uh...Monk Jessup. The code is I-P-9-5-3. Everything is fine. I was—" Oh, hell, Izzy hooked her fingers into the waistband of his pants. "Uh...showing Ms. DeRosa how to work the alarm and we didn't turn it off in time."

Connie let out a sarcastic snort. "Sure you were, Monk."

He'd never live this down. As soon as they hung up she'd be on the phone to the rest of his team and they'd call his cell constantly for the remainder of the night.

"You two have a lovely evening," she said.

Peter stabbed at the button, tossed the phone over his shoulder, and it hit the wood with a crack.

"I think you broke my phone," Izzy said.

"I'll buy you a new one."

He reached down, hooked his hands under her arms and hauled her up against the wall. Their eyes met for a second and the heat nearly scalded him. Now it was his turn to make her crazy. And he'd enjoy every damn minute of it.

"Born to Run" blasted from his pocket into the quiet of the house. Connie worked quick. *Let the games begin.* He retrieved his phone, shut it off and turned his attention back to Izzy.

Her eyes were closed.

Nuh-uh. She'd closed her eyes. *Crap.* "Look at me, Izzy." Hope nestled in the back of his mind. Not to mention other parts of his anatomy.

She didn't open her eyes, but dragged him against her and kissed him, nearly swallowing him. She worked at it, doing everything she'd been doing just a few minutes earlier. But this kiss lacked the spontaneous heat of the others.

The mother of all hard-ons, and Creepy Izzy comes home. Rotten luck.

His whole body deflated. Well, maybe not his *whole* body, but it came damned close. Her words from earlier in the week nearly drowned him. *It's a coping thing.*

Could anything destroy a great lay like a woman needing a coping mechanism to endure it? He doubted it. Particularly when all he wanted was to get said woman in a bed and send her into the atmosphere.

He backed up a step, his breath heaving. She slowly opened her eyes and the only thing there was a big neon vacancy sign. She'd flipped the switch.

"What?" she asked, grabbing him, but he backed away again.

"Creepy Izzy."

She stepped closer. "It's okay, Peter. It's what you want. It won't make a difference. It'll still be good." She hit him with the man-killer eyes and ran her fingers across his chest. "I promise."

And, holy hell, the profound weight of what he was dealing with hit him. Staring into those barren eyes nearly gutted him, because she had no capacity for sex beyond the physical act. Nothing. She was probably a silver bullet in the sack, but had to emotionally shut down to do it.

Did she even enjoy sex?

More than that, when did he become such an honorable guy that he'd turn down a hot woman because of her emotional detachment? Seriously, seriously fucked-up. That's what he was. Totally off his rocker.

He grabbed her hands. "It makes a difference to me. I want you involved, not mentally out to lunch. I'll wait for Fun Izzy."

She dropped her hands, sighing. At least he wasn't the only one suffering.

"We talked about this the other night," she said. "Fun Izzy doesn't have sex."

"Then I guess we're not having sex."

Her mouth flopped open. "You're turning me down?"

Apparently she had never been turned down. That didn't to stop her, because she slid her hands over the jagged scar on his stomach.

Uh-oh.

He *wanted* this. Bad.

"We'd be good together," she said.

He stepped back. "Please, don't do this to me."

The bright white of his shirt against the stained hardwood floor caught Peter's attention. Izzy looked down, hesitated, then picked it up and handed it over. The undershirt was somewhere, but he'd find it later.

"I wish I could give you what you want, Peter."

He attempted a smile, but he didn't have the energy to fake it. "Me too. It'll happen though."

"I'm not so confident."

"Why?"

"Outside of sex, I've never been able to give a man what he needed. They always want more than I can provide. Emotionally speaking."

He slid the shirt on and she reached to button it for him. The simple act of fastening his shirt offered an intimacy of its own, and his body turned to stone.

"We don't have to rush this," he said. "Let's take it slow. Like we talked about."

She shrugged. "I don't know if I know how. I'm not sure I can let go of myself enough to make you happy.

I'd love to change that.

He rested his forehead against hers. "Stop thinking. That's when Creepy Izzy takes over."

"But that's the problem. When things get hot between us I have to force myself to stop thinking. I need to flip the switch because I'm not comfortable with what I'm feeling. You have no idea how much that vulnerability scares me."

Yeah, actually, he did because he wasn't feeling too confident right now himself. Not after ten years of living with no emotional connections.

"You're going to push me away aren't you?" he asked.

A rush of tears filled her eyes.

Please, no tears.

"Did I ever mention how much I love a challenge?" he cracked.

Before backing away, she swiped at her watery eyes. "I'm more than a challenge, Peter."

"Even better." He kissed her quick and brought her a little closer. "I think you've conditioned yourself to push everyone away. As crazy as you make me, I like you. I can't help it. You're so much more than you think."

"Peter—"

He shook his head to silence her. "I dare you to make me not stick."

Izzy leaned in, rested her head on his shoulder and her warm breath slipped across his neck. "I know you can stick. I'm just not sure if you'll want to."

And here we go again. This woman would take some work. Lucky for him he had time.

He backed her up and extended his arms into a dance hold. "Time for your first rumba lesson."

"*Now?*"

"Might as well do something with our hips."

14

ISABELLE POURED THE LAST OF THE COFFEE INTO HER MUG. The Sunday paper lay sprawled across her kitchen table, and she settled down to scan the circulars.

Morning sunlight drenched the kitchen and she glanced out the windows along the back of the house. A great beach day loomed ahead. After reading the newspaper, she'd grab a book and let the warm sand soothe away the fatigue from her evening out with Peter.

Would he call her today? The little voice inside whispered no, but that was simply a defense. The truth of it was she'd be damned disappointed if he didn't.

Trouble.

Big trouble.

A knock sounded at the front door just as she brought the coffee to her lips. *Who is that at eight forty-five on a Sunday?* After her surprise visitor yesterday, she didn't want to hazard a guess.

She walked to the front windows and peeked out. Two men. One in a sport coat. The other, younger, in jeans and a golf shirt. Her stomach wrenched.

With the security chain still on, she opened the door an inch. "Can I help you?"

The older man, maybe mid-fifties with dark hair graying at the temples, flipped out a badge. "Villa Point P.D."

She noted the detective's shield then moved to his ID. Detective Ron Cherald. Villa Point police. Her uncle lived in Villa Point.

"Isabelle DeRosa?" the younger detective asked.

"Yes," she said, taking in the features of his face. Long nose, narrow jawline, small mole on his right cheek and dark eyes to go along with his midnight-black hair.

"We need to speak to you regarding Kendrick Edmonds."

Oh, no. What the hell was he up to? Could these two guys be impersonating police just so Kendrick could get in here? She wouldn't doubt it.

"I need to verify who you are. Hold on while I call the police station."

Cherald nodded and provided the phone number.

Yeah, well, she'd just double-check to make sure he wasn't giving her a bogus number. After closing the door and resetting the lock, she ran to the kitchen, grabbed her cell and searched online for the number.

Her stomach hitched again when the same number the detective had given her popped up on her screen. She poked at the call link, asked for the detective's squad and received her verification.

Crap. Kendrick must have decided to press charges.

She took a good, solid breath and prepped for the burden of telling the police about her history with Kendrick. She suddenly wished Peter were here.

She slid the chain off the door and opened it. "Come in, gentlemen. Sorry to keep you waiting."

"No problem," the younger man said, giving her legs the once-over.

She couldn't even wear shorts in her own house. Men. So easy to figure out. Most of them anyway.

He held out his hand and she shook it. "Detective Mark Pratt."

ISABELLE MOTIONED THEM TO THE TWO STRIPED CHAIRS IN THE living room while she took the couch. Tension bubbled inside her and she squeezed her fingers closed.

"Ms. DeRosa," Cherald said, "we have some bad news for you. Kendrick Edmonds was found dead in Abram's Park this morning."

The words pummeled her and she most definitely processed them, but the jolt forced her to slouch back. The drumming at her temples left her no choice but to close her eyes and try to quiet the madness in her mind.

The intricate stitching of her grandmother's afghan pressed into her and she remained still for a moment, absorbing the comfort.

Kendrick. Dead.

She'd wished it a thousand times, yet felt nothing. Not happiness. Certainly not sadness. Maybe he didn't warrant her feeling anything at all. "What happened?"

"He was beaten to death."

Beaten.

To. Death.

"Ms. DeRosa, where were you last night between twelve-thirty and one-thirty?"

And there it is. She was a suspect. A throbbing began in the back of her skull. She wished she had her lawyer clothes on. Sitting here in shorts and a tank top did not offer her the same armor.

She stared into Cherald's eyes. No looking away or they'd think her a liar.

"I was here. I went to a wedding last night and arrived home around twelve-forty."

"Can anyone verify that?" Pratt asked.

Peter could.

Damn. Now she'd have to drag him into a murder investigation. Her morning coffee swirled in her stomach.

"Yes. My date brought me home. We had to drop his grandmother off in Nosrum at Beach Haven Assisted Living." Cherald pulled his notepad and started jotting. "We walked her to her room. The lobby attendant saw us. We came straight here after that. In fact, we set the alarm off when we came into the house and the security company called to make sure everything was okay."

Cherald and Pratt shot each other a look.

"We'll need that phone number," Pratt said. "And the number for your date."

"Of course."

She went to the kitchen, her heart slamming so hard she thought she'd come apart from the pressure. She was a murder suspect. She'd need a lawyer. They hadn't Mirandized her yet. They were still in fact-finding mode.

She wrote down Peter's number and Taylor Security's dispatch number under it.

When she went back to the living room, Cherald took the paper from her, stuck it in his jacket pocket. "We spoke to your uncle this morning when we notified him of his son's death. He indicated you had an altercation with Kendrick."

She shot Pratt a glance then went back to Cherald. "He

came, uninvited, into my house in the middle of the night and tried to rape me."

"Did you threaten to kill him?" Pratt asked.

Her uncle didn't waste any time throwing her under *that* big bus. "It had been an emotional night. He attacked me and I said I'd kill him if he didn't stay away from me. I didn't kill him though."

Pratt cleared his throat. Clearly, he was new to this whole detective thing. And if he didn't quit checking out her boobs, she'd beat the crap out of him too.

"Uh, your uncle did mention the disagreement after you brought Kendrick home." Pratt's eyes finally made it to her face.

A disagreement. She almost laughed. She should know by now her uncle would never take her side, but she'd have to play this cool. Coming off sounding like a bitter bitch would do her no good.

Think like a lawyer.

"Your uncle said you and someone you called Peter took Kendrick home that night," Cherald said.

She nodded. "Yes. Peter Jessup. I just gave you his number."

"He was with you last night?"

Yow. This wasn't good.

"Yes. He left here around one-fifteen."

Cherald jotted a note on his notepad. "Do you know where he was going?"

"Home. He's visiting his parents in Nosrum."

More jotting.

"Had you seen Kendrick since the incident last week?" Pratt asked.

She had to tell them about yesterday afternoon. They'd

probably find out anyway. They might even know it and were testing her to see if she'd lie.

"Kendrick came here yesterday afternoon. He tried to push his way in, yelling that he needed to talk to me. But I held the door shut."

Enough. She needed to stop talking now. Telling them Peter knocked Kendrick out would be bad.

Cherald held his arms wide. "And what? He left? Not buying it, Ms. DeRosa. Not after you just told me he tried to rape you."

She shook her head. Slid a glance at Pratt. *Don't look away.*

"Peter arrived and helped."

"Helped how?"

"He gave him a tap on the temple and knocked him out."
So not good.

"He started to come out of it a few minutes later and we put him in his car to sleep it off."

Cherald's eyebrows went up. "You left him there?"

She nodded and Pratt gave his head a hard shake. She couldn't blame him. If she were them, she'd be locking the cuffs on.

"Yes," Isabelle said. "But, as I said, he was already waking up. When we came home Kendrick and the car were gone. He must have driven home."

"Did you hear from him again last night?" Cherald asked.

"No."

Cherald flipped his pad shut and stood. "Okay. I think we've got everything we need for now. We're going to verify this information. Stay around today, Ms. DeRosa. We may need to speak to you again."

If her alibi didn't check out with the time of death,

they'd have an arrest warrant. "I'll be here all day, gentlemen."

PETER DIALED IZZY'S NUMBER THE SECOND THE COPS LEFT THE cottage. Some fucking irony. That son of a bitch Kendrick got himself whacked the same night Peter had walloped him.

"Hey," he said when Izzy answered the phone.

"I can't believe it."

Her voice sounded rough, like she'd been thinking too much. Coming undone wouldn't help either one of them, but he knew she'd step up. Izzy was a warrior at heart.

"The cops just left." He grabbed the cards they'd given him and set them on the white dining table. "Pratt and Cherald."

"They were the ones who questioned me also. Please tell me someone saw you arrive home last night. I've been piecing this together. They must have the time of death narrowed to between twelve-thirty and one-thirty because that's the time frame they asked me about."

"That's what they told me too."

"I think you left here around one-fifteen," she said. "There's no way either one of us could have made it to Villa Point by one-thirty. Please, Peter. Tell me you went straight home."

Whoa. Peter sat back, shrugging off the nagging feeling tickling his neck. Was she making sure *he* didn't kill Kendrick?

"I came straight home. The security camera at the gate records whoever enters. The time stamp will be on there. Plus, Vic and Gina are staying at the cottage with me and Vic was still up when I got home."

"That's a relief. I am so sorry to have dragged you into this. I'm just stunned."

She wasn't the only one. He was supposed to be on R&R and his ass landed in the middle of a murder investigation. "Have you found out anything more about what happened?"

"I called my mother. A jogger found him in the park at six-thirty this morning. Someone beat him with a club or something."

"Did you talk to your uncle?"

"No. And I won't call either. He sent the police straight to my front door. I'm not sure how I feel about that."

Peter let out a breath. "Izzy, this is screwed. Who could have killed him?"

"I have no idea. I don't think he talks to anyone around here anymore."

He made a mental note to ask Vic how much of a hothead Izzy's dad was. Jeez, that'd be a mess.

Bad enough the cops thought *he* might have done it. As if he'd leave the body lying there. He'd have hit Kendrick with a double pop and made sure the body wouldn't be found. Forget this beating him to death shit. He wouldn't waste that kind of rage on that asshole. Nope, he'd get a gun and make it quick and clean.

"Well," he said. "The cops will do their thing and they'll clear us."

"I hope so. I feel bad enough that I involved you. What your mother must think of me..."

Peter puckered his lips. *She's a suspect in a murder investigation and she's worried about what my mother thinks?* He couldn't blame her. Stress did screwy things to people.

"My mother thinks you're great. She wasn't happy when two detectives knocked on her door wanting a download of security footage, but she knows we didn't have anything to do with this."

A long silence hung on the line.

"Peter?"

"Yeah?"

"I'm not sorry he's dead."

Peter glanced out the door leading to the tiny patio. Yellow daylilies, his mother's favorite, lit up the otherwise green landscape. A sick, familiar feeling settled on him. If he didn't say something worthwhile, Izzy would drive herself insane. He understood questioning one's moral code. Particularly when it came to taking lives.

"And you somehow think that makes you a horrible person?"

"Doesn't it?"

Too late. She'd already worked herself into the moral code dilemma.

"My take is Kendrick was sick. Clearly he hadn't redeemed himself in eleven years because someone hated him enough to club him to death and, based on his history, he probably deserved it. He terrorized you, and I don't think it's abnormal for you not to be sorry. Actually, I'd be shocked if you didn't have a sense of relief. But hey, that's just me."

More silence. He waited. Tapped his free hand on the table hoping he'd helped a little because he had no idea what else to say.

"Peter?"

"I'm here."

"Thank you for not thinking I'm crazy."

"Babe, you're about the sanest person I know."

She scoffed. "Which is kind of scary."

"Anything I can do for you?" Peter asked.

"I don't think so. I'm staying close to the house today in

case the police need to talk to me again. I'll probably sit on the beach for a while."

"The waves any good?"

He heard her open a door. Probably checking.

"No," she said. "But I wouldn't mind you being here."

"Yo," Vic said and Peter turned to see him coming down the stairs wearing jeans and a white pullover, suitcase in hand.

He went back to Izzy. "Vic and Gina are getting ready to go. I'll be over after that."

He clicked the off button and sat for a second. What the fuck was he doing? He should run screaming from this situation.

A murder for Christ's sake.

This woman would tear him to shreds. He already couldn't keep his mind off her and, with her hang-ups, there would be no way they could both get what they needed.

Ten years he'd waited for a woman to have more than a physical effect on him. His ex-wife had ripped a piece of his soul away and there hadn't been another woman since that made him want any more than a good lay. Now, with Izzy, he was thinking she'd look damn good sleeping in his shirts.

Vic sat in one of the three other chairs. "What's up?"

"I'm fucked."

"What else is new?"

No shit. Peter propped his elbow on the table and stuck his chin in his hand. "Izzy. You were worried about *me* hurting *her*? You blew that call. She's going to eat me alive and—idiot that I am—I'm gonna let her."

15

ISABELLE STOOD BEHIND THE SMALL GATHERING OF PEOPLE sitting by Kendrick's gravesite. She closed her eyes. The lack of sound, no birds chirping or leaves rustling, just the occasional squeak of a chair when someone moved, forced her pulse to hammer. Even the humid, overcast day seemed appropriate. Gray. Just like her mood.

She hated this.

The priest finished his final prayer and invited mourners to the casket, but Isabelle remained motionless. She couldn't step near that casket. She showed up. That was enough.

In the three days since Kendrick's death, she'd agonized over whether she'd be a hypocrite if she attended. But would the police think it odd if she didn't go? No good answer.

Digging deep, she decided to make an appearance. After all, she had loved Kendrick once and, in an odd way, seemed to be mourning the person she had cared for. Not that the funeral gave her any closure, but at least she made the effort.

The twenty or so mourners, mostly friends of her uncle

and a few family members, tossed their roses onto the casket and filed toward their cars. Isabelle twisted and spotted Peter parked down the road in the vintage Mustang —another car from his collection—that she'd instantly wanted to drive. The man liked his cars.

More than that though, he was a darn good man because he'd offered to drive her to the funeral so she didn't have to go alone.

She turned back to the casket and waited. Her mother sat next to Uncle Bart and Aunt Carol and would probably wait to toss her flower with theirs. Once again, her mother had sided with Uncle Bart. It seemed so petty at this point, and Isabelle found herself wishing her sister were here. Jenny would support her. But her sister was spending the summer with her boyfriend in San Diego. Lucky girl. Lucky *smart* girl because she knew to stay away from the family lunacy. At least one of the DeRosa girls was emotionally healthy. For whatever reason, Kendrick had never put his filthy hands on Jenny, and Isabelle remained thankful for it.

"Hello, Isabelle." Her mother leaned forward to kiss her and the collar of her crisp white shirt brushed Isabelle's chin. Her mother's scent—something floral—seemed in contrast with the stark navy suit she wore.

"Hi, Mom." *I wish you would have stood with me.*

Her mother narrowed her eyes slightly and ran a hand over Isabelle's cheek. She sucked in a breath, felt it shatter inside.

"Are you all right?"

No. I'm not all right. I want us to be better than we are. I love you and want to trust you.

Isabelle shook off the thought. She and her mother had a stable relationship. They weren't close, but they occasionally went shopping or to dinner and it worked. She didn't want to disrupt that.

"I'm okay," Isabelle said because that's what she always said. And what her mother wanted to hear.

Her uncle stepped up, regal in his three-thousand-dollar suit and graying hair. "Isabelle," he said, while his wife ignored her.

Hating these people would be easy. They were so smug. "Hello, Uncle Bart. Aunt Carol. I'm sorry about Kendrick."

With that, Carol turned away and Uncle Bart followed without another word.

Lovely exchange.

"I have to go," her mother said. "I came with Bart."

Of course you did.

"Are you all right?" her mother asked again.

"I'm okay."

She watched her mother walk away and then turned back to the casket. It seemed odd that she and Kendrick were the only ones left.

"Ms. DeRosa?" someone said, and Isabelle shifted as two men approached.

Two men she'd never seen before. In suits. But wait... The tall one. He seemed familiar.

Cops.

Had to be.

A long breath escaped and her heart thumped faster.

The police had not contacted her since the day after the murder. Could be good, could be bad. Maybe they had cleared her. Or, maybe they were building a case.

Prickly pins badgered her arms. She couldn't think about it now. She threw her shoulders back, called up her neutral lawyer face. She could do this. Peter sat just down the road. He'd help her if need be.

"I'm Isabelle DeRosa."

The taller man flipped open his ID and three big letters jumped out at her.

FBI.

What could this be about?

"Special Agent Wade Sampson," the taller man said. "May we speak with you a moment?"

Sampson wore a black suit with a white shirt and patterned red tie. His dark hair was combed straight back from his face and, with his angular cheekbones and square jaw, she imagined he used those assets to his advantage. She'd have to keep that in mind.

The shorter man held out his hand and Isabelle shook it. "Kirk Watson."

Watson looked older. Maybe around fifty. His salt-and-pepper hair and long face didn't have the impact Sampson's did. And then it hit her. Special Agent Wade Sampson had been the man sitting in the car parked at the beach entrance last week.

The FBI was watching her.

"What's this about?" A bird chirped from overhead and Isabelle glanced up.

Sampson took the go ahead. "You're the cousin of Kendrick Edmonds, correct?"

"Yes."

The lawyer in her would offer nothing other than what they asked for.

"We understand, prior to his death, you were invited to stay at his home in Ohio?"

She nodded. "Yes. I refused."

"We're aware of that also," Watson said.

What the hell was this about? She swallowed once to pop her ears and clear the sudden echo of every microscopic sound.

"Ms. DeRosa," Sampson said, "we have an opportunity we'd like to speak with you about.".

This should be good. Kendrick and the FBI?

"What opportunity?"

"We'd like your assistance with a case involving Kendrick Edmonds."

Assistance. That could mean a lot of things. She swung another glance at Watson, but Sampson seemed to be in charge. "Are you involved with the murder investigation?"

"No, ma'am," Sampson said. "The local P.D. is handling that."

A noise came from beside them and Isabelle turned to see several caretakers coming their way. She so did not want to witness Kendrick's body being lowered into the ground. Time to get to the point. "If you're not investigating Kendrick's murder, what do you want from me?"

Sampson's cocoa brown eyes sparked with amusement. Some men appreciated an aggressive woman.

"We believe there is illegal activity in Mr. Edmonds's compound."

When Isabelle realized her jaw had dropped open, she snapped it shut. Kendrick doing something illegal didn't shock her, but Kendrick doing something illegal on a federal level, surprised the hell out of her. He just never seemed that motivated. She shot another look at the casket. The caretakers stood beyond the row of headstones trying to be discreet, but she knew they were waiting for them to leave before getting on with their work.

She turned back to the FBI agents. "Let's move to the road."

When she reached the street, maybe twenty feet from where Peter was parked, she stopped, saw him staring and held up her index finger. He waved in response and, content he'd stay where he was, Isabelle turned back to the agents. "Gentlemen, before last week, I hadn't spoken to Kendrick in years. Even then it was only to say hello at family functions."

"We're aware of your history with him," Sampson said.

The words slapped at her. A *history* with him. That's what they wanted to call it? "You know he sexually abused me?"

Sampson kept his face neutral. No smile, no frown. Nothing.

"Yes. We also know he came here last week and you had an altercation."

Isabelle scoffed. "I kicked his ass. And I'd do it again. Kendrick may have been my cousin, but he was a sick child that grew into a sick man. He belonged in a jail cell."

"Which is why we're here," Watson piped up.

She tilted her head toward the overcast sky and blew out a breath before returning her gaze to the men in front of her. "What do you need from me?"

"As I stated," Sampson said. "We believe there is illegal activity inside that compound. You were invited there, we suspect, to help them with any legal issues that might arise from their activities. We'd like you to see if you can manipulate that into an extended stay in the compound."

"You want me to be an informant?"

"We like to call them sources," Sampson said.

"No," she said. "I wouldn't know the first thing about that kind of work. Find someone else."

"Ms. DeRosa," Watson said, "we'll provide as much security as we can from the outside."

"What good will that do if they catch me poking around?"

Sampson held up a hand. "We believe the children within the compound might be in some danger."

Children. A hammering began behind her eyes. "There are children involved?"

"Yes. Mostly girls."

Dammit. "Wow. You guys are good. You come here, to this man's *funeral*, knowing he sexually abused me, and you throw that out there. What a tactic."

"We also believe someone from inside the organization may have murdered Mr. Edmonds."

The pounding behind her eyes crept away. Now she saw where they were going with this. "I've been questioned by the P.D. in this case. They won't have a problem with me leaving the state?"

"We'll take care of that."

"Because this is a federal case and it trumps theirs?"

No answer.

"Okay then. Am I correct in assuming that if I go in there and dig up something that leads you to the murderer, it clears me?"

"Possibly," Sampson said.

Isabelle tilted her head. "The police have probably already cleared me."

"True," Watson said, "but they won't make it public. The news media will probably continue to mention your name in connection with the case."

The sharp end of a hot knife seemed to puncture her spine. She'd spent most of her life hiding her secrets and didn't want her name to be forever associated with Kendrick's murder. It might happen anyway, but not if she could help it.

16

PETER WAS GETTING IMPATIENT. HE PULLED THE CAR CLOSER to where Izzy stood talking to the feds. They had to be feds. He saw them pull up in a Crown Vic that should have had a sign on it reading law enforcement.

Part of him didn't want to know what was going on, but he also didn't like the idea of her being alone with these guys.

After parking the car and shutting the engine, he contemplated getting out when an unsmiling Izzy, her face drawn and blank, turned her head toward him.

The taller dude angled to see what had captured her attention. Peter waved.

Dude said something to Izzy and she did a bobblehead impression.

What the hell's going on here?

Izzy finally stepped away and walked toward the car, teetering when her heels dug into the grass. The two feds nodded at Peter as they drew closer, but the taller one glanced back at Izzy. A dormant sting of jealousy blasted Peter, but there was no denying she had an effect on men.

Any red-blooded man would be a fool not to take a second look.

He got out, swung around to the passenger's side and opened the door for her. "Are you all right?"

"Yep," she said, but the crispness in the word confirmed she lied.

He slid back into the driver's side. "Feds?"

She slapped her hands over her eyes. "How'd you know?"

"Pretty obvious, Iz."

She hesitated. "I probably shouldn't discuss it with anyone."

Yeah, right. "Oh, you'll tell me about it."

He gave her the hard stare until she folded. "They think Kendrick's charity is into something illegal."

"Well, hot damn." He pulled out of the cemetery. "Where to?"

"My office. I need to make some calls."

"What do they think Kendrick was up to?"

Izzy shook her head. "They don't know. They want me to leverage Kendrick's invitation to visit so I can get into the compound." She slouched down in the seat. "Peter, they want me to be an informant. A *source*."

A sudden burst of shock made his cheeks hot. "*O*-kay."

"Exactly."

No way she could handle that. Not with her emotional issues. She'd have to go into the home of her abuser, be among his things. Batshit central. "What did you tell them?"

She rubbed her fingers across her forehead. "I said I'd get back to them."

"*What*? It would be emotional suicide."

She turned to him, those gorgeous eyes snappy and mean. "You don't think I know that?"

He held up a hand before turning right onto Broad Street for the last half mile to her office. "Sorry."

"Drop me off in front." When he pulled into the circular drive, she said, "There are kids there. At Kendrick's. Girls."

"Ah, shit." Peter shook his head. Friggin' feds went right for the jugular.

"How do I turn away from that?"

"I have no idea."

"Well, when you figure it out, let me know."

THE EARLY EVENING SUN EASED OVER ISABELLE'S CHEEK AS they cruised down Ocean Avenue in Peter's Mustang, and she decided being chauffeured around wasn't a bad thing. He'd picked her up from work, brought her home to change and informed her he would be making her dinner at his place.

The man could cook. Who'd have thunk it? Peter Jessup continued to be chock full of surprises and, for once, she didn't mind.

When they pulled onto the Jessup estate she once again marveled at the palatial surroundings. These people were loaded. Filthy rich.

They passed the main house, drove around the tennis court and pool to a small cottage five hundred yards below. A simple two-story structure painted a vibrant white with pale blue trim, it had four windows lining the front with a porch that spanned the length of the home. Two white rocking chairs gently moved with the wind.

"So, this is it?" Isabelle asked as Peter pulled around the side of the house to the small driveway.

"Yep."

"It so homey."

"It's a two bedroom. My mother wanted to make sure there'd be enough room for people with children." He laughed. "It's not like she has any extra room with the ten bedrooms in her house."

He held open the car door and she followed him along the path to the front door. "Why don't you stay in the main house?"

After flipping through his keys and finding the right one, he jammed it into the lock. "Because my family doesn't understand the meaning of privacy. If I stay here, I'm not underfoot all the time."

Isabelle stepped into the cool air and chill bumps peppered her bare arms. The large, open living room and the casual sectional, upholstered in a beige cotton, immediately drew her attention. Two vivid blue chairs in the same fabric sat opposite the sofa. The walls were a lighter beige, and she breathed in the coziness around her. The decorators earned their money on this job.

She dropped her purse on the floor and followed Peter to the small kitchen, but he promptly settled her on one of the iron stools by the breakfast bar.

"Anyway," he said, "back to the feds. What are you thinking about this informant thing?"

He pulled a plate of partially cooked chicken from the fridge.

"I don't think I can do it. What do I know about that sort of work?"

After pouring olive oil into a skillet, he said, "Good. Tell them no."

He retrieved two small bowls from the fridge, dumped the contents into the pan and the sizzle brought the aroma of onions and garlic.

"I can't believe you know how to cook."

He shrugged. "Marguerite taught me. All those years of being punished resulted in me sitting in the kitchen most evenings. Eventually, I started to help. No big deal."

Maybe not to him.

"Anyway, I'll tell the feds no. I think that's what I should do."

"Good," he said again and a fuse inside her blew.

"Are you going to say anything other than 'good'?"

He glanced over his shoulder, his eyes narrowed. After a minute he stopped sautéing and turned to face her. "Do you *want* me to say something other than good?"

"Well, I'd like your opinion. We've had all afternoon to think about it. Besides, you know more about this type of thing than I do."

He scrubbed his right hand over his face, took a deep breath and went back to cooking. The smell of the sautéing onions and garlic wafted her way and she let the comforts of a home-cooked meal settle her.

"I'm not sure," Peter said. "Part of me is relieved that you'll say no. I think they're withholding information until they get a commitment from you. They'd be stupid to give you any details about an ongoing investigation until you've agreed to work with them. Plus, they think there's a murderer in there, and I can't wrap my mind around you being on your own.

"The other part of me, the part that drives most of what I do, is telling me this op could clear you of murder. And let's not forget the kids."

The children. *Mostly girls.* That's what the agents had said. Probably girls just like she had been at eight years old when she discovered the male anatomy long before she should have. Her stomach clenched.

"You think I should do it."

He twisted around to the fridge again, grabbed a bottle of white wine from the bottom shelf and, without measuring, poured some into the pan. Amazing. Next came some sort of broth. She guessed chicken.

"I didn't say that," Peter said. "I think you need to decide for yourself, but whatever you decide, I'll help you."

She glanced up at him. "Help me how?"

"Not sure yet. I'm still processing it, but there's no way you're going into that circus alone while a murderer is running around."

Lemon juice went into the pan next and then some chopped greenery. Parsley? "Peter?"

"Yeah?"

"What are you making?"

He forked the chicken into the skillet, turned each piece to coat it and covered the pan. "Chicken Limone."

Her stomach growled. Roared actually. "Yummy."

"We'll eat in a little while." He came around the breakfast bar and reached for her hand. "Let's have a rumba lesson while I think about this FBI deal. I want to work on your hips. You won't let yourself go and it's holding you back."

A rumba lesson? *Now*? "Are you insane?"

He laughed and dragged her with him to the living room. "Vic seems to think so. He took all my guns."

He tried to make it a joke, but something in his tone said otherwise. Could this be him wanting to open up about what happened on his last assignment?

"Do you want to talk about that?"

He punched a button on his phone and Southside Johnny and the Asbury Jukes' version of "The Fever" wailed from surround sound speakers.

"That's a little loud," Peter said, turning it down a decibel. "This song will work though. Let me move this coffee table."

Moving to the center of the room, he shoved the coffee table toward the breakfast bar to give them room.

"You didn't answer my question," Isabelle said.

"Nope."

"Nope, you didn't answer or nope you don't want to talk about it?"

"Yep."

He held out his arms for her, but she fisted both hands and shook them at him. "Why won't you talk to me about this?"

Something in his stance changed. He still stood with his arms outstretched, but his shoulders sagged. "I'd really just like to dance with you."

Shutting down. She understood it and now realized how frustrating it could be for those who cared enough to want to help. She had forced away many people with her own version of shutting down and it suddenly seemed like an awful form of rejection to bestow on someone.

"Fine."

The million-dollar smile split his face and he reached for her, hauled her forward and kissed her in a way that had nothing to do with gentility. Rough. Needy. The scorching heat drilled to her core.

No. No. No.

Flip the switch. He needs something you can't give.

Maybe, but her hands found their way into the waist-band of his shorts and landed on his butt, while Southside Johnny whined about having the fever for a girl. Southside had no idea the fever brewing in this room.

Peter pulled away from the kiss, streaked kisses down

her neck as his hot hands roamed under her tank top to her breasts.

No. No. No. *Don't let him touch you like this.*

Too late. His fingers were inside her bra, playing with her nipples and it felt sooooooo good. Something pooled deep within her, and she grabbed his face for more kisses. She needed them. Needed to be close to him.

Flip.

The.

Switch.

He moved his calloused fingers down her body until they reached the bottom of her shirt. "Get this off," he said, still devouring her mouth.

The shirt went flying and he unclipped her bra, tossed it, before grinding his hips into hers. His erection poked at her and his eyes turned the color of the ocean during a raging storm.

Oh, baby. This would be good.

Flip. The. *Switch!*

But she moved her hands under his shirt, pulled it up and over his head, taking the do-rag off with it, before exploring the hard planes of his chest and the nasty scar on his upper abs. Remembering his weak spot, she went for his neck. His palms pressed against her nipples, shooting more heat into her.

What was happening? This crazy need for...something. Not just the sex. Something else. Something she couldn't define.

No. Don't think. She closed her eyes, concentrated on smothering his neck with kisses.

"Izzy, you're killing me."

The edginess of his voice seeped into her and she

moaned. The swirling tension looped tight, forcing the breath from her.

Peter finally shoved her backward, onto the couch, and his swarming hands moved into her pants while he trailed kisses over her breasts.

Can't breathe.

Flip the switch.

What will be left if you give yourself over?

Closer. If she could just get closer, maybe her mind would go silent.

The room contracted. No air.

She locked her arms around him and pulled him close. "Kiss me. Please, Peter."

Anything to make the panic disappear. She couldn't do it. Couldn't make this feeling of losing herself go away.

She closed her eyes one last time, let herself enjoy the tumbling, downhill fall these moments of pure lust brought. Lust that only Peter seemed to be capable of giving her.

A sob caught in her throat as she opened the door for Creepy Izzy.

FINALLY, FINALLY, FINALLY. FUN IZZY WAS IN THE HOUSE AND looking for some serious nookie. Peter would have liked to hop around the house like Daffy Duck screaming *Woohoo! Woohoo! Woohoo!* but he couldn't risk giving Izzy even a second to think about flipping that goddamned switch.

Nope. In the next minute and a half, he'd have her pants off and Fun Izzy would get a shagging that neither one of them would forget. Happy day.

Dinner would be trash by the time he got done with her, but this qualified as a good reason to ruin Chicken Limone. Holding himself up with one arm, he reached for the button on her denim shorts, felt the heat of her stomach under his fingers and nearly ripped the damned shorts in two. His head—make that *heads*—wanted to erupt. Literally.

All because Monk Junior was about to meet Izzy up close and personal. Very personal.

Something clicked. Not in his brain either. By the door. The lock tumbling?

Shit.

But Izzy. Right here under him. He shot a look at the door—nothing moving yet. He lowered his other arm, pushed himself up on both hands and spotted Izzy's closed eyes.

Dammit.

"Open your eyes." He needed to make sure Creepy Izzy hadn't gotten nosy. Before she could comply, the front door opened.

"Peter?" his mother called.

The sound of his mother's voice at this exact moment should have sent every stinking bit of his hard-on bye-bye. He launched himself off the couch, gawked at a half naked Izzy—those glorious breasts just waiting for his hands to be on them again—and nearly cried. He finally made it to her face and almost laughed at the horror displayed in her eyes. In total contrast, her lips were pressed tight to conceal a smile.

Holy shit. His mother just busted them about to have sex.

"Mom," he yelled when he heard the door close, "don't take another step"

She skidded to a stop. "What is it?"

From the corner of his eye, he saw Izzy slap her arms across her chest and try to bury herself deeper into the couch. He retrieved his shirt from the floor, tossed it to her and hauled ass to keep his mother from coming any closer.

"You *have* to stop walking in on me," he said.

The twinkling blue of his mother's eyes faded in confusion. "Why?"

Why? He dropped his chin to his chest, saw his still raging hard-on tenting the thin material of his basketball shorts and burst out laughing.

This could not be happening.

"Hi, Mrs. Jessup," Izzy said from behind him.

Going up on tiptoes to look over his shoulder, his mother's smile immediately softened his angst. His mom liked Izzy.

"Hello, Isabelle. How are you, dear?"

Now they were going to exchange pleasantries while Monk Junior waved a white flag. Peter scrubbed his hands over his face. Could this get any worse? At least Izzy was clothed now.

"Oh my," his mother said, angling from Izzy back to him, her face seeming to grow longer by the second. "Am I interrupting something?"

He cleared his throat. "Uh, sort of."

The lightning bolt of realization flashed over her face. She focused on his bare chest and then, oh crap, her gaze dropped to his crotch.

Oh, no. Oh, Jesus. His mother was staring at his engorged dick. Someone needed to plunge a dagger into his heart. *Right fucking now.* Death would be the only suitable escape.

How he could still be hard, he had no idea, but his shriveling intestines—at least *something* was shriveling—told him he'd just suffered a rare humiliating moment.

Mom slammed her eyes closed. Like that would wipe away the vision of her oldest son in flagrante delicto.

"I am *so* sorry," she whispered, her voice cracking.

"Like I said. You have to stop doing this." Peter heard Izzy moving around behind him. "Iz, would you turn off the stove please? Before dinner goes up in flames."

Like everything else.

He grabbed his mother's wrists and squeezed before she stroked out. "Relax. It's all right. Just knock next time. Please. If the door is locked, there's a reason."

Finally, she scrunched her nose and brought her gaze to his. He wanted to hug her, but with his current state of Señor Raging Hard-On there was no way he'd move any closer. Oh, damn, that had such an ick factor to it.

"I just wanted to see what you were doing for dinner," his mother said. "Your father is working late and Marguerite is off tonight. I thought maybe we could go out." She held up her hands, started for the door. "I didn't know Isabelle was here. I only saw your car outside."

"Uh, Peter?" Izzy said from behind him.

He grabbed his mother's arm to keep her from running. "Yes?"

"Maybe your mom can join us?"

Now didn't that just verge on the truly hysterical? *Gee, Mom, that's a great idea. Why don't you join me, Izzy and Monk Junior for some chow?* Yeah, it definitely just got worse.

"There's plenty of chicken," Izzy said giving him a wide-eyed, make-your-mother-happy look.

He spun back to his mom; whose pale cheeks suddenly morphed into a rosy slice of hope. "Great idea. I made Marg's Chicken Limone. I just need to do some pasta and we'll be ready to eat."

Going to tiptoes again, his mother peered over his shoulder at Izzy. "You don't mind?"

"Of course not," she said from behind him, and his heart

nearly blew right out of his chest. If anything, Izzy, standing there in his T-shirt, should have been beside herself with embarrassment, yet she invited his mother to stay.

He could be in love.

After bobbing her head up and down, Mom angled toward the door. "I'll just run up to the house and get a nice bottle of wine. It'll give you two a minute to...uh...well, you know."

Peter snorted a laugh. "Yeah, we know."

He reached around and opened the door for her, but when she got outside, she whipped back to him and stepped closer.

"Peter?"

What now? He let out a breath. "Yes, Mother?"

She scooted even closer and pointed to his crotch. "You should use a condom, dear."

He reeled back, the horror of the situation stomping around inside him. "Mom," he shouted. "Knock it off. You're freaking me out."

She held up her hands. "Just a suggestion."

He gritted his teeth, and the pressure nearly snapped his jaw. "Go. Get. The. Wine."

Before I murder my own mother.

17

"I'M GOING TO WALK MY MOM UP TO THE HOUSE," PETER SAID when Isabelle picked up the last pot to be dried.

"Good night, Mrs.—uh—Lorraine."

Lorraine grinned her approval at the use of her given name. Isabelle couldn't help forgetting to use it. The woman was formidable and deserved the respect.

"Goodnight, Isabelle. Thank you for inviting me."

A flush of heat burned Isabelle's cheeks. She'd done the right thing by suggesting dinner together, and she suspected, in some way, she brightened a lonely woman's evening.

Isabelle knew loneliness and Peter's mother was smothered in it like manure at a horse track. Oh, she did a good job of putting on a cheery face, but Isabelle sensed a gaping hole in this woman's armor. She knew about that too.

Lorraine put up her finger when Peter held his arm to her. "One last thing." She stepped closer to Isabelle, her eyes unwavering. "I wanted to tell you how sorry I am about this business with your cousin. It's just horrible."

Finally, the elephant on Isabelle's back had lumbered

away. Lorraine, dressed in her fine beige slacks and matching silk blouse had done well pretending the Kendrick issue didn't exist, but they all knew better. Still, her eyes were warm and nonjudgmental, and the sudden gush of relief left Isabelle stunned by its force.

"Thank you," she said. "It *is* horrible. And I'm sorry Peter got caught up in it."

Lorraine reached for her son's arm. "That's unfortunate, but you couldn't have a better supporter."

He grinned at her. "It'll be all right. The cops took the security footage from the gate. They'll see what time I got home and they'll clear us both."

For a few seconds the room and everything in it, including Lorraine faded to a whitewashed background and Isabelle and Peter were alone. Just the two of them. Together. He wrapped his hand around the back of her head and stroked gently while a voice deep inside her whispered, *Yes.*

What's that about?

"Well, I should go," Lorraine said, breaking the spell and bringing the room back to focus.

Peter glanced at Isabelle. "Be right back."

Walking his mother home. How wonderful. She would be perfectly safe walking five hundred yards on her own property, but he wanted to be sure. A good man.

With the dinner dishes cleaned up, Isabelle flopped onto the sofa and stretched into the wide cushions—not too over-stuffed—just enough for a weary body to sink into.

How they all enjoyed a meal after Mrs. Jessup—Lorraine —found them half naked proved a mystery. Of course, it didn't hurt that everyone had their rightful clothes on. A giggle bubbled inside, an odd sensation of mischievous joy she'd never felt as a teenager.

Isabelle flipped to her stomach and inhaled the clean scent of the soft cotton. She closed her eyes.

She liked Peter's mother.

She *liked* how the woman wore silk blouses and dress slacks for a simple dinner with her son. She *liked* how easily Lorraine recovered from awkward situations and the obvious affection she held for Peter, even if he didn't always see it.

Yes, Lorraine Jessup was a living, breathing powerhouse.

How nice it would have been to grow up with a mother like that? One that would support her child during the ugly stuff. Mrs. Jessup had her issues, but the woman, regardless of the situation, would defend her family.

Isabelle sighed a little, the soft fabric abrading her cheek, just a gentle massage to help relieve the stress. *Sleep.* Right here. Her body begged for it.

A few minutes later, her mind and body drifting, she heard the door open and stuck her arm out to wave. She didn't quite make the wave. It was more of a hand flop.

"Are you a sleepy girl?" Peter laughed softly and trailed his fingers over her head before scooping up her feet and planting himself under them.

"Probably the wine." She rolled over so she could see him.

"What a crazy night," he said. "A real bohica."

"Bohica?"

"Bend over, here it comes again."

She snorted. "My life seems to be a series of bohicas lately."

He skimmed his fingers up her leg and she glanced at him, their eyes connecting for a second, sparking that same frenetic intensity between them. *Here we go again.* He made a move toward her, but shoving her bare foot against his chest stopped him cold. She wanted some answers before they got into another make-out session.

Over dinner, Lorraine had casually mentioned someone kept knocking over the bush in front of the house. She knew this because half the dirt was missing from the pot. During the conversation, Peter had grown quiet and Isabelle's mind wandered back to the day he admitted his hatred of the bush.

"What's up with you and the fiddle leaf fig?"

SHIT. PETER LET HIS FACE SETTLE INTO HIS BEST I-HAVE-NO-idea-what-you're-talking-about look. "What?"

She nudged him with her foot. Well, maybe it was more like a kick. He rested his head against the cushion, staring at the ceiling.

"Spill it. I know it's you knocking over that bush. I just can't figure out why."

Caught. Like a bear in a trap. He could blurt it out, no problem. He'd never been embarrassed to voice his thoughts, but this was different. Before now he never thought his head was fucked.

Then she aimed those Caribbean green lasers at him. "Oh, jeez."

When she dug her heel into the crotch of his thin—extremely thin—basketball shorts, his eyes crossed.

Yow.

With extreme care, he lifted her foot off his parts and started breathing again. "You don't have to get mean about it."

"Clearly, I do."

The echo of his thumping heartbeat rattled in his head as her eyes drilled into him. Waiting. *Damn.* The quiet of the house folded in and his body stiffened. He had to say some-thing. Something she'd believe, but he wouldn't lie. Not to her.

He should just tell her. With all her demons, she'd understand.

"I keep thinking someone is hiding behind it." He inched closer to watch for any sign of ridicule about to come his way. Nothing. Only a slight puckering of her lips.

"As in someone trying to do harm to your family?"

"Yes."

She nodded, but made no other attempt to comfort him. Good, because he didn't want to be poor-babied. All he needed was to get on his game and back to work.

"You told me about Roy," she said. "Was his killer hiding behind something?"

"No." He let out a sarcastic laugh. "I went crazy in a different way on that one."

"How so?"

More questions. He shifted his eyes to her, then away again. Maybe if he stayed quiet she'd take the hint and leave him alone.

"Peter, what happened to you over there? Let me help you."

That plan failed. She wanted to help. And why not? Somebody had to because, according to his friends, he was cracking up. He slouched into the sofa, misery caving his head in.

"I couldn't sleep after Roy died. Well, I *could* sleep, but the nightmares were brutal, so I stayed awake."

Her perfect eyebrows shot up on that one. "For how long?"

"Four days." *Take that, baby.*

"Wow."

"Yep. Then Billy, he's one of the guys on my team. A real smart-ass. He started cracking jokes about me not sleeping. I went nuts and beat the hell out of him, which I now feel bad about, but he's a prototypical pain in the ass. It was nothing unusual for him to mouth off and I couldn't take it anymore. Before I knew it, word had gotten back to Vic and he put me on a plane home."

"He convinced you to come home?"

"Hell no. He told me he had another assignment for me, and I was damned glad because I didn't want to take a chance on killing Billy. The minute I got back to Chicago Vic put me on R&R."

Isabelle nodded. "Okay. No potted plant issues on *that* one. How did Tiny die?"

Bingo. We have a winner.

"He got shot."

"Was the shooter hiding behind a potted plant?"

He shook his head. "A crate of cereal boxes."

She rocked forward, smacked him on the leg a few times. "There you go. You're not crazy. You've lost two good friends in less than a year. You're exhausted because you've been working yourself into the ground trying to forget about Tiny and—*bam!*—Roy dies. It's not rocket science. You're grieving. In case you're not familiar with it, it's something we mortals do."

Another smart-ass. Flipping her off, as he'd done his brother, didn't seem appropriate. He reached over and pinched her thigh just below the hem of her shorts. Not hard, but enough for her to know she'd hit a nerve. "Okay," he said. "Fine. I'm not crazy, but that plant is driving me batshit."

She shrugged. "Ask your mother to move it until you get beyond this initial stage of anxiety."

"Oh, Lord. No way. *No way.*"

She slid over, snuggled in beside him, pulled his do-rag off and trailed her hand through his hair. "You can't escape this. You've been trying for the better part of a year now and it's catching up. You need to let yourself experience the pain so you can get past it."

A blood rush seized him. He didn't want to talk about this. Not now, not ever. He could escape it. He could. He just had to try harder.

He patted her leg. "Hey, we never did get that rumba lesson in."

She didn't move.

Shit.

He shook his head, huffed a breath. "I hear what you're saying. And it makes sense. I don't know how to give in to it."

"News flash, Peter. No one does. You just have to let it be. When you're pissed be pissed, don't try to push it away. When you're hurt, be hurt. Trust me, you cannot play hide and seek with your emotions. Just ask Creepy Izzy. You will fail miserably."

She knew.

Maybe in a different way, but she understood running away wouldn't work.

Besides that, unbeknownst to her, she'd started helping him the second his horny ass landed on that elevator with her. The nightmares didn't happen as often. Now he dreamed of her and his list of sexual fantasies continued to grow at an alarming rate.

Plus, when they spent time together, he didn't feel so useless.

"Thank you," he said.

She cocked her head and twirled his hair around her finger. "You'll get there if you give yourself a chance. Talk to your mother about the plant. She adores you. She'll move it."

He turned sideways, brushed his hand down her bare arm. The faded strawberry tank top she wore had some miles on it. He laughed. Izzy, outside of her top-notch lawyer clothes, sometimes dressed like a homeless person. They could look homeless together.

"My mother likes you," he said.

Izzy grabbed his roaming hand and entwined her fingers with his. "You're changing the subject."

He grinned. "Yep."

The lecture would begin at any minute. One, two, three seconds and...nothing. She leaned forward, her breast rubbing against his arm, and brushed her lips against his. The hair on his arm tingled and old one-eye woke from his slumber.

She moved closer, and smoothed her hand down the front of his T-shirt. "Hmm," she said, still moving that hand up and down, up and down and—oh baby—his thoughts were definitely going south.

"Izzy?"

Her lips parted and—oh, man—he wanted to feast on them.

"Yes?" she said.

"I'd really like to fuck your brains out."

18

In Peter's opinion, her deep belly laugh could have been the sun peeking out on a gloomy winter day. Heaven. And he hadn't experienced much heaven lately.

She straddled him and dragged her thumb over the scar near his mouth. "You're the one who's insisting on waiting for Fun Izzy."

"I had her for a while." These small hills of emotional and physical progress kept him from going insane.

"Yes, you did. It's getting better, don't you think?"

She continued to rub her thumb over his cheek and Monk Junior came awake. *Jeez.* This woman would kill him yet. And, unless she'd lost all feeling in her lower body, she couldn't miss the hard-on.

"Oh, my," she said.

Nope. Her lower body was just fine. In all aspects.

"Uh, better how?" Peter asked, trying to get back to her question.

Or, they could do it her way and she could nibble at his neck. *Oh, man.* Totally frickin' haywire.

"It took Creepy Izzy a while to catch up," she said, while

his thoughts played demolition derby in his head. "Usually it happens right away."

Her gaze settled on the scar. He should tell her and dissolve her curiosity. Everyone imagined he'd gotten the scar in some war-torn country. *Sorry to disappoint, folks.* "The coffee table."

She bolted to spine-stiffening attention, the pressure causing a riot with Monk Junior who wanted to be released for pillaging.

"Excuse me?"

"The scar on my cheek. I was ten. Stephen and I were fighting and I crashed into the edge of a marble coffee table. That's why it's L shaped. Needed ten stitches."

Leaning forward, she grazed her lips across the scar and his body hit overdrive again. Searing heat scalded him, but something else, maybe the quiet tenderness in her kiss left him wanting this every night. With her.

"I've been wondering," she said, rolling her hips into him.

Unfortunately for him, Fun Izzy had already left the building. The inflection in her voice clued him in. Fun Izzy had a silly way of being sexy where Creepy Izzy turned into a purring seductress.

But, what the hell, he kissed her. Even held her head in place while his tongue explored her mouth. She didn't seem to mind so much.

If he had to endure the torture of not being able to ram his aching body into her, he might as well get some enjoyment, and kissing Izzy would never be a bad thing.

He backed away, stared into those sparking green eyes and the internal battle began.

Creepy Izzy wanted him.

His *body* wanted her, but the rational part of him, the

part that knew she didn't trust men to be anything more than sex-seeking pigs, told him to back the fuck off.

Any sane man would give in to the obvious talents of Creepy Izzy. Not that Peter was sane right now, but he knew enough that he couldn't settle for less than all of her. He wanted her body, mind and heart. Every inch.

"What's the problem?" she asked, sliding her hand under his shirt.

She knew the damn problem. "I want the entire Creepy Izzy-Fun Izzy package. The whole you, rather than this compartmentalized version, would be worth the wait for both of us. You're not there yet."

Her shoulders didn't sag, they plummeted. Too bad Monk Junior didn't go with them. Nope. That bad boy was still on the prowl.

"I'm sorry."

He kissed the tip of her nose. "Yeah, me too. We'll get there. Just not tonight."

"I'm afraid you'll run out of patience."

Oh, hell, he'd gone way beyond being out of patience.

AT SIX-THIRTY THURSDAY MORNING, PETER PULLED INTO Izzy's driveway, parked and retrieved his board from the cargo area of the Explorer. According to the charts, high tide would be in soon.

He hefted the board and hauled ass to the back of the house. Izzy was probably awake by now—she liked to get up early and work out—but he needed the water and would catch her before she left for work.

To his surprise, he found her sitting on the deck wrapped in a blanket, fighting the morning chill while the ocean breeze smacked against her sleep-rumpled hair.

Damn, she looked cute curled up in that lounge chair. His body's radar went *beepbeepbeepbeepbeep.*

Yeah, I hear you, but there's nothing I can do about it.

"Hey, beautiful," he said, still holding his surfboard. "I'm gonna catch a few."

She jerked her head. "Tide chart says six forty-five. I checked it last night."

Something about her checking the tide charts for him forced him to grin. "You okay?"

"I'm going to do it," she said. "The FBI thing."

No.

Peter dropped his board in the sand, stepped onto the deck and sat on the edge of her chair. "You sure?"

"I was up half the night. I can't get the kids out of my head. I keep thinking about Creepy Izzy and the havoc she's causing between us. I might be able to save one of those girls." She brought her gaze back to him, misery mapping her face. "Don't I owe them that? A chance for them to be—as you said last night—whole?"

"I was talking about you. You and me. Don't let that influence this decision. Two totally different things."

She drew in a breath. "Maybe so, but those children could become adults and turn into me. I wouldn't wish that on anyone."

Peter scrubbed his hands over his face wishing he'd kept his big mouth shut. He couldn't help admire her willingness to jump in, but she could get hurt. Or worse. And then what? "It's not your responsibility."

"Says the man who has taken on my problems."

"That's different."

"Actually, it's not."

"The FBI can find someone else," he said.

"But I have a chance to get in there faster." She sat up,

grabbed his hand and the blanket slid off her shoulder, revealing a white tank top adorned with pink flip-flops. "I've made up my mind. I'm going to call Sampson and tell him I'll do it."

A nagging itch trailed the back of Peter's neck and he tugged on his wet suit's zipper leash. *Yeah, that's the problem.* The *zipper* was causing the itch. "You realize you'll have to take time off of work, right?"

Yes, he wanted to talk her out of it. He wanted her safe, and sending her into that compound where all kinds of depravity could exist jeopardized that.

"You don't want me to do this."

He jerked a shoulder and searched her eyes for self-doubt, but he didn't see much of it. No, he saw determination. "I understand why you want to, but for selfish reasons, I'd rather you not."

She brushed her hand down his arm. "It'll be fine, Peter. I'll tell my uncle I'm taking a leave of absence. The Parker trial will start soon, but someone will to take my spot."

A seagull landed on the sand at the foot of the deck in search of food, but Peter's gaze went to the shoreline where high tide rolled in. The pounding waves offered an invitation to lament this on his board. Probably a good move before he said something stupid. He turned back to Izzy. "Sounds like you thought it out last night."

"I did. It's the children. I can't get past that."

He stood. "Okay then. I'm going to catch some waves and think about how I can help you."

"Peter—"

He held up a hand. "I'm done talking about this right now."

He scooped up his board while fast-moving thoughts nearly fried his mind. How the hell was he going to avoid her entering that compound alone? On top of that, in his fucked-up mind-set, could he keep her from getting hurt?

The way his luck was running he'd create more problems for her.

His involvement would also send Vic into freakville, which wouldn't get him back to work any time soon. Another happy day in paradise.

The bigger issue would be Izzy staying in one piece, and if she didn't, Peter would have to live with it.

AT QUARTER AFTER TWELVE ISABELLE SAW AGENT SAMPSON stroll around the path in Fireside Park, a quiet, heavily wooded area a few miles off Route 35 in Woodbridge. He had chosen the place and given her directions when she'd called him that morning. Of course, a woman alone shouldn't walk in this park. Too many places for bad guys to hide. Maybe that was just her own paranoia, but she couldn't deny her relief when Sampson came into view.

He spotted her and smiled just enough that the dimple in his cheek winked at her. His suit, a gray one this time, fit in all the right places and his hair was combed back with perfect precision. One handsome man.

And he knew it.

"Ms. DeRosa," he said, giving her a little bow before he sat next to her on the bench.

She snorted at the gesture. *Yep. He's a slick one.* "Agent Sampson."

Their eyes connected for a few seconds. Weren't they a pair? Two people unashamed to barter their looks for what they wanted. She liked this guy. Even if he was about to throw her life into a pit of anthrax.

Isabelle circled her sweaty hands over her black slacks,

the sleepless night dragging on her like cement. "How can I help you?"

He pulled a photograph from the inside pocket of his jacket and handed it to her. A young woman with silky auburn hair smiling into the camera.

"Nicole Pratt," Sampson said. "Xavier University student and the daughter of Congresswoman Monica Hollis."

Yes. The daughter had disappeared a few weeks back. "She's missing, right? Something happened to her while she was traveling?"

"That's the story the press has. We believe Nicole went into Kendrick Edmonds's compound and something happened to her there. She told her mother she'd be traveling all summer with her friend Kaitlin. When her mother couldn't reach her by cell phone, she tracked down Kaitlin's parents and found Kaitlin at home in Ohio. Nicole wasn't with her. Nicole told Kaitlin she was staying in Cincinnati for the summer to take classes."

Isabelle handed the photo back. "She lied?"

"Yes. We don't know why. Kaitlin said Nicole had been volunteering for a group called The Organization for the Underprivileged. Kendrick was the founding member. The compound is outside of Cincinnati."

"I'm assuming you questioned Kendrick."

Sampson nodded. "Yes. We questioned anyone who had contact with her. Kendrick said Nicole had helped with some fundraising, but they hadn't seen her since May."

"And you think he lied."

Sampson leaned back, just a regular Joe enjoying his lunch hour. "We *know* he lied. Her phone is GPS enabled. I checked her records and the GPS puts her on the compound three days before her mother reported her missing. That was the last time the phone was used.

Kendrick didn't think about the cell phone giving us her location."

A flickering snapped at Isabelle's skin. "Kendrick was a pervert for sure, but murder? What could they be up to that he'd kill someone for it?"

"We know they lure people on welfare by telling them they can get off public aid. The residents go through an approval process before they're allowed to live on the property."

"Does this organization really exist?"

"We think it's a front," Sampson said. "They recruit volunteers, let them do the bucket drives and the phoning. The residents are also required to do the fundraising."

She held up her hands. "Hang on. I'm confused. What's the point of this group if they aren't helping the needy?"

"That's what we need to know."

Isabelle knew she was staring, but this was just too much. None of it made any sense. Or maybe she was naive, but *that* had never been an issue before. "I find it hard to believe bucket drives help them raise enough money to support this compound."

Sampson touched his nose with his index finger. Score. "Seth Donner—the number two guy—has money of his own. He's in his forties and has been steadily working as a software engineer. Plus, he inherited some money from his deceased parents. The other fundraising seems to be a bonus. Still though, why would this guy be the sole supporter of this group if there wasn't something in it for him?"

"Right," she agreed.

"We need to get an agent in there, but that'll take time. You were invited to the compound and might be able to get in faster."

Isabelle, still facing front, needed a second to absorb this.

He turned toward her, eyes sparkling, and she got a large dose of his dangerous charm. This guy was good. Anyone walking by would think they were an ordinary couple stealing a few minutes alone.

"Look," he said, "we don't know if it's some sort of domestic terrorism or sex slavery, but something is going on in that compound."

She breathed in and let the insanity work into her brain. "Bizarre."

"Yes, it is."

With Kendrick's sexual history she could connect him to some sort of sex slavery ring. And the FBI wanted her, with her hang-ups, to get into the middle of it.

Heaven help her.

Risking the career she'd been building was one thing, but her emotional stability—or lack thereof—was something else. In the end, could she walk away from this a better person?

Or would she crumble from the pressure and forever turn into Creepy Izzy?

She just didn't know.

Leaving her life in Jersey and temporarily relocating to Ohio wouldn't be easy. Isabelle turned to Sampson and crossed one leg over the other, trying to appear casual to anyone who might be watching. "Xavier U is in Cincinnati. I thought you were based out of Newark. Why isn't the Cincinnati field office handling this?"

He mirrored her position. "The congresswoman requested me."

Ah-ha! Sampson had a thing with the congresswoman.

Isabelle clucked her tongue. "Friends in high places, Agent Sampson?"

It didn't seem possible, but his eyes darkened. "Meaning, am I screwing the congresswoman?"

Isabelle held her palm up.

"No," he said. "My brother is her senior aide. She trusts me to find her daughter."

Shame rose inside Isabelle. Obviously, all men didn't use sex as a tool. "Sorry, if I insulted you."

"Under the circumstances, I suppose it's a legitimate question. And for your information, I don't mix business with pleasure. It gets too complicated in my line of work."

She snorted a laugh. "Good to know I don't have to worry about you hitting on me."

His eyes met hers. "At least not until this case is over."

Her mind immediately went to Peter in his beat-up clothes and do-rag. Putting him next to Wade Sampson's tailored suits and model perfect looks would be quite a comparison.

Peter though, had more understanding and patience than any man she'd known. Were they a couple? She didn't know, but she didn't want to jeopardize the tenuous early stages of what might be something special.

A *relationship*.

Her chest felt as if someone had parked a bus on it. Special relationships were few and far apart for her. She generally couldn't give enough of herself to make it work and the men eventually walked away. She never blamed them. Sometimes she wanted to walk away from herself.

"You should know I'm involved with someone," she said.

He nodded. "Peter Jessup. The guy at the cemetery the other day. We checked him out."

She rested her elbow on the back of the bench and

fiddled with her nails. "He's a good man. He saved my butt with Kendrick a couple of times."

Sampson nodded. "He's also an ex-Navy SEAL—with two Silver Stars—who does contract work for the government."

Silver Stars? The man had a gift for shocking her. A tickle of pride blossomed inside her.

"With his background," Sampson said, "this guy is my worst nightmare. As long as he stays out of my case, I don't have a problem with him."

Good luck with that.

Isabelle shook off a laugh. Peter didn't have it in him to mind his own business. "How is this going to work? Do I just walk up to the compound and knock?"

"That's exactly what you do. Seth Donner probably knows Edmonds invited you. If not, you simply tell him that's why you're there. That you wanted to see the place. He may turn you away. My hope is that he'll take one look at you and invite you in. Once there, help out, get friendly with the residents. Find someone you connect with and work the relationship."

"And if I get in? What then? Do I have to stay if I'm not comfortable?"

"No. This is completely voluntary. You can walk away whenever you choose. It could be dangerous."

What he didn't bother to add, and they both understood, was her place on the murder suspect list still existed. Even if her alibi checked out, she could be in line for a conspiracy charge.

A bird landed on an overhead branch causing Isabelle to jump. She glared at it. Dumb bird. She turned back to Sampson. "I won't wear a wire. Not at first."

"That's a problem," he said.

Peter had warned her Sampson would push back. Heck, she wouldn't have thought of it had Peter not brought it up. He'd convinced her it would be better for her to gain the trust of the members before wearing any kind of recording devices. What if they searched her and found the wire?

"It's my only condition. If you want me, it's without a wire."

Sampson did a yes-no thing with his head. "Let me float it."

"Knock yourself out."

For some reason, he laughed. "What else?"

"How should I contact you?"

"Call me from a secure phone outside the compound. I'll be working out of the Cincinnati office. Generally, I don't give my sources a lot of information. If you appear to know too much, the group members will get suspicious."

That sounded reasonable. She'd rather be in the dark anyway. She didn't want to filter information. All she wanted to be was the messenger.

The alarm on her phone beeped and she reached to silence it. "I need to get back. I'll call you in a day or two."

She rose from the bench and Sampson followed, holding out his hand for her to shake.

"We're going to be working together, so you might as well call me Wade. And thank you."

Staring down at his hand, she took it, and the soft skin reminded her of Peter and his calloused fingers. "Don't thank me yet. I haven't done anything."

"Yeah, but something tells me you will."

"ARE YOU SHITTING ME?" VIC ASKED.

Peter stood in the middle of his mother's picture-perfect lawn talking to Vic on his cell. He didn't have time for this crap. All he wanted were his guns and some information. Bad enough he was too paranoid to make this phone call from inside his car or the house. What if the cops bugged it?

"Yeah. I'm *shitting* you. I have nothing better to do than mess with your head. Why would I make this up?"

"I talked to you two days ago and suddenly Isabelle is going undercover for the feds? What the *fuck*?"

Peter pinched the bridge of his nose. "Okay. Once again. I'll try to speak slowly so you can understand."

"Oh, fuck you," Vic hollered.

Peter laughed because, although it wasn't funny, it was still funny. "The feds showed up yesterday. She talked it over with me last night. I did my best to stay neutral, but I did try to sway her not to do it."

Rustling leaves drew his attention and he swung his head right, his eyes shifting to locate the disturbance. A squirrel darted around the base of the hundred-year-old oak tree. A squirrel. Peter unclenched his ass and rolled his eyes. Yes, his nerves were so fried that if he'd had a gun, the terrorist squirrel would be toast.

Get a grip.

"They got to her on the abused kids, right?" Vic asked.

"Yes. When I showed up to surf this morning she told me she wanted to do it. She met with the agent in charge this afternoon and we're off."

"Un-fucking-believable. Who's the agent? I'll call Lynx and check him out."

Pay dirt. Lynx, a former army buddy of Vic's, worked for the State Department.

"Wade Sampson is his name. He's based out of the Newark office. He seems like a straight up guy, but who knows."

"Got it. What else?"

Peter shook off the drumming in his head. He would *not* go there. Even if every instinct pushed him that way.

"You still there?" Vic asked.

"Yeah. Ask Lynx if this guy has a history of getting personally involved with his sources."

So much for not going there. He had to though. For Izzy's sake.

Right. For his own damn sake because he wanted to be sure Mr. Slick wouldn't steal his girl.

"He moved on her already?" Vic sounded incredulous. "Even I never worked that fast."

Peter pulled the phone down, banged his knuckle on it, and brought it back to his ear. "Hey! Can we focus here?"

"Sorry," Vic said. Peter heard a tapping noise. Probably Vic smacking his pen against the desk. He did that when his brain got active. "What's the plan? She's going to Ohio?"

Peter tilted his head back, closed his eyes and let the late afternoon sun warm his skin. A perfect beach day. "Yep. I'm going with her."

"No."

His muscles spasmed. "Excuse me?"

"You're on vacation. A *mandatory* one. She has to go in there alone anyway. The feds will lock you up before they let you anywhere near this case."

Peter ground his teeth together at the reminder of his mandatory R&R. "Are you stoned? She can't go there alone. Even if I won't be able to go in with her, I can be around. The feds can't keep me from being in the area. I'll get a hotel room and lay low. At least she'll have someone close if she gets into trouble."

More tapping from the other end.

"I'll send someone else," Vic said. "You stay put."

Someone else? Negatory.

Peter shook his head so hard he got woozy. "She trusts *me*. She doesn't need someone else. Someone she doesn't know. It'll just add to her stress. I'm fine. Unless you count wanting to kill my mother last night, but I get a pass on that because it wasn't my fault."

"Your mother is a sweetheart. Leave her alone."

"Remember that when she uses a key to walk into your house and finds you with your shorts tent-poled."

Vic didn't just laugh. He howled. And Peter gave up the fight and joined in. Last night it was horrible, but today it was funny.

"Besides," he added. "I'll be better off with Izzy than sitting here wondering if she's all right. That would really make me nuts."

Let's see him try and argue that one.

"I don't know," Vic said.

Dammit.

More tapping. "Okay, but I'm sending someone with you."

A babysitter. *Shit.* Vic didn't trust him. Peter hated to admit how much that bothered him, but if he needed to prove himself again, the best way to do that would be to have someone there to witness it.

"Fine."

"I'll send Billy."

Son of a bitch. From bad to worse. Peter fisted his free hand until the knuckles burned. Billy. The guy he beat the shit out of, thereby landing his ass on R&R.

"I'm beginning to think you *want* me to go insane," Peter said. "Send someone else."

"No. I like this idea. You two will settle this bullshit and I won't have to check my blood pressure every time I send you on an op together. It's either Billy or I haul your ass back here and give you paperwork so I can keep an eye on you."

Blood gushed in Peter's veins and he slammed his eyes shut, dug his fingers into them. He should quit. Tell Vic to stick the job. Go to work somewhere else. With his skills, anybody would take him.

Taylor Security got the government's cherry assignments though. The oddball stuff that kept things interesting. Plus, he liked it there. A lot.

At least until recently.

"Billy it is then," Peter said.

"Good. And if one of you assholes kills the other, so be it. At least I won't have to put up with you girls fighting."

"I want my guns back. Even the throwaway you robbed from my safe."

Vic sighed. "I didn't *rob* it. Confiscated maybe."

"I want them back. Send them to Ohio with Billy. If you don't, I'll buy new ones. I'd prefer to have my own though."

Vic would understand that. Gina often joked the other woman in Vic's life was named Sig because he practically slept with his .45.

"Okay. I'll send Billy to Ohio on the jet, and we'll load him up with some toys."

Peter gazed down at the grass, digging his bare toes into the thick green blades. "Thank you. You may think I'm nuts, but this is a good call. You know I'll take care of Izzy."

"It's the only reason I'm letting this happen. If I thought for one second you'd be a hazard to her, I'd shoot you myself. When this is over though, you *will* take that vacation and you *will* deal with your issues over Tiny."

Tiny.

Another one chiming in on his dead friend. What was with these people playing Freud? Why did everyone think his problems were about Tiny?

Maybe because he was kicking over potted bushes?

"Izzy told you?"

"What?"

Oooh, shit. He shouldn't have said anything. Besides, there was nothing to be ashamed of. Vic had experienced his own meltdown about Tiny and Peter helped *him* with it.

"Izzy thinks I have an avoidance problem about Tiny getting killed."

"I think Isabelle is a genius." Vic stopped, letting out a heavy breath. "Buddy, I know it sucks. It doesn't go away, but as soon as you give up fighting, it'll get better. I've been there myself. Gina dragged my ass through it, and I bitched and moaned because all she wanted was for me to fucking talk. Talk, talk, talk. I mean, kill me now."

Peter grunted because he'd had a ringside seat to those battles. Back then, they were just a couple of pissed off guys. Now though, it almost made sense. Gina wanted Vic to recognize the grief and not shut down. She forced him to face the pain.

And if he hadn't, he probably would have gone nuts on his friends.

The front door of the main house opened and his mother stepped out, waving to him. She must have stayed home today because she wore a pair of walking shorts and a collared shirt. Her casual look.

"I gotta go," Peter said. "I hear what you're saying. I'm working on it."

"Just take care of Isabelle. I'll get you whatever you need. Later."

Vic hung up and Peter stood staring at the phone in his hand.

"Yeah, including Billy."

20

THIRTY MILES OUTSIDE OF CREEKWOOD—AKA, HOME OF THE now very dead Kendrick Edmonds—Peter pulled Izzy's Audi into the airstrip parking lot.

They had crossed the Ohio border over three hours ago, and Peter was damned sick of being in a car.

On the bright side, Izzy sat next to him wearing cotton shorts and a tank top that showed enough cleavage to make him a happy guy. The midafternoon sun shined bright in a baby blue sky that stretched over miles of open land and pastures. Nothing but lush green plants and an occasional lonely tree.

Yep, Monk and Izzy, just a carefree couple out for a Saturday drive.

At least until they found Billy, the guy who sent Peter into a life-altering, homicidal rage a few weeks earlier.

Good times all around.

Fuck.

"There it is," he said, gesturing to the gleaming white Gulfstream parked in front of a hangar.

Billy was probably waiting inside. The sudden pain in

Peter's jaw seemed to indicate he needed to lighten up on the teeth grinding.

This would be no picnic, but if he didn't square things, Vic wouldn't let him back to work. Peter opened the driver's side door. Might as well get it over with.

"Get the food, Iz. I'll get the drinks. Let's see if Billy is on the plane."

Izzy grabbed the two bags of food sitting at her feet courtesy of Bob's Burger Heaven. Considering they'd skipped lunch, Bob's burgers, no matter how they tasted, would indeed be heaven.

They marched into the small office, nodded to the person behind the desk and headed straight for the tarmac. A guy had to love private airports. No security hassles.

As they approached the plane, the side door opened, the stairs descended and Billy stepped out in baggy hood-rat jeans and a black T-shirt. His shoulder-length brown hair bounced as he jogged toward them, and Peter questioned—for the millionth time—the man's need for long hair.

Billy didn't look any worse for wear considering the last time they'd seen each other Peter left him rolling on the floor coughing up blood. He cracked his neck. Billy, pain in the ass that he was, didn't deserve that vicious beating.

Said pain in the ass stopped a foot in front of Peter—but turned his attention to Izzy. "A beautiful woman carrying food." Billy dropped to his knees. "Marry me?"

When Izzy laughed, Peter rolled his eyes so far up they should have shot out the top of his head.

"Isabelle, meet Billy."

"Hi, Billy," she said, grinning at him in that way women did when instantly smitten.

Sickening. He needed to break this shit up quick. Peter

shoved the tray of drinks at Billy, who was still on his knees. "Hold this."

When he obliged, Peter took the two bags of food from Izzy. "Now I'm holding the food. Still want to get married, you jackass?"

Billy rose from the ground, his eyes narrowed. "Not on your life."

Peter grunted. "Has that last beating faded from your memory?"

"You got lucky that time. You had rage on your side."

"Guys," Izzy said, but Peter kept his focus on Billy.

"Keep talking and I'll have rage on my side again."

"Hey!" Izzy said. "I thought you were friends."

They both turned to her, but Billy's what's-her-problem look won the prize. "Of course we're friends," he said. "We're just pissed at each other."

Her mouth dropped open.

Women.

Billy shifted back to Peter. "Vic says we should kiss and make up."

"Do we care what Vic says?"

"No."

"Then we'll kiss and make up when we're ready."

That must have been okay because Billy shrugged. Not that Peter didn't want to square things. By now, they should probably get over it and move on, but Peter had no interest in talking about Roy. And making up with Billy meant doing just that.

Izzy flapped her hands between them. "How can you stand this tension?"

Peter laughed. "What tension?"

"Ugh!"

"Get used to it, babe. This is life with Billy. He's a royal pain in my ass."

Billy ignored him. "What'd you get me to eat?"

"Bacon, double cheese, ketchup and mayo. No onions, lettuce or tomato."

Billy shot him a sideways glance. "Just the way I like it. Maybe I'll marry you after all."

"Listen, Billy, quit flirting with my man or I'll hurt you."

The sound of Izzy's words stopped Peter, but she and Billy kept walking. He knew he was smiling. Couldn't help it. Izzy had just staked her claim on him and he kinda liked it. Loved it, actually.

Billy clamped a friendly hand around the back of her neck and squeezed. "I heard. You know, I love a woman who can fight."

"Ha!" Peter hauled ass to catch up and nudged her with his elbow. "Maybe he should spar with you first. See how he feels then."

She nudged him back. "You boys. You are too good to me."

Heh-heh. She had no idea how good he wanted to be to her.

First though, they had a missing girl to find.

21

On Sunday afternoon Izzy knocked on the adjoining motel room door. Peter and Billy had just checked in after sleeping at a different rattrap motel the night before. All of them arriving on the same day would have been the equivalent of carrying a we-are-traveling-together sign. Peter had made sure to request the corner room because he knew Izzy had the one next door.

With only five cars in the motel lot the front desk clerk had given a jerky shrug and handed over the key.

Piece. Of. Cake.

The place wasn't so bad. He could live with the circa 1970 swirl rug and avocado green curtains because the sheets and bathroom were clean. The lone double bed was a problem since he and Billy were sharing the room. No wonder the clerk snickered when the two of them had checked in. Small town minds.

Izzy knocked again, and Peter opened the door to find her standing there wearing heavy black eyeliner and loads of inky mascara. Then he made the mistake of looking down. Short—really short—cutoffs and a deep—*really* deep

—V-neck T-shirt. He stood frozen for a second before his gaze traveled from her head to the monster amount of cleavage.

Holy.

Holy.

Shit.

He'd seen her bare-chested that night his mother busted in on them, and her rack—although beautiful—didn't pack that kind of firepower.

She held out her arms. "What do you think?"

"Uh," he said.

Billy materialized next to him. "Hello, Izzy's boobs."

Peter shot him a glare. "Yo. Take it easy."

She held up both hands, fingers spread wide. "You noticed. Perfect."

Every part of Peter's body began to itch. He didn't know where to scratch first, so he started on the back of his neck. What the hell was she doing dressed like a hooker?

"Honey, they're..." He waved his hands toward her chest.

"Big," Billy suggested.

Peter gritted his teeth, turning toward him. "Shut up."

"It's the new Miracle Bra," Izzy said.

Billy grunted. "It's a miracle all right."

"That's it. You're outta here." Peter pushed him to the door. "Come back in ten minutes."

"Come on, Monk." Billy stole another look at Izzy's rack. "She doesn't mind. Do ya, Iz?"

"*I* mind," Peter said. "Beat it."

The door closed with a loud click. He threw the safety and marched back to Izzy. "Okay. What the hell is this?"

She put her hands on her hips and huffed out a breath, causing the miracle boobs to bounce.

Oh, baby.

Monk Junior roared to life. Peter's luck was nothing but bad lately. And son of a bitch if he didn't need to add that bra to his Izzy list of sexual fantasies.

But, right now, for the first time ever, he wanted to have a conversation rather than think about sex.

"Sampson," Izzy began, "told me there might be some kind of sex slavery thing going on in the compound. I figured I should try and use my, uh—" she waved her hands down her torso, "—assets when I go there."

This from the woman who didn't want to be thought of as a sex object. Baffling. Simply baffling.

"You don't agree?" she asked.

Tricky territory. He did agree. On a professional level. If these guys were into sex-related activities, Izzy, with her perfect cheekbones and body that would bring a dead man to life, would make one hell of a prospect.

On a personal level, she wasn't leaving the room. Putting aside the idea of her going in there alone, and his inability to help her if she got into trouble, he didn't want those sick fuckers looking at her the way *he* looked at her.

The sex-kitten outfit was probably the right call though.

Obviously disappointed, she dropped her chin to her chest, spotted his hard-on and, with puckered lips, lifted her head again. The man-killer gaze connected with his. They stood there for what had to be ten minutes. Her looking at him. Him looking back. She finally stepped closer and reached for him, her hands sliding around him as she nuzzled his neck.

"I guess my idea worked."

When she ran her tongue behind his ear, he breathed deep and tilted his head back so she could work her magic. He imagined nailing her right there. Yep. It would take a week to get rid of this boner.

He gripped her arms and pushed her away before he lost all semblance of coherent thought.

Creepy Izzy—no surprise there—stared back at him. "They'll see you and think you want to get laid. Can you handle it?"

She closed her eyes and the only sound drifting between them was the John Wayne movie Billy had been watching.

"I don't know," she finally said. "But if it'll get me in, I'll deal with it."

He brought her into his arms and she rested her cheek against his chest. Damn that felt good. "You can still tell Sampson to screw off. After you go there today, it'll be harder to back out."

"No. I need to do this. I'll be fine. As long as I know you're here. I'll be fine."

"You can take care of yourself, but I won't let anything happen to you. We'll give you a ten-minute head start and then follow. I won't be able to get too close, but we'll be around. If you have trouble, text me a 9-1-1 and we'll bust in there."

She stepped away. Threw her shoulders back. "I can do this."

"I know you can."

He just didn't want her to. "You ready?"

"Yep."

She smiled at him, but the weariness of it didn't sit well with him. She bit her bottom lip. "Um, Peter?"

"Yeah?"

She pointed to the top of his head. "Can I wear that? For luck?"

He slid his do-rag, the faded blue one with the American flag on the sides, from his head and handed it to her. "This has to be love if I'm giving you my favorite do-rag."

When her gaze shot to the floor, his mind reeled. What'd he say? He ticked the last bit of conversation off in his head —*got it*—and nudged her chin up to kiss her. "It's just an expression. Don't freak out."

Filtering every word would take some getting used to. Either that or they'd spend most of their time with her perpetually scared or pissed off. Fun stuff.

He wrapped an arm around her waist and, when she made no attempt to move, kissed her again, this time slower, deeper, enjoying the feel of her before she left to face whatever waited at that compound. She nipped his bottom lip before backing away.

"I need to go," she said. "Just get it over with."

"Yeah."

"I can handle it. It'll be worth it if we find Nicole."

He sure hoped so because none of them had a clue what she was walking into.

22

Isabelle turned into the driveway and stopped. With her foot firmly on the brake, she double-checked the address Sampson had given her. Thirteen forty-two. That's what the street side mailbox said.

This was it.

A shot of panic seized her, slashing at her insides with the fury of a deadly tornado. She sucked in a breath.

Calm down. You're just saying hello.

Isabelle considered the wide-open iron gate a sure sign from above. She glanced at the intercom. She could push the button and ask to see Seth, but why take a chance on not getting in?

The gates *were* open.

Up the long winding driveway, at the top of a slight hill, sat a huge white Victorian with a wraparound porch that extended to the back of the house.

Good Lord. Sampson could have warned her it was so big. Big and beautiful. Windows framed by mossy green shutters lined the front of the first floor. A turret poked high into the sky, and Isabelle's mind drifted to her favorite child-hood fairy tales.

What a shame. No fairy tales here.

Even the landscaping, pretty flowers in pinks and purples and blues, had been seen to. Leave it to Kendrick to come up with a place so welcoming. The idea of something illegal happening within those walls was criminal in itself.

With an intake of breath, she levered her foot off the brake, coasted through the gate and headed up the drive.

She hadn't called. She and Peter discussed it and came to the conclusion she should just show up and introduce herself. Why not? It would give her an opportunity to at least check out the house rather than calling and risking Seth Donner declining her visit.

When she pulled to a stop in front of the steps, she shut the engine down and took a long look.

The front door opened and a young blonde woman stepped onto the porch. She couldn't have been more than twenty, yet her belly swelled with pregnancy.

"May I help you?" the woman asked, her voice not so welcoming.

Here goes. Act natural.

Whatever natural was when undercover.

"Hello," Isabelle said, sliding out of the car and moving up the brick steps. "I'm Isabelle DeRosa. Kendrick's cousin."

"Oh."

The woman squinted and, combined with rigid shoulders, her body language screamed of mistrusting people. Isabelle knew the feeling.

"I'll get Seth," the woman—girl really—said.

She turned and hurried back into the house. A slow, snaking feeling crawled up Isabelle's arms, but she stood motionless in case they were watching. Finally, needing to move, she stepped toward the porch rail and leaned against it.

After two of the longest minutes of her life, the front door opened again, and a man of about her height with a thick mass of light brown hair came out. His cheeks were round and ruddy and his nose too big for his face. He offered a plastic smile, but the skin around his drab hazel eyes didn't bunch. Nothing genuine there.

He extended his hand. "Isabelle. How wonderful to meet you. I am so sorry about Kendrick. What a tragedy. We're all still in a bit of shock around here."

She shook his hand, and the bit of moisture there turned her stomach. He clasped his other sweaty hand over hers. *Ew.* The snaking feeling left her arms and went right to her midsection.

She smiled anyway and made sure it was big enough to appear natural. No sense in him seeing a fake smile as well. "You must be Seth?"

"I am." He eyed her car's Jersey plates. "Have you been driving all day? From New Jersey?"

"No. I drove out yesterday. I'm on my way to Chicago to visit a friend." The cover story she and Sampson had come up with. "I thought I'd take a detour." She stopped, rubbed her hand over her forehead and prayed she wouldn't vomit all over this nice porch.

She glanced up at Seth and lowered her eyes again. "I wanted to see where he lived. I'm not sure why."

Seth nodded. "I understand."

"I don't think you could. I don't understand it myself."

This wasn't a total lie because standing on Kendrick's porch was the absolute last place she wanted to be.

"Kendrick never said much, but I know your relationship with him was awkward."

Awkward. Is that what they were calling it? Isabelle stifled the urge to slap him.

Seth reached forward and Isabelle steadied herself so she wouldn't flinch when his hand touched her arm. The taste of metal filled her mouth and she swallowed hard.

Then he did it. His nasty little gaze went to her boobs and lingered there a few seconds longer than necessary.

Jackpot.

Normally, at this point, she would have given him a thorough inspection, zeroed in on his crotch and then scoffed.

For a moment, her mind drifted back to when she'd first seen Peter in the elevator. The first man in history to take the insult in stride. She moved her hand over the do-rag on her head.

Don't think about him now.

As much as she wanted to pound Seth into the ground, she kept her eyes glued to his face. Even managed a smile.

The churning in her stomach curled upward and she swallowed the bile back.

Just get inside. That's all you have to do.

Seth eventually stopped gaping at her boobs and looked her in the eye. And—*yow*—what she saw there, that burning heat, forced her to throw her shoulders back. Probably not the best action because it made her chest stand out all the more. He must have taken it as an invitation because he grinned like a pervert at a peep show.

"Why don't you come inside? Have some lemonade?"

Double jackpot. Now *she* smiled. "I'd love to."

Peter checked his watch. "She must be in."

This would be the one and only drive past the house in the banged up eighty-five Camaro he'd paid cash for at a corner car lot near the airport. Of course, having his fake identification back, courtesy of Vic, moved the transaction along.

"Guess so," Billy said from the passenger seat. "Let's find a place to wait."

A quick punch to the gas pedal and they cruised down the two-lane country road. Hundred-year-old trees surrounded them on both sides and seemed to go on forever. Lots of wooded property around here.

Plenty of places to hide a body.

Half a mile down, Peter pulled off the road and parked the car on the grass before shutting down the engine. He might just keep this relic and see if he could rebuild it.

"I'll pop the hood," Billy said.

"Pull the distributor wire while you're at it."

If any nosy cops came by, they could prove the car wouldn't start.

"Done," Billy said as he got back into the car. "You bring any snacks?"

"We just had lunch."

"You know I need snacks."

"Listen, Lucy, we won't be here long. I told Izzy to make it short so she doesn't seem too anxious to stay."

Billy stuck his foot out the open window. "What's with you two?"

"Don't know."

"Liar."

"Dickhead."

They both laughed.

"Have we kissed and made up yet?" Billy wanted to know. "This being pissed at each other is a lot of work."

"I'm not apologizing for kicking the shit out of you. You were dogging me."

Billy shrugged. "I always dog you."

Yeah, well, you never did it after one of our guys died and I was on four days of limited sleep.

"Chalk it up to a bad day." Peter reached under the seat to make sure his nine-millimeter was still safely hidden in case those nosy cops came around.

His gun. Vic had sent it back. Along with the throwaway he'd confiscated from the safe.

Somehow, having the guns back made Peter feel like his old self. Like someone who could be useful in keeping people alive.

"You're not gonna shoot me are you?" Billy laughed at his own joke. "You just got the damn thing back."

So, okay. That was funny. Peter took a second to enjoy the rumbling laugh. He hadn't really laughed much lately. Except with Izzy. She made him laugh. When it happened his world became a better place.

And he wanted to stay there awhile.

Seth Donner held the door open for her.

All Isabelle had to do was step in. To Kendrick's house.

She mentally settled herself. Letting Seth see discomfort would blow the whole thing before she'd even gotten started.

She stepped into the foyer and took in the mahogany woodwork surrounding the tiled entryway. On her left was a large dining room painted a dark blue and, to the right, a library—*Kendrick had a library?*

In front of her, the staircase had been stained the same deep color of the trim.

Seth led her down the hallway. "Right this way."

"What a lovely home," Isabelle commented truthfully.

She followed Seth down the hall, replaying Peter's words.

Don't ask a lot of questions. Let him do the talking. Don't appear too interested. Try not to lie. The lies are hard to remember after a while.

Seth led her to a two-story family room at the back of the house. The hunter green walls were outlined with more mahogany trim and the matching hardwood floors left her wondering if they'd hired a decorator. An oversized stone fireplace sat nestled in the corner. This house had to be big bucks.

Isabelle stopped in the middle of the room. "The house looks new."

Seth turned right and headed to the kitchen. "It's only three years old. Kendrick and I purchased it from the builder."

"Wow. Great yard." She moved to the door and scanned the property.

The children's swing set nearly came to life and pummeled her. Children. Kendrick and children under the same roof. Suddenly the swing set spun and she placed an arm on the door to steady herself.

"Isabelle?" Seth stood next to her holding a glass of lemonade. "Are you all right?"

She shook it off, took the lemonade and, rather than gulp it down, as she wanted to, took a dainty sip.

"I'm fine. I think it's the heat. Maybe coming into the cool air from outside."

Seth motioned her back to the family room. "Let's have a seat."

The young pregnant woman wandered in from a doorway off the kitchen, and Seth shot her a hard, scolding glare.

Interesting.

Isabelle rose from her chair, approached the woman and held her hand out. "Hello, again. I'm Isabelle DeRosa."

"I know," the young woman said. "You told me on the porch."

I'm not giving up until I get a name.

Finally, she shook hands, but made it quick. "I'm Courtney...Masterson."

Gotcha.

Before turning back to Seth, Isabelle drilled the name into her brain for Sampson to check.

Seth, with yet another of his plastic smiles, looked beyond her.

"I just needed some water from the fridge," Courtney said.

Isabelle retrieved her seat, but glanced back at the younger woman. Might as well engage her and see what else she could find out. "It must be hard being pregnant in this heat. When are you due?"

"Uh." Courtney's gaze went to Seth then back to Isabelle. "In about a month. Give or take."

"Well, good luck to you."

Courtney glanced at the floor and appeared unsure how to respond. *Just say thanks, hon.*

Seth cleared his throat. "Thank you, Courtney."

Dismissed.

What was with this guy? Was he the baby's father? Maybe he and Courtney were a couple and he didn't like her talking to people? Talk about emotional abuse.

Seth settled back into his chair. "Isabelle, what brings you here?"

She shrugged. "As I said, I'm not really sure. After Kendrick's funeral I decided to take time off, visit a friend in

Chicago. I thought the drive would be nice." She faked a laugh. "Turns out it's boring as hell."

Seth chuckled, but again, his smile, so small and unyielding, appeared fabricated. Gave her the creeps.

Then his eyes wandered to her boobs again.

"Anyhoo," she said, forcing herself not to adjust her shirt so she wasn't so exposed. "I stopped for a coffee at the rest area by the Cincinnati exit and remembered I had the address in my purse."

"Did Kendrick give it to you?" His tone may have been casual, but his stiff shoulders said something completely different.

"I'm sure Kendrick told you we weren't on good terms."

"He did mention it, which is why I'm surprised to see you. He really did want to reconcile that with you." He rested his head back against the chair. "I still can't believe he's dead. We built this organization together."

Right. She had to remember this guy was grieving his friend. Even if that friend was a sick son of a bitch. Isabelle cleared her throat and wondered just how much Seth knew about her. "It has to be overwhelming for you."

"It's a shock."

"The day he came to my office he said if I changed my mind I should call him. I was curious and did an internet search on your foundation. The address was listed."

Not a total lie. She did research the foundation's name after Sampson had given it to her.

"I see," Seth said.

"I hope that isn't a problem." She scooted to the edge of her seat, leaned over a little so he could see down her shirt. Men could be easily distracted. Once she had his attention she bolted upright. "Oh, wow. I'm sorry. This is your home and I just barged in." She stood. "I'll go. You don't even know me."

He jumped from his seat. "No, no. It's all right. I do remember Kendrick saying he had invited you to visit. It makes sense now. Please. Don't go."

She glanced down at the chair she'd just vaulted out of. *Don't seem too anxious.* "Well, maybe just for a few more minutes. Then I should go."

"How long will you be staying in the area?"

"I'll probably head to Chicago tomorrow morning. It is quite beautiful here though. I may take a day and do the farm tours in the area. Maybe do some picking. I don't know."

"The farms around here are wonderful. We take the children every now and again."

"Children?" Isabelle asked trying hard not to throw up.

He thunked himself on the head. "That's right. Kendrick mentioned he never got around to telling you what we do here."

"No. We never got that far, but the articles I found said you helped the poor."

"Yes." He bobbed his head and his cheeks jiggled from the force. "If you have time, I'd be happy to tell you about it."

Oh, I have plenty of time. You rat bastard. "I think I have a few minutes."

"HOW THE HELL LONG HAS SHE BEEN IN THERE?" PETER KNEW it had been over an hour. Specifically, seventy-eight minutes.

He was going apeshit. Sweating like a damned sprinter and he wasn't sure if it was the heat or aggravation.

They were still parked half a mile down the road with

the hood up. A few cars had passed, but nobody offered to help. And what was up with that? Not that he wanted help, but didn't people have common courtesy anymore?

With the condition of this car, it wouldn't be a shock they'd broken down. The body of what was once a hell of a nice ride looked like it had been blasted with BB gun pellets. Dents and paint chips ran amok. The wheel wells were also rusted out and nearly cried from abuse.

And the front hood was white, which wouldn't be bad if the rest of the car didn't happen to be gray.

But hey, the car ran damn well.

He glanced at his watch again. All that thinking ate up another ninety seconds.

"You have got to chill, man," Billy said, still sitting with his foot hanging out the open passenger side window. "She'll come out when she comes out."

"It's so friggin' hot," Peter said, opening the door and stepping out. The temperature hovered around ninety-five even without the sun, and the humidity left him drenched.

He leaned against the driver's side door, folded his arms. Kicked some pebbles. Checked his phone.

Nothing.

"She'll call when she calls," Billy said.

"Yeah, thanks, Confucius."

"Huh?"

Peter shook his head. "Never mind." He bent down and looked at Billy through the open window. "Didn't I tell her to only stay an hour?"

"Gee, Dad, I don't know. You threw me out because I was staring into Hooterville."

Peter flipped him the bird. Asshole. His own fault for letting Billy see his weakness regarding Izzy. After three years of Billy's smart-ass comments, he should have known better.

Take a walk. Get away from him.

Wandering down the road, he made mental notes about car parts needed to rebuild the piece of shit Camaro. Anything to keep his mind off Izzy, dressed like a stripper, amping up the sex with Seth Donner. His head began to pound, the throb settling behind his eyes.

Tormented. That's what he was.

And it was only day one.

He moved back toward the car, squatting down to examine the rear bumper.

"Hillary Hooters coming our way," Billy shouted from the front seat.

Peter peeked around the bumper and spotted the white Audi cruising toward them.

Thank you.

He stood when she drove by and gave him an inconspicuous finger wave. Making himself useful, Billy fixed the engine, lowered the hood, and they both jumped back in the car.

"Hillary Hooters?" Peter asked while hooking a U-turn. "What's that about?"

Billy grinned. "Izzy's alter ego."

Peter laughed. He couldn't help it. The irony of Billy unknowingly giving Izzy *another* alter ego was too mortifying. Now he'd have to deal with all three of them. Hillary Hooters, Creepy Izzy *and* Fun Izzy.

He'd never survive.

23

PETER TOSSED HIS KEYS ON THE CRAPPY MOTEL DRESSER, WENT straight for the locked door separating the two rooms and tapped on it.

One minute later the door opened and Izzy stood in front of him wearing long cotton shorts and a crew neck T-shirt.

Praise God.

He wouldn't be able to stand looking at her in the stripper getup.

"Well, hell," Billy said from behind him. "Why'd you change? You are just no fun, Izzy."

Peter spun on him. "You wanna get bounced again?"

Billy responded with a toothy pain-in-the-ass grin.

"Children," Izzy said, "I've had a rough day and I'm not in the mood."

Pushing past her into the room, Peter said, "What happened? You were in there way too long."

She made a low growling sound. "Don't hassle me."

"Yeah," Billy said.

Maybe Peter should have tempered his statement.

Women didn't understand man-speak for "I was worried about you."

The hideous yellow-and-brown striped side chair beside the bed suddenly looked inviting and he dropped into it. This could get ugly. Butt ugly.

He bit down hard on his bottom lip, felt that nice little zing of pain and let out a huff. Billy had formed some twisted alliance with Izzy and now he'd have to battle both of them.

"Have a seat, Billy," she said, waving him to the other disgusting chair.

Izzy boosted herself on top of the long dresser rather than sitting on the bed.

"Here's the deal," she said. "He invited me back tomorrow. I told him I wasn't sure, that I wanted to sightsee. He gave me his cell number and told me to call him when I was done."

"Why did he invite you back?" Peter asked.

"Mainly because he couldn't stop staring at my boobs."

Ouch. Peter closed his eyes. Did he need to hear that? "I guess the T-shirt worked."

"He had to have been blind for it to fail," Billy offered.

Izzy fired Billy a warning glance before Peter could blast him.

"I pretended to be interested in their cause," she said. "He explained they help people on welfare. They have ten cabins on the property and they let people live there while they get back on their feet. Sort of a halfway house. The tenants are screened and, once accepted, they're required to do fundraising for the organization and pay a small rental fee. He didn't give me specifics, but said they try to secure employment for the residents. The goal is for them to be self-supporting as

quickly as possible so they aren't at the compound long.
"

"How many people live in the main house?" Peter asked.

She shook her head. "No idea. I met a woman. Her name is Courtney Masterson and she can't be more than twenty. She's eight months pregnant and all indications are that she lives in the house. There's a swing set out back and Seth confirmed there are children living there."

The idea of children living with Kendrick must have been killing her. Peter could see it in the pasty color of her face. "Give Sampson her name. He'll run it."

Izzy nodded. "My guess is Courtney went there when she became pregnant. She seems healthy enough. I'm assuming she has medical care, but she left quickly. It seemed like she was afraid to say anything. She kept looking at Seth to gauge his reaction."

"Maybe he's the father?" Billy asked.

"Could be," Izzy said. "But nothing about the way they acted indicated they were a couple. It was very strange."

"Where are the cabins on the property?" Peter asked.

"Just beyond the house. I could see the roof of one of them from the back door, but the property is wooded and the trees block the view. There's a narrow dirt road. The other cabins must be along the path."

Billy stuck his bottom lip out. "You thinkin' you want to do a sneak and peek?"

Bet your ass.

"I'd like to know what's on the back end of that property. Sampson needs to get us some land surveys so we can check it out."

Izzy scoffed. "Good luck. He doesn't want you within ten miles of that place."

"He'll change his mind as soon as we give him something he couldn't get by playing fair. When you talk to him, ask him about the surveys."

"I have to check in with him today. Besides, I really want to know how Courtney got there. She must not have a family."

Peter shrugged. "You never know about women from these small towns. With no real employment opportunities, she might have conveniently wound up pregnant hoping to land the baby's father as a husband. The guy probably bailed on her."

Izzy's eyebrows nearly hit the ceiling. "Well, that's an interesting theory. Did you even hesitate to consider she might be lonely? She could be searching for companionship and *accidentally* wound up pregnant. Why does she have to be a hustler?"

Holy crap. Somehow he was back in the Izzy minefield again. She was working at staying neutral, but those green eyes were snappy. "I'm not saying she's a hustler. You have to admit, it's a possibility."

"That's true," Izzy conceded. "But you shouldn't make presumptions about her motives."

"Yeah, well," Billy said. "You two can fight about this all you want. It bores the hell out of me. I might as well go for a run. I'll need some form of entertainment while we're in this rathole."

When Billy left, Peter wandered to where Izzy sat on the dresser. "What did I say that pissed you off?"

She stared down at her fingers wrapped around the edge of the dresser, tight enough for the skin to stretch. Yep. Izzy had something working her over.

She finally looked at him, squirmed, and dropped her head back. "When I was in high school I slept with just about any male who came within twenty feet of me, and it had nothing to do with trying to snag a husband."

"That's different."

"No. It isn't. Maybe this girl is searching for the one person that will make her feel *something* during sex. That's all I wanted. Someone to make me feel like it was more than a fuck. I wanted someone to love me for more than the sex act. I finally gave up when it didn't happen."

Minefield. By now he should be getting better at detecting it.

He sat next to her, stretched his legs in front of him and slid a hand down her back. "I'm sorry I made assumptions."

She pressed the heels of her hands into her eyes and laughed, but nothing seemed funny.

"You just don't get it, Peter."

SHE MOVED OFF THE DRESSER. "I'M TAKING A SHOWER."

The invisible film of lustful grime from Seth ogling her all afternoon had sunk into her bones and left her feeling a gear behind.

Plus, she couldn't stand the way *Peter* was now watching her. Men. They always stared at her for one reason or another.

Time alone with no one analyzing her. That's the way her world worked best and maybe, for once, Peter would leave her be. She hurried to the bathroom, and shut and locked the door. If the bathroom had a window she'd probably climb out.

What had she just done? He probably thought her a whore and Peter had standards in that area. He wouldn't touch her after *that* little admission.

Maybe that's what she wanted.

She breathed deep craving the sensation of air filling her lungs.

Taking off her clothes, she tossed them on the cracked tile floor. The bathroom, with its brown vanity and drab green sink, was an extension of the rest of the motel and she hated every bit of it. Or maybe it was simply being there she hated.

After turning the shower on full blast, she stuck her hand into the stream and waited for the hot water.

The door flew open and crashed against the wall with a bang that rocked her. She clutched the shower curtain for balance and turned as Peter stepped into the bathroom.

"What the hell, Peter? You scared me!"

He slammed what looked like a metal pick on the sink and got within an inch of her. His blue eyes locked on hers and the steel there could have broken cement. Hard, hard eyes.

"I'm naked here," she shrieked.

But the sickening vulnerability had nothing to do with being naked.

"You don't say something like that and walk away," he yelled. "If you're pissed, you need to tell me why. I'm not a goddamned mind reader."

Isabelle shoved the curtain back and twisted the shower knob. The faucet wasn't providing the only steam in the tiny bathroom. She turned, gave Peter a shove and reached for the towel hanging on the rack.

"And *I* deserve some privacy." She wrapped herself in the stingy towel.

Peter, to his credit, kept his eyes focused on her face. *He must really be mad.* Most men would have at least snuck a peek by now. Or maybe he was trying not to piss her off any further. That theory made much more sense.

She angled around him, stormed out of the bathroom and shut the adjoining room door. All they needed was Billy wandering in with her wrapped in a swatch of cotton barely bigger than a hand towel.

Peter followed her. "What's this about?"

Damn him.

They needed a distraction. She spun to face him and the towel came loose. She should reach to tighten it, but maybe…if she just let it sink to the ground…his mind would move elsewhere.

Sex she could handle.

Even if she didn't want their first time together to be manufactured because she was too terrified to admit she was losing herself. Was she that pathetic? Obviously so.

"Don't even," he said, somehow knowing exactly where her mind had gone. "You're not getting out of talking to me. I've been stepping in all kinds of shit this past week and I'm pissed." He huffed out a breath, and bit down hard enough that the muscle in his jaw flexed. "I know you're intentionally doing this. I can see it in your eyes. Creepy Izzy is barking at you and I'm trying to stay cool, but dealing with you on an emotional level can be a nightmare."

Oh, my God. Give up already. How could he still be standing here after all she'd subjected him to? Crazy. That's what he was.

She scoffed. "That's not it."

He stuck his hands on his hips and puckered. The silence hung between them, daring her to say something, but she'd wait it out. Part of good lawyering meant knowing when to keep quiet.

Peter slowly shook his head. "You're trying to frustrate the crap out of me so I'll give up on you. Classic move, Izzy, but you're *busted*."

Her breath caught, backed up into her throat and she gasped. No air. No air. *Breathe.* But she couldn't. Not with her nerves chewed raw. He wouldn't go away. Wouldn't leave her to this agony of being stuck between two worlds.

"Shut up," she said.

"Talk to me."

"Shut. *Up.*"

The pressure behind her eyes intensified and she jammed the heels of her palms into them. The pounding wouldn't stop, so she dropped her hands and looked him square in the eye.

Back him off.

"I hate you," she said.

He didn't flinch.

"No you don't. You're scared. Big difference."

Hot tears began to pour from her eyes and she swiped at them, ran her wet hand down the towel. *Dammit. Dammit. Dammit.* How could she have let this happen?

"I just handed it over to you," she blurted.

He stared back at her. Clueless.

"What?"

"I told you about being promiscuous. I shared that with you."

"So what?"

"See! You don't get it."

Peter dug both hands into his hair and pulled. "Holy, holy shit. I don't have a clue what you're talking about."

Isabelle began to pace, keeping one hand on the knot in the towel. "Telling you not to make assumptions had nothing to do with Courtney. It had to do with me giving a piece of myself to you and wanting you not to judge me. You totally missed it. I've never done that before and you *missed* it!"

A sob punched free, and she covered her mouth as if that would make it stop. *Just great.* The emotional torture clearly wasn't enough because now she got to be humiliated too.

Peter finally moved. In three strides he reached her, but she retreated and the back of her calves bumped the ugly side chair.

Trapped.

Back him off.

She swatted at him when he extended his arms.

"Stop," he said. "Please."

But the panic still roared at her, screaming that she should run.

Shut him down.

Fast.

All this stress and hurt couldn't be good.

He stepped an inch closer, blocking her from moving. She wouldn't look up, but let him put his arms around her, her breath hitching from the tears.

"It's all right," he said, squeezing her tight. "I'm sorry I missed it. I understand now. I do."

The heat of his skin flowed into her and she inhaled to quiet the madness in her mind. "I told you I'm not good at this. I don't know how to do relationships. It's too hard."

"That's crap," he said, holding her in place when she tried to back away. "You're driving me crazy. Seriously nuts."

She tilted her head a little. "I tend to do that. I haven't met a man yet that knows how to deal with me."

"One that can stick you mean?"

She shrugged. "Seems as good an explanation as any."

"I think you don't want anyone close to you. In any way. You know people, but how many of them are friends? Probably not a lot. If they're around too much, they might start to ask questions about your personal life. You can't have that."

"Peter—"

He jabbed his hand out. "Not done yet. You've been pushing me away since the day I met you in that elevator." He held up a finger. "You did it with that staring at my package trick—and that's another conversation, because I'm amazed some egomaniac hasn't decided to prove what he's got after you've dissed his dick. But I digress."

He held up a second finger. "You push me away every time you flip the Creepy Izzy switch because you know I'm sensitive to it."

"But, Peter—"

"Hold up. Being scared is one thing. I can handle that, but be honest when something's working you over."

She rested her forehead against his chest, and let her hands wander under his shirt, around his waist to the solid comfort there.

"I'm worried you think I'm a whore. The sleeping around was a way to deal with my emotional problems."

He pushed her back and held her there. "I would *never* think that. I can't even say the word to you. You were betrayed by people who meant the most to you and you still grew up to be an amazing woman. You did that on your own. However you got there, you got there."

His blue eyes, so focused, nearly blistered her. She lowered her head to his shoulder and tried to concentrate on slow breaths. Crying again. With relief maybe? She didn't know, but he needed to see. Needed to know what his acceptance meant to her.

She smiled through soppy tears.

"Are we okay?" he asked.

She nodded. "I'm sorry."

"Nothing to be sorry for. We'll figure it out. One step at a time."

His cell phone started ringing. The real one. Not the disposable he'd bought earlier in the day. Peter threw the adjoining door open and hustled to the phone on the bedside table. Private caller.

"Jessup," he said.

"This is Special Agent Wade Sampson. There's a convenience store on the south side of town. Meet me there in ten minutes."

Click.

Peter laughed. This should be good. Simply for the pain-in-the-ass factor, he'd make it fifteen minutes.

He stuck his head into the room and found Izzy still standing there hanging on to her towel. "You can take your shower now. I'll leave you alone." He grinned and wiggled his eyebrows. "Unless you need me to scrub your back."

That got him a half smile at least.

"Rain check?" she asked.

"You bet. That was your buddy Sampson. He wants to see me."

"Uh-oh,"

"Nah," Peter said. "He probably wants to throw his federal weight around. I've been waiting for his call."

"Well, don't make him mad."

He laughed and walked out the door.

Thirteen minutes later, the convenience store lights called like a beacon on the deserted country road where only darkness surrounded him. The lack of moonlight sent a familiar buzz through his system. Dark nights like this were perfect for an op, and the longing for his normal life hit him square in the chest.

He pushed the Camaro to eighty-five.

Getting Izzy home safe had to be the priority. Then he'd tell Vic he wanted an assignment. And no wouldn't be an option.

Peter pulled into the store's parking lot. The sign said Open Twenty-Four Hours, but considering how quiet this town was, the place couldn't make any decent money at night.

Sampson, wearing a suit sans the jacket, leaned against a black Chevy at the far end of the low-lit parking lot and stood taller when Peter drove toward him.

He parked the Camaro, got out and strolled over.

"You're late," Sampson said, taking in Peter's do-rag and combat boots.

"You didn't give me much notice. What can I do for you?"

"Mr. Jessup," Sampson said. "Or should I call you Monk?"

"Peter works for me. I'm surprised it took you this long to contact me. You federal boys are way too predictable."

The sarcastic laugh from Sampson proved Peter hit his target. At least until Sampson got in his space. Of course the fucker had an inch on him and that always sucked. Not that Peter would give Mr. Slick any room to intimidate him.

"Stay out of my case," Sampson said.

Interesting body language here. His voice was harsh, yet he stood with his hands in his pockets.

Peter crossed his arms. "Or?"

Sampson shrugged. "Or I lock your ass in jail."

"I'm offended, *Special* Agent Sampson. I'd think the FBI would welcome a person with my skills to their investigation. I can bend the rules where you boys have to play by them."

"Stay out of it."

"No."

"Are you out of your friggin' mind?"

Peter grinned. "My boss thinks so. Makes it all the more fun."

Sampson gave him a confused, narrow-eyed look. "Don't make me lock you up. You're a war hero, but I'll wreck your life if I have to."

Peter stepped closer. Got right up in his grill. "You think I care about my life when you're sending Izzy into a situation where you don't know what the fuck is going on? You know as well as I do the congresswoman's daughter is probably dead, her murderer probably in that compound—Kendrick's too—and you think I care what happens to me? I think you're the one out of your mind."

"We'll protect Isabelle."

"There's nothing you can do for her once she gets inside. She's on her own."

Sampson broke eye contact and stepped back.

Cornered.

"*Don't* fuck up my case."

Hmm. Time to play. To rattle Sampson's cage some.

Peter laughed, waved a finger. "I think you'd enjoy locking my ass up. If I'm in jail you can steal my girl."

Sampson's rock-hard expression didn't say much. He was definitely pissed, but was he pissed that Peter caught his attraction to Izzy or that he refused to stay out of the case? Both maybe?

"I wouldn't do that," the lying sack of shit said.

"Yeah, you would."

"No. I'd lock you up, close my case and *then* steal your girl."

The answer, sudden and without warning, hit Peter like a drive-by shooting. He'd expected Sampson to deny the accusation. Props for a good comeback. And son of a gun if Peter didn't kind of like the guy. At least he was honest about his intentions.

"That sucks," Peter said. "Here I am wanting a reason to kick your ass and you go and say something that makes me think you're a stand-up guy. I hate that."

Sampson pointed at him, but he half grinned. "Stay out of my case."

"I got it. You don't have to keep saying it."

"But you're not going to are you?"

Peter shook his head. "Nope."

With that, Sampson turned and headed for his car.

"Sampson?"

He stopped, turned back.

"I won't stay out of it," Peter said, "but I won't screw it up either. I want this case closed as much as you do. The sooner it's done, the sooner Izzy gets home safe."

"At least we understand each other."

Oh, we understand each other.

And you can't have my girl.

Fucker.

24

PETER WHITTLED AWAY THE TIME IN THE CRAPPY MOTEL ROOM playing chess with Billy. They'd found the game at the five-and-dime on Main Street. He hadn't realized five-and-dimes still existed.

He checked the digital clock on the end table. One o'clock and Izzy was still locked behind her motel room door. She'd spent the morning at some you-pick farm because she wanted to give Seth Donner a real story. The strawberries she brought back were damn good—a nice side benefit—but she'd been back almost an hour and Peter had no idea what she was doing in there.

Sending her alone on her strawberries run had not been in his plan but she'd insisted, and he couldn't disagree with her logic that they couldn't keep coming and going at roughly the same times or people would notice. Most of the rooms were empty and the nosy desk clerk constantly sat by the window.

"So," Izzy said, pushing open the adjoining motel room door. "I just called Seth and he said I should come out to the compound."

Peter glanced up from the chessboard and saw exactly what she'd been doing. The stripper look again. Heavy black eyeliner, low-cut shirt and yet another pair of microscopic shorts. The only part he liked was his do-rag sitting on top of her silky dark hair.

He'd get no sleep again tonight thinking about her dressed like that in front of Seth Donner.

"Did you call him on your cell?" Peter asked.

"No. I used the room phone."

"Good." Peter rose from his chair and moved to the dresser where he retrieved a cell phone from the top drawer. "Leave me your phone and take this one."

She stared down at the new phone. "Why?"

"If they search your stuff," Billy said while contemplating his next chess move, "you don't want them to have all your contacts."

Her face blanched. Leave it to Billy to freak her out.

Peter rolled his eyes. "It's not a big deal. We use these prepaid phones all the time. Billy and I each have one. I've programmed those numbers into this phone. I'm number one and Billy is number two. I didn't put our names in. Try not to call our regular cell phones."

She nodded. "Got it. Um... Can I talk to you a minute?" She gestured to the other room. "In private?"

He held a hand toward her room and trailed her there. "You okay?" he asked after she closed the door behind him.

"I'm fine. I just...well...I know you're not happy about my clothes and I don't want you to be upset."

He smiled and brought her in for a hug. Clearly he'd done a piss-poor job of hiding his disgust over her getup. "I'm not upset. Not really. It's weird seeing you dressed this way, but if I didn't feel about you the way I do, it wouldn't faze me."

She squeezed him tight and all that soft, exposed flesh pressed against him.

Hellooo, baby.

"It makes me sick," she said. "The way he looks at me. It's not like you. You look at me and I know you have sex on your mind, but I also know you care about *me* and not just the miracle boobs."

Peter smiled. "The boobs are a bonus."

That got him a snort.

He pulled back, cradled her cheeks in his hands and kissed her quick. The kiss may have been simple, but the buzz simmering under his skin was anything but. "I don't know how he looks at you, but I'm glad you see the difference."

"I'm not sure when I'll be back, so don't worry."

"If you can, send a text or something so I know you're okay. With these prepaid phones they won't know who you're texting."

She jerked her head. "Okay. If I'm going to be back after, say eight o'clock, I'll text you."

"Do you want me to call Sampson and tell him you're there?"

"No. I called him from a pay phone on the way back from the farm."

"Be careful, Iz. Remember, don't seem too curious."

She smiled up at him, wrapped her hand around the back of his neck and dragged him down for a lip-lock. He couldn't help it if his tongue slid into her mouth. She'd started it. Monk Junior began singing a wake-up tune and Peter broke away from the kiss. The last thing he needed was a hard-on when she was leaving.

"Yeah, you should go now. I have this whole stripper-Izzy-giving-me-a-lap-dance fantasy going on."

She laughed. "You're a pig."

"You started it, sweetheart."

But that lap dance thing wasn't a bad idea. He'd add it to his list.

She picked up her purse and turned for the door. "Bye, Peter."

"Bye, Iz."

The door closed with a loud click that seemed to rattle around in his head. Did he just let her leave to send another man into a sexual stupor?

A sexual stupor that could get her hurt? Maybe killed.

What the hell was wrong with him letting her do this alone? They knew next to nothing about these people *and* a young girl was missing after having been seen at the compound. She was probably dead. Call him a fatalist, but the odds weren't good they'd find this girl. There would be no way he'd let that happen to Izzy. Not after losing Tiny and Roy. No way.

He strode into the adjoining room, grabbed his gun and keys from the top drawer of the dresser. "Let's go."

"Where?" Billy asked.

"We're gonna have a look around the back end of that property and find a way into the compound."

"Isabelle, how nice to see you again," Seth said, smiling that plastic smile as he opened the screen door.

The porch overhang offered shade from the afternoon sun and the slight breeze against her bare skin calmed her jitters.

Smile.

Stepping into the house, she grinned at him. "Thank you for inviting me. I hope it's not interfering with your day."

He wore tan slacks and a weathered red golf shirt. Was this his normal work attire? Or was this casual for him? Either way, he dressed too much like Kendrick for her comfort. His hand came to rest on her lower back as he guided her into the house. A warning flare shot from her brain, and her shoulders stiffened.

She had to learn to control that.

Seth snatched his hand back. "I'm sorry."

Don't lose him.

The last thing she wanted was his hands on her, but her clothing and mannerisms probably said something completely different. And wasn't that the whole point? Considering the FBI thought they were running a sex slavery ring out of this place.

Get it together.

She closed her eyes and let Creepy Izzy take the wheel. When she opened her eyes again, she stepped an inch closer than her own boundaries would normally allow.

"Please don't apologize." She squeezed Seth's forearm. "I've been out of sorts lately."

His gaze landed on her boobs again and she forced herself to smile as the acid in her gut churned. Damn Peter for making her feel things that would never have bothered her before.

"I'm sure," Seth said. "Come in. I believe I promised you a tour of the property. The golf cart is out back."

"I would love to meet the residents. I do some pro-bono work for a shelter at home. Maybe I can help in some way."

He slid her a sideways glance and an oily half grin glossed his face. "Maybe you can."

They wandered through the kitchen, complete with maple cabinets and granite counter tops that she failed to notice the day before. *Wow*. Granite? For a place that was reportedly about serving the underprivileged?

A woman and three young girls sat eating sandwiches at the oversized L-shaped breakfast bar.

"Hello," Isabelle said, smiling at the woman first and the girls next.

The woman's dark gaze tore into her for a second before they did a quick survey. The downward turn of her lips indicated displeasure. No surprise there. Women tended not to like Isabelle's looks. Especially women dressed in stained, threadbare T-shirts and baggy cotton shorts that had seen the inside of a washer too many times.

The tension from this woman felt different. Her face read like a roadmap of a hard life. Craggy lines around her lips and eyes left her haggard when she probably hadn't reached forty.

"Mary Beth, this is Isabelle DeRosa. She's Kendrick's cousin," Seth said with raised eyebrows and a tilt of his head.

It appeared Mary Beth had just been given warning number one. This guy had some serious control issues.

"These are my daughters," she said.

The oldest, a pretty blonde teenager, rose from the chair and shook Isabelle's hand. "Nice to meet you. I'm Rebecca."

"Very nice, Rebecca," Seth said. He turned to Isabelle. "We've been working on manners."

Isabelle wasn't sure what was more shocking, Seth creating a Stepford community or Rebecca's protruding belly. Whatever was in the water around here must be making all the women pregnant.

Seth introduced her to the other girls before they went on their way, stopping briefly to speak with Courtney, who had found a shady spot on the patio to read a magazine.

"It's awfully warm out," Isabelle said. "Aren't you roasting?"

Courtney glanced at Seth first and then at Isabelle. Her mouth split into a defiant grin. "I'm fine. I've only been out here a few minutes."

A four-person golf cart was parked twenty feet away. "Seth is going to show me the property. Would you like to join us?"

Courtney's blue eyes stayed fixed for a second. Measuring.

"I wouldn't mind," she said.

"I don't mind either." Isabelle unleashed what Peter called her man-killer eyes on Seth. "You don't mind, do you?"

"Of course not," he said, but nothing in his crabby tone revealed happiness.

Isabelle had just scored a major victory with Courtney and she'd need to step lightly. Something niggled at her—a warning perhaps—that Courtney didn't miss a trick.

Getting her to reveal those tricks would be the challenge.

"Thank you for dinner," Isabelle said. "You've all been very kind."

She glanced around the kitchen as she stacked plates next to the sink. This group had a definite routine. Mary Beth washed, Rebecca put away, the girls cleared the table and Courtney wiped down all the counters.

Seth, of course, parked his lazy ass on the couch in front of the television in the adjoining family room.

"You're welcome." Mary Beth didn't bother to glance up.

Okay. Now this was starting to make Isabelle's skin itch.

She'd been cordial to Mary Beth and had gotten nothing but scorn in return.

As she turned to leave the kitchen she walked right into Courtney and her big belly.

"Oh," Isabelle said, reaching for Courtney's arms. "Are you all right? I'm so sorry."

Courtney drew her eyebrows together. "I'm fine. Sheesh. I'm pregnant, not an invalid. I'll never understand why people think being knocked up means I should be treated like glass."

A laugh bubbled in Isabelle's throat. In another place and time, she'd probably like Courtney.

She held up her hands. "You're right. I'm sorry."

"Great. Now, I've got this dripping rag in my hand, so if you don't mind, could you get out of my way?"

"Watch that mouth," Seth said from his throne in the family room.

Isabelle stepped sideways. "She's right, Seth. I was in her way."

"She doesn't need to be rude about it."

Isabelle wandered into the family room and perched on the chair across from his. "I should go. I'd like to be back before dark. These country roads are confusing enough. I had a wonderful day though. You've put together a lovely home here."

Oddly enough, she wasn't lying. Any person would be thrilled to live in such a home. Even the one-bedroom cabins, although small and minimally decorated, appeared quite comfortable.

Too bad something sick was probably going on.

"So, this is goodbye then? Are you leaving tomorrow?" Seth asked.

Where was this going? Had she said something that

indicated she'd be leaving tomorrow? She'd better go with it. See where it landed.

"I'm not sure. My friend in Chicago is expecting me. There's something about this area though, maybe all the open land, that's peaceful." She shrugged. "I have three weeks off and the motel is starting to get on my nerves. It's desolate and way too quiet."

But Peter's there and he gives me sanctuary.

What was that all about?

"You should stay here," Seth said. "One of our residents moved out a couple of weeks ago and we have an empty bedroom."

Success. *No turning back now.*

"And, of course, there's Kendrick's room," he continued. "But I don't feel that would be appropriate. All of his things are still in there. I'm waiting for his father to tell me what he wants done with them."

The idea of even stepping foot into Kendrick's bedroom nearly made her cough up dinner. "I don't want to impose."

Seth waved her away. "You can stay as long as you'd like. And maybe I can convince you to do some pro-bono work for us." He winked at her for effect.

Great. A winker. It worked for some men. On Seth it was smarmy.

She steeled herself and smiled the you're-a-gift-to-women smile. "I'm not licensed here, but I could advise you."

The triumphant grin on his face almost drove her to hysteria. The idiot didn't even know she'd played him.

"It's settled then," he said. "We'll have the room ready for you in the morning. Just come whenever you're ready. You could even stay tonight if you wanted."

Tonight? She wasn't ready for that. She wanted to see Peter. Talk to him about this.

"That's not necessary. I don't have any clean clothes. I'll come back tomorrow."

"All right then." Seth rose from the chair. "I'll walk you to your car."

After getting what she needed, she suddenly couldn't leave fast enough. She spun around and spotted Mary Beth at the sink boring visual holes into her. *Why does this woman hate me?*

"Goodnight, everyone," Isabelle said and made her way to the front door.

With Seth on her tail, she stepped into the steamy evening air and the humidity wrapped around her. She missed the ocean and the cool evening breezes that billowed through her back doors.

"Isabelle, I hope you don't mind, but could I ask a favor?" Seth said.

"Of course."

"Kendrick had mentioned he ran into you and Peter Jessup in your office."

Oh, no. Had Seth somehow seen Peter with her at the motel. "Yes?"

"I'm not sure if you know this, but his mother runs an organization that gives grants to worthy charities. She's quite a fundraiser from what I hear. She has all the right corporate contacts with Jessup Industries."

Isabelle swallowed. Peter's *mother?* "And?"

"I've been thinking we should apply for a grant from her foundation and wondered if you might be able to put in a good word for us?"

25

THE OUTSIDE DOOR TO IZZY'S ROOM SLAMMED CLOSED, AND Peter threw the television remote on the end table, rolled off his bed and got to his feet.

"Peter?"

He pulled open the adjoining door without bothering to put on a shirt. "I'm here."

She marched over to him and wrapped herself around him in a bone-crushing hug. *Ho-kay.* Not a bad greeting at all. The clean smell of her shampoo lingered on her hair despite the do-rag.

"You okay?" he asked.

"I need to talk to you. Where's Billy?"

"He went in search of nose strips. His snoring is killing me."

Izzy laughed and her breath tickled his neck in a way he hadn't felt since his wife left him, but over the past couple of weeks had come to enjoy. "You two really are an old married couple."

"There's a thought." He set her back to arm's length,

checked out the sagging luggage under her eyes. "You're tired."

She nodded. "This mental bedlam over whether I'm saying or doing the right thing is exhausting."

He pulled her in again, kissed the top of her head and wished he could be the one in that compound. "Unfortunately, you get used to it. Did it go okay?"

"Yep. Two big things."

"Two? Sampson will be delirious."

She snuggled into his neck again and Monk Junior started to stir.

"I'm moving out of this dump and into the compound."

Talk about an instant soft-on. Peter stepped back with an odd mixture of excitement and dread. "He invited you?"

"Yes. And I think I made some headway with Courtney. She's the pregnant girl. The *first* one I met. Lots of pregnant people in that place."

"You're not going back there tonight are you?" Because there was no way he wanted her leaving so soon.

"Heck no. I can't take any more tonight. There's a weird tension there and I don't know what it is."

"You've got time, don't be too aggressive. They'll get suspicious."

"I know." She turned, dropped onto the bed, and stretched that amazing, toned body.

Yow.

Peter coughed once. "What was the other big thing?"

Besides, of course, that he wanted to have hot monkey sex with her for the next fifty years.

He cracked his neck side to side. Could he honestly be thinking long-term with her? The woman whose emotional capacity ranked in the negative numbers?

"It involves you," Izzy said.

How appropriate. The burst of laughter came right from his toes. He couldn't help it.

She lifted her head. "What's so funny?"

"Nothing. My mind was wandering."

"Well, pay attention."

That was the problem. He paid *too* much attention. And it was slowly killing him. He moved to the bed, laid on his side and propped himself on one elbow.

"What involves me?" He dragged the do-rag off her head and played with her hair.

She inched closer. Snuggled against him and he could see this going all sorts of good places.

"Your mother actually," Izzy said.

He laughed again. "You certainly have a gift for killing the mood, Iz."

She slipped her leg over his. *And then getting the mood back.*

"Sorry. Didn't mean to bring your mother into it, but Seth apparently wants to apply for a grant from her foundation. He wants me to clear the way. I had no choice but to tell him I'd ask."

Peter rolled to his back, away from Izzy. He needed his brain for this. Being horny as hell never amounted to anything good in the thinking straight department, and he definitely wasn't comfortable with Seth Donner anywhere near his mother.

Obviously deep in thought, Izzy ran her hand down his bare chest, and he stilled it because—holy hell—every skin cell caught fire.

He shook his head and focused on the foundation issue. His mother always toured all potential properties.

Maybe this could work.

Peter, still holding Izzy's hand, rolled to his side. "Tell

him you'll do it, but the application requires an on-site visit."

Her head lolled forward. "You're sending your mother in there?"

"No. My *mother* is sending *me* in there. I just won't tell her about it."

Izzy sat up. "How will you keep it from her? Won't she get the application?"

"Not if you get it from Seth and give it to me. He'll never know the difference. Tell him to fill it out, email it to you and you'll send it to me. My mother will never know."

"Not a good idea. Too dangerous."

Too dangerous? *Please.* He held off rolling his eyes.

"This is a good idea, Iz."

She waggled her head. "But I'm nowhere close to figuring out if they're doing anything illegal. What happens if I fail and leave the compound? Seth will think the application is still pending."

Peter sat up and brushed the back of his hand against her cheek. "If the place is legitimate, I'll forward the application to my mother and tell her to approve it. Seth will get his money and we're out of there."

"I don't like it."

"I do. It'll get me inside the compound. Billy and I went out there this afternoon and found access from the rear of the property, but it's so big we couldn't get close to the house. I need those land surveys. I could probably get them by going to the town hall, but I don't want to call any attention to myself."

"I'll ask Sampson. We've been playing phone tag."

"Don't push it. It'll piss him off."

"I'm not a dope."

"I know that. Didn't mean it that way. If you can get me

inside the house with this grant idea, I can poke around while you keep Seth occupied. I'll stay a couple of days and, maybe by then, we'll have something Sampson can work with."

"Sampson will freak if he knows you were there."

Peter shrugged. "Don't tell him."

"What were you searching for at the compound?"

He huffed out a breath. "I could be wrong, but I don't think Nicole is alive. Everything I pulled up on the internet indicates she's a responsible girl. Something happened to her or she'd be in contact with family or friends."

Isabelle pressed her lips together. "And what? You think the body is on the property somewhere? Kendrick was a disgusting pig, but he wasn't a murderer."

"Maybe Kendrick didn't kill her. Aren't there a bunch of people living there?"

She thought about that a minute. "At least six people live in the main house. I've met them over the last two days. There might be more that I don't know about."

"What about the cabins?" Peter asked.

"Today I met ten—" she stopped, counted on her fingers. "No. Eleven people from the cabins. There are more because those eleven were only from two families. That leaves eight cabins where I didn't meet anyone." She twisted her lips. "There could be fifty or sixty people living there."

"And if you get me in there, I'll have a reason to talk to every one of them."

The outer door to the adjoining room slammed shut.

"Honey! Did you miss me?" Billy yelled.

Peter boosted himself off the bed. "Our pain in the ass is back."

He strode into the other room, spotted Billy rummaging in a small paper bag. "Did you get the strips?"

Billy looked over at him and tucked his hair behind his ears "No."

"Dammit."

"Peter?" Izzy poked her head in. "I'm going for a soda, but all I have is a twenty. Do you have anything smaller?"

He swiveled to her. "In my wallet. And your phone rang a few times while you were gone."

"Thanks," she said. "I've been neglecting my voice mail. I'll check it."

Peter went back to Billy. "What happened with the strips? Did you even try?"

"What the fuck? Of course I tried. I went to four places. Two were closed. I guess the stores here don't stay open past six. The one place didn't carry them, and the other place was fresh out."

Peter shoved his hands into his hair and contemplated another sleepless night. "After tomorrow it won't matter because Izzy is moving into the compound. We'll have her check out and I'll take that room."

Izzy.

His wallet.

The fantasy list.

Shit.

All movement around him halted, his ears whooshing as he angled toward her to find the nightmare materializing before his eyes. She stood with the wallet in her right hand and the slip of white paper in the left.

His hands immediately went in the air. "Don't freak."

Billy laughed. "Uh, oh."

"Shut up," he shot back.

Izzy took the singles and the list, but dropped the wallet before spinning around and hauling ass to her room.

Peter grunted. Another fucking landmine. *Goddammit.*

"Izzy, hang on." He followed her into the room, closed the door behind him and caught up with her.

When he tugged on her arm, she whirled on him and all the softness in her face disappeared. "No."

The growl in her voice smacked at him, but he didn't let go of her arm until she shoved him back a full step. *Whoa, strong woman.* She turned toward the door, but he jumped against it before she got it open. "Let me talk to you."

Squaring her shoulders, Izzy stepped back from the door. "Get away from this door before I hurt you."

"No."

She held her closed fist in front of his face, the crumpled paper sticking out the bottom like a death sentence. "What is this?"

Oh, hell. From her perspective it would look bad. A woman with trust issues regarding sex finds a kinky list in his wallet. He was a dumbass for carrying it around. At the very least, he should have committed it to memory.

"Did you have a specific person in mind with this list or would any random woman do?"

The quaking strain in her voice warned of her emotional state, but her eyes were glued to the floor. *Please don't let her be crying.* He stuck his finger under her chin and pushed up. The glistening green of her eyes knifed into him. *I'm an idiot.*

"It's nothing sick."

He tried to draw her in for a hug, but she pushed back. "Don't touch me."

"Remember I told you about the nightmares? The nightmares that kept me from sleeping and started this whole mess with Billy?"

She jerked her head, but continued staring at the floor.

"The day I met you, the nightmares eased up. They

weren't nearly as bad and then I started dreaming about you. And, well, in the dreams we had sex. Crazy good sex."

The list suddenly hit him in the face. She'd thrown it at him. *Nice.*

"Among *other* things," she said, red faced and mad enough to carve him to pieces.

He heaved a breath and blew it out. "Yes, among other things."

"Damn you!"

"I didn't talk to anyone about it, I swear to you. It made me happy to think about it and, at the time, I didn't have a lot to be happy about. I was grasping at any piece of sanity. You became that sanity."

"That's bullshit, Peter. You're trying to charm your way out of this."

"No. It's the truth. I couldn't wait to go to sleep because I'd dream about you. The problem was the dreams were coming fast, and I was losing track of the good stuff."

"I don't want to hear this."

"Yeah, you do. The list is my version of Creepy Izzy. You use her to cope. I cope by having dreams about you. It's so much better than Roy getting his head blown off." He waved his hand in the air. "Anyway, I started losing track, so I wrote it down. I thought if things went my way, maybe we'd get to a point where we trusted each other enough to talk about the list and maybe we'd do some of the things on it. That's all. Just me wanting to remember what made us both feel good in my dreams."

Her gaze darted around his face, but he stood still while his heart nearly beat out of his damned chest.

"Are you lying to me?"

"No. We've come too far for that. We may or may not manage a relationship, but it won't be because I lied."

He cupped her face in his hands, but after a second, she backed out of his grasp. "You should have told me about the list. It would have avoided this."

Chalk that up to a lesson learned.

The list sat on the floor between them and she bent to pick it up. She smoothed it in her hand and read it while Peter stood like a second grader in the principal's office.

She ran her fingers over her forehead before looking up at him. "I'm sorry I jumped to conclusions. I'll try not to do that anymore." She handed him the list. "I'm not good at this. I've been alone a long time. I don't trust people. Men in particular."

"For good reason."

The heat in her eyes evaporated. "I can't imagine you wanting to share your life with me. I'm a lot of work."

He smiled at her. "We're in this together."

She bit her lip and closed her eyes for a second.

Thinking.

Come on, Iz. Take a risk.

She opened her eyes, wobbled her head a bit and said, "Will you put the list somewhere safe until we're ready to discuss it?"

"You bet I will."

26

THE AIRPLANE LANDING IN THE MOTEL ROOM TURNED OUT TO be Billy's snoring.

Crap.

Peter glanced at the digital clock's bloodred neon numbers. Three-oh-six. Another sleepless night. He couldn't take any more. He needed some serious shut-eye or he'd go ballistic.

Again.

On Billy.

Irony at its best.

The adjoining door to Izzy's room was unlocked. He'd told her to shut it, but leave the bolt off in case they needed to get into either room in a hurry.

Maybe he'd crash on the floor in her room. She wouldn't mind. Unless she was still steamed about the sex list. Billy let out another honk and Peter rolled his eyes. He should have killed the son of a bitch when he had the chance.

He stomped to the adjoining door and pushed it open enough to get his head through the gap. "Izzy?"

"Hmm?"

A soft night light behind one of the butt ugly chairs threw shadows across the room. Apparently she didn't like to sleep in the dark.

"Iz, I'm coming in," he said being careful not to get too close or he'd startle her. He'd learned that lesson years ago when one of his navy buddies almost shot his head off because he tried to wake him up while standing too close to the bunk. Once you've been at the wrong end of a .45 you don't make that mistake again.

She sat up, shoved her hair from her face and smiled a sleepy smile that forced him to breathe deep because she was major league shaggable.

"Finally," she said pulling off her tank top.

"Ho!" he said, a little louder than he wanted to. He reached back and shut the door so Paul Bunyan didn't wake up. "What are you doing?"

Could she still be asleep? Sleep stripping? He snorted a quiet laugh.

The covers went flying and she wiggled out of her shorts. The night light offered enough of a glow for him to know her body, with its gently sculpted muscles, would be the death of him.

Help me.

She tossed her shorts at him. "It's about time, Peter. I can't believe it took you this long to give in."

"Huh?" Malfunctioning brain. Had to be.

She walked over to him, completely freaking naked, and started pulling his T-shirt up. Monk Junior stood at attention howling the war cry.

Peter had to stop this before it went too far. He grabbed her hands. "Are you awake?"

"Completely."

"Then hold up here. A few hours ago you were lambasting me for my sex list and now you're all over me."

Yes, this woman might possibly be certifiable.

But he most likely loved her.

Did that make him certifiable as well? Maybe Vic was right about him being a nutcase.

She squeezed his hands and leaned back to see his eyes despite the shadows in the room. "I apologized for that. My mind was working overtime. I thought we settled it."

"Yeah, but I got the impression you wanted to wait. I'm confused."

"I warned you about this, Peter."

Why did he feel like he was floating in the path of a rogue wave about to break on him? "You did?"

She nodded. "My body wants things my brain doesn't. It's physical. The list is about feelings and intimacy. This isn't."

The wave broke and nearly drowned him. Sex was a function to her. He might as well be screwing a tree.

"I get it," he said, heavy on the sarcasm. "Creepy Izzy needs to get laid and I'm available."

"Peter—"

"No." He tore his shirt over his head. "This'll be *great*. Just because you don't want to be objectified doesn't mean I don't. I love a good fuck and something tells me *you* are going to rock my world." He ripped his shorts off, tossed them aside and pointed to his hard-on. "As you can see, I'm ready."

"That's not what I meant." She kept her voice low, but the vibration there could have shook the building.

Now they were both pissed. *Goddammit.* Why couldn't they ever be on the same page when it came to sex? There was always a fight brewing. He put his hands on his bare hips, wandered to the window and peeked out the blinds. Un-fucking-believable. The two of them standing here, naked as a couple of jays, and they couldn't manage a guilt-free lay.

Maybe he'd go for a run. Work some of this pissing mad out of him. Not to mention the woody.

He turned back to her. "Billy's snoring again. That's why I came in here. I wanted to sleep on your floor."

"Oh, no."

A sliver of light crossed her bare skin and the hunger crawling inside him swarmed. All rational thought evaporated. He wanted her. She was willing. *What's the problem, dickhead?*

"How humiliating," she said.

He rolled his shoulders, mentally forced his pulse to a slower pace and got his thoughts in order. "For both of us."

In two tentative steps she was in front of him, but didn't touch him. Probably a good thing, because if she put her hands on him he'd go up in flames.

"I'm sorry," she said. "I know I'm driving you crazy."

He jerked his head. "I never know when you're going to blow a fuse on me. I'm a patient man, but I have my limits. We're either going to have sex or we're not. You know my feelings about Creepy Izzy. If Fun Izzy isn't ready, we'll wait."

Instinctively he knew she wasn't ready, but he couldn't deny the morsel of hope stirring in him.

"Fun Izzy isn't ready," she said, pounding the morsel into oblivion.

"Fine." He kept his voice even and forced himself to stay rooted to his spot. She needed to know, despite his disappointment, he wasn't angry with her. He wouldn't guilt her into it. "Then let's not put ourselves in a position where we're tempted."

She trickled her fingers down his chest, heating his body again. "I'm always tempted with you though."

He stilled her hands by squeezing them. "See, this is what confuses me. The hot-cold thing."

Her gaze zeroed in on him. *Shake it off. She'll get you with the eyes.*

"Peter, what you don't understand is Creepy Izzy knows what she wants. My body has needs my brain doesn't. I've spent years solidifying my barriers. I think it's unreasonable for you to think they'll fall just because you came along."

"I don't think that."

"So, it's okay for you to call the shots when it comes to not sleeping with Creepy Izzy, but it's not okay for me to self-protect?"

"What do you mean?"

"Just because you don't want to have sex with Creepy Izzy doesn't mean *I* don't want to have sex with you. Why do you get to decide when it's right?"

"That's not what I'm doing."

"Yes, you are."

He fisted his hands. "No, I'm not. I'm more than capable of having casual sex. I've been doing it since I got divorced."

"But?"

He laughed, but the sadness in it made him sick. How the hell had they gotten to this point? He'd been divorced ten years and hadn't missed this empty, frustrated feeling that came from two people not understanding each other. And the pisser of the whole thing was, if he told her how he felt, she'd freak.

Well, too fucking bad. He wouldn't spend the next century circling her fear of rejection.

"You're different," he said. "It won't be casual with you. I'm going to want every piece of you. And I'll expect you to give it me. I'll expect you to be with only me. Maybe that's not fair to you, but I have a right to my own self-protection."

She stepped an inch closer, searched his eyes for something. Damned if he knew what.

"Stalemate then?" she asked.

Truth time. Put it all on the table. Screw the consequences. "I know I said I never lied to you, but that's not true."

Despite the dim light he saw her flinch. He put his hands on her hips—very naked hips—and held her there. "The other day, when I gave you my do-rag, I made that crack about it being love. I lied when I said it was a joke. That was me firing a warning shot. When you panicked, I backed off. But that's where I'm headed. In love with you. And you're not going to be able to handle it."

Isabelle's vision swam and the tension seized her into a tight ball.

Caught. That's what she was. She could remain in her safe zone or she could throw open the door and let in the sun that came with him.

You can't give him what he needs. He'll take what little you have. Stupid Creepy Izzy making this harder than it needed to be. Hadn't he proved he could be trusted? Isabelle had put this man through hell and he always came back stronger.

She couldn't give him what he needed. Not completely. But maybe, over time, she'd learn to give it all.

Maybe.

She cupped his cheeks, glided her thumb over the scar she found so fascinating. "I'm crazy about you. You have to know that. I lay in bed night after night and I think about having you there with me. When I'm with you, I'm at peace. I almost know where I fit in this world because I don't have to pretend with you. You know I'm nuts and you still stay."

He grunted. "Yeah, but I'm slowly dying from it."

"I wish I could tell you Creepy Izzy will go away. I don't know if she will, but I know, emotionally speaking, this is the furthest I've come with anyone. It might not seem like much, but I've shared my problems with you. I've never done that before. I let men think I'm distant. They never know about Kendrick or Creepy Izzy."

"Then they aren't paying attention and don't deserve you."

She grinned at him. "That's what I mean. You *get* me. It's like my own piece of heaven and I'm not sure what to do with it. I know I want to do *something*; I just don't know what."

Peter ducked his head. Kissed her. Hesitant at first and then, with a sweep of his tongue, surer. *Yes.* He tried to back away, but she pulled him closer and the kiss deepened. Her mind wandered to the bed and getting him over there.

"I know what I want," she said. "I can't promise Creepy Izzy won't take over, but, at this second, it's Fun Izzy and I really want you to love me."

He grunted, and backed her up until her legs hit the bed. "Convenient that we're already naked."

"How about that?"

They both laughed as she landed on the squeaking bed and he dropped beside her. "You want to be in charge?" he asked.

"I want *us* to be in charge." She rolled over, straddled him, felt the heat of his erection against her inner thigh. "Wow. Peter. It's a powerful thing to know I do this to you."

He slid his hands up her torso, across her breasts, and

she threw her head back, concentrating on the sensation of his hands on her.

Don't give yourself over.

Stop thinking.

She leaned forward and kissed him. Kissing him always quieted her rioting brain.

"Don't think," he said, gliding his hands down her back. "Just let go. I'll take care of you."

"I know." She trailed kisses down his neck, wanting only to feel him inside her. Maybe he'd be the one that could help her find that part of her that had been missing for so long. *Please let it be him.*

"Condoms," he said.

Isabelle sat up and leaned over him to the bedside table while he put his tongue to work on her nipple. "That's cheating."

He pulled back. "You don't seem to mind."

She dangled a condom in front of him. "I was expecting you."

"I love a woman who's prepared."

AND HE COULDN'T WAIT TO GET STARTED. HE HAD TO BE brain-fried because he couldn't come up with a single reason not to spend the next four hours banging the hell out of Isabelle DeRosa. The woman who was slowly killing him.

After slipping the condom on, he rolled on top of her, shoved her hair out of her face and held it while he got lost in those sea green eyes that, in a darkened room, shined bright.

He wanted her. And it wasn't just the sex. He wanted the whole nutty package.

She hooked her hand around his neck, pulled him down

and kissed him. Hot, needy. His weight sunk into her, the miserable bed squeaking again. He used his knee to spread her legs and settled himself there, pulling away from the kiss and nipping her jaw.

Her welcoming giggle left his mind swirling and she clamped her hands on his ass, slid them across his hips, up his back, all the while arching under him. Wanting him.

"Please, Peter."

She shivered under him, but didn't object when he pushed into her and let the hunger he'd kept at bay run loose.

After she bolted her legs around him, he dared to look at her, watching her eyes and the heat there as her hands moved all over, driving him to madness. Damn, he loved her.

Faster, he thought, and plunged again, surrendering to his baser needs, but wanting to give what her pumping hips so clearly wanted. Yes, he'd given in to Creepy Izzy. He'd let the emotions of that same rogue wave devour him as he thought about the two of them, together, in this bed, the scorching heat between them firing like a hot zone until he couldn't hang on anymore. With one hand, he touched her face. She opened her eyes, blew him a kiss, and his body exploded from the force of it.

"HOLY SHIT," PETER SAID.

Isabelle caught her breath for a second before she remembered to let it out. She laughed and dragged her nails lightly against his back. "Uh-huh."

"Just so you know," he said, "I usually last longer than ten seconds."

Like she cared. At this moment, her pleasure couldn't be diminished. "I wasn't counting."

"Yeah, but I know you didn't—"

"It's all right."

He pushed himself up, his wavy hair a curling mess around his face. "It's not okay."

Here we go again. Another explanation. Would it ever stop?

She made a move to roll away, but his arms kept her in place. She sighed. More humiliation. "It doesn't always happen for me." Too much baggage occupying her mind. But she'd never say that to him. The one who asked for all of her.

"Unacceptable."

She laughed.

"I'm serious," he said, still hovering above her. "How is that fair to you? We're in this together. Why is it okay for me to have an orgasm and not you?"

Oh, Lord, she thought, wanting to find the nearest closet to hide in. He didn't get it. She reached and brought him down to her, brushed her lips against his. "I'm fine without it. I'm used to it."

Rolling to the side, he propped himself on one elbow and moved his hands over her breasts. "I don't believe that."

The heat of his hands drew her closer. "But I love you touching me."

He kissed the top of her head and glided his hands down her torso. "I'm not done with you yet."

Typical man, needing to prove his point. What was it with men? They just couldn't accept that she wasn't equipped for an orgasm every time.

She grabbed his roaming hand. "It's not about you not doing something. It's me."

"I don't understand."

The way he focused on her; told her he wouldn't give up until he comprehended the problem. She blew out a breath, prepared for more humiliation.

She shook her head and swallowed the bile in her throat. She hated this. Hated the shame that came with being honest.

"Iz?"

Here goes. Another first. "With Kendrick, I would have orgasms. At the time, I was too young to understand what they were and he told me it happened when people enjoy sex."

"Son of a bitch," Peter said.

She ignored that and pushed forward. He wanted to know and she'd already started, so she might as well finish. "It's hard for me to think about those times. It makes me sick because I know I was turned-on, and I'm ashamed of it. How could I have liked it?"

He sat up. "Honey, you were a little girl. You didn't know the human body reacts to that kind of...well...stimulation. You didn't get off because you liked it. You got off because it's the way the body is supposed to respond. And nobody had the right to mess with that."

"I know, but I've spent years separating my mind and body. When I have an orgasm, the shame strangles me. I don't want to live with that reminder. It's easier to disconnect."

Peter stared at her for a solid minute. He wasn't running for the door yet, so that was a good sign. She had to admit she felt some relief after having shared that nasty little secret.

"You deserve better than this, Peter. I'm broken and will frustrate the hell out of you. There will be times when you think I'm getting close to an orgasm and—*poof!*—it'll be gone. You'll feel like a failure and I'll feel guilty. It's a vicious cycle."

He sat back against the pillows. "Here we go again. You're trying to scare me off."

"I'm not. It's the truth."

"It's *your* truth. How about you let me decide how I feel?"

"I wasn't—"

He held up a finger. "Sshh! One step at a time. Do you agree that you should let me decide how I feel?"

She rolled her eyes. "Well, of course, but that's—"

"Sshh!"

Insane. He had to be insane.

When he leaned over, put his arm around her and pulled her close, she didn't fight it. She simply rested her head against his chest and enjoyed the comfort of being held. No shame.

"One step at a time, Iz. We'll figure it out."

27

Sunlight streaked between the cracks in the window blinds, and Isabelle concentrated on remaining still. Peter slept soundly beside her, his chest rising and falling just inches in front of her face. They had fallen asleep, arms and legs entangled, and she found she didn't so much mind waking up that way.

She breathed in slowly as her brain and body sent conflicting messages.

Ignore it.

Knowing she'd told him her secret terrified her. But she liked it. Sort of. Why deny it? She had handed over more weakness by admitting her orgasm issues and he didn't make her feel like a freak.

Damned Peter. Screwing up her life. Literally. His eyes popped open.

"Good morning, sunshine," he said, grinning like a madman.

"Morning."

She snuggled into him.

"I can hear you thinking," he said. "You okay?"

"I am." And, at that moment, she was. "Thank you for understanding."

"No prob. I like to process the problem before I tackle it."

"I'll keep that in mind."

"So," Peter said. "Today's the day. Moving into the compound."

The compound. She didn't want to. She wanted to stay in this bed, with Peter, and not think about the blasted compound.

Then again. The sooner she got in, the sooner she'd go home and figure out where he fit in her life. Not to mention saving her job. A job that her uncle, via voice mail, threatened to relieve her of unless she returned his calls.

"Yep. Today's the day."

"Before you go, I'm gonna teach you how to pick a lock. That's one skill that always comes in handy."

Isabelle nodded. "I'm up for that. I'd also like to get a workout in before I leave. It'll relax me. Get me in the right frame of mind. Maybe I'll go down to that gym you guys found in town."

"Sure." Peter rolled sideways and put his feet on the floor. "Billy will probably go. Time it so he gets there first."

"Why?"

He turned back to her. "The guy that owns the place is a meathead and tends to hover around the women. He'll be all over you, so unless you want that, Billy will make sure the meathead stays away."

If ever a comment deserved an eye roll it was that one. "You know I can take care of myself."

"Yes, but possibly beating the crap out of the guy, and calling attention to yourself when you're supposed to be undercover, won't make your buddy Sampson happy."

She hadn't thought of that. And just to make sure Peter

didn't start channeling his inner caveman, she'd better be up front about the agent's presence in Ohio.

"Speaking of Sampson, how did your meeting go?"

Peter shrugged. "He wants me to stay out of his case or he'll lock me up. He'll come around after I start feeding him information he can't get legally."

Izzy sat up. The cold air smacked into her and she contemplated burrowing back. "Please don't get in trouble over this. I couldn't stand it if you wound up in custody."

He quickly snapped off one of the bright smiles that transformed him from a regular Joe to movie-star hand-some. "Not a chance, Iz. Sampson gets no free passes when it comes to you."

A disturbing tension buzzed. Free passes? What the hell did that mean? "I'm not sure I understand."

He let out a sarcastic laugh. "Izzy, come on. You're telling me you haven't noticed he'd like to nail you? He practically admitted it to me."

Wait. They were discussing her? Talking about sex? With her? Couldn't be. Peter wouldn't do that. Would he?

"I...I...hmm." She gave her head a hard shake.

The pressure of the blood barreling inside her made her head pound. She had to relax. Think about this logically before she tore into him. Could Peter have done this to her?

"What?" he asked.

She breathed in, jabbed both hands at him. "I'm trying to make sense of this. I'm busy turning my life upside down and you two are talking about who gets to have sex with me? Are you *kidding*? *I* decide who gets to be with me."

An agonizing panic shot up the center of her ribcage.

"No, no, no," Peter said. "You are *not* gonna do this. I've learned a few things from our prior arguments, and you are *not* making this about me treating you like a sexual object."

"I don't do that."

"Actually, you do. It's a defense mechanism. It's how you push people away and I'm not biting this time."

She opened her mouth to speak, but he held up two hands. She closed her mouth.

"Listen up," Peter said. "Sampson and I did not, I repeat, did *not,* discuss who gets to have sex with you. I wouldn't do that and you know it. The conversation had nothing to do with sex." He turned so his body faced her. "I don't think you're an object. You're smart and caring and driven to do what's right. Most people don't even understand the concept. The thing with Sampson was me being an asshole. I can't stand the idea of anyone else touching you. So, you can be mad at me and call me a caveman for wanting to keep you for myself, but that's it."

The quiet of his voice soothed her barking temper and she closed her eyes, let the feeling fill her. Allowing herself to get emotional about Peter had been her first mistake, a slippery slope. And she couldn't pinpoint where she'd let go of the anchor to her emotional stability. Even if it was only a little bit of a slip, she'd permitted it.

"Iz?"

She scooted forward, threw her arms around his shoulders and hung on tight. "I'm stuck, Peter. It's like you're trying to drag me out of a window and I'm digging in, fighting it because I'm terrified of what's on the other side. That's never happened to me. I never wanted to go to the other side."

"I think you *want* to be terrified," he said into her ear. "I think you're sick of Creepy Izzy having the power. And, for whatever reason, I'm the lucky guy who happened to be in the right place at the right time."

She rolled her eyes at that one. How the hell hadn't he

given up on her yet? "You call this lucky? You need more help than I thought."

Peter sat back and entwined her fingers with his. "The only way to get past the fear is to experience it. It won't kill you, Iz. It *won't*. It sucks, but once you beat it, you'll be free."

Free. She wanted to be emotionally free. More than anything she wanted to feel, really feel, the highs, maybe the lows too, of loving a man and being loved in return.

She sighed, tilting her head to the side. "I want to tell you I'm trying, but that sounds weak."

"I know you're trying. Let's take it slow."

That sounded nice because this psychological warfare, if she wasn't careful, would suck her dry and leave nothing to put into a relationship. She squeezed his hand. "I like that idea."

He cracked off another movie-star grin and stood to stretch his chiseled body. "Great."

When he started toward the bathroom she watched him go, enjoyed the way the taut muscles in his back rippled, but something nagged at her. His insecurities about Sampson's attraction to her couldn't be ignored. She walked to the bathroom, pushed open the partially closed door and pretended to ignore the fact that he was peeing.

He shook his head. "How about a little privacy?"

"I have to meet with Sampson today. Do you want to come?"

He flushed the toilet and moved to the sink to wash his hands, but his eyes stayed on her, checking out her naked body from head to toe.

"No."

"Peter, I have nothing to hide. Particularly at the moment." She laughed at her own joke, enjoying the ease of having a conversation with him while butt naked. "I don't mind if you join me."

After drying his hands, he grabbed her for a lip-crushing kiss. "It's okay. Sampson and I will work it out. Having me there will only piss him off. If he makes a move on you though, tell him he's too late." Peter laughed. "He'll *love* that."

A little zip went up her arms. How high school. Was she seriously turned-on by his possessiveness? Peter Jessup, caveman-at-large. "Should I tell him about you coming to the compound?"

He nudged her out of the bathroom and smacked her on the ass. "Not unless you want him to blow a gasket. Tell him after I'm there. There's nothing he can do about it then."

Withholding information wouldn't make Sampson happy, but Isabelle knew having Peter inside the compound would help. And the more help she received, the sooner they'd find out what happened to that missing girl. "Okay. I'll do it your way."

"Good," he said. "Now get back in bed so I can screw you stupid. *Again*. My work is never done."

ISABELLE WANDERED INTO MAISIE'S FAMILY RESTAURANT a little after three o'clock that afternoon and spotted Wade Sampson sitting in a corner booth toward the back. She'd only ever seen him in a suit, but today he wore a crisp white pullover and no jacket. Trying to blend in. *Good luck with that, GQ boy*.

Maisie's, on the other hand, resembled every other fifties-style diner and came complete with vinyl red booths along the walls and mini-jukeboxes on the tables. Ten or twelve worn veneer tables sat between the lunch counter and the booths.

Most of the tables were empty, but two elderly men seated at the counter gave her the once-over. She smiled at them and they both hooted.

To think she'd opted for a plain T-shirt and baggy shorts to avoid attention.

She slid into the booth across from Wade and he nodded. "Ms. DeRosa."

"I thought we were doing away with the formalities."

He grinned. "You are correct, *Isabelle*."

"Thank you."

A server dressed in a bright pink polyester dress with a plastic nametag that read Joy sidled up to the table. The capper had to be the matching lipstick and electric blue eye shadow. The place was a throwback, but the comforting sense of simplicity couldn't be ignored.

"More coffee, handsome?" Joy asked Wade.

A slick smile stretched across his face. "You bet. Thank you."

"No problem, hon."

After Joy took their order, Isabelle rolled her eyes. "Shouldn't you be trying to keep a low profile? I mean, flirting with the waitress?"

"I'm being nice."

"Please." She waved him off. "What do you need from me?"

He sat forward and leaned his elbows on the table. "Have you been to the compound today?"

"Just came from there. I'm all settled in."

"Good. Anything you can tell me?"

She sucked in a breath and released it. "I tried to open my bedroom window. It's sealed shut."

Wade stayed silent.

"Plus," she said, "all the bedrooms have double key locks on them. Not exactly comforting."

"If they're running a sex trade operation, they probably lock the girls in there with johns. Who has the keys?"

"Courtney told me Seth has them. No shock there because he seems like a control freak anyway. Oh, and I refuse to drink the tap water because it's making the women pregnant."

Wade screwed up his lips.

"Go ahead and laugh, but I've met at least four pregnant women there. Two live in the main house and two live in the cabins. And I'm not done meeting everyone yet. I'll try and get to the others tomorrow."

"What about Courtney?" he asked, reaching for the container of multicolored sweetener packets.

"She helped me move my things in. Her bedroom is on the other side of mine and we have a shared bathroom. She's either incredibly neat or Seth does white-glove checks on all the rooms. He definitely has creepy tendencies."

Wade stopped messing with the sweetener packets. "How so?"

"He's always on the girls about minding their manners, yet he stares at my chest like he's hypnotized."

Of course, Wade's gaze moved to her chest. Typical man. "Stop it."

He laughed. "Sorry. Reflex."

"Yeah, well, knock it off."

Joy stepped up, refilled his mug, slapped an iced tea in front of Isabelle, turned on her squeaky sneakers and left. *That Joy is a regular queen of efficiency.*

After she watched Wade dump three packets of sugar in his coffee, Isabelle's stomach rolled.

"You should get close to Courtney," he said.

"Why?"

He cocked his head a second and clucked his tongue. Isabelle remembered him telling her he didn't share much information because it could put his sources in danger.

"Yeah, I get it. You don't want me blurting out something I shouldn't know, but I want to fast-track this assignment. My job is in jeopardy, and I need to be back in two weeks. Just tell me what you've got. I'll be sure to control all babbling."

With a sip of his coffee, Sampson contemplated her, those dark eyes narrowing. He set the cup down. "She has an arrest record."

Of all the things Isabelle expected to hear, that wasn't one of them. She slouched back in the booth, her bare legs sticking to the cheap vinyl. "For what?"

"Four months ago she stole a protein bar and bottled water from a convenience store."

"She was pregnant four months ago."

"Yes. She told the local P.D. her boyfriend took off and, since she'd been laid off from her job a month earlier, she had no money."

"She was hungry." A sudden anger flamed up her throat. "Trying to take care of herself, and her baby, and they *arrested* her?"

Wade held up his hands. "I know it sucks, but she broke the law."

Deputy Do-Right. "They couldn't let her slide on a three-dollar theft? She's twenty years old. She was probably terrified."

"Don't bitch at *me*. I'm telling you what I know."

She leaned forward again. "Sorry. What else?"

"She caught a judge who's a single mother. Got probation, but the judge told her she needed counseling to figure out how to take care of herself and a baby."

"I like that judge," Isabelle said.

"Courtney went to a center called—" he pulled a notepad from beside him on the booth and checked his notes. "—Tomorrow's Family Network. They sent her to the Organization for the Underprivileged."

"Seth and Kendrick."

"Yes. She's been there ever since."

"What about the baby's father?"

Wade shrugged. "No idea. I don't think he's around. The point is she's been living there four months and knew Nicole Pratt. I questioned Courtney myself when Nicole disappeared. They were friends. Maybe you can get something from her."

That made sense. "I see where you're going with this. She told me she doesn't have a car and occasionally needs a ride into town. Seth usually drives her, but she has to wait until it's convenient for him. I told her I'd cart her around while I'm there. I'll see if she wants to run to the store with me after dinner tonight. Maybe she'll open up."

"Don't push too hard," Wade said, sounding like Peter.

Yeesh. They didn't give up.

Speaking of Peter... She sipped her tea to hydrate her suddenly parched throat. This should be interesting. "Can you get me land surveys of the property?"

His eyes fused to hers. "Why?"

Play dumb. She wouldn't lie to him, but she wouldn't give him anything extra either. "There's a lot of property there."

"And Jessup wants to see it?"

Jig's up. No sense denying it.

"Actually," Isabelle said, "he's already seen it."

One of the men at the counter barked out a laugh and

she looked over, relieved for the distraction while she waited for Wade to lecture her. She turned back and found him staring out the filmy window, his lips curled in.

"Knew it," he said.

The best thing for her to do would be to stay silent. Very silent. Peter and Wade needed to exhaust this quest to pulverize each other. She got that. She just didn't want to be in the middle.

Wade's gaze met hers and the disappointment on his perfectly angular face could not be ignored. "Mr. Jessup didn't follow my advice to stay out of my case?"

She grinned. "He can be stubborn. You'll learn that."

That got her a stony look. "No. I won't. I'll have another talk with him."

Her cue to leave. She so did not want to be around for that. Isabelle wrapped one hand on the end of the table and boosted herself from the booth. "Well, best of luck to you. I need to get back. The drive is long and dinner is served promptly at five-thirty. I shan't be late."

28

Peter sat at the banged-up imitation wood desk in the motel room doing an internet search for all things related to Kendrick's foundation when "Born to Run" screamed from his phone. Wrong damn phone. He wanted it to be the prepaid one because Izzy should be calling to let him know her meeting with Sampson had ended. He'd spoken to her on the way to the meeting, and was none too pleased with the sealed windows and locks on the doors development. His rampaging blood pressure had, in fact, nearly driven him to psychosis.

He glanced at the phone sitting on the desk. Blocked number. Usually it was Vic calling from his cone of silence, but sometimes he got a surprise. "Jessup."

"Wade Sampson."

"That didn't take long," Peter said.

"Huh?"

Sampson was a little slow on the uptake. "For you to call me. I guess you just finished with Izzy."

Did she mention you should keep your slick fucking hands off her?

"I thought I asked you to stay out of my case," Sampson said.

"You did." *Enough said on that subject.* "Can you get me the property surveys for that compound?"

Silence. Peter waited for Sampson to blow his stack. He spun the chair and motioned for Billy to lower the volume on the porn movie he'd rented. Porn, at this point, could create chaos because it meant Billy was bored, and when that happened, he got busy doing all sorts of shit he shouldn't be doing.

What they *should* have been doing was helping Izzy figure out what happened to the pretty college student, but nothing was popping. Blanks everywhere. Instead he was listening to some woman moan about Carl the lizard man and his amazing tongue.

"You're kidding, right?" Sampson finally said in his best you-are-nuttier-than-a-fruitcake voice.

"Nope. It's a lot of property. I'd like a guide."

Sampson laughed. At least he had a sense of humor.

"I'm not getting you those surveys. I can't chance you screwing up evidence."

"Oh, man," Billy howled from behind him and Peter spun around again.

"Shut that thing off. I'm on the phone."

Billy waved him away. Perfect. Peter shot him the bird and wondered where he put his gun. He might need it in the next thirty seconds.

"Hello?" Sampson said.

"Yeah, I'm here." *I'm just busy trying to keep my buddy from whacking off in front of me.* "You should get me those surveys. There's a lot of property."

"A hundred acres," Sampson replied.

Hey, at least the guy was talking. Maybe he needed to be

convinced by way of a boot in the ass. "Lots of places to bury a body."

"I know."

Progress. Not only was Sampson talking, he was listening. "The faster you get probable cause, the faster you get a warrant to search the place. I'll get you probable cause. You'll have to turn your back for a while, but how bad do you want it?"

More silence. *Yes, Agent Sampson. Keep thinking. You'll get there.*

Peter counted off in his head. Ten seconds tops and this guy would crumble.

"I'll get you those surveys."

Haza! Eight seconds. Not bad. A tough guy.

"I knew we could agree on this," Peter said.

Sampson released a breath. "I'm on a limb here, Jessup."

Peter could respect that. A man like Sampson didn't play outside the rules. Particularly with a case of this magnitude. A congresswoman's missing daughter might make or break his career, and Peter couldn't blame him for not wanting to be the agent who screwed the pooch.

"My reasons for being involved are different than yours, Sampson, but we agree on what the results should be."

"Just don't fuck me."

Sampson did a half sigh. Probably because he knew, deep down in that part of him that yearned for the greater good, he needed help. They weren't so different after all.

"No problem," Peter said. "You're not my type anyway."

Isabelle spotted the Dipsy-Do Ice Cream Shop as she drove along the rural route heading back to the compound. Trees and crops surrounded the road, but the Dipsy-Do, with its bright white paint and neon sign, stood smack in the middle of all that lush farmland.

After dinner, she and Courtney had taken a trip to the five-and-dime so Courtney could stock up on essentials. Seth, surprisingly, didn't argue. He was probably relieved he didn't have to take her. The Dipsy-Do would provide another opportunity to endear herself to Courtney.

"This place reminds me of one of those old drive-ins. How about we stop?"

Courtney shrugged. "Fine by me."

This girl had a steel coat and cracking it could take a while. Maybe more time than Isabelle had.

"I love a good vanilla soft-serve," she said.

"Whatever."

All right. Maybe she should make Crabby Courtney pay for her own damned ice cream. Isabelle chuckled to herself. Crabby Courtney meet Creepy Izzy.

Five minutes later, they settled down on one of the wooden picnic tables to enjoy their ice cream cones as Isabelle's mind went to work.

Having Courtney alone was an opportunity to cull information, but Isabelle would have to use caution. This girl was no fool and would see right through an influx of questions. Isabelle licked a drip off her cone, glanced at the setting sun and wished she were sharing this time with Peter.

Don't think about him now. Concentrate on the task.

"This is a great place," she said. "I'll have to take a picture of it."

Courtney's gaze stayed focused on Isabelle's as she licked her chocolate-vanilla twist. She took a second lick, but her measuring stare remained.

A gentle bubbling under Isabelle's skin indicated a shift of energy between them, and she willed herself to remain still. Being a good lawyer meant understanding the rhythm of a situation, and speaking too soon might cause Courtney to retreat.

"I used to come here with my friend."

Isabelle took another slow swipe of her cone. "It's not far from the compound."

"That's why we liked it."

Hmm. A lot of past tense going on here. "It doesn't sound like you come here anymore."

Courtney shook her head. "My friend moved out."

Ba-da-bum, ba-da-bum, ba-da-bum. Isabelle's heart pounded and she steadied herself against the pressure in her chest. Could they be talking about Nicole Pratt?

What would a congresswoman's daughter be doing living in a glorified homeless shelter?

Deep breath. Confirm the information. Act natural.

Isabelle bit into the cone and focused on the crunch rather than the near heart attack she was having. "That's too bad. Were you roommates before you moved into the compound?"

Courtney popped the last of her cone into her mouth and wiped each finger with her napkin. "No. We were at Seth's together. She moved in a few weeks after I did. You're in her old room."

Holy, holy cow. Stay calm. Breathe.

"Ow!" Courtney smacked at her arm. "Damn, bugs. They'll swallow you whole."

No kidding on that one. Isabelle had already used half a bottle of bug spray. "Do you need spray? I have some in my purse."

"No. I'm afraid it's bad for the baby."

"We can go back if you'd like."

Courtney shook her head. "I like being away from the house."

Didn't take a neurosurgeon to understand that. "Yeah, I needed some air, too."

"I guess you've had it with the Queen Bee wishing you'd melt."

Isabelle snorted a laugh. "You caught that, huh?"

"I'm knocked up, not blind. Don't sweat it. She does it to any new woman that comes along."

"Why?"

Courtney's eyes shifted. *She knows something.*

Isabelle waited the near one hundred hours until Courtney shrugged. "She's a nut."

Not exactly case-breaking information. "Maybe we'll just stay here until everyone goes to bed."

Courtney rolled her eyes at the bad joke, but Isabelle wasn't sure she was kidding. Spending the evening with Seth staring at the wonder boobs was not high on the to-do list.

And yes, she knew it was her own fault for playing up her assets, but if it got her enough information to find Nicole, she'd do it. In intervals.

"It's nice that you get your own room at least," she said.

"The timing worked out. I'm hoping to be gone before anyone else comes in."

"When are you leaving?"

Courtney shrugged. "After the baby comes."

Now wasn't that interesting? Where was she going to go with an infant? And no job to support them? "Do you have something lined up? A place to live for you and the baby?"

"I...uh...no." She stood for a second, stretched her back and sat again.

"I see." Isabelle tried to keep her voice level, but Courtney caught the surprise and eyed her.

"I'm giving the baby up. It'll just be me I need to worry about, and I've managed so far."

Courtney rubbed a hand over her belly. "She'll be better off with someone else. I want her to have a good life."

"You're having a girl?"

"Yep. And I think she'll be a feisty one too. She kicks all the time."

A rare, wistful smile took over Courtney's face and the sadness plunged into Isabelle's heart. Courtney wanted to keep her baby.

"Courtney?"

The girl stared at a young couple passing. "What?"

"This is none of my business, and feel free to tell me to screw off, but are you sure you want to give up your baby?"

She twisted her lips and then said, "Sure, I'd like to keep her, but how can I do that? I don't have a job, a place to live or health insurance."

"What about your family?"

"I ran away when I was sixteen. I haven't been back since. I call my mother once in a while, but I don't expect them to help me. I won't go back there anyway."

"What about the baby's father?"

"Took off three months ago because he didn't—" Courtney made air quotes, "—sign on for this." She laughed her derision. "Maybe he should have thought about that before he stuck his dick into me." She slapped her hands over her face. "I'm sorry. It's the hormones."

Isabelle reached her hand across, but unsure how Courtney would respond to her touch, set it flat on the tabletop. "Don't apologize to me about men. I don't understand them myself."

Except Peter. Him I understand. Most of the time.

"Anyway, I'm giving up the baby." Her gaze shifted to the couple again. "I'm only twenty. I have a lot of time for children. I want my children to have a good life, with a mom and dad who love them. The best thing is to give the baby to someone who can do that."

Courtney's plan sounded reasonable, but the look on her face as she rubbed her hand over her belly said something different. Regret. And the baby wasn't even gone yet. What would this girl be like when her child was being raised by someone else?

Isabelle thought of Peter's mother and her foundation. Maybe Lorraine could help? Maybe *Isabelle* could help. She could certainly line up a job. And she had contacts at the women's shelter back home. Maybe they knew of an assistance program.

"Courtney, we don't know each other well, but maybe I can help you find someplace else to live. I'm not trying to talk you out of giving up the baby, but this is a big decision and you don't seem convinced."

The frigid look Courtney leveled on her forced Isabelle to lean back. *Wow. That pissed her off.*

"Don't you think I know it's a big decision?"

"I didn't mean to be patronizing."

Courtney huffed. "It doesn't matter anyway. The decision is made."

What did that mean? "You have time yet."

"No. I don't."

"The baby isn't due for six weeks. You can line something up. I'll help you. I would hate to see you make a decision like this and regret it later."

The young couple left their table and walked to the parking lot. Courtney watched with a longing that Isabelle recognized. Loneliness. *Don't go there. This is a job. Leave the emotion out of it.*

After a long minute, Courtney turned back. "You're right. You don't understand. I already regret the decision, but it's too late."

The last of Isabelle's patience dropped away, but she made sure to keep her voice at a reasonable volume. "How can it be too late when the baby isn't here yet? Even if you've talked to an adoption agency you can still change your mind. You're the birth mother. You have rights."

A moment, maybe two, passed in silence before a loud engine from a passing car caught Isabelle's attention. She stayed focused on Courtney and another minute elapsed while Isabelle waited for the girl, so lost over this decision, to talk to her.

Courtney bit her bottom lip and turned to her with drippy eyes. "I can't talk to you about this. I'm sorry."

Isabelle exhaled. *So close.* With caution she reached for Courtney's hand and the girl didn't pull away. Progress. "I don't mean to pressure you. This is your decision, but if you want to talk about it, I'm here. There are always choices."

She fiddled with the crumpled napkins on the table then scooped them up. "We should get back."

"Sure," Isabelle said, not sure at all. "I have to talk to Seth when we get back anyway."

"Lucky you," Courtney said in that sarcastic way that meant *un*lucky you.

"You don't like him much do you?" Isabelle asked when they got to the car.

Courtney slid into the passenger seat and buckled up. "He's a controlling asshole, but that's just my personal opinion."

She liked Courtney. "You're entitled."

"Kendrick was at least nice to me."

The sound of Kendrick's name caught Isabelle off-guard and she stiffened. "Kendrick wasn't my favorite person."

"I figured that out. How come?"

A car raced by and honked and Isabelle yelped as she rolled to a stop at the exit. Getting a pregnant woman killed wasn't on the to-do list for the day either.

The distractions with this assignment were plentiful, and there always seemed to be a tough choice to make. Courtney wanted to know something Isabelle had spent a lifetime hiding. She could make something up and risk getting caught in the lie, thereby losing any chance of this girl trusting her. Or she could admit it. Which she'd only done a handful of times, under specific conditions.

Courtney waited; her features frozen in a perpetual I-don't-give-a-damn mask. "You don't have to tell me."

Do it. She had to gain Courtney's trust and if being truthful did that, it would be worth the risk. A burst of air exploded within her, willing her forward. "He sexually abused me when I was a kid."

"Oh, ouch," Courtney said. "Rat bastard."

Isabelle choked a laugh. Nothing in Sampson's file indicated sexual abuse, but Courtney understood betrayal. Her simple reaction—maybe the lack of judgment or the honesty in which it was delivered—eased a smile from Isabelle. Twice now, the first time with Peter, she'd admitted her abuse to a near stranger, and shame didn't sit on her like a rotted carcass.

Odd, she thought, the most unlikely people seemed to identify with her.

"Thank you, Courtney."

Courtney tilted her mouth into a smirk. "For what? I didn't kill him."

29

Isabelle slipped out the front door of the compound with her prepaid cell phone in hand. The sticky night air surrounded her and moisture beaded along her spine as she stepped away from the porch.

She needed to get away from the house and its lunatic inhabitants for a few minutes. The whole thing was just damned weird. Seth couldn't stop staring at the miracle boobs, which, of course, was the point, but Isabelle still wanted to pop him. Throw in Mary Beth giving her the constant hairy eyeball, and Isabelle had a brain-frying headache. The three ibuprofens she'd slammed didn't forestall the pounding behind her eyes, and she pressed her thumb and middle finger into them trying to gouge the pain away. No luck.

What was Mary Beth's problem anyway? Just because Seth found another woman attractive? Mary Beth could have him. The bigger, nagging issue though, was whether Mary Beth's dislike had something to do with her very pregnant fifteen-year-old daughter. Isabelle had spied Rebecca and Seth talking quietly on several occasions and it led her to wonder if Seth had fathered Rebecca's unborn child.

Sick, sick, sick. Maybe Kendrick and Seth were both sexual terrorists. If so, he'd better back the hell up because she'd do whatever it took to put him in jail.

Even if it meant dealing with Mary Beth.

Isabelle stopped in the middle of the lawn and glanced at her phone—anyone inside the house would think she was searching for a good signal—and kept walking as she dialed Peter's number.

"I need to see you," she said when he answered. Where this sudden neediness came from she had no idea, but the richness of his voice only intensified it.

Normally, when the angst overtook her, she'd kick the hell out of her heavy bag. She would wind up paralyzed with fatigue, but the negative energy would be long gone.

No heavy bag here. No salty ocean air. Just humidity and the stench of something vile.

"What's wrong?" Peter asked.

"I think Nicole was staying here. Courtney told me." Isabelle stopped, turned toward the house in case anyone came out. Even if they did, from this distance they wouldn't be able to hear.

"Just like that? She offered it up?"

"Courtney doesn't offer anything up. She measures every syllable. When we were having ice cream she mentioned she used to go there with her friend. I asked leading questions. I *am* a defense lawyer you know."

That defense lawyer line wasn't necessary. The man was asking a question and she jumped on him like a commuter chasing a train. "I'm sorry, Peter."

"Forget it. Why the hell would Nicole be living there? I thought she was a volunteer."

"That's what Sampson indicated."

"He may have intentionally kept it from you," Peter said. "Or maybe he didn't know. I checked her mother out and she's loaded. Jessup kind of loaded."

"I don't know about any of that. All Courtney said was that her *friend* had moved out." She hesitated. Jammed her fingers into her eyes again as the pain roared back. "I told her about Kendrick abusing me."

"You *did*?"

"I had to. I need her to trust me. I need someone in this miserable house to trust me."

"That had to be hard for you."

Nearly gave me a heart attack. "It'll be worth it. Plus, I think I like Courtney."

The soft grass tickled Isabelle's flip-flop-clad toes, and her legs wilted until she dropped spread eagle onto the grass.

Whacko-whacko-whacko. That's what the residents would think when they saw her lying on the grass with only the porch light throwing shadows across the darkened lawn.

"Don't get attached, Izzy. This is a temporary gig."

She nodded her understanding even if he couldn't see it. The queen of self-protection found herself revealing ugly details of her life with a girl she'd known only a few days. But still, she couldn't deny the kindred spirit they seemed to share. "I'll be careful."

"You're doing great, babe. Hang in there."

When her chest seized, she smacked at it and forced a breath because—holy cow—she loved the sound of Peter praising her. Since when did she need a man for that? How did she let *this* man come to mean so much to her?

Tears moistened her eyes. *No. No crying. It's just the stress. No. Crying!*

But Kendrick's house, the sealed windows, double key locks, Seth, Mary Beth, a girl missing. It was all too much for someone lacking any form of emotional stability.

"Izzy? Are you all right?"

"No. I've never been all right though, so I don't know what this is. I hate it."

Weakness.

After Kendrick, she'd never allowed herself to be vulnerable. She had strengthened the foundation, shored up the walls and, for years, she'd been fine. Now Peter Jessup and Courtney Masterson understood her, and who were these people? She barely knew them and yet she shared the horror of her childhood with them. Left herself exposed to their derision. Their judgment. What had she been thinking?

"Izzy, can you get away from there for a while? I'll meet you."

Yes. She didn't have her heavy bag, but Peter could help. He'd open his arms to her and she'd snuggle into him, breathe in his strength, and it would quiet the havoc in her mind.

Maybe she'd fuck him. Get rid of this swirling panic and take control again. She'd spent half her life interchanging sex with power. If she hadn't let the weakness take over, she would have realized she could fix this.

"I need you inside me," she said.

"Helloooooo, Creepy Izzy." *You pain in my ass.* "When did she show up?"

Peter stood on the balcony of the motel staring at the illuminated parking lot and the adjacent pool with its slimy green water. Billy had just flipped for another lap.

Poor bastard must be desperate for something to do to swim in that muck. Although, they'd taken dips in a lot worse.

With Billy driving him batshit and Izzy going Section 8, he wondered who in this twisted threesome would *not* have to be committed.

Shagging Izzy would never be difficult, particularly after they'd experienced it last night—a few times—but this had nothing to do with sex. This was her trying to manipulate a situation she couldn't get comfortable with.

He gripped the phone tighter. "You're dealing with a lot. If Creepy Izzy helps, use her, but we're not bringing sex into it. Sex between us will never be about control."

A sniffle came from the other end of the phone line. "Are you crying?" he asked.

"I think so," she said, and he burst out laughing.

Only Izzy.

"Honey, it's a yes or no thing. You're either crying or you're not."

She laughed then too, but it was a weird sort of snot-filled laugh.

"Peter, I'm freaking out. I don't know if I can do this. It's bringing up too much baggage. Being here, talking about Kendrick. It makes me feel powerless. Like I'm that vulnerable girl again. I despise that."

Leaning over the rail, he said, "Did you ever hear Vic say 'pain is weakness leaving the body'?"

"No."

"That's what you're experiencing. Your compartments are imploding and everything is running together. It's similar to what you told me that night at the cottage. You have to let yourself feel it before you can get past it."

"But I didn't expect this. I didn't expect to miss having

you with me. Telling Courtney about the abuse intensified it."

She missed him. Damn, if that didn't make him smile. It sucked that she considered it a bad thing, but he'd take it. "I'll be there the day after tomorrow. Tell Seth the Jessup Foundation got his paperwork, but that my mother doesn't do the visits. She's sending me instead. We'll do this together."

"Okay. That sounds good."

"For now, you had a major breakthrough with Courtney telling you about Nicole."

"I *think* she meant Nicole. She never said a name."

"Doesn't matter. It's a start. I'll call Sampson and let him know. You're going to bring this girl home Izzy. Remember that."

A car drove by, its rotted muffler drawing his attention.

"Peter?"

"Yep?"

"I think I love you."

A soaring, screaming ball of relief settled him. For weeks now he'd been captivated by her. Add being frustrated beyond belief and worry over her current situation and it equaled a dangerous combination.

One that took him ten years to find.

"I think I love you too. It's good." *But I want you out of that place.*

Izzy sighed. "I know."

"It scares the hell out of you. I can deal with that. I'm not going anywhere. You need to not think so much about it though. You start to freak out when you think too much and *hello,* Creepy Izzy."

"You're right. I trust you. I hope you know that."

That alone couldn't be easy for someone like her.

Someone who had been betrayed in the evilest way by someone she should have been safe with. "We're good, babe."

For a few seconds the only sound was Billy flipping for another lap. Christ, he'd be out there all night.

"By the way," Peter said, "your phone, the one you left here, rang a few times. Do you want me to check it?"

"Yes. It might be something important. Or my uncle is threatening to fire me again."

"Screw your uncle," Peter said, wanting to rip the son of a bitch's heart out. He walked into the motel room, retrieved the phone from the top drawer of the dresser and read the missed calls to her.

"Yep," she said. "It's my office. And my father."

"Call them from a pay phone tomorrow," Peter said. "Don't use the cell I gave you."

If Seth checked her phone he'd have her father's phone number. The office he didn't so much care about because Seth knew where she worked, but having Izzy's personal contacts out there would not be copacetic.

"Speaking of tomorrow," she said. "Seth has a business lunch about twenty miles from here. Cannonsville, I think he said. He invited me to ride along so I could shop while he's at lunch. Apparently they have some touristy stores there. The car ride would be an opportunity to talk to him."

Peter fisted his hand and clamped his eyes shut. As much as he wanted to tell her to stay away from the guy, he knew this was why she was there. "Just stay alert."

"I will."

"Who's the lunch with?"

"I don't know."

Hmmm. Peter sat at the desk, opened his laptop. "Cannonsville?"

"Yes."

He went to MapQuest and got a visual. "I want to know who he's lunching with. What time are you going?"

"We're leaving at eleven-thirty."

Peter sat back, drummed his fingers on the scarred desk. This could work. "We'll drive into Cannonsville tomorrow. Call me after Seth goes into the restaurant. I'll send Billy in there for some takeout so he can see who Seth is with."

Izzy's moan floated over the phone line. "I don't know. What if Seth sees you and then you show up here the next day?"

"Seth isn't going to see me. I'll stay out of sight. Once Billy gets a visual, we wait for the person to leave, and we follow them. I want to know what kind of *business* this guy is doing."

30

THE NEXT MORNING, AFTER A FITFUL SLEEP, ISABELLE WAITED on the bottom step of the front porch for Seth to pull his car around.

The lunch was an hour away. That meant two hours of being alone with Seth. Not something she relished after he'd dragged his hand over her ass at breakfast that morning.

The man was ratcheting up his mating signals. This flirting tactic of hers had to be dealt with carefully. She had to give him just the right amount of encouragement, but not so much that he would think she intended to have sex with him any time soon.

A fine line.

Seth pulled his sparkling sedan around front and she got in, grateful she'd purposely worn knee-length shorts that didn't ride up as she sat. The pink crew neck summer sweater she paired with the shorts gave her an added defense against Seth's wandering eyes.

He gave her a once-over and nodded. "Nice sweater."

She nearly laughed at his disappointment at not seeing

any cleavage, but checked herself. For all she knew, he'd pull off on some deserted road and try to force himself on her. At which time, she'd kick his pathetic ass.

"Thank you for letting me tag along."

Seth smiled and lifted his foot off the brake. Mary Beth appeared on the front porch and he waved to her. She waved back, but her blasting gaze was on Isabelle.

Yikes.

"Mary Beth doesn't like me," she said.

"She doesn't like most people. She's had a tough life. We're—" Seth stopped, shook his head. "I can't get used to Kendrick not being part of this anymore. It's odd. I know you had your differences with him, but he was my partner and friend. He did a lot of good around here."

Isabelle found that hard to believe. "I'm sure." She stared out the window at the sun dappled pasture across the street while her stomach did a quick pitch and roll.

Seth turned onto the road and hit the gas.

"Thank you for setting up the meeting with Peter Jessup. I know your influence got their attention. The funding from outside sources is vital to what we do."

"That's how you support this place? Outside funding."

He nodded. "Yes. Corporate sponsorships, grants, that sort of thing. In fact, I'd like to take you up on your offer of legal help. Would you read a few sponsorship agreements? I've been holding off sending them to our attorney because he's expensive and I've been watching our money."

Perhaps this would get her into his office to snoop in his files. "Of course. I can do it today if you'd like."

Seth smiled, clearly pleased with himself. "I have the agreements on the computer in my office."

The computer. Even better.

"You know," she said. "I've been meaning to ask you

about the bucket drives you mentioned. Do they provide enough money to help an operation of this size?"

"The bucket drives are a way for the residents to take some responsibility. They're expected to help. In turn, we offer assistance in finding work so they can move out on their own. This grant from the Jessup Foundation would be exceptional. We could do a lot of good with that money."

A sliver of guilt sliced her. If this guy were as honest as he played, she'd feel like a first-class dope for setting up this ruse about Peter's visit.

"Seth, I'm just the messenger when it comes to the Jessups. I sent Peter the application and that's all. I don't think I know enough about your organization to vouch for you. I was happy to get the process moving because you've been kind to me, but we're talking about a lot of money. Peter will do his own research. And he *will* be thorough."

Seth glanced at her, his drab hazel eyes intent. "We have nothing to hide."

"You have nothing to worry about then."

"Does Peter know about your history with Kendrick?"

The question landed with a thud. What the hell business was it of his? "Excuse me?"

"I'm not prying—"

"You don't think?"

Seth rolled his eyes and she nearly climbed over and smacked him.

"I think I have a right to know if Peter Jessup has formed opinions regarding my organization. If you've told him about your relationship with Kendrick, he might not look upon us so favorably."

Her *relationship*?

"Peter is fair. Whatever his thoughts about Kendrick are, he won't hold them against you."

"What exactly is your relationship with Peter Jessup?"

Where the heck was this going? "Why do you ask?"

He made a left turn onto another rural road, pulled over and parked. Isabelle swung her head left and right, surveying the surrounding area. No houses, no other cars.

This is it.

She wrapped one hand around the door handle, ready to yank it and run. Spotting her grip on the handle, Seth punched a button on his door and the thump of the lock engaging vibrated against her hand. Locked in.

With her hand still on the door, she turned to him. "Why are we stopping?"

Seth scooted an inch closer and she backed away while escape scenarios materialized and she readied her free hand for a palm strike. "What are you doing?"

His gaze dropped to her chest. "I think you've noticed I've developed an attraction to you, and Peter Jessup is coming to my home. I'd like to know what to expect so I can avoid any complications."

Holy cow. He flopped that right onto the table. Complications. This butthead didn't have a clue. "Peter and I are friends."

You jackass.

He reached a hand toward her breast, a half grin plastered on his face. *Don't let him touch you.* With her free hand, she grabbed his wrist and held it. If necessary, she could flick it backward and twist until the pain left him begging for mercy. "What do you think you're doing?"

"We're never alone. And since you just told me you and Peter are only friends, I thought we could take a few minutes." His grin widened. "Get better acquainted."

Could this guy be any more arrogant? He certainly wasn't the most handsome man she'd ever run into, but he carried himself with self-assurance. Like she was a shoo-in. Then again, she'd probably given him every reason to think so.

She'd have to backpedal. She squeezed his wrist making sure to press her nails into his skin. A low groan came from his throat—the perv liked it. "I don't think that's a good idea. Not here in the middle of a road where anyone can come along." She released him. "I enjoy your company, but next time, ask if you can touch me in an intimate way. That, I insist on."

Seth rubbed two fingers over the spot on his wrist where she'd punctured him. "You are a puzzle, Isabelle. I rather enjoy this game of yours."

Idiot.

He shifted front, his challenging stare never leaving hers. "I'll be sure to ask permission next time."

"Probably a wise move," she said.

THAT EVENING, AFTER LOADING THE LAST OF THE DINNER plates into the dishwasher, Isabelle straightened to find Mary Beth staring at her. Hard. This woman made Creepy Izzy look like a Girl Scout.

"What?" Isabelle asked.

Mary Beth shook her head. "Thank you for helping."

That was weird. Still though, nice of her to say. "If I eat, I help clean. Besides, with Rebecca not feeling well and in bed, you needed the extra hands." Unlike Seth who left the cleaning to the womenfolk. Isabelle's mind wandered back to Peter standing at the kitchen sink the night she had dinner with him and his mother. *He* didn't have a problem washing dishes.

Feeling Mary Beth's eyes on her, Isabelle folded the

dishrag that had been haphazardly thrown on the counter and wiped her hands on her shorts. "I think we're done here. I promised Seth I would review some papers for him."

She'd tossed it out there with nonchalance but, if her plan worked, Mary Beth would wait a few minutes then turn up in the office. With luck, she would pull Seth away and Isabelle could search his office.

When she got to the stairs, she thought back on Peter's earlier phone call informing her they'd followed Seth's lunch date to a maximum-security women's prison an hour away.

Maybe some of the prisoners, upon their release, came to live at the compound?

It made sense, in an odd way, but then again, these women must have committed harsh crimes to be in maximum security. She made a mental note to ask Seth about his screening process. Isabelle hoped the prison system reformed people, but the criminal defense attorney in her knew that wasn't always the case.

Could one of the released prisoners have been staying at the compound and had a falling out with Kendrick? Could she have killed him?

Isabelle climbed the stairs to the second floor thinking about the five families with young children living in the cabins on the property. Would Seth put those children in danger by possibly allowing unreformed inmates to come here? She just didn't know.

She strode down the hall, past her room and Courtney's, then Mary Beth's and her daughter's rooms. At the end of the hallway, on the left, Seth's office door was slightly ajar. She rapped twice.

"Come in," he called, and she stepped in to find him at his desk writing on a legal pad.

The office held the same casually elegant decorating style as the rest of the house. The wood trim gleamed and the burgundy walls brought hominess to the room. The desk lamp replaced the fading sunlight streaming through the large window.

Isabelle sat on one of the black leather chairs in front of the desk and Seth's eyes locked on her with the anxious hunger of a man needing to get laid. The oily slickness dripped over her and, despite her forced smile, an inward groan traveled down her throat. He was definitely stepping up his aggression.

"I thought I'd check that paperwork for you," she said.

An odd look crossed Seth's face and his eyes narrowed. What? Did he expect she was coming to have some quiet time with him?

Not.

"Oh, right. I forgot." He swiveled to his computer, grabbed the mouse and began opening files. "I'll print them for you."

"I can read them on-screen if you'd like. Save the cost of paper and a tree." She fisted a hand in the air. "Go green."

Come on, Seth. Go green with me. We'd save the earth and I'd search your computer files.

He smiled. "Go green. Absolutely."

Yes! A *rat-a-tat-tat* of victory started in her head and Isabelle smiled before moving to the other side of the desk. All she needed was to get him out of the room for a few minutes and she could peruse his hard drive.

Seth stood and spun the chair for her to sit. "I've opened all three files for you. Let me know if you have questions."

When she scooted the chair closer to the screen, he plopped his hand low on her shoulder, the tips of his fingers grazing the rise of her breast. *Hold it, fella.* Her instincts took over before her brain could engage and she stiffened against the unwelcome touch. This jerk just loved testing her.

He snatched his hand away. "I didn't mean to make you nervous."

Sure you did. She breathed deep and thought about her behavior the last few days. She'd been leading him on. Sick as it was, she knew he wanted her, and she'd manipulated it by wearing revealing clothes and prolonging the eye contact. *And let's not forget laughing at his bland jokes.*

Yep. Seth had been reading all those come-hither signals and, after the incident in the car earlier, he was ready to make his move.

The speed of this process left her needing to back him off before he started to question her motives. He probably already had questions about her visit. She'd explained those away as confusion over her strained relationship with Kendrick and her quest for closure.

Now though, this man expected her to jump in the sack with him.

Stall him. She could do it. Sex was a tool she knew the intricacies of.

"Isabelle?"

She glanced up at him. "It's my fault. I didn't mean to flinch. I should have explained when we were in the car today, but I have issues with people touching me. It stems from my mistrust of people."

Ack! Wrong thing to say. *Backpedal.* "Not that I don't trust *you.* I do, but it's ingrained and totally unfair to people who have been kind to me."

Seth's dull hazel eyes softened, and he folded those wandering hands in front of him. "I'll be more careful."

She nodded. "Thank you for understanding."

Their gazes locked for a long moment. She refused to

look away. To waver. Giving in to a man like Seth hadn't been part of her repertoire for years. He finally broke the eye contact and held up his hands. "I didn't mean to make you uncomfortable. It wasn't my intention."

My butt, Isabelle thought because she never heard an apology.

A knock sounded at the door and they both turned to see Mary Beth hovering in the doorway. Finally. Isabelle refrained from blowing out a breath.

Seth grunted and Isabelle sensed the negative energy swirling around her. Old Mary Beth didn't disappoint.

"What is it, Mary Beth?" he asked.

"Can I see you a minute?"

"We're busy."

Isabelle spun back to Seth. "I don't mind. I'll get started on these agreements."

Mary Beth smiled, but it didn't resemble anything close to happiness. This smile was all about her winning a perceived battle. *Knock yourself out, Mary Beth. Just get him out of here for a few minutes.*

"Fine," he said. "I'll be right back."

Isabelle turned to the screen. "I'll be here."

Reading your files.

The second he hit the doorway she reached for the mouse, quickly opened the file directory and scanned it. One was labeled Org Undr Priv and Isabelle double clicked. Various names popped on the screen in front of her. Nothing on Marshall Correctional Facility.

Voices from the first floor—Mary Beth's daughters— drifted up the stairs and Isabelle's fingers stilled on the mouse. Were they coming up?

She heard the front door close and the voices went silent. Must have gone outside.

She clicked on the main directory. Several more folders to review. One marked Business. She clicked on it. Password protected.

Dammit. What could the password be? Birthday? Someone's name? On a whim, she tried Rebecca. No dice. Too simple. Seth wasn't that dumb.

"Isabelle?"

She yelped and the sound rattled around inside her brain.

Caught.

She turned to see Courtney in the doorway. *Deep breath. Slow and deep.* Her heart slammed a vicious thump against her ribcage and she pressed her hand over the spot. This 007 stuff wasn't easy.

"Startled you, huh?" Courtney said, her lips quirking.

Isabelle faked a laugh while she closed the directories she'd been scanning. "Holy cow. You scared me."

Just then Seth stepped into view. "What's going on?"

"Nothing," Isabelle said. "Courtney snuck in and startled me."

"I didn't sneak. I walked."

Isabelle laughed again. "Whatever. What's up, Courtney?"

"Never mind that," Seth said, his voice harsh. "Something has come up and I need to go out. You can do this tomorrow, Isabelle. There's no rush."

"Is something wrong?" She vacated the desk chair so Seth could shut down the computer.

He slid her a sideways glance. "Rebecca is not in her room. Her sisters can't find her and think she's taken off somewhere."

A young, pregnant girl alone in a rural area. Dangerous.

"Can I help you search? Courtney and I can go in my car."
And if I find her first, maybe she'll tell me something.

Seth finished with the computer. "That would help.
Thank you."

Ninety-eight minutes later, Isabelle and Courtney
returned to the compound after receiving the call from Seth
that they'd found Rebecca. Courtney's normally irreverent
mouth had remained firmly shut during the search, and
Isabelle was sure the young woman knew something. She'd
have to work on that later.

She strode into the house, heard voices from the kitchen
and came to a halting stop when she turned into the room
and found Rebecca seated on one of the counter stools, her
feet hooked around the top rung, her shoulders stooped and
her arms wrapped around her torso. The girl was as closed
up as her pregnant body would allow, but Isabelle could still
see her shivering.

What the hell?

Seth stood to one side while Mary Beth flanked the
other. Isabelle stepped forward. "Rebecca, are you all right?"

"She's fine," Seth said.

Isabelle ignored him and focused on Rebecca. She
shoved the girl's long hair out of her face. No blood or
bruises. At least that she could see. Thoughts of a pregnant
girl being beaten slammed into Isabelle and the insidious
rage smothered her. She whirled on Seth. "What
happened?"

"This doesn't concern you." His voice held the flat, life-
less tone of someone barely tolerating her presence.

And oh, how she wanted to hurt this man. Just let him
have a good, solid palm strike. Because deep down, where
her once-healthy soul used to be, Isabelle knew he'd done

something to Rebecca. Looking at him now, his total disregard for her or Rebecca, she saw a truly disgusting person.

"She is shivering, clearly terrified and you want me to mind my own business? I don't think so." She reached a hand to Rebecca and slowly, inch by inch, the girl raised her gaze. Isabelle's pulse hammered. Creepy Izzy eyes. Just dead. Nothing there. This is what Peter sometimes saw.

"No," she whispered.

Rebecca squeezed her hand. "I'm okay."

No, honey, you're not. But Isabelle knew she'd get nothing out of her. That alone made her ill, but there was nothing she could do. Not with Seth hovering. "Are you sure?"

"Yes."

Isabelle nodded, straightened up and left the kitchen because, after staring into those dead eyes, she'd just glimpsed her past.

PETER SNATCHED HIS CELL PHONE OFF THE DRESSER. IZZY'S number. "Hey."

"He did something to her," she said in a rush of words that instantly set Peter on edge.

He closed his eyes, concentrated on slowing his heart rate. "What are you talking about?"

"Rebecca ran off and we all went looking for her. Courtney went with me; Seth and Mary Beth went in the other car. They found her first, brought her home, but she's inside shivering. She's practically in the fetal position. I know he did something to her and I want to kill him."

The words flew at Peter and he took one, two, three deep breaths. Calm.

But Izzy was seriously hopped up. And he couldn't get to

her. Nor could she leave the compound. Not with that girl possibly in danger.

Izzy was on her own.

The alpha dog's nightmare scenario. Right here. "Where are you?"

"On the front lawn. I had to get out of there. Peter, you should see her. She's a mess. I couldn't see any bruises, but I *know* something happened to her. What can I do? How do I get her to talk to me?"

"Whoa, hang on. You're way too strung out. If you go at her, she'll get scared and clam up."

"I don't know what it is... The way Seth just stood there, not caring that a pregnant teenager was shivering made me nuts. I saw Creepy Izzy in her eyes, Peter." She drew a hard breath. "I saw what you see and I hate it. Kendrick and this man did something to her."

Kendrick? WTF? "Iz, you need to calm down. Right now. Close your eyes and get your shit together because if you go back into that house this way, you will screw up."

Peter, his head throbbing, covered the phone with his hand and spun back to Billy. "Something is fucked-up over there."

"Don't *you* get nuts," Billy said. "You've got that psycho Monk look. Chill."

"Peter, I have to go. Seth is coming outside."

"Iz, don't hang—"

The line went dead.

Crap. "Izzy?"

Listening to nothing, Peter lost it. That same boiling anger that triggered the beating to Billy snapped at him. Teased him. Poked him. Insisted he set the beast free.

"Oh, son of a bitch," Billy said. "Here we go again. You touch me and I'll lay you to waste."

Peter stepped back. Then moved sideways. Then back the other way. Just random, haphazard movement. Anything to vent the rage filling him, because he was so fucking useless. He couldn't help Izzy. He'd let an emotionally tortured woman go into a place where who knew what kind of sexual depravity existed.

And for her, that would be suicide.

He made a move for the door, but Billy jumped in front of him. Made himself one hell of a big, tempting target.

"Forget it," he said. "You'll blow this whole thing if you go there. Let her work it out."

But the rage kept coming, coming, coming, and Peter stepped back. He needed to hit something and unleash the insanity devouring him. He opened his mouth, sucked huge gulps of air. *Don't hit him. Don't hit him. Don't hit him.*

"Work it out," Billy said, tossing a pillow at him.

Peter clutched the pillow between his hands, curled his fingers into its softness and squeezed until his body quaked. He needed to destroy something. Go absolutely fucking apeshit and get rid of this pummeling agony. Total nutcase. Suddenly, feathers flew into the air, just—*poof!*—because, apparently, he'd ripped the pillow in half.

Feathers floated on the air and Billy put his hands on his hips. "I'm not cleaning this shit up."

But Peter stared down at the remaining halves of the pillow still in his hands. His straining muscles quivered and he released the tension in his arms, let the assassinated pillow fall to the floor. *Wow.*

Then his phone rang, the sound piercing the turmoil in his brain before he saw Izzy's name on the screen. He fumbled and punched the button while his pulse triple-timed. "Are you okay? Don't ever hang up like that. Leave your phone on so I know what's happening."

"Shhh! I have to hurry. Seth apologized. He's trying to put me off. No chance. I'm heading inside to check on Rebecca."

Peter pounded a fist against his head. "Listen, you need to take a couple of minutes before you go back in. Settle down some. Please."

"I will. I'll feel better when you're here."

Peter glanced down at the mangled pillow. "Yeah. Me too."

"I need to go, but I'm okay. Really."

"Call if you need me."

He hung up, tossed the phone on the bed and dropped onto it himself. Feathers leaped into the air, a not-so-subtle reminder of what an insane asshole he was. He dug his fingers into his head. Too much pressure.

"Dude," Billy said. "You gotta stop thinking you can save everyone. Izzy is a smart girl. She's a survivor. And if you don't quit trying to manage a situation that's beyond your control, you'll give yourself a coronary. And get her hurt."

Peter reclined his aching, spent body and spread his arms wide. "You may find this hard to believe, but you're right. I don't know how to stop though."

"It's simple. Stop trying to control every damned thing."

Peter snorted. *It sounds simple.*

31

Isabelle pulled into the gravel parking lot of the so-called regional airport, an airstrip really. The morning sun's rays danced over the steering wheel and her twitchy hands.

Right now, all she needed was to set eyes on Peter in one of his nutty do-rag-combat boot ensembles. Some sense of normalcy would help the hollow agitation she'd been experiencing the past two days.

She spotted him sitting under the overhang of the office, his arms stretched casually across the back of the bench, and the voice in her head said *yes*. Peter made everything in her life easier.

She knew he had been sitting there for almost an hour. Billy had dropped him off early because they didn't want to chance Isabelle being followed and someone seeing Peter getting out of the car rather than a private plane.

Peter rose from the bench, straightened his slacks—*dress clothes*—and grabbed his duffle and jacket. He smiled that million-dollar smile and all Isabelle wanted was to get her hands on him.

She loved him in his quirky do-rag outfits, but seeing

him in tailored black slacks and a French cuffed shirt kicked her heart into overdrive.

Hot, hot, hot.

Steamy hot.

Like her body had gone through an incinerator.

She punched the air conditioner up as he opened the door and tossed his duffle and jacket into the back seat. Normalcy. Maybe normalcy meant Peter. Regardless of what he wore. Her stomach dropped.

"Hey," he said.

Unable to keep from touching him, she popped the release button on her seatbelt, leaned over the console and kissed him until her toes curled. Her midsection caught fire when he started that sweeping thing with his tongue and slid his hands under her shirt. The rough texture of his fingers glided over her back, made her think of the night at the motel and what it felt like to have those fingers inside her.

The voice in her head again whispered *yes*. Fun Izzy.

But Creepy Izzy burst forward. *Don't give yourself over*.

Controlling the physical and emotional with Peter was becoming a hassle. Particularly after the I-think-I-love-you-thing. Did she even know what she was doing anymore? She backed away from him before she climbed over the console and did him right there in the airport lot.

"I'm guessing you weren't followed," he said, his eyes sparkling, "because if you were, they just got a good show."

She grinned at him and rebuckled her seat belt. "I wasn't followed. On these quiet roads I would have noticed. Plus, I explored a little bit and found a dirt road in the middle of a farm that's in foreclosure. I would definitely have spotted someone."

"Izzy, you're getting good at this."

She put the car in gear, gave him a head to toe once-over. "Buckle up. And, can I just say, you are sizzling today?"

He laughed. "Is this your way of trying to get me to dress up more?"

"Not at all. I'm just wondering if you and Billy went shopping yesterday."

"Hell no. I don't buy dress clothes off the rack. I had Vic overnight me some stuff from my closet."

He doesn't buy his clothes off the rack. That cracked her up and, after the drama of the night before, it felt so good to laugh. "How very blue blood of you."

She floored the gas pedal, and the tires spun against the gravel parking lot. The country roads made driving a whole lot more fun because she could push the pedal.

"Hey," Peter said, "I'm a guy who paid twelve ninety-nine for his last pair of shorts, so don't think I'm a snob. I'm not comfortable in dress clothes. If I'm going to wear them, I'm getting them made for my body. I don't want to think about if they fit right. Plus, people won't look at me funny because I have the wrong shirt on with my pants."

This from a man who wore combat boots with his shorts. Isabelle glanced over at him, but quickly brought her eyes back to the road. Only Peter could be secure enough to admit his weakness with dress clothes. "I hope you never stop surprising me. I love that about you."

He gave her a happy grin. "I am who I am, babe."

Fine with her. As long as he kept kissing her and rubbing those big hands over her like he just did.

Oh, boy. She shouldn't have gone there because, yes, the itching in her legs started again.

What the hell?

This could not be happening. *No. No. No.* Her body was *not* craving this man. No sirree. Her *mind* always decided on sex. Always. *No fair changing the plan.* She didn't need a man. Men were tools. A means to an end. When she wanted sex, she got sex. Sometimes it was good, sometimes not, but that was before Peter Jessup marched into her life and screwed the whole thing up.

Damn him.

Panic crawled up her body gobbling all remnants of rational thought along the way. Her chest collapsed and she gripped the steering wheel harder.

Concentrate. Flip the switch.

She came upon the abandoned farm, pressed the brake and swung a hard left onto the dirt road in the middle of an open field.

"Whoa," Peter said. "I love a good ride, but let's not get killed in the process."

The crumbling barn she'd spied on the trip out came into view and she braked again, turned onto the patch of dirt in front of the barn and, because the doors were thrown open—a sign from the universe for sure—she drove straight in and slammed the car into park.

Peter snorted a laugh and looked at her like she'd just run naked through a nursing home. "Nice barn?"

For what she needed, yes it was.

She left the car running, climbed over the console and straddled him as the blast from the air conditioner hit the back of her thighs. Her micro-miniskirt dug into her and she hiked it up. Peter drew his eyebrows together and backed away, but the seat kept him from going anywhere.

"Iz?"

"Don't start yammering at me." She reached down and started on his belt buckle. "I don't want to hear about Creepy Izzy or Fun Izzy because I don't know who the hell I am right now. It's all jumbled in my head, and it's your fault." She stripped the belt from him, tossed it to the back-seat and started on his pants. The sudden swell of his erection poked at her inner thigh.

Oh, yes. Come to mama.

He grabbed her wrists, but she yanked free, caught sight of his wild, freaked-out eyes and fisted his shirt in her hands. "I need you. With you it feels good and I need to feel good. Now. Right. *Now*." She gripped his shirt tighter. "Can you do this for me?"

"Iz?"

"What?"

"You're wrinkling my shirt."

Tears flooded her eyes and she pounded on his chest. "Screw the shirt. I know you think I'm crazy. Maybe I am, but I can't do this anymore. Nothing in my world is in my control and I hate it. But I need to get rid of this panic and you are the only person that does that for me. I hate you for that. I hate you for throwing my life upside down and making me think I need you. I don't know who I am anymore."

She smacked him on the chest again, but he sat there calm as could be. How incredibly humiliating that she should fall apart.

Over a man. A man that would probably eviscerate her.

Then the stupid, blasted sobbing started and she struggled to take a breath, one measly breath. That's all she needed. But no. She couldn't do this. Could. Not. Do. This. It hurt too much.

But then Peter whipped his arms around her, pulled her against him. "I know who you are. *I* know."

She tried to push away, but he locked his hands together and held her close.

"Stop," he said. "I'm not going anywhere." The warmth

of his breath against her ear, that steady reassurance he was so good at, silenced her and she snuggled into him.

"It's okay," he said.

She inhaled, let it back out slow and dropped her head to his shoulder. "I need you inside me and I don't want to be analyzed."

"Iz?"

Dammit. "What?"

"I'm not...you know...*prepared* for this."

The relief ravaged her and she sat up. "Condom?"

He nodded.

"I've got one." She reached for her purse on the back seat.

He grinned and popped the seat to recline. "That's what I love about *you*. Crazy as a loon, but always prepared."

"Shut up and get your pants off."

"Yes, ma'am."

He lifted his hips, slid his pants down, then shoved his hands under her skirt and helped her push her panties off. Sex in the front seat of a car, a small car, was no easy feat and she banged her knee against the doorframe. "Ow."

"I'll see if I can fix that for you."

His fingers were suddenly inside her and she sucked in a breath, exhilarating in his touch. "Fix what?"

"Thought so." But he pulled his fingers away—*darn*—so he could tend to the condom. Could he not multitask?

He grinned at her again. "Don't be smug," she said.

"I guess you riding me like a rodeo queen can come off my fantasy list."

Oh, yes, she thought when he entered her, the mixture of his groan and her sigh filling the car and comingling with the radio. He dug his fingers into her thighs, pushing her down and she rocked her hips, needing him deeper and deeper until they reached that part of her that had been locked away so many years ago. The part she never knew she'd been waiting to offer someone.

She vanished in the feel of him, his body under hers, the wanting from both of them until her core caught fire. The coiling inside her began to unwind and everything, except the two of them loving each other, faded.

Peter's hands went under her shirt and bra to her breasts. The chaotic spinning started over again and she groaned.

Too much.

Please let him be the one.

Rob Thomas's voice from the radio floated around her. Something about being touched by a loving hand. Yes. Finally. A man that loved her.

Peter closed his eyes, "Ah, shit. I can't wait."

She smiled. "It's okay."

But he reached down, used his fingers to search for the spot that might send her over the edge. *Please. Please. Let it happen.*

A blast of sparking colors erupted around her. She dug her fingers into his shirt while layer upon layer of pressure rose inside her. It climbed higher and higher until it reached her throat, captured her breath.

Let me be normal. Just once.

The breath she'd been holding blew apart. Her body turned liquid, and the kaleidoscope of colors erupted behind her eyes. A low, guttural moan sounded in her throat as her body and mind—yes, all of her—wrapped around the sensation of total release.

Finally.

Hot tears shot down her cheeks and she sat forward to

get even closer and feel his breath on her skin. *Please, no shame.* This was too perfect for the shame.

Peter seized and cried out with the force of his own orgasm, and Isabelle snuck her hands under his shirt to the hot skin. She did this to him. This crazy, mind-blowing thing she couldn't yet describe. "I love you." She cuddled into him, and the scent of his soap lingered when he slipped his arms around her.

The *kuh-kunk* of his heartbeat bounced against her ear and she smiled. She'd finally made love to a man. Fun Izzy wasn't a virgin anymore. And it couldn't have been more perfect. Even if it did happen in a deserted barn that would probably collapse on them at any second. At least she'd die happy.

"I love this," she said.

He laughed. "Me too."

She sat up slowly to preserve the last few seconds of their bodies being joined. He grazed his finger down her cheek and kissed her with a tenderness that touched her soul.

"I'm terrified," she said. "Should it feel like this?"

"Absolutely."

Peter pulled his sunglasses off and whistled as Izzy turned into the compound's driveway. This being his first up-close survey of the place, he wanted to sear it into his brain. The magnificent white Victorian, complete with covered porch and high turret, must have been five thousand-square-feet. The healthy shrubs surrounding the porch were obviously well cared for, and Peter wondered just how much cash Seth and Kendrick had dumped into this palace.

He glanced up and counted the windows on the first and second floor.

"Which room is yours?" he asked.

"Second floor. Third from the right. Although, you'll be staying in that room and I'm moving in with Courtney. No more rooms at the inn."

He shot a look at the second floor. "That room is where?"

"Right next door. There's an adjoining bath."

"Second window from the right?"

"Yes. Why?"

He shrugged. "Giving Billy the layout."

Izzy parked the car in front of the wraparound porch. "What's he doing while you're here?"

"I have him checking out that women's prison. Something's bugging me. You need to get into those protected files on Seth's computer."

She rolled her eyes. "No fooling, Sherlock. I'm working on it."

Seth Donner stepped onto the porch wearing navy pants and a collared white shirt. "He always dress that way?"

"Every day," she said. "Why?"

"Just curious if he dressed normally for a visit from the Jessup Foundation." Peter opened the door and checked his fly. Yep. All good. Considering Izzy damn near humped him to a good death. He snorted a laugh, got out and reached into the back seat for his duffle and jacket while shoplifting a look at Izzy's ass when she stepped from the car.

He grunted. This woman got him stoked.

"Hi, Seth," she said in that purring voice she used when she amped up the sex on some poor schmuck.

He shook off the thought and stepped around the car to see Donner's eyes on her in a way that tore into Peter's flesh.

Ho-kay. She had told him her plan that first day when

she'd marched in wearing the stripper clothes. She had a body that affected men and, if it could get her what she needed, she'd use it. He knew this. He did. Didn't make it any easier to watch. He'd have to suck it up. Stay focused on the mission.

He extended his hand to Donner. "Peter Jessup."

"I'm Seth. Welcome."

Peter glanced up at the house. "Nice place."

"Thank you. We've put a lot of work into it." Seth stepped back and waved Peter and Izzy by. "Come inside. Isabelle will show you where you are staying and we can get started."

We'll get started all right, Peter thought as he climbed the steps of the big Victorian.

32

LATER THAT DAY, AFTER TOURING THE PROPERTY AND TALKING to any available residents, even those staying in the cabins, Peter wandered back to the main house to snoop. Izzy was right about the abundance of pregnant women.

Hell, maybe her theory about not drinking the water was spot-on. He might want to keep his hands off her while here or she'd wind up with a bun in the oven. A vision of her athletic body swelled with pregnancy flashed in his mind. Normally that vision would scare the ever-loving shit out of him, but for some reason, today, he thought it kind of hot.

If he did his math right on the number of pregos running around the compound the count would be five. Two of whom were teenagers and included Mary Beth's daughter. The other was a sixteen-year-old girl living with her parents and two younger siblings in one of the cabins.

That girl's father didn't just have a bug up his ass, he had a pterodactyl up there. Peter couldn't blame the guy. Out of work, drowning in debt and busting his ass doing fundraising calls for Seth's organization. The guy barely had time to breathe and his anger came off him like a monster truck on the warpath.

Peter reached the back door and spotted Courtney and Mary Beth in the kitchen preparing dinner. He had to forget about the guy from the cabin and concentrate on these two.

"Hello, ladies," he said stepping into the large open kitchen. Sunlight bounced off the granite countertops. Izzy had told him about the granite and he was equally baffled at such an expense for a non-profit.

He stood on the other side of the large center island trying not to stare at the permanent scowl carved into Mary Beth's face. The woman had some miles on her for sure. Her dark, gray-speckled hair was held back by an elastic band— an elastic band?—and only accentuated her perpetual state of pissed off.

Then there was Courtney. When her bowling ball-sized blue eyes grabbed hold, a man had to look. Had to. It was ingrained. Plus, she seemed like a girl who would take someone down or die trying. He liked it. Considering he often felt that way himself.

He'd intended to ask a few questions, but he caught sight of a door just off the kitchen. Seth had neglected to show him that area on the earlier tour of the house. He walked over and tried the knob. Locked. He rapped a knuckle against it. "What's this door?"

"The basement," Courtney said.

"Why is it locked?"

She hesitated. And rubbed her nose. *Let the lying commence.*

"Seth keeps personal stuff there. He doesn't want people poking around," Mary Beth said.

"The door is always locked?"

She shot him a what-the-fuck look. Okay. Now he definitely needed to know what was behind door number one.

"Seth has the only key," Courtney said. "Well, Kendrick had one also, but I'm not sure where it is now."

The vibe in the room morphed into a charged current and Peter's ears began to buzz. These ladies were not comfortable. Mary Beth had gone into rigor mortis and Courtney suddenly avoided eye contact.

Obviously, they didn't want him asking about the basement. He absolutely had to get his ass down there. Peter copped another look at the lock. A dead bolt. On a basement used for storage? Not buying it. Lucky for him he knew how to get by a dead bolt.

He smacked his hands together and moved to where the women stood. "Can I help with dinner?"

Courtney laughed. "You're kidding, right?"

"Nope."

She blew out a breath. "You want to ask questions."

A girl after his own rebellious heart. No wonder Izzy liked her. He grinned. "That's true. But I do like to cook."

Mary Beth stared at him, her eyes showing nothing. Nada. This woman might as well have been comatose for all the body language she offered. "Let's wait until Seth is here."

Peter slid his gaze to Courtney. "Well," she said, "*I* want to get it over with. Rich boy, have at it."

Rich boy? Heh. She had a monster set of stones on her. All he had to figure out was just how rebellious she could be. Could he push her hard enough that she'd rat on Seth? That's what they needed. Izzy was having trouble getting into Seth's computer, and Peter's own investigation of the residents had turned up squat so far. They needed a stool pigeon. And Courtney just might grow a damn nice set of wings.

.   .   .

Isabelle, wide-awake and all too aware of Peter's presence on the other side of the bathroom door, studied the ceiling. She glanced at the digital clock sitting on the nightstand between the two double beds in Courtney's room. Eleven forty-seven.

On the other bed, Courtney's breathing came in soft jolts, and Isabelle smiled at the girly version of snoring. She sat up. The bathroom light snaked under the door. Peter was still awake.

It took her three seconds to slip out of bed and get to the bathroom. With one last peek at Courtney, she closed the pocket door on their side and slid Peter's door open.

His head snapped up but he remained seated on the bed with a book cradled in his lap. He was bare-chested—*my stars*—with the sheet thrown over his lower body, and her blood turned to a hot, syrupy mess.

"Hey," he whispered. "I thought you were sleeping."

She padded into the room, sat on the edge of the bed. "No luck."

After tucking a strand of hair behind her ear, he said, "You need to shut your brain off." He tossed the book aside, scooted over and held the sheet up. "Get in. I'll rub your back."

She laughed, but kept it low in case anyone happened to be in the hallway. "That's the last thing I expected you to say."

"I know. It's shocking."

With her heart thumping, she crawled into the warm sheets and rolled to her side, her back facing him. "Peter?"

"Yeah?"

"Please tell me you have pants on." Because if he didn't, she'd want to jump him.

"Shorts. I can make them go away."

But then, as promised, his hands were on her back kneading away the knots, and she wanted nothing more than to stay just the way they were. "This is nice."

"Sure is." He kissed the back of her shoulder. "You okay?"

She nodded, letting her body float into the glory of his hands. "I keep thinking about how I can get the computer passwords from Seth. I was in the office with him today, but I was too far away to see when he typed in the password. He doesn't trust me yet."

"Iz, lighten up on yourself. You've been here less than a week. Give it time."

That was the problem. She didn't have time. Three weeks was all she had and then, if she didn't get back home, she could kiss her job goodbye. Besides, she didn't think she could handle three weeks of this place. She'd already chewed her fingernails to the quick.

"How do I get into that computer?"

"I was thinking about that." He drove his thumb into her shoulder.

"Ow."

"Ooh, honey, that's a killer knot right there."

No lie there, but the piercing pain from him working the kink evaporated and the subsequent release felt sooooo good.

"I need to talk to our computer specialist at Taylor Security, but I think we can send Seth an email that's embedded with a virus that'll download all his files. Then I can have Janet hack into them."

Mmmm. Hacking. Right.

Isabelle stretched a little. "That's good."

He stopped rubbing. "Are you listening?"

"Not really. No." She patted her shoulder. "Keep

rubbing. Please."

"Nope." He rolled away. "My turn."

So not fair. She groaned her protest and sat up, ready to repay her debt, but unlike him, couldn't get enough leverage from her spot beside him to do a decent massage. "Lay on your stomach." He did as he was told and she straddled him.

"Yay, me," Peter cracked.

That earned him a smack on the head before she went to work on his shoulders.

"What do you know about the basement?" he whispered.

"Nothing. Haven't been down there."

"I'll do a sneak and peek. Courtney got cagey with me today when I asked her about it."

"She's always cagey. Plus, she's uptight about the baby. I don't think she wants to give it up. I'm afraid she's making a mistake."

"Okay." He lifted his head. "You need to get off me. My mind is everywhere but on this conversation, and shagging you here is a bad idea." She climbed off him and he shot her one of his movie-star smiles. "You tend to moan."

A horrified breath lodged in her throat. "I do *not*."

"Yeah, you do. It's a constant loop in my brain. I'm a walking hard-on most of the time."

Oh, now that formed a picture. Isabelle leaned in and trailed her tongue down his neck. "And the problem with that is?"

He pushed her away. "I'll discuss the intricacies of it at another time. Back to Courtney. She got here through a counseling center. Tomorrow's Family Network?"

"Yes."

"I sent Billy there today. Told him to say his girlfriend

was pregnant and he wanted to know about adoption possibilities."

If Billy found something that would give them a lead they could get this thing moving and she could go home. With Peter.

Creepy Izzy started her normal chatter. *Don't be thinking long-term. He's a restless spirit and will be gone as soon as Vic clears him for work.*

Screw off, Creepy Izzy. At least momentarily. "Did he find anything?"

Peter rolled over, wrapped an arm around her and pulled her close. "They told him to bring the mother in and they'd discuss it. That place isn't right. I can feel it."

"They could have talked Courtney into giving the baby up for adoption. She did say the decision has already been made. I thought that was odd since she could still change her mind."

"I'm gonna push her on that. She'll probably clam up on me, but we'll see."

Isabelle inched closer, ran her hand over the springy dark hair on his chest. "She's scared. She has nowhere to go. No family or job. I told her I'd help her, but she backed off."

Peter grabbed her hand and squeezed. "You like her?"

"She's spunky. Tells it like it is. Most people make you wonder what they're thinking. I think she can do more with her life, but she needs a step up."

Silence hung between them for a second.

"If you want to help her," he said, "we can move her to Jersey and hook her up with my mother and her foundation. If that's what you want."

Isabelle sat up, and the wonder of being able to change Courtney's life took hold. "Your mother would do that?"

He batted his eyes. "If we ask nicely."

"Don't tease me. I could have wound up like Courtney. Angry, promiscuous and mad at the world, but my parents —my father specifically—wouldn't give up on me. Courtney doesn't have that."

He leaned over and kissed the tip of her nose. "I'm not kidding. It's no free ride, though. If Courtney screws up, she'll be cut loose. My mother is big on education. She'll want her to have some sort of career plan. Does Courtney even have a high school degree?"

"No. But she's taking an online GED class. She's almost done."

He smiled. "Good for her."

Getting Courtney out of this place, and giving her the opportunity to live a fulfilling life, one where she would know she deserved more than some quasi halfway house, suddenly became Isabelle's mission.

"Yes. That's what I want to do. If she agrees."

Peter nodded. "I'll talk to my mother. Now you need to go back to your room because I'm gonna break into the basement."

33

Long after he sent Izzy back to her room, Peter tossed his book aside. Everyone had to be asleep by now.

He rolled off the bed, retrieved his T-shirt from the floor and pulled it on. After jamming his cell phone and microflashlight into the pocket of his cargo shorts, he slipped on running shoes and crawled under the bed. Upon arriving, he had loosely sewn his gun into the box spring in case the room got tossed while he was away.

Always paid to be cautious.

He secured the gun into his waist holster and draped his T-shirt over it.

His lock-picking tools were next. They were stashed in the lining of his duffle bag along with a few pairs of latex gloves. He snatched the tools and a set of gloves and shoved the bag back into the closet.

Ready to roll.

He flipped off the light and let his eyes adjust to the darkness before opening the bedroom door and sneaking a look into the hallway.

Off to work.

The silence of the house set his senses buzzing as the sweetness of adrenaline devoured him.

Thank you. He still loved the rush. Maybe he wasn't losing his edge.

He slammed his eyes shut. *Concentrate.* Fuck the negative thoughts.

The thick carpeting absorbed his footfalls as he descended the stairs with slow, deliberate steps. He picked up his pace, eyes darting left and right, until he reached the bottom, swung around the railing and moved down the hall to the kitchen doorway.

A peek around the corner.

More darkness.

And silence.

Nobody awake.

Nice.

Moonlight through the back windows lit the path to the basement door. *Talk about a sign from above.* He made the sharp right into the alcove and went to work on the lock.

Fifteen seconds and he'd be in.

Ten...eleven...twelve...boom.

Daddy's home.

With gentle hands, he turned the knob and pulled, but the door stuck to the frame and made a scraping noise. He gritted his teeth. *Dammit.*

He stood motionless, waiting for any sound from the second floor.

Nothing.

Go to work.

Once behind the door he slipped on the latex gloves. He had touched the outside of the door earlier in the day so his prints on the knob were easily explainable. Once the gloves were in place, he flipped the lock. Considering his dumb luck, he wasn't taking a chance someone would wander by and spot the unlocked door.

The staircase was standard issue with uncarpeted steps and he made sure to step lightly. He reached the bottom, pulled his flashlight and turned it on. A white tiled floor came into view under the light's beam.

Finished basement.

For storage?

He swept the light up and around the room. Stark white floor-to-ceiling cabinets with glass doors sat on one end with some sort of supplies. He stepped closer as the hum in his bloodstream kicked up.

The beam of the light landed on a shelf loaded with gauze bandages, stethoscopes and some kind of salad-tong looking things. Also in the cupboards were bottles of saline, basins, alcohol wipes and a few boxes of iodine pads.

He spun toward the countertop and spotted jars of cotton balls, cotton tip applicators and a couple boxes of gloves.

The drawers were unlocked and he opened the top one, aimed the flashlight on the contents; K-Y jelly, a prescription pad and a wheel chart that said Birth Date Calculator. *What the hell?*

Peter spun and shined the flashlight across the room. It landed on an examining table.

He hauled ass to the table and flicked the light across it. Stirrups in the upright position.

Thoughts hammered like dozens of live missiles and he surveyed the room once more. The cabinets, the supplies, the stethoscope. The exam table. Ladies and gentlemen, an OB/GYN office in the basement.

A closet on the right drew his attention. The door was unlocked, but inside he found four shelves with three drawers on the bottom. He opened the top drawer and found hospital gowns. The next one held paper blankets for covering patients. The bottom drawer was locked and Peter put his pick to work. Within seconds, he slid the drawer open, shined his light on the contents and saw women's clothing. Carefully, he pulled out a roomy white shirt, blue shorts and a pair of white underwear. Definitely maternity clothes. A golf ball-sized stain covered the crotch of the underwear and instantly he knew.

Blood.

Footsteps sounded above and he shot a look at the ceiling. The sound halted somewhere around the kitchen-family room border.

A sudden burst of voices, then immediate quiet filtered through the floor. The television volume being lowered.

Fuck me. Someone was watching television. At 3:00 a.m.

Un-friggin-believable.

Peter stuck the flashlight between his teeth, set the garments back and, using his pick, relocked the drawer. He dug out his cell phone and fired a text to Izzy. *Please hear your phone buzz*. Otherwise he'd be stuck in the basement all night and everyone would wake up in the morning wondering where he was.

Shit.

Thirty seconds later his phone vibrated in his hand. *Yes*.

With swift fingers, he replied: *Stuck in bsmnt. Someone watching TV. Get them out of there.*

The answer was a swift and decisive *Okay*.

"That's my girl."

He stood in the center of the basement listening for footsteps. Five minutes had passed, so any time now, she should be hitting the first floor. The sudden click of heels tapped above him. She must have put sandals on so he'd hear her. Smart girl.

He tracked her steps to the kitchen, then heard muffled voices. After a few minutes, the clicking heels started again. This time toward the front door. And then silence. He held his phone in his hand waiting for it to buzz with a text that said no go, but nothing happened.

She must have gotten the person out of there. At least he hoped so.

He made his way up the stairs, silently flipped the lock and peeked out. The kitchen light had been turned off. Nobody there. *Good signal, Iz.*

After stepping out and making sure he was alone, he used the pick to lock the basement door. That took longer than he would have liked, but he finally nailed it and, with his back to the wall, crept into the kitchen and took a gander around the doorway. Nothing. The front door was open a crack and he heard Izzy's voice.

On the porch. Damn, she was good.

He started up the stairs and heard Seth say, "I'll get more lemonade."

Son of a bitch.

Peter spun around and made like he was coming down the steps just as Seth came in.

"Oh, hello," he said, his squirrely face a cross between guilty schoolboy and oh shit!

Peter continued down the stairs. "I heard voices. Everything all right?"

"Yes. I was watching television and Isabelle came down for some lemonade."

Lemonade. Right.

He walked past Seth, stuck his head out the door and saw Izzy sitting cross-legged on the porch swing. She kept her eyes squared with his, completely unfazed. Peter checked on Seth, but he was already in the kitchen.

"Sorry if we woke you," Izzy said, half-grinning at him.

He nodded. "No problem. Just wanted to check."

"Everything is fine," she said, heavy on the eye contact.

Yep. She had this handled. Still though, he'd wait in his room until he heard her shuffle back to bed. If she didn't come up in half an hour he'd figure out a way to get her back upstairs.

"Don't stay up too late," he said.

Several minutes later he crawled into bed with the vision of that medical office and the bloody underwear glued to his brain.

Could Nicole Pratt have been pregnant? If so, was she killed because of it? And were those her clothes?

34

At eight-thirty the next morning, with the sun pounding onto the patio bricks, Peter held the back door open for Izzy.

He stalked toward the middle of the grass and slugged a shot of coffee from his mug.

More. Coffee.

Sleep had eluded him after the sneak and peek, and mainlining coffee would be the only way to boot him up. The overload would make him irritable as all hell, but life sucked that way. After all these years he was used to it.

"Where is everyone?" he asked.

"Seth took Mary Beth and the girls into town. They should be back by lunchtime. Courtney is in the shower. Where are we going?"

"Away from the house. I don't want to be overheard."

He stopped in the middle of the backyard where the swings rocked in the wind. This fucking place. It looked like Fantasyland, but nothing about it sat right with him. And the doctor's office in the basement was just the tip of it.

These assholes weren't even trying to hide the money they threw around. What the hell would a non-profit be doing with five thousand dollars worth of granite counter-tops? Not to mention the fancy appliances and flat screen television.

He turned to Izzy. Her eyes were puffy from lack of sleep and edginess filled him.

"Nice work last night," he said. "I'm not happy Seth is so taken with you, but it worked."

He gulped more coffee. Seth Donner wanted Izzy. Simple fact. Nothing shocking considering her unbelievable hotness, but having her flaunt it to get what she needed was tough to watch.

She knew how to get the job done, but he didn't want her using her body to do it. Or at least he wanted her to be uncomfortable about it. And he didn't seem to be getting his way in either case. Which pissed him off.

Don't judge.

Reminding himself of her sexual abuse and the resulting birth of Creepy Izzy kept him from going insane. She thought of sex as a weapon in her arsenal. Nothing emotional about it.

Maybe this pissed-off-at-the-world attitude was about Seth. Or, maybe Peter was freaking exhausted. Not so much physical exhaustion. He could go a couple of days on minimal sleep. But the mental shit was eating him alive. He wanted Izzy out of this place and away from Seth. Something fucked-up was happening here, and she didn't have the undercover experience to recognize danger.

"What did you find in the basement?"

Peter inclined his head, taking in his favorite do-rag wrapped around her head. "It's a medical office."

This information must have slammed into her with the force of a category five hurricane because she stepped back. "In the *basement*?"

"It's set up like an OB/GYN office. Medical supplies. An examining table with stirrups. The whole bit. Where does Courtney go for her doctor's appointments?"

Izzy shook her head. "I don't know. I offered to drive her, but she said it's not a problem."

Peter exhaled a sickening breath. "Probably because they're doing them in the *basement*."

"But who's playing doctor?"

"Don't know." He drained the last of his coffee and rolled the mug between his palms. "I found a set of women's maternity clothes and underwear with some blood. Not a lot, but enough."

Izzy put her hands over her face and slid them down. "Oh my God."

"We need to know if Nicole Pratt was pregnant when she left here. If she left."

Then I want to get you the hell out of here.

Peter had broken the supreme rule of not getting emotional about an op. Knowing he could screw up and get Izzy hurt plunged into him.

Billy's advice about not trying to control every damned thing filtered back. *Focus on the mission.*

"I talked to Janet at my office. She'll send you an email to forward to Seth. She'll plant a virus in the email that should let her grab what's on his hard drive. In the meantime, we need to ask Courtney about the basement. See what she has to say." He inhaled sharply as the full brunt of the coffee attacked his empty stomach. "This coffee is killing me."

Izzy eyed him. "*I'll* talk to Courtney. You're crabby and I don't want her upset."

Peter shrugged. "I'm not going to upset her."

But he would push her. Hard. No problem there. Not if it meant finding Nicole Pratt. A vision of a dead pregnant girl flashed into his mind. Jesus, he'd never get that out of there.

"She's skittish. If you intimidate her, we'll get nothing."

The patio door opened and Courtney, dressed in an oversized sleeveless maternity top and shorts, came outside. The strap of the top slipped down her shoulder and she righted it before approaching them.

"Hey, Isabelle," she said. "Rich boy, you're dressed down today."

Peter glanced down at his khaki shorts and golf shirt. If she only knew. "Yeah. This is more my speed."

Courtney's gaze swung between them. "What are you guys doing?"

"I was having coffee before heading down to the cabins to find the residents I missed yesterday."

Izzy nodded. "He's trying to get all his interviews done today because he's leaving in the morning."

Yeah, he had one day to wrap this shit up and get her out of here.

He was so screwed.

Unless someone—like Courtney—started talking.

Courtney shifted back to Peter. "How's that going? The interviews?"

"Well, I'll tell ya," he said in a tone Izzy clearly didn't like because she shot him a WTF look. *Sorry, babe. Business to transact.* "I'm getting a weird vibe."

"Peter—" she said.

But he ignored her and kept a hard stare on Courtney. "Like something's not right in Oz. You have any thoughts on that?"

Courtney swayed a little and Izzy reached a hand to her. "Are you okay?"

She bobbed her head up and down and sent her long blond ponytail bouncing. "I'm fine. Just a dizzy spell. It happens sometimes."

"Courtney?" Peter needed answers and she had them. He was sure of it.

"Why would I know anything? I'm just minding my own business until I have this baby and can leave."

"Right," he said. "When's your next doctor's appointment?"

Courtney's eyes went wild. Literally shifting all over the place. "Why?"

"Okay." Isabelle grabbed Courtney's arm. "We're done here. Peter can go do his interviews while we have breakfast."

The two women started toward the house and Izzy hurled him a sneer over her shoulder. *Yep. She's pissed.* Nothing he could do about that.

"You ladies do that. I'll be back in a while."

And I want some goddamned answers.

"YEESH," COURTNEY SAID AS SHE AND ISABELLE WALKED TO the house. "What's his problem?

Isabelle snorted a not-so-amused laugh at Courtney's mind reading abilities. "I was thinking the same thing."

They entered the kitchen and Isabelle went to the fridge and grabbed the eggs and some cheddar cheese. "Omelet sound good?"

"Sure," Courtney said. "High protein."

Isabelle started cracking eggs into a large bowl. She blasted one and the shell disintegrated. *Take a breath.* She fished the pieces of broken shell out of the bowl. "I'm sorry about Peter. His radar is beeping on something. He's worried he's going to give half a million dollars to a charity that doesn't deserve it."

Courtney gagged. "Half. A million."

"You can see why he's concerned. Half a mil is half a mil, and Peter is a smart man. Even if he acts like an ass at times."

"Wow."

Isabelle cracked the last egg, threw the shell away and started scrambling with a ferocity that should have rocked the house. "Courtney, I don't know what Peter is sensing but his instincts are good."

Courtney wiggled her head back and forth. "I don't know anything."

Isabelle held up a hand. "Relax. I just want you to know if you need something, you can come to me. I have no loyalties to Seth. Frankly, I came here to close the door on my own demons and I'm not sure it's working. I'm leaving soon, but I'll give you my numbers. Even if I'm not here, it doesn't mean you can't come to me."

The stiffness in Courtney's shoulders melted, and she collapsed against the back of the stool. She brought her gaze to Isabelle's.

Thinking.

Isabelle put the bowl aside and reached across the counter. "I'll help you."

Tears moistened the girl's eyes and the air stilled in contrast to Isabelle's pounding heart. Courtney had something to say.

What is going on with her?

"I'll help you," she repeated.

Courtney swiped at her tears. "I can't. I just need to have this baby and get out of here."

"I'll help you after you have the baby. *Peter* will help you. We'll find you a job and put a roof over your head. You can leave this all behind. If you change your mind and want to keep the baby, we'll help with that also. There are plenty of single mothers out there."

But Courtney did the panicked head shake again. "No. The decision about the baby has already been made."

A whipping anger smacked at Isabelle. "You keep saying that. Are you not allowed to change your mind? I change my mind five thousand times a day over inconsequential things. Give yourself a break. If you want this baby, then keep her."

She bit down on her lip and stepped back. *That* was something. Regret licked at her for shooting off her mouth.

"Screw you," Courtney said. "You don't know what you're talking about. Go ahead and leave."

"Courtney—"

"Shut up!" Tears ran down her cheeks. "I don't need you telling me my life could be different. I don't have your education. I'm just trying to survive and you're going to mess it up!"

"Hold on," Isabelle said, coming around the breakfast bar. Courtney stood and squared off with her, her eyes cold and hard, like the light had been snuffed. Isabelle knew that kind of cold. She'd been living with it for years.

She took a tentative step closer and waited. Courtney stood stone still. No movement. Good. She slowly put her arms around the frightened girl and the hard lump of Courtney's belly pressed against her midsection.

They remained in the quiet of the kitchen, swaying a little in the embrace. "I'm sorry I made you angry."

"You can't help me," Courtney said, her voice hitching with tears as she hugged back. "It's too late."

And with that, she broke away from Isabelle and hurried from the room.

Isabelle exhaled. Almost. She almost had her. Courtney wanted to talk.

She just didn't know it yet.

35

After Seth had returned home with Mary Beth and the girls, Isabelle walked into the kitchen to find the women preparing lunch while he did his usual disappearing act. Mary Beth stood at the stove browning meat and wearing a baggy T-shirt that said Go Ahead, Make My Day. How appropriate.

Isabelle nodded. "Can I help?"

"No. I've got it."

"Fine." She glanced around the kitchen, stepped into a stream of sunlight from the glass door and tilted her face up. She suddenly yearned for the normalcy of going to her office every day.

She needed to *do* something. The morning run-in with Courtney had churned her into a sour mood. She was so far over her head she should be staring up at the curb.

"Have you seen Peter?" she asked.

"I think he's down at the cabins."

Isabelle pulled the door open. "I'll find him."

Where could he have disappeared to? Being a smart man, he was probably hiding from the tongue-lashing she wanted to give him. She whipped out her cell phone and sent him a text while she tromped down the path toward the cabins. The exercise gave her muscles a long overdue work-out, but these little snatches of exercise didn't compare to the ass kicking she usually gave her heavy bag. The heavy bag helped her cope and her mind and body craved the release.

A few minutes later her phone beeped and she punched the button to read the text. Peter. *Talking to a family in the last cabin. Almost done. Wait.*

Great. She kept walking. Thick hundred-year-old trees separated the cabins and offered shelter from the sun's heat. Five minutes later Peter emerged from the cabin. She picked up her pace to meet him by the end of the path. "Where've you been all morning?"

He waved his hand toward the cabins. "I've been talking to all these people. One lost his job and got his house fore-closed. One is on disability and can't support her kids. One has cancer and can't afford the medical bills."

"I know," she said. "It makes me appreciate my life."

"No shit." Peter jerked his thumb at the cabin he'd just come from. "Did you meet this guy? He hated Kendrick. Apparently, Kendrick had a thing for his teenage daughter."

"Oh no."

"It's fine. He told the daughter to stay away from Kendrick. She's a good girl and did so."

"Did you meet the family with the pregnant sixteen-year-old?"

Peter scoffed. "Yeah. That guy. He was interesting. Did you know they got here through the same place that sent Courtney here?"

Wow. "I *didn't* know that."

"They're all good, hardworking people. They don't

deserve this." He shook his head. "This place is a breeding ground for the downtrodden."

"They're trying to make—"

Breeding ground.

"What?" he asked.

Isabelle ran her fingers over her mouth and focused on the tree behind Peter. *Breeding ground.* What an odd way to put it, but she supposed he was right. At least they had shelter, food and an opportunity to find work from Seth's organization. Even if it was a front.

Breeding ground.

She tilted her head and silently replayed her conversations with Courtney.

"What?" Peter repeated.

And the way they'd all grimaced when she made the crack about not drinking the water because it made everyone pregnant.

The medical office.

Peter snapped his fingers in her face. "Izzy?"

The decision is made.

"I think I know," she said.

How could they have not seen this? She slid her hands down her face and wiped away the salty moisture of her sweat. *No. No. No.* It couldn't be. Her eyes nearly exploded from the pressure behind them. "Could they be breeding babies? Selling them on the black market?"

Peter squinted and she reached out, grasped his wrists. "That's why Courtney keeps telling me the decision has been made. All the pregnant girls? The OB office in the basement? He probably has a doctor come in and pays all of the medical expenses out of the fees he collects for the babies."

Sickness swelled in her throat, and she stepped away in

case she vomited. "I read about a black-market baby ring in one of my law journals. The babies can go for up to a hundred thousand dollars."

"And he's got five of them on the way."

"Courtney and the other girl came here from that counseling center. Maybe they're in on it."

And... *No.* Isabelle stretched her arms and fingers wide in front of her as paralyzing thoughts banged around inside her skull. "The prison you followed Seth's lunch date to," she croaked. "Maybe Sampson can find out how many pregnant women have been there and gave their babies up for adoption."

"Oh, Christ," Peter said. "That can't be."

She shook her head to free her brain from badgering thoughts of prisons and counseling centers and defeated young women. "I need to get into Seth's computer. Fast. There must be something on there." She turned and started up the path. "I'm going up to check my email. Maybe that message from your office came."

She'd see if she could borrow Seth's computer to check her email...and forward him a corrupt file.

SETH STOOD IN FRONT OF THE FILING CABINET READING A report. He wore that same basic outfit of chinos and a collared shirt and Isabelle was absolutely sick of him. He turned to her and his gaze locked onto her chest.

Sick of that too.

But she needed to get onto his computer and forward him that file.

"Hi," she said. "Can I check my email?"

He glanced at the computer. "Of course."

"I'll just be a second." She scooted by him, felt the brush of his hand against her leg and bit down to keep from screaming at him. Her own fault for flirting and encouraging his behavior.

That would end soon. For now, she looked over her shoulder and forced a smile.

She logged into her email account. Lots there, but nothing from Peter's office. She gritted her teeth while closing her email. Where the hell was that corrupted message? Now, more than ever, she needed to see what was on Seth's hard drive. If this man was demoralizing women and selling their babies, she wanted to obliterate him. She wanted to watch the FBI handcuff the bastard and lock him up. She wanted to watch Seth Donner, disgusting, vile human being that he was, lose the life he knew.

"Problem?" Seth asked.

She slowly spun the chair. He stared at her a minute. She stared back. Oh, she knew what he wanted. If only she could trade what *he* wanted for what *she* wanted. If slimy bartering would get her into that computer and help find a missing girl, she'd call it a done deal.

Even she wasn't twisted enough to believe Seth would give her the passwords in exchange for sex. And if Peter knew she was even thinking it, he'd go crazy.

But she needed answers and those answers were somewhere in this house.

Maybe the computer wasn't the answer.

Hadn't Kendrick come to her seeking legal advice? Perhaps Seth still needed that advice and, lucky him, here she was. All she needed was for him to tell her why Kendrick sought her out. It would be a start.

This could be a plan. She'd seduce him, get some pillow talk going and who knew, maybe she'd walk away with a nugget that would lead to answers.

Besides, Creepy Izzy could take the wheel. Her skills were more than adequate in that department.

Hang on. Could she really be thinking this?

Seth inched closer. He wanted her. Yes, she was really thinking this. She could work him until he was so crazy with need he'd confide in her. That, combined with the email to copy his files, could be all they needed. Maybe she'd find out whose panties Peter found in the basement.

"I have a lot to do," she said, answering his question and loading him up on eye contact.

And there it was. That casual stance coupled with the lusting focus on her. She'd seen this predatory hunger in men for years now. *Here we go.*

"You are an exceptional creature, Isabelle."

The chaos in her mind began to tick and she closed her eyes.

You can do this.

Creepy Izzy. *Thank you.* She opened her eyes—Peter called them man killers—and gazed up at Seth.

She'd make this quick and simple. Just shut the door behind her, confess her deep longing to screw his brains out, blah, blah, blah. She'd tell him how much she'd been enjoying her stay and would, after all, like to spend some time with him.

Alone.

At which point, he'd look at her tits again, and she'd step closer instead of drawing away.

Then she'd kiss him. Let him pull her shirt off and...a sour taste flooded her mouth.

No. Don't think.

This could work. With Peter still down at the cabins the whole thing would be easier.

Forget him. Find Nicole. Help Courtney. That's all she had to do. Sex was nothing for Creepy Izzy.

She stood and took the few steps toward Seth.

"Did you need something?" he asked.

"If you're not busy, I thought we could spend some time together."

His ruddy cheeks bunched with a knowing grin, and Isabelle swallowed hard at the vision of Peter's strong face flashing in front of her.

Don't think about him.

Seth reached behind her and closed the door. "I'd like that."

Wait. She was supposed to close the door. This was *her* plan. Not his. No. *She* needed to control this situation.

Instead of walking to his desk, he motioned Isabelle to the black leather sofa and sat next to her. Seth was having no problem with her I-want-to-screw-you signals because he scooched closer and draped his arm behind her head.

A skittering angst shot up her arms at the personal space invasion. *You can do this.* She shifted sideways, crossed one leg over the other and let her top leg rub his knee. "I wanted to tell you how much I've enjoyed it here."

He dropped his hand on her leg, his stubby, sweaty fingers rubbing and working up...up...up. Too fast. He inched closer and with her heart pounding, she found herself backing away. Something felt...off. She placed her hand over his to stop its movement.

Stick to your script. She needed to kiss him first.

He took a long, analyzing perusal of her legs and half grinned as he squeezed the inside of her thigh and nudged his hand up. "I think you know I've enjoyed having you here. And I think we're both going to enjoy you staying a little longer."

This is it. She licked her bottom lip, saw the shock of pleasure in his smile and leaned forward. He met her halfway and kissed her, gently at first and the feel of his dry, nasty lips against hers sent her stomach into a full-blown churn.

She squeezed her eyes closed, prayed for Creepy Izzy to stay put. Seth opened his mouth wider, jammed his tongue into her mouth and leaned over her, his bigger body pressing her backward.

Sickness devoured her, filled every pore, and she squeezed her eyes even tighter. The tears were building, coming too fast.

Nothing about this felt right. When Peter kissed her, she felt happy and light. This kiss, the aggression, that disgusting tongue in her mouth, invading her, caused bile to pool in her throat.

Peter would never kiss her this way.

She retreated, pressing on Seth's chest to give herself some room and take a breath. To organize her plan and get Peter out of her head. Bad enough she'd have to face him when this was over. She'd have to look into those beautiful eyes and know she'd destroyed him. Thrown away every decent thing he'd given her.

For what? She wanted to find a missing girl, but to what end? How many lives would she obliterate to get there? No, she couldn't do this. Even as Creepy Izzy, it was more than she could handle. Peter would be too much of a sacrifice.

Isabelle turned away, her back almost to Seth, but he knew what he wanted and grabbed her hip, digging his fingers in to hold her in place.

He laughed. "You're not going anywhere."

Back him off.

She hooked her fingers around the arm of the chair to pull herself from his grasp just as the door slowly opened.

Peter. A swelling panic submerged her, its violence stealing her breath. His face held a harshness she'd never seen. His gaze traveled to Seth's hand as it landed on her ass. *You've lost him now.*

"Don't you knock?" Seth asked, his hands still on her.

No reaction from Peter.

But the shame she'd been hording for so long surged, and her mind went back to the day her uncle walked into his study and discovered his son's ugly secret. She pushed the thought away. *Control this.* She glanced up to Peter, who stood impossibly still.

"Are you okay?" he finally asked.

Immediately, she understood. Peter didn't know what he'd walked into. Was she being attacked or was this part of her game?

He waited for her to answer. If she said no—not a complete lie because at this moment she was far from okay —he'd haul her out of there. She'd convince him it wasn't her fault. With the way Seth was hanging on to her, she could let Peter think she hadn't willingly used her body to get information. Even if it hurt him, she could do it.

Or she could be one hundred percent truthful and answer yes because she'd never lied to Peter.

"Are you okay?" he repeated.

And Seth laughed. "Oh, she's just fine, aren't you, honey?"

She had to say something because Peter, being Peter, wouldn't stand there forever. He didn't have it in him to be idle. Not with Seth taunting him. No, if his wiggling fingers were any indication, in a few seconds he would take control of the situation.

"Yes, I'm okay."

He straightened and took a step backward. His expression hadn't changed—not much anyway—but for a brief second he pinched his lips tight and the hurt and anger reached her.

"Peter—"

"I need to borrow your car."

Isabelle scrambled to her feet, spotted Seth's smug grin of satisfaction and almost slapped him. But she blocked Peter's view because the last thing she needed was more tension thrown into this mess.

"Next time knock," Seth said.

Peter winced. Isabelle waved him out the door before he did major damage. "My keys are in the bedroom."

Spinning away from her, he marched down the hall and she hurried after him. "Peter—"

"Outside," he said. "Get your keys and meet me outside."

She ducked into the room, wrapped her hands around the keys and stopped. *Deep breath*. She needed to make him understand. That's all. If she explained it to him, he'd understand.

Maybe.

She raced down the stairs and out the front door where she found Peter standing on the lawn out of earshot. Seth would be watching from somewhere. She knew it, but to him, it would seem like a lover's quarrel. He'd most likely find pleasure in it.

"Not here," Peter said. "Side of the house. I don't need an audience."

"It's not what you think."

When they reached privacy, Peter folded his arms, his fingers digging into his skin. "Enlighten me."

He knew.

She held her hands palm up. "Peter."

The need to make him understand balled inside her. She had to make him see the logic. "It wasn't me. I flipped the switch. It was Creepy Izzy. The email from Janet hadn't come and I was frustrated. I thought if I could get him to relax maybe he'd give me information that'll move us along. That's all. I was just trying to get him to confide in me."

Peter's jaw dropped and hung there for a few seconds while he absorbed what she'd said. He began stomping around, back and forth, back and forth, his face transforming to nothing but hard angles.

"And what?" he said, keeping his voice low. "You think he'll scream the passwords while you're blowing him? Are you out of your *mind*?"

"Peter—"

"No!" He gaped at her as if she'd become a vile whore. Some piece of trash stuck to his shoe. "I can't believe you did this."

She had to make him understand. "It wasn't about the passwords. I thought it would get me closer to him, and that's where we need to be."

Peter stopped moving—just halted right there. "Is that where we need to be, Iz? You prostituting yourself? That's so goddamned far from where we need to be we're not even on the same planet anymore." He threw the heels of his hands over his eyes. "Fucking insanity."

When he bent forward and rested his hands on his knees, she put a hand on his shoulder, but he jerked away. The lightning-quick rejection tore into her and she snatched her hand back. She held her breath a second too long and the air suddenly burst free. His repulsion to her touch had been a natural response, and the sudden fear washed over her.

Wait it out. Don't panic. Maybe he'll accept it.

But she knew better. Caveman Peter would never accept her using sex as a tool.

After several moments he stood and faced her. The tightness around his mouth forced her to realize she pushed him too far.

"I need to get out of here and think about this. I'm too wound up now."

But she didn't want him leaving the house.

Leaving her.

Flip the damn switch.

"Isabelle, I can't believe you would want to get with this guy."

The sound of her given name coming from his lips made her ears ring, and she fought to keep her feet under her. He just didn't get it. She fisted her hands and shook them at him. "I didn't *want* him. You've seen Creepy Izzy in action. You know, without a doubt, there is nothing emotional about Creepy Izzy. Don't make this about you, Peter."

His head lolled forward.

"No. I didn't mean that."

But he snatched the keys from her hand and started toward her car.

She grunted. *Dammit.* How could she, a highly educated twenty-six-year-old criminal lawyer, be so painfully awful at relationships? Maybe because she'd never had a good one. Or at least one she wanted to fight for.

She ran to catch up with him. "Peter—"

But when he stopped moving he didn't face her. Not even a glance. No. He looked down at her hand on his elbow and curled his lip. She made him sick. What else should she expect?

A tiny piece of her heart, the one she'd let him thaw out,

shattered and a whimpering sound erupted in her throat until she forced it back.

Flip the switch! Don't let him hurt you.

"Guess what, sweetheart?" he said. "You've finally pushed me away."

36

HE CHARGED AROUND THE SIDE OF THE HOUSE AND SHE closed her eyes. *Flip the switch*. No hurt. No pain. Nothing.

Her mind wandered to her cottage on the beach, the smell of the salty air and the sunrises she watched from her deck. All of nature's beauty for her to enjoy. After a few deep breaths she imagined all the pain from Peter's rejection being stuffed into the tiniest box she could find. Crammed it down as far as it would go. She slammed the lid on the box and locked it.

There.

All better.

She opened her eyes, but the image of Peter walking away from her blew the lid right off the damn box and she came apart as if someone had hacked at her with a meat cleaver. *Whack, whack, whack.*

Her lungs strained with the need for air and she dropped to her knees. She hadn't even gotten the chance to tell him she couldn't go through with it. That he'd demolished Creepy Izzy.

The gravel path dug into her skin and she sucked air, but

the tears still came, shooting down her face and she shoved them away.

No.

Flip the switch.

She could handle this. Had been handling it all her life. People she loved had been disappointing her for years. This would be no different than every other time. She'd just bury the pain. Even if it was still alive and screaming.

No. She imagined a bigger box this time. Steel plated. Nothing could escape this box. She shoved everything inside. Her tears, her broken heart, this house that made her think about Kendrick and his sick ways, she pushed it all in the box.

Now the lock. A big one. Industrial sized. A mental image formed of her snapping the lock closed.

There. Just try to get out.

She focused on a tiny rock on the ground and her fingers dug into the gravel, the dirt piling under her nails. *Deep breath.* She released her fingers, let them rest against the loose dirt. *Relax.* A chirping bird and the sudden flapping of its wings drew her attention. She glanced up, watched him fly away. *Calm.* Time to move forward.

Rising to her feet, she used the backs of her hands to wipe away the tears and started toward the front door. Peter could do what he needed to and so would she. When this was all over, maybe they'd find their way back to what could have been, but right now, Nicole Pratt was still missing. Along with Kendrick's murderer.

She watched her car turn out of the driveway. She'd have to let Peter go. Her emotional issues would not keep her from getting this job done and getting home. If she was right about this baby-brokering scheme, she had to break it up.

Before Courtney gave birth.

. . .

PETER PULLED INTO THE MOTEL PARKING LOT, JAMMED THE CAR into park and banged his palm against the steering wheel. The rampant fury licked at him and scalded his skin.

Son of a bitch.

He could have called Billy on the phone—as he'd intended—but after walking in on Izzy about to offer her body to that scumbag, he had to get his head together. What a moron he'd been to think he could handle working with her.

Wasn't that the number one rule? Don't get emotionally involved. Well, he'd blown it this time. And worse, he'd have to put it aside until they figured this baby thing out.

He turned the car off, got out and locked it before climbing the motel stairs to the second floor.

Billy had been poking around trying to find information on the family planning clinic Courtney had visited. So far, he hadn't been able to connect them to anything illegal, but this new theory of Izzy's about the baby brokering could blow it open.

It made sense that the clinic would refer down-on-their-luck pregnant women to Seth's organization. They'd get shelter, food in their bellies and a chance to make a life for themselves and their children. Assuming Seth wasn't selling those children.

Jesus.

Izzy's theory might not be far off. He didn't want to think what she might be doing while he was gone. The thought of her naked body, all that toned flesh, under Seth made his eyes throb. How the fuck did he get to this place?

Shake it off. Deal with it. Izzy's thinking got screwed. Maybe she'd come to the realization that fucking a man blind wouldn't find a missing girl. Then again, if anyone could bring a man to heel, it would be Izzy and her sexual skills.

Goddammit.

He stopped on the landing, bit down hard and grunted. Okay. *Settle down, chief.* One hour to calm down. That would do it. Then he'd be functional again. He hated leaving that compound, but he'd be no good in this condition.

He dialed Billy and waited for him to answer. "I'm coming in the room. Don't shoot me."

"Roger."

Peter slid the key, an actual key, not a keycard, into the lock and stepped in. Billy, dressed in jeans and a sleeveless T-shirt, had his head buried in the laptop.

"What are you doing here?"

Peter tossed Izzy's keys on the dresser and sat on it. "I needed some air. Izzy came up with something and I wanted to fill you in."

"How is she?" He sat back and propped his feet on the desk.

Probably getting laid right now. There's a thought. *Shit.* He plunged his fingers into his eyes to relieve the exploding pain.

"You okay?" Billy wanted to know.

Fucking peachy.

"Headache," Peter said. "Anyway, Izzy thinks, and I tend to agree, that Seth is selling infants on the black market."

Billy's head snapped back. "Holy crap. Is Courtney selling her kid?"

"Don't know. Courtney's not talking. I went at her this morning, but Izzy got pissed at me and pulled her away."

"That's why you're here? You had a fight with Izzy."

Sort of. "I told you, I needed some air."

"Sure." Billy shrugged in that annoying way he did when he was about to be sarcastic. "The two of you cooked up this baby thing and then you took her car and left her there —*alone*—to deal with it. Nice work, Monk."

He left her there. Alone. His worst fear and he made it happen. "It's complicated."

"Not really. Since when do you, of all people, leave a teammate because the situation is complicated? What is *wrong* with you?" He held up his hands. "Wait. What did you fight about?"

Right. Like he'd tell *Billy*? Peter swallowed the string of insults begging to be hurled. "It's complicated."

"Bullshit. The truth is you broke the fucking rule and got emotional about an op." Billy put his feet on the floor and went back to the laptop. "Deal with it and get your ass back there. She needs you now."

Peter shook his head. "Not this time."

"Waa, waa, waa."

"Fuck you," Peter yelled because he'd had enough of the armchair psychology. Let Billy walk in on his girl about to bang some guy simply to get information. Then he could offer an opinion.

"No." Billy said. "You signed on for this. Vic wanted to send somebody else. You told him you could do it."

"Well, I can't," Peter mumbled because defeat never came easy. Or was it weakness? He didn't know. It sucked though. He jammed the heels of his hands into his eye sockets. "You're right. I admit it. I got emotional. Happy now?"

Billy pushed the chair back and got large. "I should kick your ass. You need to suck it up and get back there. You took her car! Which proves to me you aren't thinking. I know there's no way you'd leave her without wheels."

No lie there.

He'd panicked. He couldn't stand there and watch her play Seth right in front of him.

"You know," Billy said, "this is still about you not getting your way. Every time you can't control a situation you get pissed off. You got pissed off when Tiny went down and you got pissed off when we lost Roy. Like somehow *you* should have saved them. Listen up, asshole. We're all pissed. We all lost friends. We *all* feel responsible. You can't reserve the corner on that."

Peter braced himself, willed his body to relax. If he didn't get out he'd go apeshit on Billy.

Again.

He didn't need this. "This is crap. I'm leaving."

Billy waved him off. "Of course you are."

And that ripped it. Peter lunged forward, grabbed Billy by the shirt and got in his face. "What is your fucking problem?"

Billy shoved him off. "You're my fucking problem. You haven't been right since Tiny died. We all knew it and gave you slack, but now you're being a pain in the ass. You're so bent on proving you can save someone that you're screwing up. What makes you think you could have saved those men? Christ, you weren't even there when Roy died." Billy stepped back. "Let me say this so you can understand it. You couldn't help them. But you can help Izzy. Why you're here, arguing with me, I don't have a clue."

He could help Izzy. The words shattered Peter's rage and he backed up, sat on the bed, curling and uncurling his fingers.

"Yo," Billy said, "somehow you got it into your head that you didn't do something that could have saved them. Accept the fact that you're hurting. We all know it. You're the only one who doesn't. Take some time and deal with it. It wasn't your fault those men died. I was there both times and I know there was nothing we could have done to save them. You did *not* fuck up."

Peter stared at his hands. "All I know is my teammates are dying."

"Yeah, they are."

"That's all you've got?"

"I can't think too hard about it or I'll wind up like you. And I'd rather put a bullet in my head."

No shit.

"Whatever happened with you and Izzy, you'd better set it straight. She's good for you. You're not some insane asshole when she's around."

Peter snorted a laugh. "Trust me, I get it, but I can't compromise on what we fought about."

"Maybe not, but here's what you need to do."

Peter rolled his eyes. Great. More advice from Billy.

"Hold up," Billy said. "This isn't bullshit."

Peter waved his hands to urge him on. Might as well. Considering he was at a dead loss. And how many times had that happened in his life? Not many.

Billy wagged a finger. "You have to learn to cooperate but not lose your nuts."

Why, why, why did he think Billy could help? "What the hell does that mean?"

"It means you can't agree to anything that will compromise what you stand for. Tell her you don't mind cooperating, but not if it means giving up your non-negotiable terms. Think about it. If you didn't have a list of terms you'd be living in constant fear of being hosed."

"That's the problem, jackass. I know my terms."

This couldn't be making sense. Not from Billy.

"Stay specific with her. Don't make it a huge list, but be

honest. Women like that. Besides, if it's a short list, she's more likely to give in."

Izzy giving in? Doubtful.

"Okay, genius, what if she doesn't like my terms?"

Billy shrugged. "Then you're fucked, but you've got to try and make her understand."

37

Once inside the house, Isabelle ran up the steps to her room in search of privacy. She couldn't face Seth right now. He'd want to pick up where they left off and, well, not going to happen. Nope. The only thing she needed now was time alone to think about repairing things with Peter and getting in touch with Sampson about the baby-brokering scheme. But, with Peter taking her car, she couldn't go anywhere. And hadn't he told her to never call Sampson from her cell phone?

She'd just call Peter, find out when he'd be back and then she'd find a pay phone to call Sampson. Excellent plan. Two birds, one stone. She flew into the bedroom, where Courtney sat on the bed reading a magazine and nearly rocketed off in surprise. "Isabelle! You scared me."

She held out her hands as Courtney shook off the scare. "Sorry. So sorry. Are you all right?"

"I'm not going to pop this baby because of it, but, wow, you just blasted in here."

"I know. I'm sorry." She rushed to the dresser. "I...uh...

need my phone. Important call." She dialed Peter's number, held the phone to her ear. One ring, two, three. Nothing.

Not taking her calls. Should have known. She jabbed the disconnect button, fired off a text and waited for his response. Come on. Come on.

"What is it?" Courtney asked.

Isabelle turned to her and saw the curiosity in those big blue eyes. "Nothing for you to worry about."

"Is there an emergency?"

Yeah. A big one. *I just jettisoned the only guy that makes me feel like a living, breathing woman. The one who was man enough to keep working with me until he cracked the code.*

The full force of what she'd done finally hit her. By being an idiot, she'd annihilated her shot at what could possibly have been the most fulfilling relationship of her life.

"We had a fight." Izzy continued to stare at her phone, but the panic—that pecking that ravaged her nerve endings —began to take hold.

Come on, Peter. Call me back. Please.

"Who?"

"Uh. A friend."

"The rich boy?"

"Yes."

She shouldn't have admitted that.

"Must have been some fight," Courtney said.

Isabelle willed the phone to ring, but nothing came. He wouldn't call her. She could 9-1-1 him and he'd call back in a second. No. No tricks. That wouldn't be fair.

But was this fair? Ignoring her? Treating her like an expendable piece of meat? No. That wasn't fair either. Yes, she'd hurt him. She knew that, but ignoring her? After she'd given herself over to him? She shouldn't have done it. If she'd kept her emotions locked in the box—the damned box—she wouldn't be feeling this...this...raging skewering of her heart.

She threw the phone on the bed. "Dammit."

"Yikes," Courtney said. "I'm guessing you and the rich boy are doing the nasty. Did he dump you?"

Wasn't this perfect? Courtney trying to dissect this crazy situation. The irony of it was that Courtney had been dumped in the worst possible way and could probably relate.

"I screwed up and he won't talk to me. And he took my car, so I can't even try to get to him."

A sob clawed free from the steel-plated box and Isabelle spun to the sealed window, stuck her face in the path of the sun's rays and allowed the heat to penetrate. She would not cry.

Please call me back.

Who was this whimpering, pitiful girl? Images of herself as a fifteen-year-old girl standing in her uncle's study with her pants down knifed into her brain. *That* was the pitiful girl. The scared one who didn't know what to do as Kendrick pulled up his jeans while his father screamed at them.

This Isabelle, the grown up one, didn't allow men to control her emotions. No. She kicked their asses. Emotionally and physically. Not much to be proud of, but still...

She counted three breaths and turned back to Courtney, but the panic continued to bubble, and tears formed in her eyes. Done. Cooked. No sense fighting it anymore.

She lowered her head into her hands. The air came too fast, her head spun, and her ribs ached.

Catch your breath.

But the sobs came instead and her body shook with it,

shattering over the agony, and, suddenly, Courtney was next to her, stroking her shoulders, offering comfort. All Isabelle wanted was her life back. Her house, her beach, heck, even her job.

She wanted Peter.

"This is stupid," she said. "He probably just didn't hear the phone. He has my car so he has to come back."

She breathed deep, let the calm inch over her.

"He's probably cooling off," Courtney said. "Besides, I need him to come back, too."

Huh? Isabelle swiped her hand over her face and shifted to Courtney. "How come?"

"Well, I was...uh...thinking...about what you guys said."

Oh, please. Please. "Yes?"

"About helping me?"

A burst of hope whipped at Isabelle, but she dialed it back. She snatched a tissue off the bedside table and blotted her face as her meltdown faded to the background. "Of course. You know we'll help you."

"Yeah. But, it's bad." She glanced at the closed door.

"Whatever it is, I'll get you out of here. We'll walk away. Right now."

Shock. No. Pure joy lit Courtney's face and her eyes turned a shimmering, sparkling blue. "You'd do that for me?"

This poor girl had grown so accustomed to being disappointed by people she didn't trust kindness. They really did understand each other.

"Yes. We'd have to wait for Peter to bring my car back, but yes. Absolutely."

"Uh. There's a problem."

"What's that?"

The joy slipped away, and Isabelle sensed Courtney

retreating. Giving in to the fear. No. *Don't lose her.* She sat next to her on the bed, draped an arm over her shoulder. "You and I, we're a lot alike. The world, at times, has been shitty to us. We're survivors though. We always come back. Whatever it is, I'll help you."

Isabelle shut her mouth as Courtney's mental war raged on. The only sound came from a bird outside the sealed window. Isabelle waited. Didn't speak. Someone would give in.

"I have to sell my baby."

The thundering behind Isabelle's eyes wouldn't stop. This was it. "What do you mean you have to sell her?"

"I told them I would. I'm so ashamed, but I didn't know what else to do. The lady at the counseling center called it a private adoption. And when you have no job and no place to live, it makes sense. I was scared."

"And the counseling center sent you here?"

"Seth and Kendrick made it sound like a perfect option. They said they'd support me, get me a doctor. Then after the baby came I'd walk away from here with some money. Plus, I could make a childless couple happy. It seemed like a no-lose situation."

"Until you changed your mind?"

Courtney nodded. "I was afraid to tell them. I didn't know what they'd do."

"Well," Isabelle said, squeezing her arm and standing up. "You're not going to have to worry about that because I'm getting you out of here."

38

PETER'S PHONE BUZZED AND HE UNCLIPPED IT FROM HIS BELT. Two seconds later Billy's went off. Peter checked his screen. *Oh, shit.* He'd missed a call and now a text from Izzy. A 9-1-1. He'd left her alone, without her car and she was in trouble. His heart nearly exploded because his worst fucking nightmare wouldn't end.

Son of a bitch. He snatched the keys off the dresser and hauled ass as he dialed.

"Right behind you," Billy said.

Izzy's phone barely rang before she answered. "Where are you?"

"At the motel. You all right?"

"Yes. Courtney just told me everything. We're going to walk out of here together. She's packing her things and I need your help when Seth tries to stop us."

The guilt settled on him, nearly drove him into the ground. "I'm sorry. I had no idea. I figured I could leave for an hour and get my head together."

"It's not your fault. I didn't know this would happen. I

had a meltdown and unloaded on Courtney. She unloaded back."

"Are you okay?"

"Let's talk about it later. In private. Right now—"

"Yeah. We're on our way. Don't do anything until I get there."

He bolted down the stairs, but hollered over his shoulder at Billy. "Follow me to the compound, but stay on the road. Don't drive onto the property until I figure out what's going on. I'll open the gate for you with the remote Seth gave Izzy."

Peter jumped into the Audi and started it. "You still there?" he asked Izzy.

"Yes."

"I'll be there in ten minutes. What's happening?"

"It's what we thought. Seth is running a black-market baby ring. I have to call Sampson. Courtney is willing to talk to him."

"Don't hang up, Izzy. We'll call Sampson once you're both out of there."

"No. I'll be fine. We're in our room. Call me when you get close. We'll walk out and you can pick us up in front."

He didn't like hanging up. Not for one second. But she needed Sampson more than him right now. Sampson could get the cops crawling all over that place. The weight of Peter's nine-millimeter, hidden at his waist, reminded him he hadn't gone completely loco. At least he remembered to grab it before he'd gone into that office and found Izzy with Seth.

"Izzy, don't move from that room until I call you."

"Seth is at the door," she whispered. "I have to go."

The line went dead.

· · ·

"SHOVE THAT BAG IN THE CLOSET," ISABELLE WHISPERED TO Courtney. "I'll get rid of him."

Courtney leaped to her feet with amazing speed for a woman eight months pregnant. She stowed the duffle in the closet and dove into her bed. "Tell him I'm tired. Don't say sick or he'll have a doctor in here."

The knock sounded again. "Isabelle? Courtney? Everything all right?"

Isabelle reached for the door, straightened up and gently pulled it open for him to see in the room. "Hi, Seth. Sorry. Courtney wasn't decent."

After spotting Courtney in bed he stepped into the room. "Are you sick?" His voice remained flat, like this was nothing but a bother.

"No. Just tired. Isabelle is keeping me company."

Seth fired a glance at Isabelle still standing at the door. "What's going on?"

"Nothing. After Peter left, I came back to check on Courtney." Isabelle grinned at him. "I was about to come back and see you."

If his locked jaw were any indication, Seth wasn't buying it. Not this time. He turned back to Courtney. "Lunch is ready. Why don't you both come down and eat."

"I'm not hungry," Courtney said.

"Courtney—" he began.

"Seth," Isabelle said, "we had a late breakfast while you and Mary Beth were out." She held the door open a little wider. The universal signal for get the hell out.

"Fine. We'll save you some."

"Thank you," Isabelle said.

When he left, she shut the door and went to the closet to retrieve Courtney's duffle. Her own bag sat on the floor packed and ready to go. She had never bothered taking the things out of it after switching rooms. Peter's things! She wouldn't be able to carry it all. He'd have to come back for them.

"Okay," she said. "Peter is on his way. Billy too."

"Who's Billy?" Courtney threw the covers back.

Oh, right. She didn't know about Billy. "I'll explain later."

She dialed Sampson. Peter had told her to hold off, but she needed something to do while waiting. Voice mail. *Figures.* She left a message that Courtney was willing to talk and they were leaving. Maybe they could sneak out without Seth knowing. They'd have to be quiet though.

The distinctive grind of a key sliding into a lock sounded and Isabelle ran back to the door and pulled just as the lock engaged. *No.*

"Rich boy's room," Courtney said, her voice a hissing whisper.

Isabelle shoved open the pocket door only to find Seth pulling the bedroom door closed.

"No!"

"Yes," he said from the other side of the door as he flipped the lock. "I'll be back for you after lunch and we'll finish what we started."

She slammed her open hand against the door. "Unlock this. Now!"

He laughed. "Be ready for me, Isabelle."

"Seth, open this door or I'll call 9-1-1."

"No you won't," he said, his voice fading as if he were walking away. "Courtney has a lot to lose if you do."

"Seth!"

No answer. That rat bastard locked them up. The press of tight air closed in and she spun to face the window.

Sealed. She gripped the doorknob behind her and concentrated on the cold metal.

"He locked us in," Courtney said from the bathroom.

Isabelle snapped her head around. "Don't worry."

"Well, that's kind of tough since we can't get out."

"Yes, we can." Isabelle pushed by her and went to her suitcase where Peter had sewn lock-picking tools into the lining. She tore open the lining, pulled out what he called a tension wrench and the pick and held them up. "Pray I can do this."

"What's that?"

"Peter taught me how to pick a lock. If I can do this, we're out of here."

Her phone rang. Peter. She moved to the far corner of the room in case anyone with big ears was in the hall. Still, she'd keep her voice low.

"Are you here?"

"Two miles out. Get moving."

"That might be a problem. Seth locked us in."

"*What?*"

"I'm going to try and pick the lock, but if I can't do it, you'll have to get us out of here."

"I'll kill that son of a bitch. Forget the lock. I'll kick in the door when I get there. You're done, Izzy. Time to pack it up."

"No, Peter. If I can get the door open, we'll try and sneak out. It'll give us a head start and, hopefully, by the time Seth comes back, we'll be long gone. Let me work on this lock and I'll call you back. If you don't hear from me, expect us to come tearing out the front door in the next few minutes."

She hung up, shoved her phone in her pocket and breathed in to let the oxygen clear her rioting mind.

Concentrate.

Imagining Peter standing next to her, instructing her as

he'd done at the motel, Isabelle inserted the tension wrench into the lower part of the keyhole. She turned the wrench counterclockwise and it stopped. Wrong way. She turned it the other way and the cylinder gave a little. *That's it. Clockwise.* She inserted the pick to the top of the lock.

"Do you know what you're doing?" Courtney asked.

"I'm trying to think here. Remember clockwise."

"Why?"

"Just remember it."

She focused on the pick, felt something on the end and assumed she'd hit what Peter called the pins in the lock. She needed to push the upper pin out of the cylinder before moving on to the next pin. A barely audible click sounded and the shock of actually succeeding hit her.

"That's one," she said. "I need to do the rest."

After repeating the process for each pin, she glanced at Courtney. "Clockwise?"

Courtney nodded.

Isabelle turned the cylinder clockwise, hoping she was right or she'd have to start over.

The cylinder turned.

Tools still in hand, Isabelle jumped backward and waved her arms. She picked the lock. Not wanting to waste any more time, she turned to Courtney. "We're going down the stairs and right out the front door. Don't stop for anything. Can you carry your bag?"

Courtney nodded. "Let's go."

Isabelle opened the door and peeked out. No life. Perfect. With one finger against her lips, she jerked her head for Courtney to follow. "Whatever happens," she whispered, "don't stop. I can handle Seth. You just get out to the car."

They moved down the hall and the sound of voices carried from the first floor. A dish clanged. They must all be in the kitchen at the back of the house. She picked up her pace, but made sure Courtney was still with her.

After inching down the staircase, they stopped at the bottom. To their right was the kitchen, to their left the front door.

"I'll get it," Isabelle heard Seth say and she nudged Courtney toward the front door only a few feet away.

Almost there. Please let Peter be pulling up.

Seth stepped from the kitchen, spotted them and froze. "How the hell did you get out?"

Could they not get a break today? Isabelle swung to Courtney. "Go."

"Hold it," he said as she darted for the door.

Isabelle jumped between Seth and the younger woman. "I said go!"

"She's not going anywhere." He sidestepped and grabbed for Courtney, but Isabelle sent a sharp elbow to his ribs

"Uhhh." He stumbled back, bumped the staircase and doubled over.

"Courtney, go," Isabelle shouted, but Courtney stood poleaxed just feet from the door.

Seth sucked a deep breath and stood straight. "You stupid bitch."

He faked a lunge at Courtney, but instead tackled Isabelle at her waist and they hit the floor with a *thwack*. Isabelle crashed onto her back, her breath catching with the force of the blow. Seth landed on top of her, recovered and tried to straddle her.

No. She sat up, launched a hard palm punch under his chin. *Scrunch.* His jaw snapped back like a Pez dispenser. He rolled to the side, shaking his head. *Bastard.*

Isabelle sprang to her feet, glaring down at him. "I could

have broken your neck. Now back off! I beat the crap out of Kendrick and I'll do the same to you."

Suddenly Mary Beth came flying from the kitchen. She stopped, glanced down at Seth and slowly retreated.

You'd better go back.

On his knees, Seth slowly raised his head, eyes glowering. "Kendrick was a stupid fuck." He looked to Courtney, then down at her protruding belly before raising his gaze to her face again. "I didn't let Kendrick go, and I'm not letting you go either."

Isabelle froze, but her mind raced. What did he mean? She concentrated on the words. *I didn't let Kendrick go.* "You...Kendrick?"

Isabelle turned to Courtney. The young girl still stood motionless. What was she waiting for? "Go!"

Jolted, Courtney ran and groped for the doorknob.

Still on his knees, Seth shook his head hard, probably clearing the fog. Like cannon shot he bolted to his feet, lunged past Isabelle and grabbed for Courtney. "No!" He grasped Courtney's baggy T-shirt and dragged her to one knee.

Isabelle tackled him from behind, chopping at his arm to loosen his grip on Courtney. He let go and they hit the floor again with Izzy's arms wrapped around his knees.

Take him out. Take him out.

"Run, Courtney." Isabelle increased her grip on Seth because who knew what he'd do next.

She needed Peter. He should be here by now. Seth wrenched a leg free, kicked her hard in the shoulder. Her vision blurred as the pain exploded into her neck. Releasing her grip, she fell on her back.

Each jagged breath scraped at her throat like tiny slivers of broken glass. *Recover. Don't let him win.*

She closed her eyes for a second, letting the fury build. She'd finish this.

"Ow!" Courtney cried.

Isabelle sprang to her knees. Seth had hold of Courtney's ankle. The bastard would not win this.

PETER TORE UP THE DRIVEWAY.

Where were they?

He parked, left the car running and hauled ass. When he pushed open the front door, he crashed into Courtney with Seth hanging on to her leg. *Whoa!* Peter jammed his foot into Seth's wrist and he howled in agony before rolling to his back.

A large duffel bag and Izzy's suitcase had been thrown to the floor next to Courtney.

Izzy, on her knees, heaved for breath. Her head was down and he couldn't see her face as Mary Beth tore around the kitchen doorway with something in her hand.

An iron skillet. Un-friggin'-believable.

He pulled his nine-millimeter and lined up his shot. "I wouldn't."

She skidded to a stop.

"Good girl." He jerked his head to Courtney. "Get in the car. Now!"

She snapped to attention and scooted behind him. His gun still on Mary Beth, he stepped forward to help Izzy, but she'd already gotten to her feet, her squinted eyes focused on Seth. She lunged for him, but Peter snaked an arm around her waist, and hauled her backward. "Leave him be. Billy will watch him until the cops get here. Sampson is on his way."

The rage had gotten to her and his words didn't penetrate. He knew the feeling.

Izzy pushed against his arm, her breaths coming in fast, hard grunts, and it took a hell of a grip to keep her from breaking away.

Her leg shot out in a wayward kick near Seth's crotch. "You son of a bitch!"

Too bad she missed.

"Ssshh," he said dragging her to the door while his arm muscles strained against her. Damn she was strong. He kept his gun on Mary Beth and that skillet as they backed out the door.

Once on the porch, he hauled Izzy down the steps. "In the car."

"I couldn't get into the back," Courtney said from the passenger side. "I'm sorry!"

Izzy slid into the rear seat so Peter could drive. "It's all right."

"Everybody okay?" Peter asked ramming the car into gear before grabbing his phone and dialing Billy.

"Yes," Courtney said. "Isabelle, holy crap, you're like the bionic woman."

Peter brought his eyes to the rearview mirror and glanced at Izzy. Her head was back against the seat and she had closed her eyes. The comedown was a bitch.

Billy picked up on the first ring. "I hope this is you driving Izzy's car down the driveway."

"Yeah. Watch the house. I've got Izzy and Courtney with me. Izzy went apeshit on Seth and he's in bad shape."

"I missed it again? That is *so* hot."

Peter snorted a laugh as he turned onto the road and floored it. "Sampson should be showing up any time. I called him on the way here. He said he'd get some agents out here ASAP."

"I wish I could have seen her in action," Billy said.

Peter hung up and exhaled.

"What?" Izzy asked, still with her eyes closed.

"He's pissed he couldn't watch."

She rolled her head side to side. "He's such an idiot."

"Stop!" Courtney yelled.

ISABELLE BRACED HERSELF AGAINST THE BACK OF THE DRIVER'S seat as Peter hit the brakes in front of a deserted farmhouse about a half mile from the compound.

"What the hell?" Peter said.

Courtney paddled her hands toward the empty house. "Turn in here."

"What for?"

"Please? There's someone else."

"Courtney?" Isabelle said, her energy suddenly roaring back.

Peter pulled into the driveway of the ramshackle farmhouse. The sagging covered porch, with its peeling paint and missing first step, should have collapsed by now.

Courtney turned to her. "I'm sorry. I couldn't tell you, but I can't leave her here."

Dust kicked up around the car and Peter came to a stop in the driveway. "Who?"

But Courtney was out of the car already, half walking half running to the front door. A tattered orange no trespassing sign hung in the front window and indicated the house was in foreclosure.

"Iz?" Peter said as he got out of the car.

"Beats me." She grabbed his hand so he could pull her

from the backseat and they ran to catch up with Courtney who had already entered the house.

They stepped into the house and the oppressive heat and stagnant air hit Isabelle like a full speed garbage truck.

"Are you here?" Courtney yelled. "It's me. It's okay."

The slap of a screen door came from the back of the house and a hugely pregnant young woman with greasy auburn hair stepped into view.

"Holy cow," Izzy said.

39

Isabelle backed against Peter and leaned into him, because holding up her own body suddenly became too much.

Could this be...

Yes, the girl looked different from the glamour shot Isabelle had seen, but her hair color—not brown, not red, with flecks of gold—was the same. The cotton maternity shorts and grimy white top she wore strained against her ballooning belly.

"Please tell me you're Nicole Pratt."

The girl stayed silent, but Courtney nodded. "How'd you know her last name? I never told you."

Isabelle spun around, threw her arms around Peter's neck and squeezed. She shut her eyes and breathed in and out, in and out, in and out. "Am I dreaming?"

He backed her up and gripped her arms. "You *found* her."

Alive.

Isabelle turned and faced the two girls. Courtney stood still, her gaze bouncing between Peter and Isabelle.

Obviously, an explanation was owed. "I'm sorry I had to lie to you, Courtney. I've been working with the FBI to find Nicole. After Kendrick was killed they asked me to come here." Izzy glanced at Nicole. "Your roommate told the police you'd been volunteering at the compound. They didn't know you were living there. Your mother is frantic."

Nicole brought her hands over her face and Izzy glanced back at Peter who shrugged.

"Courtney, what's going on?" Izzy asked. "What is she doing in this house?"

But Courtney stiffened.

Defiance.

A reaction Isabelle understood all too well. She'd have to reassure her. "Nothing has changed. We're still going to help you. Both of you. Now more than ever, but you have to be honest with us."

Courtney wrapped an arm around Nicole's boney shoulders. "I trust them."

The air grew hotter and less breathable, but Isabelle waited while Nicole considered them.

She finally said, "I found out I was pregnant just after Christmas. I couldn't tell my mother. When I began to show I started wearing big shirts and didn't go home for spring break. I stayed at school and told my mother I was going home with a friend."

"You didn't think you could tell her?" Isabelle asked.

Nicole shook her head. "My mother is the highest-ranking Republican in Congress. She's an ultra-Conservative who has spent her career talking about family values. She wants to run for president. A pregnant, unmarried nineteen-year-old doesn't fit."

And Isabelle understood. After all, she'd been protecting her own family secret for years. "I'm so sorry."

Nicole stared at the floor. "I didn't know what to do. I was afraid to have an abortion. I didn't *want* to have an abortion. I figured I could give up the baby, but I was afraid the press would find out. I went to Tomorrow's Family Network and gave them a fake name. They sent me to see Seth and Kendrick. I knew it was illegal, but it meant no one would know. I told my mother I wasn't coming home for the summer and I told my friends I was. No one knew where I'd be and I would have the baby before school started. It seemed like my only option."

Isabelle glanced at Nicole's very large belly. "When are you due?"

"Next week."

"Next week!" Peter said. "What the hell are you doing in this rat hole?"

"That's the problem, rich boy. She decided she wanted to keep the baby, but Seth and Kendrick wouldn't let her go. They were afraid she'd go to the police and told her it was too late, that they'd already made the deal."

"Why didn't you call someone?" Isabelle asked.

"They threatened her. Said they'd kill her and the baby before they let her leave. Then Seth took her car keys and cell phone."

Nicole nodded. "I couldn't risk my baby."

Isabelle's mind raced. "When did he take the phone?"

"A few days before I ran."

Isabelle turned to Peter. "He must have shut the phone off. That's why the feds couldn't get a location."

Peter shifted to Nicole. "Where's your car?"

"I don't know."

"I think Seth dumped it," Courtney said. "The car disappeared two days after Nicole left."

"Peter, could he have hidden it on the property somewhere?"

"Who knows with that dumbass. Nicole, how did you get out of the compound with the sealed windows?"

"They weren't sealed then. Seth had it done after I ran. Courtney helped me climb out my window and she lowered me to the porch rail. It wasn't that far, but it was a little awkward with my belly."

Isabelle's mouth flopped open. She couldn't help it. "How on earth?"

"We waited until everyone was asleep, tied a couple of sheets together and wrapped them around her like a sling. I wrapped the other end around me to anchor her, and she lowered herself over the edge of the roof to the porch rail. She's pretty tall so it was only a few feet."

Two pregnant women doing this? They both could have gotten hurt. Desperation must have driven them to it.

"Girls," Peter said, "that was way too dangerous."

"We had no choice," Courtney yelled.

Peter raised his hands. "Don't get mad."

Isabelle glanced around the room. The empty, filthy room. "You've been here the whole time? How have you been surviving?"

"Courtney has been sneaking me food and water. The water here still works, but I didn't want to use it in case the utility company noticed and figured out someone was squatting. I'd kill for a shower right now because sponging off with bottled water doesn't quite do the job."

"Wow," Isabelle said.

Nicole shrugged. "Courtney sneaks down here once a day. It was only supposed to be for a few days until I figured out where to go. Then Courtney said my picture was all over the news. That's how Seth figured out my mother is a congresswoman. I didn't think about the press. If I went to a shelter, someone would recognize me."

Peter turned to Courtney. "You didn't know who she was?"

"Not until her mother reported her missing and her picture hit the news. That's when Kendrick panicked. I overheard him and Seth arguing one night. Kendrick thought they should hire an attorney because he was sure Nicole would run to her mother and tell her about the illegal adoptions. Then Seth disappeared for a couple of days and Kendrick wound up dead. It doesn't take a genius to figure that one."

"Hang on," Isabelle said. "You suspected Seth was a murderer and you didn't call the police?"

Courtney looked at her like she was hanging upside down. "Are you crazy? If the guy killed his friend he wouldn't think twice about making us disappear. I figured the police would at least *question* Seth about it and they'd find proof. Then he'd be arrested and Nicole and I would be free, but nobody even *talked* to him. What kind of investigating is that?"

Peter rubbed his hands over his mouth and after a few seconds said, "The feds told the P.D. to stay away from the compound because they were sending someone in undercover. A congresswoman's daughter trumps Kendrick."

I could use your legal expertise. That's what Kendrick had said to Isabelle in her office that first day. Isabelle's stomach launched upward.

She spun to Peter. "That's why Kendrick came to see me. In his sick, demented mind, he thought he could hire me as his lawyer."

Peter raised his eyebrows. "Crazy son of a bitch."

"Yeah, he was," Courtney said. "He knew if they got

caught he'd get in trouble for the adoption thing, but he was more worried about statutory rape."

"What?" Isabelle tried to process the information before she plummeted to the floor in shock.

"Rebecca's baby is Kendrick's. Rebecca told me her mother made her do it. Mary Beth had a baby last fall and wanted to stay on because they had nowhere to go. Plus, Mary Beth doesn't want to get a job. She had the bright idea that Rebecca should get pregnant. Kendrick was happy to help."

Isabelle pressed her fingers into her forehead. "Is that why she ran last week? She wants to keep the baby?"

"All she knows is she doesn't want to be a baby-making machine. Especially after Seth beat her."

Tears bubbled inside Isabelle as the sickness terrorized her. "He beat her?"

Courtney nodded. "He gets off on whipping rule breakers with his belt. He does it on the back so no one sees it."

"Jesus," Peter said.

"Then he panicked because she started spotting. They hauled the doc in when you left to pick up the rich boy at the airport. The doctor left ten minutes before you pulled up."

Isabelle turned to Peter. "The clothes you found must have been Rebecca's. I didn't see her before I left so I didn't know what she was wearing. This is so sick."

If she'd exposed Kendrick years ago, this would never have happened. She was partly to blame.

But Peter stepped behind and enfolded her in his arms. "It's okay."

The sound of his voice, his breath against her ear, eased her battered mind and she melted into him, let her head fall back on his shoulder. "I can't believe this. It's too twisted."

Her cell phone's ringer pierced the silence in the room, and Peter reached into her front pocket, pulled it out and handed it over. His roughened fingertips brushed hers, reminded her of his hands on her body, and all she wanted was for everything to be right between them. For him to still love her after what she'd done. She glanced at the phone's screen. "It's Wade."

"Tell him where we are," Peter said. "Sorry, girls. Time is up. You have to tell the feds."

"Hi, Wade," Isabelle said into the phone. "We're just down the road. Head south. There's an abandoned farmhouse. You'll see my car in the drive. Get here fast. You won't believe it."

"Isabelle," Wade said, "I'm on a seriously weak limb here. I've got agents locking down that compound. Courtney better be ready to talk."

She glanced at Courtney then Nicole and triumph overtook her sadness. "Trust me. That limb will hold."

40

Late that night, Isabelle knocked on the motel room's adjoining door. She knew the door wasn't locked, but waited for either Billy or Peter to open it. She glanced at Courtney, asleep on the double bed with her hand sloped across her protruding belly.

Isabelle swallowed her uncertainty and the ensuing rush of tears. They'd make it work. With Nicole on her way home to her family, Courtney would also get to keep her baby and have a life.

The door swung open. Billy stood wearing only a towel while his shoulder-length dark hair dripped fat drops of water down his chest. The guy needed to be on a beefcake calendar.

She didn't notice his rock-hard chest. Really. She didn't.

"You all right?" he asked.

"Yep. Where's Peter?"

"I don't know. I was in the shower. His wallet is here. Maybe he went for a pop or something."

"I need to find him. Will you watch Courtney? She's

sleeping, but she's pretty strung out from all the questioning and might wake up in a panic."

"No prob. Leave the door open so I can hear her."

"Thanks."

"Iz?" he said when she started to turn for the outside door.

She stopped and moved back to him so their voices wouldn't wake Courtney. "Yes?"

"Whatever happened this morning with Monk—before the shit hit the fan—it freaked him out."

Isabelle nodded. "I know. I want to fix it."

"That would be good. I mean, it's none of my business, but you guys fit. Ya know?"

"I know. I think I pushed him too far though."

"Yeah, well, I've pushed him too far before and look at us now." Billy blasted her with what Peter called his "chick-magnet smile" and crossed his fingers in front of his face. "We're like this."

She couldn't help laughing at him. He, more than anyone, knew Peter's wrath and yet they still managed to be friends. Maybe it was a testament to both of them and their can-do attitudes.

Whatever it was, it gave her hope.

"So, I'd really like to hug you right now, but with you in that towel, I don't think it's appropriate. And, with my luck, Peter would walk in and blow an artery. But thank you. For everything."

He jerked his head and sent more water drips flying off. "You bet. I am still pissed at you though for not waiting for me when you laid Seth to waste. That would have been better than porn."

She rolled her eyes. "You're a dope, but I like you."

"Story of my life." He flicked his thumb toward the outer door. "Go find him and let's get this ship sailing again."

"That seems to be the story of *my* life."

"Waa, waa, waa," he said.

Dope.

But she was smiling when she opened the outside door and—*voilà*—there was Peter, leaning on the metal railing, talking on his cell. He wore his trademark do-rag and cargo shorts with a plain white T-shirt that was just tight enough to set her mind on a path to somewhere else. At least he'd forgone the combat boots in favor of flip-flops. He glanced over at her, held his finger up, and she stepped onto the balcony where her bare feet hit the warm cement.

"I know," he said into the phone. "I'd like to have given you more notice, but it didn't work out that way...Right... Okay...Talk to you tomorrow." He hung up, lopped his head forward.

"Everything okay?" Isabelle asked.

He pocketed his phone. "My mother. I was filling her in on Courtney."

Isabelle held her breath for a second. Mrs. Jessup's help wasn't crucial, but it would move them along in the Courtney-needs-a-life plan.

"She'll help," Peter said. "I told her I'd bring Courtney by when we got back to Jersey."

Isabelle closed her eyes. "Thank you. I've been watching her all night trying to figure out what we were going to do."

When she opened her eyes again Peter had his elbow propped on the rail and was watching her.

"You like this girl, huh?" he asked.

She took a tentative step toward him. He didn't flinch. A good sign. "I see parts of me in her. The not so good parts. I want to pound them out of her. Smooth out the edges, I guess. She's never had anyone who cared."

Peter rubbed both hands over his face. "I can't stop imagining that pregnant girl falling off a roof and Courtney tumbling out after her. This whole thing is bizarre. I mean, it shocks me—and that's saying something—that Nicole didn't feel she could go to her own mother."

"Oddly enough, I get it. I know how the fear of the truth can paralyze someone. Even someone who is rational and normally level headed. It's crazy."

Their eyes met and held for a second before he rested both elbows on the rail and looked out over the parking lot.

Now or never. Here goes.

"About this morning," she said.

"Yeah. I knew this was coming."

What?

"Peter, I was wrong. It was a dumb plan. I just didn't realize it at the time. I was too caught up in getting answers."

He turned to face her. "But that's the problem. We're in different worlds when it comes to sex. The abuse taught you to treat sex as a function. *I* don't see it that way. For me, it's about trust and intimacy. I don't want to be in bed with you staring into Creepy Izzy's eyes. I want more than that. And I want it all the time. I can't always be stepping onto land-mines. It'll shred me, and with my job, that won't work. This is a deal breaker for me."

The words wrestled around in her mind and she closed her eyes. *Talk to him.* She needed to tell him things she had no idea how to translate. Her heart knew what to say, but by the time it reached her brain the filtering started.

"I couldn't do it," she blurted. "With Seth. I didn't get a chance to tell you earlier, but when you walked in, I was in the process of getting out of there."

He narrowed his eyes. "What?"

"I know you don't want to hear part of this, but I think you have to. When I took that run at Seth and he...well...he wasn't turning me down, it made me sick. I tried to flip the switch, but it didn't work. All I could think about was you touching me. And suddenly, I couldn't deal with him. I couldn't make my body do it."

Peter pressed his fingers into his eyes and she stepped an inch closer. Testing. He didn't move.

"You've ruined Creepy Izzy," she said half laughing. "And now Fun Izzy isn't so much fun because she's in this emotional nightmare and doesn't know how to get out. I think *you* can get her out. I want you to get her out. It's like you said, I'm terrified, but I *want* to be terrified. All of a sudden, when it comes to you, I like how terrified feels. I like knowing I can depend on you. That you understand my own special brand of insanity and don't judge me for it."

"Iz—"

"For the first time in my emotionally fractured life, I've experienced giving myself to someone who loves me. Someone who makes my body come alive in ways I've never known. More than that, I love when you hold me and that's never happened before. So, I'm asking you to forgive me. I ignored how important it was to you that I not encourage Seth. It sounds dumb to me now, but this morning it seemed like the way to get information from him. I was wrong. I understand now. It will never happen again."

He shook his head, let out a little sigh. "I knew you'd shred me. Early on, I told Vic that."

Oh, boy. This didn't sound good. Isabelle closed her eyes.

She concentrated. Hard. She deserved whatever he was about to say, but her heart pounded and the ache almost broke her. So she stood a little taller and waited for Peter to toss her on her ass.

A cricket's chirp from the trees next to the motel drew Peter's attention. He shook his head and turned back to her.

"Izzy, I broke every rule with this op. Given how I feel about you, I shouldn't have been here. I was so bent on keeping you safe and proving Vic was wrong, that I wound up putting you in danger because I couldn't control my emotions."

Isabelle waved her hands. "But it all worked out okay."

"Yeah, it did. *You* made it happen. You didn't need me."

She started to protest by shaking her head, but he wrapped his fingers around her skull to stop the motion. "It's okay that you didn't need me. It makes me realize I can't fix everything. Billy went at me today over Tiny and Roy, and it actually made sense. Shocking as *that* is. I can't take responsibility for everyone anymore." He laughed. "It's so much damn work."

"That it is." She stepped closer and grabbed his hand, entwined her fingers with his. "But Peter, I did need you. You kept me sane. You listened when I talked, you let me be the raw, stripped-down version of me who doesn't always make sense. And through all of it, you didn't treat me like a freak. I've never had that kind of emotional connection."

With a crooked grin, he pulled her into his side and kissed the top of her head. A head kiss. Not good. But she wrapped her arms around his waist and squeezed, because if he was dumping her she wanted to hang on for just a few minutes more.

A curling stream of panic wormed into her chest and she swallowed hard.

Talk to him.

"So, what now?" she asked.

"This may surprise you, but I have a plan."

They both laughed and he pulled her a little closer. "My plan is to go back to Jersey, finish my vacation and give myself a break. I think I need to grieve for my friends, and the only way to do that is to stop for a while. Hell, maybe I'll take my mother to lunch a few times so she stops being a pain in the ass."

When he turned and looped both arms around her the curling panic slipped away. "That'll make her happy," Isabelle said.

"But more than anything, I'd like to spend time with you. Normal time. Going to dinner, and hanging out on the beach for what's left of the summer."

He wanted her. And not just for sex.

Relief, in all its weightlessness, swarmed her. "You want to start over?"

"No. Starting over means forgetting what we've done together. We know too much to start over. I want to pick up right where we left off. How's that sound?"

Where did this man come from? After all the torment, he still came back strong.

Yes. He's the one.

Thank you, Fun Izzy.

She threw her arms around his neck, kissed him hard, the way he liked it. With everything she had, holding nothing back.

"I guess you agree?" he asked while he kissed her.

"I love you, Peter."

He inched back, cupped her cheeks in his hands and their eyes fused together for a long moment. "I love you, too."

But he stepped away, knocked lightly on the motel room door and Billy answered.

"I need my wallet." Peter ducked into the room for a second. "You're on Courtney for a while."

"Sure." Billy closed the door leaving Peter and Isabelle alone on the balcony.

He grabbed her hand, dragged her toward the stairs while her bare feet slapped against the cement. "Where are we going? I don't have shoes on."

"You don't need shoes. I'm getting us a room so we can screw each other stupid all night. Plus, you haven't had a rumba lesson in a while. This'll just be a horizontal one. We'll work on that problem with your hips."

41

THREE WEEKS LATER

ISABELLE SAT AT HER KITCHEN TABLE ABOUT TO CLICK THE send button on her laptop. She paused, staring out the French doors to the ocean's glistening surface. The midafternoon sun flooded the kitchen with heat and light, and she loved every second of it.

Home.

When her iPod offered her new favorite song, she straightened in her chair. Her thoughts drifted back to the old barn, and Peter's hands on her, as they made love in the front seat of her car.

She sang along and clicked send.

Her resume was now on its way to Jorgensen Bradford, the *second* largest defense firm in the state.

Part of her still couldn't believe her uncle had actually fired her. She showed up for work the day after she'd gotten back to Jersey and found her personal items neatly stacked in a box on top of her desk.

That was it. No conversation. No thanks for finding my son's murderer.

Nothing.

Bastard.

The front door lock tumbled and she turned to see Peter stride in, the key she'd given him still in his hand.

Her heart did that weird slamming around in her chest thing it did whenever he came into a room. Of course, the tight T-shirt and ripped Levi's didn't hurt. All topped off with the battered do-rag he'd taken back because it was his favorite.

She loved this man.

Clunky boots on her wood floors and all.

"Hey," he said, dumping her mail on the table in front of her.

She grabbed him by the shirt, hauled him down and kissed him. "You look too good today, Peter."

That wicked movie-star smile of his nearly melted her bones.

I love this man.

"You know I like hearing that," he said.

When he pulled her to her feet she didn't resist. She snuggled into him, her head bumping his chin as she nestled into his neck. The best place to be. Ever.

"Where's Courtney?" He slid his hand into the back of her jeans.

Peter wanted some. So did she. But Courtney was in the guest room. Well, her room now because Isabelle had moved her in. She couldn't stand the thought of Courtney, at this time in her life, trying to find a job and an affordable apartment.

So they made a deal. Courtney would have her baby,

finish her GED and get a job. Until then, this would be her home.

It helped that Nicole Pratt's mother, the congresswoman, set up a trust fund for Courtney as a way to thank her.

Truth be told, Isabelle enjoyed the company. And having a friend. Courtney knew more about her than most and, somehow, it seemed right for her to be here.

"Would Courtney mind a little moaning?" Peter asked.

Isabelle snorted a laugh and glided her hand over his cheek. "She's going with your mother later. Something about meeting the director of volunteers at the women's shelter."

"Excellent. The Lorraine Jessup school of getting your life together." He tilted his head toward her laptop. "Working on the résumé?"

"Yep. Gotta find a job."

She had to find a way to pay the rent and stay in the house she loved. Even if she had to beg her mother to take her side and not let her uncle throw her out.

"Mmm," he said, pulling out of her arms—*darn it*—and walking to the door leading to the beach.

"I...uh...talked to Wade this morning," Isabelle said.

"And what did Agent Sampson have to say?" Peter reached up and rubbed the tips of his fingers over the wood trim above the door.

What's with him?

"If we hadn't figured it out, I've been officially cleared of murder."

Peter snorted. "Gotta love the feds. I guess the DNA came back a match."

"Yep. They've got Seth from the skin found under Kendrick's nails." She picked up a pen from the table and twirled it in her fingers. "Between murdering Kendrick and the black-market babies, he's broken enough laws to keep him locked up for a long time."

Peter turned to her, leaned against the door and folded his arms. "What about the others involved?"

"The doctor that came to the house, the woman at the counseling center and let's not forget the prison. That's probably the most sickening of all."

"No shit," he agreed.

A prison official had worked with Tomorrow's Family Network to place inmates' newborn babies up for adoption. In reality, Tomorrow's Family Network sent the babies to Seth and Kendrick. Everyone, the prison official included, took a share of the profits.

Thanks to Courtney, they were all in jail.

"You did good, Iz."

She grinned. "Thank you, Peter. That means a lot to me."

But he turned his back to her and looked out the door again. *What is wrong with him?* "Going surfing?"

"Nah. Low tide. Maybe a run though."

After three weeks of downtime he was restless. He'd been avoiding talking about it, but she knew by the way he became so easily distracted. A man like Peter couldn't be tamed for long. The adventurer in him didn't allow it. And he wasn't kicking over potted plants anymore.

He'd be leaving her soon and it would obliterate her.

Your own damned fault.

Shut up, Creepy Izzy. Go away.

"You can say it," Isabelle said, still standing by the table.

He puckered his lips and eyed her. "What?"

"I know you've been keeping it from me. Just say it."

He propped a hip against the counter. "Uh—"

The phone rang and she glanced down at the ID. "It's my mother."

He nodded, the relief evident on his face. "You'd better take it. I'm gonna go change."

"We're not done here." She hit the talk button. "Hi, Mom."

"Hi," her mother said, her voice tinged with excitement.

What could *this* be?

"What's up?" Isabelle watched Peter make his way down the hall.

"I called to tell you about your new landlord."

Sqreeeeeee! Did a freight train just come skidding to a halt in her kitchen? Isabelle's spine turned to steel. "Excuse me?"

"He's on his way over there."

New landlord? What the hell? "Mom, are you telling me you sold my house?"

"You're going to love him. He's handsome. In an odd sort of way."

Her knees wobbled and she locked them to keep from crumpling to the ground. Could her mother seriously be trying to hook her up with some guy who'd just bought her house? The house she dreamed of spending her life in? The house she'd put so much energy into making a home?

Tears filled her eyes. Her mother had betrayed her. Again. "How could you do this to me? Knowing how much I love it here."

"Isabelle the new owner is—"

She couldn't have this conversation. Not right now.

She punched the off button, threw the phone across the room and watched it shatter as it hit the floor.

What if the guy wanted this as a summer home? Isabelle would be out in a heartbeat. Plus, she had Courtney and the baby to think about. The baby was due any day now, and she'd promised Courtney she'd have a roof over her head.

"Why?" Isabelle said as the tears spilled over.

No job. No home.

She had to do something.

"Iz?" Peter said from the hallway, his gaze shooting to the destroyed phone.

"She sold my house. My own mother is putting me on the street." She stalked the room like a caged animal. "It never ends with her. The disappointments. They just keep coming and coming and coming. As soon as I think I'm settling in, she pulls out that big sledge hammer and—*bam!*—she bashes me on the skull."

"Iz, it's not what you think—"

What? Oh no. *No. No. No.* He could *not* be taking her mother's side. She put her hand up as all the blood rushed from her head and the room whirled in front of her. "Don't, Peter. Please. I can't take it right now. My mother just told me the new landlord is on his way here. I have to figure out a way to make him let me stay until I can buy my house back. Dammit." She dug her fingers into her hair and yanked. "I'll never get a mortgage. I don't even have the down payment I'd need. Not for oceanfront property."

She would not ask Peter for money. Absolutely not. They hadn't even discussed what the future held for them, so how could she possibly ask for a loan?

He stepped toward her, grabbed her arms and held her in place. "Stop a minute. Please."

"She sold my house!"

"To me!"

She jerked her head back. *Huh?*

"*I* bought the house. For you. Not for me. Your mother wanted to tell you. I knew she'd screw it up, but she insisted."

"But—"

"You were worried your uncle would toss you out. And, after he fired you, it wasn't a stretch, so I contacted your mother and told her I wanted to buy the house."

Isabelle stepped back, out of his arms. A bizarre mixture of relief and fury tore up any chance at rational thought. How could he do this without talking to her?

"I knew you wouldn't take money from me," Peter said. "And if I told you what I was planning you would have said no. You're stubborn that way. You're so damned independent you don't let people help you. Now you don't have to worry about paying the rent."

The thought of it eased into her brain. "Holy cow."

He nodded. "If you're not comfortable with me being the owner you can buy it back. As soon as you get a job, I'll sell it to you. That's not what I want, but I'm learning to accept not getting things my way." He grinned.

She laughed at that because it had to be difficult for the Emperor of Fix-It Land, as his brother called him, to admit it.

"You really are the Emperor of Fix-It Land."

"No. I'm not. I'm trying to get shit done. I want you happy because Vic cleared me for work and I have to go back soon."

"That's what I thought you were hiding from me. I didn't know you were hiding this other thing too."

He waved that off. "Yeah, well, the thing with Vic just happened last night. I've been working on the house for a couple of weeks."

He put his hands on top of his head and huffed out a breath. "Everything feels like a mess. I have to go back to work. I *want* to go back. And yet, I can't leave you while you have so much going on. No job, Courtney with a baby on the way. I figured if you didn't have to worry about being thrown out of the house you'd feel more settled." He laughed. "The only thing I know for sure right now is that I'm a landlord willing to accept sex—lots of it—in lieu of rent."

She scoffed. "That's a no-brainer."

"Plus, I have to decide what I'm doing about living in Chicago because I know you won't move. And I wouldn't ask you to."

"Thank you," she said, because all other words seemed lost in the recesses of her mucky brain.

"So, I guess I just figured it out. If you want, I'll move back here."

Yes. Absolutely.

She nodded. "I'd love that."

He held up his hands. "Don't freak about me owning the house. I mean, my hope is, eventually, we'll live here together but I'm not pushing you on that. I know you need time and that's fine." His lips curled into a playful grin. "For a little while at least. But you *are* going to marry me at some point. I'm only good at compromise for limited intervals."

He wanted to marry her. Could it be that simple? *It'll never work.*

Shut up, Creepy Izzy.

She stepped forward as the sun shined into her kitchen —their kitchen—and the dream of a life in her grandmother's house morphed into a variation of its original shape.

"Yes," she said without thinking.

Peter welcomed her into his arms. "Yes what?"

She squeezed her eyes shut and breathed in the woodsy scent of him that would never leave her. "Yes everything. I don't care. As long as you're here. Even when you can't physically be here, just knowing you're here for me. Yes. I want it all."

"It'll be hard with me being gone, but I'll try to cut back

on the travel. Maybe Vic can get me some local gigs with the New York big shots."

An old Tom Jones song came from the iPod.

"Oh," Peter said, moving his hips into the now familiar rumba. "Perfect song."

And yes, she realized, it was. She pulled him closer, their hips rocking in perfect unison as fire blasted her core.

She loved this man.

"Well, look at you," he said, twirling her backward, but then pulling her close again.

Side.

Forward.

Replace.

"It's easier now," she said.

"That's because you're not thinking so much. You've let go. *Finally*."

She pressed her hand into his shoulder and pulled closer. "I trust you. I know how your body moves with mine now."

"Lucky me."

Box step.

Their eyes connected and something changed. Their hips moved in perfect time; their bodies pressed together so tightly that her mind could only go one place. And it involved him naked and on top of her.

But he dipped her back, dragged his free hand down her chest, across her breasts and drew her back up.

"I love this dance," she said. "You can never do it with anyone else. I mean that, Peter."

He cleared his throat and when she glanced up he'd thrown his head back—concentrating probably—and closed his eyes.

"You know what they call it, right?"

She laughed. "As long as your hands are on me, I'm not sure I care."

He stopped, tangled his fingers with hers. "They call it the dance of love."

"How appropriate." She glided down the front of him, rocking her hips back and forth as she traveled south and then back.

"Whoa," he said. "I didn't teach you that. Very *hot*."

"I saw it on the internet. I've been practicing. *Alone*."

"That's a damn shame."

"I wanted to get it right."

He grunted and yanked her hips closer so she could feel the swell of his erection. "I think you've got it."

"Eh-hem!"

Courtney's voice crashed into their little love fest and Isabelle jumped back. She would have to get used to having a roommate before she and Peter did a throw down on the kitchen table.

Ooh, that could be fun.

"Will you two ever stop?" Courtney asked.

Peter laughed. "I hope not." He turned away. Most likely to avoid Courtney seeing his erection.

"My water broke."

Nothing ruined a mood like *that* announcement, but a sudden explosion of excitement crackled in the air, and Isabelle stared at Courtney's saturated maternity shorts. "Really?"

She nodded.

"Okay then," Isabelle said. "Let's call your doctor and see what's what." She turned to Peter who wore the million-dollar smile that made her think of happiness and having a man, this man, to come home to.

She *loved* him. How he managed it she didn't know.

Creepy Izzy was no pushover, but the light and warmth Peter brought to her otherwise barren life came in huge waves that left her paralyzed by fear yet wanting only more of whatever he offered.

"We're having a baby," she said.

"I should be so lucky," he said.

———

Want more of the Private Protectors series? Read on to enjoy an excerpt from *Relentless Pursuit.*

RELENTLESS PURSUIT
BY ADRIENNE GIORDANO

Enjoy an excerpt from *Relentless Pursuit*, book five in the
Private Protectors Series:

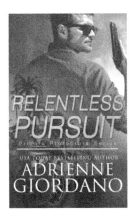

Billy Tripp nudged the nine-millimeter holstered under his
suit jacket and decided this might be as good a time as any
to meet his maker.

All he needed to do was slide that baby out, prop it
under his chin and—*bang*—the misery would be over.

After all the death-defying experiences he'd had, killing

himself in a hotel ballroom would be sub-par. Supremely sub-par.

Plus, he'd be dead.

"Cheer up, jagweed," Monk said, slapping him on the back.

"Why?" Billy glanced around the massive room at the sea of men and women dressed in sharp tuxedos and sexy, low cut gowns. As ballrooms went, Dante's ranked in the top ten. Funky red walls and icicle chandeliers gave it a more contemporary feel, but it was still a ballroom. And he'd seen plenty of them.

"It could be worse. This job is almost complete."

Billy scanned his immediate surroundings. "Yeah, but, dude, I'm guarding a *necklace*. There's not even a body attached to it."

Monk grinned. "You shouldn't have let your passport expire."

Dick. Head.

"First of all, I didn't *let* my passport expire. It just happened. An accident."

"You fucked up. Admit it." And then Monk started humming.

Humming? Really? Of course Monk was in a good mood. He'd just returned from overseas where he played with guns and blew crap up. Billy had been scheduled to take the next two-month shift, but got caught up in this expired passport mess.

How had he, an ex-Army ranger working for one of the country's most elite private security firms, forgotten to renew his fu—fudging passport?

And why the hell had he picked this month to promise his mother he would stop swearing? She'd asked him to do it and deserved his attention to the matter, that's why.

Even if it was slowly destroying him.

A woman in her fifties wearing a monster low-cut black gown—*that thing has no business on her body*—wandered to the table and locked in on him. *Cripes.*

"Fabulous, isn't it?" she asked.

He glanced at Monk, who rolled his eyes and stepped away to check his phone. "It is." Billy kept his focus on the room and any potential bad guys. The woman pressed a note into his hand. Great. Another one slipping him her number.

Ceasing conversation, he waited until the woman left and tucked the paper in his pocket with the other two. He'd get rid of them later. This routine, like most things, had lost its novelty long ago. Wasn't *that* a travesty? Early on, he'd enjoyed the steady stream of attention that accompanied women throwing themselves at him. He was a guy. And guys liked to get laid. Pretty simple.

Except it got old. The strange women. The *crazy,* strange women who parked themselves on his doorstep or called him night and day. Hell, he never misled anyone about his intentions. He always told them what it was.

"That was Vic." Monk grinned. "He said to say hi."

Not biting, Billy kept his gaze on the packed room. "Fu—fudge off. I could have had a new passport in a day or two, but Vic wanted to break my balls."

"He's teaching you a lesson. Next time, you won't forget. Besides, we've been in a lot worse places than a fundraiser in South Beach. In December."

Monk might as well take another hit off the crack pipe because he wasn't getting it. "Every time I turn around, Vic is hauling me into his office. And he had to bring up that little infraction when you beat the crap out of me last summer. Christ sakes, you nearly kill me and *I* get in trouble? All because I was ragging on you?"

A couple in their twenties stepped up to the table and Monk nodded. "Evening."

Billy stayed silent but shifted closer to the table. As ticked off as he was about this job, there would be no way he'd let that necklace disappear. Not on his watch. Soon he'd be out of here. Gone.

When the couple moved on, Monk turned back to him. "You're not grasping the point of this assignment. This is punishment for being a grand fucking pain in the ass all the time."

That was his theory? "Then why are you here? What are you being punished for?"

"I asked for it. I'd been gone two months, Izzy is on vacation for a couple of weeks and we're doing a long weekend. I got no problems with this assignment."

Yeah. There's the difference. Billy turned his attention back to the ballroom. "You're on vacation with your Victoria's Secret model of a girlfriend and I'm in purgatory."

A strawberry blonde, her thick hair falling in soft waves around her shoulders, stepped out of the crowd wearing a peach gown with a baggy, draping neckline, but the rest of it —*humina, humina, humina*—clung to her ample hips like snakeskin. "Whoa."

She'd never be called skinny. Not with those hips and a rack that could give a man vertigo. But chunky didn't suit either. Statuesque maybe. Hot, most definitely. Jeepers, he might be hearing angels singing over the orchestra. He elbowed Monk. "Check out this smoker coming our way."

Monk swung his head in the sexy blonde's direction. "That smoker is Kristen Dante. She runs this place. I met her when I got here yesterday."

The boss? She couldn't have been thirty years old. Billy let out a low whistle as Kristen Dante, her sumptuous body balancing on mile high heels, came closer. Damn, the woman had to be six foot in those shoes.

He nudged right up to the table. A woman like her could make a guy like him lose focus and he'd wind up with a missing million-dollar necklace.

"Hello, gentlemen," Madame Hotness said, pushing her hair off her shoulder.

In contrast to the body that made him want to reach out and touch, she had a face sent straight from heaven. Soft and round and sweet with dynamite green eyes. Amazing that she lived in Florida, because her fair skin would get crispy in the sun. Toss in the reddish-blond hair and Billy decided the whole fudging package worked. Big time.

Monk held out his hand. "Hello, Kristen."

The two of them shook hands and Hotness turned back to Billy. "We haven't met, I'm Kristen. Welcome to Dante."

Kristen stood with her hand extended waiting for him to say something. This was a big boy and, given her height, she didn't get to look up at a man very often. Not to mention the Calvin Klein model good looks. He wore his collar-length, dark hair fashionably shaggy and his slick Italian suit fit his long body just fine, but he apparently hadn't learned to speak. His sparkling blue eyes communicated their appraisal quite well, however, and she forced herself not to hunch. Her lifetime of weight issues didn't permit comfort when people stared.

This man made an immediate impression though. With those eyes, she imagined he could get into all sorts of mischief. The pinging in her head warned she should run screaming. He had player tattooed all over him.

Peter, the man Vic Andrews called Monk, nudged his partner with his elbow, and the guy wandered back to Earth.

"I'm Billy. Billy Tripp. Sorry. Mindsnap."

O-kay, then. She could only hope this guy had a bigger attention span than what he'd displayed introducing himself. Considering there was over ten million dollars worth of jewelry in this room.

She turned back to Peter. "Do you need anything?"

"No, ma'am. We're fine. I'm doing the rounds and checking in with our men. All is quiet."

Familiar slivers of unease curled around Kristen and she turned to see Mr. Mindsnap's gaze plastered to her chest. *Here we go. Yes, they're real.* Again, she focused on standing tall, but the effort drained her, forced her to concentrate on anything but her oversized body.

Peter cleared his throat and Billy flicked his attention back to the ballroom.

"We have men by the main doors and by each table," Peter said. "We're rotating every half hour. Were you expecting this big of a crowd?"

"We expected three-fifty, but we're over four hundred. It's a good cause and everyone loves to see millions in jewelry." She pointed to the necklace propped on the stand. "This one will be auctioned tonight."

Billy leaned forward and something in his twinkly eyes had her girly parts on full alert. *Trouble.*

"I'll keep it safe," he said.

But he was staring at her again, taking in her face and her hair, and the pressure of that hungry gaze forced her shoulders down. If only she could ball herself up to hide from the inspection. Did she have food on her face or something? Wouldn't that be perfect? A fat Amazon with food stuck to her cheek.

Her assistant appeared next to her. "Sorry to interrupt. Can I see you a moment?"

If she didn't already cherish Dee, this interruption would have sealed it. Anything to get out from under Billy Tripp's eyes. "Absolutely. Excuse me, guys."

Once Madame Hotness—M.H. as she would heretofore be known—left, Billy waggled his eyebrows at Monk, clutched his heart with both hands and gasped. "This could finally be the end. Tell my mother I love her."

Monk cracked up. "What are you doing?"

"Holy shi—sorry, Ma. Holy crud. Do I have drool on my face? Seriously, dude, I'm fudging dumbstruck here."

"I see that. You were staring. She thinks you're an asshole. I tend to agree. If you screw me on this assignment I'll beat you worse than the last time. All I want is a quiet weekend with my girl."

Kristen appeared again, her lips pinched. "Guys, I have..." She motioned to Billy's hands still at his chest "Are you okay?"

"Crap," Monk muttered.

Oops. Billy dropped his hands, stood tall and scanned the room. "I'm fine. Heartburn."

Her gaze bounced between him and Monk before she finally shook her head. She held up the phone with her left hand. No wedding ring. *Perfect.*

"Something has come up in another part of the hotel. If you need me, call my cell."

Oh, sweetheart, Billy thought, *you've got yourself a deal.*

Kristen charged through the lobby doors and was met by two uniformed Miami police officers. "I'm Kristen Dante. I understand we've had a theft."

"Yes, ma'am," the taller officer said.

A young guy in his twenties with slicked back hair stepped up. "My Range Rover was stolen."

She shifted to maintenance mode. "I'm terribly sorry, sir. Was it valet parked?"

"No, it was in the lot."

At least the car hadn't been touched by one of her employees. "Are you staying in the hotel?"

"I checked in yesterday. I should sue your ass."

Sue them? He parked the car himself. How could it be their fault? But he was a guest. "I apologize for the inconvenience. I'll be sure your hotel bill reflects our gratitude for your business. We will, of course, arrange for any transportation you may need."

The guy pinched his thin, little lips tight and the veins in his neck popped. Kristen folded her hands in front of her and waited. *Don't scream at me, you weasely man.*

"I'll be in the bar," he said and stormed off.

"Nice guy," the officer said.

Welcome to the hospitality business. She turned back to him, checked his nametag. "Officer Jackson, what can I do?"

"If we could get a look at your security footage, maybe there's something there."

She nodded. "I'll take you upstairs."

After ushering the police to the security office, she phoned the victimized guest and offered use of the hotel's fleet of cars for as long as necessary. For tonight, she'd need to track down a driver.

The elevator doors opened just as her phone chirped. Kurt, her assistant hotel manager. She waved the people inside the elevator to continue without her "Hi, Kurt."

"We have a problem."

For the second time, Kristen strode through the lobby

doors and, thanks to the popularity of the two nightclubs in the hotel, ran into a crush of people. A gust of wind blew her hair in front of her face and she tucked it behind her ear. She sidestepped, found Kurt waiting for her and guided him from milling guests.

"You're telling me," she said, her voice strained with forced control, "in addition to the stolen guest's car, one of our Bentleys *and* a Mercedes are gone?"

"Yes," Kurt said.

"How did this happen?"

"We don't know. Both sets of keys were locked in the safe."

"Were the cars taken out tonight?"

"Yes, the Bentley was out twice and the Mercedes once."

"And there were no issues?"

Kurt held his hands palm up. "Not a one. Both drivers turned in the keys and went home."

"The police are upstairs in security. Do they know?"

"Yes. They're reviewing footage."

Kristen's phone beeped with a text. The auction of the diamond necklace was about to start. She should get in there.

A second squad car, lights flashing, entered the circular drive already bumper to bumper with cars. Nothing like causing a scene. What a damned night. Kristen and Kurt rushed to greet the officers and waited for them to join her on the sidewalk.

The older officer stood eye to eye with her, while she towered over the shorter one. "Hello, officers. I'm Kristen Dante."

"Ms. Dante, I'm Officer Burns," the bigger one said. "This is my partner, Officer Sams. Busy night here."

Kristen nodded. "We have a large function in the ballroom and the nightclubs, well, they draw a crowd most nights."

"Okay. Any witnesses come forward?"

"Not yet," Kurt said.

Burns's radio crackled and he stepped away.

"The other two officers are upstairs copying the security footage," Kristen said. "What now?"

Sams nodded. "We called for a detective. Someone will come down and follow up. Meantime, we'll do a BOLO—be on the lookout—for the stolen cars. Maybe something will pop. Most stolen cars go to certain locations. We'll concentrate on those areas. Any idea what time this happened?"

"Yes," Kurt said. "Both cars had been taken out this evening between seven and eight. The Bentley was signed back in at 8:45 p.m. and the Mercedes at nine. The keys were put in the safe. One of the valets noticed the cars missing at 10:15 p.m. when he parked a car in the area."

"When was the guest's car stolen?"

Kurt shrugged. "He hadn't moved the car since he checked in yesterday, but went back this evening around 9:45 to retrieve something and the car was gone."

Kristen turned to the officer. "Maybe all the cars were taken at the same time."

If that were the case, something would be on the security footage. And the hotel was busy tonight. Wouldn't someone have seen something?

Burns finished his call and joined them. "A detective is on the way."

"What are the chances we'll recover the cars?" Kristen asked.

"If these guys are any good, they know how to disable the factory antitheft devices. You have LoJack or anything?"

Kristen shook her head, almost embarrassed by it, but

between the cost of the cars, the upkeep and the insurance, maintaining a fleet was expensive. With her father's approval, they had avoided the expense of installing additional tracking systems. Now she wondered if that risk had been worth it.

They'd gambled. And lost.

"No tracking. We'd hoped the standard antitheft systems would do the job."

The officer shrugged. "You never know. You could get lucky."

Somehow, he didn't sound as if he believed it.

ALSO BY ADRIENNE GIORDANO

PRIVATE PROTECTORS SERIES

Risking Trust

Man Law

Negotiating Point

A Just Deception

Relentless Pursuit

Opposing Forces

THE LUCIE RIZZO MYSTERY SERIES

Dog Collar Crime

Knocked Off

Limbo (novella)

Boosted

Whacked

Cooked

Incognito

The Lucie Rizzo Mystery Series Box Set 1

The Lucie Rizzo Mystery Series Box Set 2

The Lucie Rizzo Mystery Series Box Set 3

THE ROSE TRUDEAU MYSTERY SERIES

Into The Fire

HARLEQUIN INTRIGUES

The Prosecutor

The Defender

The Marshal

The Detective

The Rebel

JUSTIFIABLE CAUSE SERIES

The Chase

The Evasion

The Capture

CASINO FORTUNA SERIES

Deadly Odds

JUSTICE SERIES w/MISTY EVANS

Stealing Justice

Cheating Justice

Holiday Justice

Exposing Justice

Undercover Justice

Protecting Justice

Missing Justice

Defending Justice

SCHOCK SISTERS MYSTERY SERIES w/MISTY EVANS

1st Shock

2nd Strike

3rd Tango

STEELE RIDGE SERIES w/KELSEY BROWNING

& TRACEY DEVLYN

Steele Ridge: The Beginning

Going Hard (Kelsey Browning)

Living Fast (Adrienne Giordano)

Loving Deep (Tracey Devlyn)

Breaking Free (Adrienne Giordano)

Roaming Wild (Tracey Devlyn)

Stripping Bare (Kelsey Browning)

Enduring Love (Browning, Devlyn, Giordano)

Vowing Love (Adrienne Giordano)

STEELE RIDGE SERIES: The Kingstons w/KELSEY BROWNING

& TRACEY DEVLYN

Craving HEAT (Adrienne Giordano)

Tasting FIRE (Kelsey Browning)

Searing NEED (Tracey Devlyn)

Striking EDGE (Kelsey Browning)

Burning ACHE (Adrienne Giordano)

ACKNOWLEDGMENTS

Thank you to my husband for helping me make my dream come true. And for unknowingly providing hero material. I love you.

To the dynamic duo, John and Mara, thank you for sticking with me and brainstorming scenarios.

I must, must, must acknowledge Jackie Powers and her wonderful insight when working through early characterization issues. Your advice helped me dig deep and I'm so grateful.

And, to my usual suspects, Kelsey Browning, Tracey Devlyn, Theresa Stevens and Lucie J. Charles, you continually push me to do more. Thank you!

Milton Grasle, you helped me empower Izzy when she needed to be physically strong. Nobody will mess with our Izzy.

To my wonderful editor, Gina Bernal, who encouraged me to take chances, I appreciate your faith in my ability. To the marketing team at Carina Press, you guys rock. Thanks for always answering my myriad of questions.

And, to my son, who smiles at me every day and makes my world a wonderful place. I love you.

A NOTE TO READERS

Dear reader,

Thank you for reading *A Just Deception*. I hope you enjoyed it. If you did, please help others find it by sharing it with friends on social media and writing a review.

Sharing the book with your friends and leaving a review helps other readers decide to take the plunge into the world of the Private Protectors. I would appreciate it if you would consider taking a moment to tell your friends how much you enjoyed the story. Even a few words is a huge help. Thank you!

Happy reading!
Adrienne

ABOUT THE AUTHOR

 Adrienne Giordano is a *USA Today* bestselling author of over forty romantic suspense and mystery novels. She is a Jersey girl at heart, but now lives in the Midwest with her ultimate supporter of a husband, sports-obsessed son and Elliot, a snuggle-happy rescue. Having grown up near the ocean, Adrienne enjoys paddle-boarding, a nice float in a kayak and lounging on the beach with a good book.

For more information on Adrienne's books, please visit www.AdrienneGiordano.com. Adrienne can also be found on Facebook at http://www.facebook.com/AdrienneGiordanoAuthor, Twitter at http://twitter.com/AdriennGiordano and Goodreads at http://www.goodreads.com/AdrienneGiordano.

Don't miss a new release! Sign up for Adrienne's new release newsletter!

Made in the USA
Coppell, TX
22 August 2021